SWEET HUNGER

MICHAEL BAILEY

CONTENTS

DEDICATION

To my wife Candice for your endless encouragement, patience, and belief in me.

Without you, this story would have stayed a dream.

And to every woman who has ever felt powerless, unseen, or unheard, may you remember that your voice matters, your strength is real, and your hunger for more is not a weakness, but a fire.

WARNINGS

Sweet Hunger contains themes and scenes that may be distressing to some readers.

This story explores intense psychological, emotional, and physical experiences through a dark and suspenseful lens. Content Warnings include:

Psychological manipulation

Obsession and stalking

Emotional abuse and gaslighting

Sexual situations (consensual and non-consensual dynamics)

Violence and threats of violence

Death and implied murder

Discussions of trauma and mental instability

Power imbalances and control

Ritual imagery

Body horror (mild to moderate)

Reader discretion is advised.

Take care of yourself and read at your own pace.

CHAPTER 1

*"*S*he smells like honey, warm, thick, golden. A scent so sweet it makes my senses ache. I could bathe in it, drown in it, let it soak into my skin, and consume me from the inside out. I've tasted desire before, but never like this. This is special."*

She doesn't notice me, not really. But I notice her.

Every morning, at precisely 8:17 AM, Iris steps into the elevator of The Sailboat Building.

Iris Klarelle.

She lingers in my thoughts, and I find myself whispering her name like an incantation. Iris.

I've even gone so far as to lookup the meaning of her name. Iris: it means rainbow, something fleeting and untouchable, a shimmer of color on the horizon that vanishes when you get too close. Such a perfect description of her presence, the way she moves through the world untethered, light on her feet, always just out of my reach.

And Klarelle, probably derived from Clara, meaning bright, or radiant. Like the way light catches in her raven hair, the way it gilds her skin when she stands near the elevator doors, her head tilted slightly downward, lost in thought.

She is Iris Klarelle, and I can sense l her presence before I see her.

For exactly seventeen seconds, we share the same space. Seventeen seconds to breathe in her essence, to memorize the way she tucks her hair behind her ear, to be close to her and feel the warmth of her presence. Seventeen seconds where the world shrinks down to just her and me.

She's always distracted, scrolling through her phone or adjusting the strap of her purse. Unaware. She doesn't realize how much I see her, how she makes me feel. The way her lashes lower when she reads a message. The way she shifts her weight ever so slightly in her black heels as we ascend, how she keeps her balance delicate while maintaining a posture like a string pulled taut.

That scent, honey and something else, something that lingers on the tongue. It clings to her skin, to the silk of her long hair. It makes my head light, makes my chest tighten, and makes me hungry in a way, I can't quite explain.

The elevator hums around us, the quiet murmur of the city outside fading into the background. It's just her and me, wrapped in this fleeting moment, this fragile, sacred ritual we share every morning.

She doesn't look at me. She never does. But I don't mind.

The doors slide open with a chime. Too soon. Always too soon.

She steps out, heels tapping against the polished floor. I watch the sway of her hair, the effortless grace of her movements, the way her scent lingers behind like the echo of something unfinished.

I wonder if she ever notices the silence that follows after she leaves. If she feels, even for a second, that something is missing.

She lingers in my mind, a phantom I can't shake. I catch myself checking the time, 8:17 AM, always 8:17 AM. I replay her movements like a film on repeat, the way she bends slightly to read her phone, the flutter of her pulse at her wrist when she adjusts her purse.

The elevator doors close, sealing me inside with the scent of her fading warmth. I lean against the polished wall, my fingers tracing the cool metal railing. My pulse quickens as the elevator jolts, is it just me or does everyone fear an elevator falling each time it makes a sudden jolt?

I close my eyes for a brief moment, letting the rhythm of the ascent steady me.

Ping.

The 14th floor.

The doors slide open, and I step out into the lobby of Horizon Design Group. My shoes resonating the polished marble floor as I walk down the corridor towards my office. I pause for a moment, catching my reflection in the glass, taking the moment to adjust my cufflinks and smooth down the sleeves of my jacket.

Resuming my course, I nod politely to a few junior architects who greet me with a casual "Good Morning."

I catch an argument over curtain color by an architect and a designer, bickering like an old married couple and I can't help but chuckle.

"Sebastian!" Jenna calls from her desk near the glass walls that over-look downtown Austin. Her enthusiasm is... overwhelming. Talking to Jenna not only means you won't have the chance to speak, but you'll not want to hear anyone else speak for the rest of the day either.

I offer a nod but keep walking, eyes scanning the room for something, or someone, out of place.

"Hey! You're not avoiding me again?" she teases, laughter trailing behind me like a ribbon.

I let her voice fade into background noise as I approach my office at the far end of the lobby. The door stands slightly ajar; it always does. It invites distraction yet shields my chaos from prying eyes.

Inside, stacks of blueprints and models crowd every available surface, a controlled chaos that mirrors what brews beneath my skin when I think about Iris.

What are you doing to me?

I push that thought aside as I settle into my chair, fingertips gliding over plans for a new skyscraper, sharp lines and angles promising stability in a world that feels anything but secure in this moment.

Focus.

"Wolfe!" A voice slices through my reverie. Ryan, one of my junior architects, approaches with a stack of blueprints under his arm.

I look up, forcing a smile. "What's urgent?"

He fidgets, flipping through pages as if they hold the secrets of the universe. "We need your feedback on the layout for Maple Street."

"Can it wait?" I ask.

He hesitates, sensing something in my tone that isn't quite right. "Sure... I mean, if you're busy."

Busy? I scoff lightly.

Busy, yes, I'm busy. Busy thinking about her, thinking about, Iris. My eyes dart to the entrance, hoping to see her silhouette again, her perfection, bathe in sunlight, but only shadows dance in that space now.

"Sebastian?" Ryan's voice pulls me back.

I meet his gaze and straighten my shoulders. "Let's go over it..."

As he unfolds the plans on a nearby table, my mind wanders again, to Iris and her honeyed scent, to those fleeting moments where our worlds almost touch.

"What do you think?" Ryan asks, pointing at an area I've already glanced over three times.

"It's too cramped," I say without thinking.

"Cramped? It maximizes space." He frowns, confused by my lack of enthusiasm.

"No," I insist sharply. "Add more room for flow."

He nods slowly but his brow furrows deeper as if he questions my judgment. Good. I don't care about his confusion; all I care about is finding clarity in this chaos that has become my life since Iris stepped into it.

"Right," he murmurs, scribbling notes with a quick flick of his wrist.

The lobby buzzes with chatter around us while inside I'm still trapped in that elevator with her, the smell of honey still lingering like an afterthought in an empty room.

I straighten the collar of my tailored suit, forcing my thoughts back to the blueprints sprawled before me. Each line, each angle demands my attention, but I can't shake her from my mind. Iris Klarelle. She slips into every crevice of my focus, turning every thought chaotic.

"Sebastian?" Ryan's voice pulls me from the spiralling thoughts.

I glance up. "What?"

"Can we revisit the budget? The projections—"

"Budget is secondary," I cut in, frustration bubbling just below the surface. "Focus on functionality first. It's architecture, not accounting."

He blinks, his pen hovering over the paper like a lost bird. "Right."

What does he know about vision? I push down the urge to roll my eyes and turn back to the plans. The lines blur as I imagine them rearranging themselves into something more perfect, something that reflects clarity and intention. Yet in that moment, all I see is Iris again, her laughter dancing through the air like a sweet melody that should belong to no one but me.

"I'll make adjustments," Ryan says softly.

I wave him off without looking up. "Fine."

A familiar scent pulls at my senses like a fish that has just been hooked, demanding my attention, causing my instincts flare.

I look around, darting my attention to find the source of her sweet scent, towards the elevators, I catch a glimpse of her silhouette framed by sunlight pouring through glass window.

I watch carefully, watching her speak with Alexis, a new assistant on our floor.

"Iris." The name escapes me; a whisper laced with desire.

Ryan follows my gaze, curiosity flickering across his face. "You know her?"

My heart pounds as she moves further inside, unaware of the weight she carries with every step she takes towards me. It's intoxicating, this pull between us, a thread woven tightly through every shared glance and stolen moment.

"No," I manage, my voice steady despite the tremor beneath it. "We... just seem to be on the elevator together most days."

"Seems like more than that." He raises an eyebrow but doesn't push further.

The heat of Ryan's gaze feels invasive as I fixate on Iris gliding back to the elevator, effortlessly pulling my attention like a boat yielding to the ocean.

I shake off the haze of Iris's presence, refocusing on the plans sprawled across the table.

"Ryan, if you keep looking at me like I'm about to crack the world's greatest mystery, I might just start believing it," I say with a teasing grin.

He blinks, confusion etched across his features. "I thought that was your job."

"True, but it's also my job to keep us from going bankrupt. So, let's pivot back to those layouts."

I point to a section on the blueprints, highlighting areas where flow needs improvement.

"You need to be able to navigate space like it's a dance floor," I continue. "You don't want people tripping over each other like they've had one too many at a wedding."

He chuckles, letting out a sigh of relief before diving back into his notes.

"Maybe you should teach a class on 'Architectural Dancing,' Ryan suggests with a playful smirk. "Could bring in some extra income."

"Ah yes, because nothing says, 'professional architect' like cha-cha lessons in an empty office," I reply dryly.

The laughter between us eases the tension that always lingers when projects loom overhead. I enjoy moments like this, moments that remind me I'm more than just an architect consumed by numbers and lines.

Brainstorming ideas for our upcoming meeting with investors later today, I shift my focus back to strategy, ensuring every detail is meticulously planned out.

"Alright," I say, adopting a mock-serious tone. "Let's lay down our top three selling points for the pitch: stunning aesthetics, check; sustainable materials, check; and an unparalleled sense of community, check."

"Those sound good," Ryan replies while jotting them down.

"But we need something else," I say, pacing as ideas bounce around in my head. "How about this: a rooftop garden that'll make anyone forget they're in the middle of the city? A sanctuary among steel and glass."

Ryan raises an eyebrow. "Are we pitching a building or launching a spa retreat?"

I smirk at him. "Why not both? Just think, everyone will leave our meeting wanting to book their stay!"

Ryan's laughter fades as we turn our attention back to the blueprints.

I look up at the clock, 8:43; I can feel the diminishing time before our meeting with the investors pressing down on us like a tangible force. It's not just about the design; it's about selling them a vision, convincing them to see what I see.

"Alright, let's fine-tune this," I say, leaning over the table.

Ryan nods, his eyes sharp and focused. "So, more emphasis on open spaces?"

"Exactly. And let's rework the flow from the lobby to the common areas. We need a seamless transition that feels natural, almost inevitable."

He makes a few quick adjustments, pencil moving deftly across the paper. I watch his hand, my mind momentarily drifting back to Iris and the way she moves through a room with that same effortless grace.

"Like this?" Ryan asks, pulling me back.

I study his changes, tracing the lines with my finger. "Better. But we need to make sure there's enough light. Natural light transforms a space, it makes it feel alive."

He adds a few notes in the margins, marking where skylights and large windows should go. "Got it. Anything else?"

I tap my chin, considering. "The rooftop garden. Let's make it accessible from multiple points within the building. Instead of it just being an afterthought, let's make it a destination to behold."

Ryan nods again, sketching out pathways and access points that connect different floors to the garden. His enthusiasm fuelling my own.

"There," I say finally, straightening up and stretching my back. "I think we've got it."

Ryan steps back, surveying our work with a critical eye. "Looks solid."

"It is." I nod, feeling a rare sense of satisfaction settle over me. "Now let's get ready to blow those investors away."

With one last glance at the blueprints, we gather our materials and head toward the conference room. The excitement, the anticipation, it's like butterflies lifting me lofty.

Together with Maria, our graphic designer, we gather our materials and move toward the presentation room. The corridors of the office seem to stretch on forever, filled with the hum of productivity, but I walk with purpose, each step a declaration of my readiness.

The presentation room is a canvas of glass and light, a space I designed to inspire awe. We lay out our plans across the long table, a map of the future we're about to propose for 3rd Street. The rooftop garden, the flowing lines of the architecture, the harmony of sustainability and luxury, it's all here, waiting to breathe life into an empty lot.

We just finish setting up the presentation on the computer as the clients file in.

I begin to feel the familiar adrenaline of performance coursing through my veins.

I watch them closely as they enter, noting their expressions, their faces a sea of expectation. Not to worry, I am the captain, and I know these waters.

The presentation unfolds with a seamless confidence, every phrase, every gesture meticulously designed to exude assurance and fore-sight. Ryan and Maria support me flawlessly, their segments weaving perfectly into the narrative we've crafted. The clients lean in, their eyes sparkling with curiosity, each detail capturing their undivided attention.

When the final word is uttered, the room sinks into a quiet stillness, as if the very atmosphere is pausing. It's a moment frozen in time, and then, applause erupts.

"We love it," Mr. Kallahan says, the leader of this trio of investors. "When can we get started?" He asks with a smile. The relief is tangible, a shared exhalation that fills the space with the aroma of triumph.

"Thank you," I say, my voice steady, betraying none of the elation that bubbles beneath the surface. "We're thrilled to move forward with you on this journey right away."

Mr. Kallahan and his team stand, shake each of our hands, exiting the room with smiles all around. The atmosphere among the team transitions from intense focus to exuberant festivity as we each shout "Yay!", jumping into the air in excitement.

"You know what this calls for?" I ask knowingly.

"Drinks are on you?" Maria replies.

"Drinks are on me!" I announce, already mentally calculating how much I can expense without raising any eyebrows. It's a small price to pay for the adrenaline coursing through my veins right now.

Ryan and Maria exchange an excited glance, and I can practically see the tension melting from their shoulders. We've been working around the clock on this project, and the payoff is sweeter than I could have imagined.

"Let's get out of here," I say, ushering them toward the door. The sooner we're out of here, the sooner we can truly celebrate.

The Pub is a short walk from the office, a dimly lit haunt where the architects and designers of the city come to unwind. It's the perfect place to toast our success, away from the prying eyes of clients and colleagues.

Approaching the familiar wooden door, I can already hear the low hum of conversation and the clink of glasses. This is my kind of sanctuary, a place where I can let my guard down and indulge in the simple pleasures of good company and even better whiskey.

"After you," I say, holding the door open for Ryan and Maria. They waste no time making a beeline for our usual spot in the back corner, staking our claim on the worn leather couches.

I follow close behind, the scent of hops and oak mingling with the familiar aroma of this place. It's comforting, a soothing balm to the relentless pressure of my daily life.

"Alright, what's your poison?" I ask, already heading toward the bar. "Scotch for me, obviously. And for you two?"

"Gin and tonic," Maria replies with a grin.

"Beer," Ryan chimes in. "Something dark and malty."

I nod and make my way to the bar, weaving through the crowd of patrons. The bartender recognizes me instantly, flashing a knowing smile.

"The usual, Mr. Wolfe?"

"You know it," I reply, handing over my card. "And a gin and tonic, and a dark beer for the team."

Waiting for the drinks, I let my gaze wander the room, scoping the crowd. It's a fill of the usual, a mix of creative types and industry heavyweights, all seeking refuge from the demands of their respective worlds.

"Mr. Wolfe?" The bartender's voice snaps me back to reality, and I quickly turn to accept the drinks.

I navigate the tables, moving steadily back to our spot, setting down the drinks. "One gin and tonic for the beautiful lady, and a beer for the gruff looking man." I tease, plopping myself down in the seat across from them.

Maria raises her glass, her eyes sparkling with the reflection of the city lights outside.

"To Sebastian," she declares, "the maestro of modern architecture."

We touch glasses, toasting together, the sound sharp and clear as each of our drinks collide with one another.

I sit back, taking a strong swig of the whiskey, watching Maria and Ryan taking large gulps of their drinks as we sit back and smile at one another.

I allow myself to bask in the glory of our accomplishment. But even here, in the dim light of the bar, surrounded by the clink of glasses and the low rumble of conversation, a part of me wonders if Iris would be proud.

The thought is fleeting, a whisper in the back of my mind, but it's there, a reminder that even in moments of triumph, there are still things in this world that remain just beyond my reach.

Finishing my scotch, the warm liquor burns, spreading through my chest. "Another round?" I ask, gesturing to Maria and Ryan.

"Absolutely," Maria replies, raising her glass.

"Don't mind if I do," Ryan adds, taking a long pull from his beer.

I signal the bartender, ordering another round. The whiskey feels good, lubricating the edges of the triumph, smoothing.

I finish my second scotch, savoring the smoky flavor as it burns a path down my throat. The alcohol loosens my shoulders, relaxes the perpetual tension I carry between meetings and deadlines. Ryan and Maria are laughing about something, some inside joke from the presentation, their faces flushed with victory and booze.

"Listen," I say, setting my empty glass on the table with a decisive thud. "The tab's on me tonight. Order whatever you want."

Maria's eyes widen. "Seriously?"

"Consider it a thank you for pulling off that presentation."

"Just don't celebrate too hard. We still have work tomorrow." I say, giving each of them a knowing look.

Ryan raises his glass. "To reasonable celebrations on a weeknight."

"And to unreasonable ones on weekends," Maria adds with a wink.

I laugh, standing up and grabbing my jacket from the back of my chair. "Enjoy yourselves. I've got some things to finish up."

"You're leaving already?" Ryan looks genuinely surprised. "We just scored the biggest project of the quarter."

"Which means I have even more to prepare for tomorrow." I offer them a smile that doesn't quite reach my eyes. "You two deserve to celebrate. I'll see you in the morning."

I walk back to the bar, telling the bartender to just close me out at the end of the night, taking back my card and placing it in my wallet before exiting the door.

The cool night air hits me as I step outside, clearing some of the whiskey haze. My car waits in the parking lot, sleek and patient. I slide behind the wheel, my mind already racing ahead to my destination.

The streets are nearly empty at this hour. I drive back to the Sailboat Building, my office building, its glass facade gleaming under the moonlight. The parking garage is mostly vacant, just a few cars belonging to the night security and the cleaning staff.

I take the elevator up, but instead of pressing 14 for my floor, my finger hovers over 3. Iris's floor. I press it, feeling a small thrill race through me.

The elevator doors slide open silently. The third floor is dark except for the emergency exit signs casting a faint red glow across the carpet.

Good. I anticipated the office would be completely empty by this time. I step out, my footsteps muffled as I slowly walk the office space, trying to be quiet even though there appears to be no one here.

I move carefully between the cubicles and glass-walled offices, studying each desk. Some have family photos, others display trinkets and plants. I'm looking for something specific, something that belongs to her.

A desk near the window catches my attention. It's neat, organized, with a small potted succulent and a notebook bound in soft leather. I open the top drawer and see a business card holder. I lift it, examining the name embossed in gold lettering: Iris Klarelle.

My fingers trace the embossed gold lettering on her business card. Iris Klarelle. Even her name feels deliberate, like architecture, each syllable perfectly placed.

I slide the leather-bound planner from beneath a stack of folders. It's heavy, substantial, the kind of item someone invests in rather than picks up on impulse. The cover is soft but worn at the corners, suggesting frequent use. This is how she organizes her life, how she creates order in her days.

Opening it feels like crossing a threshold. I hesitate but proceed regardless of the fact that I'm invading her privacy.

Her handwriting is precise, slightly slanted, confident strokes that don't waste space. Tuesday evenings: Singing lessons, 7-8:30 PM. Wednesdays: Violin, 6:30-7:45 PM. I run my finger along the ink, imagining her hand making these marks, planning these moments.

So, she's musical. Not just casually, she dedicates multiple evenings to it. I picture her fingers dancing across violin strings, her throat vibrating with practiced notes. This isn't dabbling; this is discipline. She cultivates herself, invests in her talents. I respect that.

Mondays and Thursdays: Gym, 6-8 PM. Two-hour sessions. She's committed to her body the way she's committed to her mind. I wonder what she prefers, cardio, weights, perhaps yoga? The duration suggests intensity, a refusal to take shortcuts.

I turn the pages, scanning earlier weeks. The pattern holds. Her life has rhythm, consistency. She doesn't cancel on herself.

The desk drawer slides open silently. A small bottle of hand lotion, unscented, practical. A pack of green tea. Three pens, identical, lined up perfectly. A small notebook with sketches, abstract shapes that could be music notes or design elements. Her mind works in patterns I want to decode.

On her desk, the succulent is healthy, its leaves plump. She remembers to water it, but not excessively. She cares for things appropriately, not too much, not too little.

A small photo frame faces her chair, a lake view at sunset. No people, just landscape. She values beauty, solitude perhaps.

Everything here speaks of someone who lives with intention. Nothing is accidental. Nothing is wasted. She and I share this quality, this need for purpose in every choice.

I close the planner, bringing it up to my face, allowing myself the opportunity to enjoy her sweet scent. It's intoxicating, like dreams made of sweet honey.

I pull the planner to my chest, holding it a moment, imagining what it would be like to hold her in the same way. I let the moment fade, my thoughts returning to reality.

I return the planner exactly as I found it, aligning its edge with the corner of her desk. My heart races with the thrill of this small transgression, this glimpse into her private world. But I can't linger. Even at this hour, security cameras are watching, and my presence on this floor would raise questions I'd rather not answer.

I move silently back through the darkened office space, retracing my steps with precision. The red exit signs cast long shadows across the carpet as I make my way to the elevator. My finger presses 14, and I watch the numbers climb, rehearsing my excuse should anyone question why I'm here so late.

The doors slide open to my floor, familiar territory where my presence won't raise eyebrows. I stride purposefully toward my office, nodding at the night janitor who barely glances up from his vacuuming. The rhythm of the machine covers the sound of my footsteps.

My office door closes behind me with a soft click. I switch on the desk lamp rather than the overhead lights, less conspicuous, and settle into my chair. The computer hums to life, the blue glow illuminating my face as I enter my password.

I open a few project files, clicking through them absently while checking my watch. Five minutes. Just long enough to establish a digital footprint, to create the illusion that I came back to finish some urgent tasks. The system logs every login, every file access, evidence of my dedication, not my obsession.

Time crawls. I straighten items on my desk, arrange pens in perfect alignment. Four minutes. I check my email, delete a few unnecessary messages. Five minutes.

Logging out, I shut down the computer and gather my things. The night security guard will remember a hardworking architect, nothing more. I leave my office exactly as I found it, leaving the room behind.

The elevator descends smoothly to the lobby. Empty now, just the night guard at his desk who offers a casual wave. I return it with a tired smile, just another dedicated employee working late.

The glass doors of the Sailboat Building slide open, releasing me into the night.

Chapter 2

Arriving at The Sailboat Building, I take a hurried step to make it through the already opened glass door being held open by Ryan instead of the busy rotating door.

"Good morning," Ryan says with a cheerful smile.

"Good morning," I reply, returning his smile.

Ryan follows close behind as we make our way toward the elevator.

I press the 'up' arrow button to the elevators, the light illuminating above us as I look up, as if uncertain the elevator will move as intended.

I see a familiar silhouette in the reflection of the polished elevator door, then a familiar scent washes over me like waves on a beach.

Honey.

The elevator doors slide open, and I step inside. The air buzzes with tension, but it's just the three of us. I glance at Ryan, who's scrolling through his phone, blissfully unaware of the magnetic pull in this confined space.

As the doors close, I focus on Iris standing across from me. She's here, inches away, and yet an unbreachable distance separates us. My heart picks up its pace; each thud reverberates in my chest like a metronome counting down the moments.

I catch her reflection in the glass. The way her hair falls just so, soft waves that frame her face, pulls at something deep within me. I notice how she tucks a loose strand behind her ear. Such a small action, yet it holds weight.

Ryan breaks the silence. "Did you see the new renderings?" His words are casual, yet they bounce around me like pinballs.

I force myself to respond, maintaining my usual composure. "Yes, they look great, but there may be a few changes that require consideration." My voice remains steady, but my attention lingers on Iris.

She glances up at me now, those eyes, deep pools of intrigue and warmth, meet mine for a fleeting second before she looks away again. My breath catches; there's something electric about that momentary connection. I wonder if she feels it too, then the moment fades as she looks away.

"I agree," Ryan says, nudging me with an elbow as he chuckles, raising both of his eyebrows, gesturing towards Iris with his eyes.

We both know that he's no longer talking about the renderings.

I show a dismissive smile, looking away from Iris directly, but keeping my gaze fixed on her reflection.

The elevator hums softly as it ascends, and for those few seconds, time stretches like elastic. The scent of honey swirls around us, intoxicating and familiar, her presence clings to me like a shadow. It makes everything else fade, the project deadlines, Ryan's chatter, all of it dims in comparison to this singular focus.

I lean slightly closer to Iris as if trying to be absorbed into her world.

I watch every detail of her reflection, the way her fingers fidget with the hem of her blouse or how her breath quickens when she shifts her weight from one foot to the other.

Ryan's voice fades out as my world narrows down to just us two. I wish desperately to shatter this delicate barrier between us, to bridge that gap and explore what lies beneath her quiet exterior.

The elevator jolts slightly before coming to a stop on her floor with a ding that shatters the moment. The doors slide open with a whisper, and she steps out, leaving my world.

As the doors slide shut behind her, I feel a peculiar emptiness, like the air has been siphoned out of the elevator. Ryan continues to talk about the upcoming client meeting, but his words are just background noise now.

I make my way to my office, my sanctuary of glass and steel. The design is flawless, but I don't believe my meticulous nature would allow me to have it any other way. Everything in its place, every line clean and deliberate. Yet, today it feels different, like there's a subtle disturbance in the order of things.

I settle behind my desk, spreading out blueprints for the latest project. My eyes scan over the precise lines and angles, but my mind drifts back to Iris. Her scent lingers in my thoughts, an echo of her presence that refuses to fade.

"Sebastian," Ryan's voice cuts through my reverie as he steps into my office without knocking, a habit I've yet to break him of. "Got a minute?"

"Of course," I reply, forcing myself to focus. I gesture for him to take a seat.

Ryan drops into the chair opposite me with a casual grace that's almost enviable. "About those changes you mentioned, what exactly did you have in mind?"

I lean back, steepling my fingers as I gather my thoughts. "The client wants something more organic, something that flows with the landscape rather than imposing upon it."

Ryan nods thoughtfully, scribbling notes on his tablet. "I can work on some new sketches this afternoon."

"Good," I say, but even as we discuss architectural nuances and client preferences, my mind keeps wandering back to Iris.

Ryan shifts in his seat, sensing my distraction. "You alright? You seem...off today."

"I'm fine," I lie smoothly, unwilling to admit the true source of my preoccupation.

He gives me a skeptical look but doesn't press further. "Alright then. I'll get those sketches to you by end of day."

"Is it that girl?" He asks probingly.

"What?" I respond defensively.

I do my best to recalibrate my thinking, how I should respond to Ryan.

"No," I respond in a calm calculated manner, "I just have a lot of different things on my mind at the moment."

Ryan nods quietly, taking his cue to leave, backing out of my office.

The room is silent save for the distant hum of city life beyond the windows. I pick up a pencil and begin sketching absentmindedly on a blank sheet of paper.

Lines and shapes take form under my hand, sharp angles soften into curves; structured designs morph into something more fluid and organic. Unconsciously, I'm drawing elements inspired by her, by Iris.

A knock at the door pulls me from my trance. One of the interns pokes her head in cautiously. "Mr. Wolfe? The clients are here for your 10 o'clock."

"Thank you, tell the HYTN associates I will be there momentarily," I say, setting down the pencil and pushing aside the sketch.

Rising from my chair, I smooth out the front of my suit jacket.

The patting of my suit releases small particles of dust glimmering in the morning rays shining through my window. With the dust, I catch one last whiff of honey in the air, a phantom scent that leaves me yearning for another fleeting moment with Iris.

Shaking off the moment, I refocus, knowing I have no room for distractions during this meeting.

I make my way to the conference room where the HengYu TongNuo Investments associates await. Each step I take is deliberate, my mind clearing as I push thoughts of Iris to the back, locking them away for later. My reflection in the glass walls reassures me, tailored suit, controlled expression, everything in place.

As I enter the room, the clients rise to greet me. Mr. Liang, a distinguished figure with an air of authority, extends his hand.

"Mr. Wolfe," he says with a slight bow of his head.

"Mr. Liang," I reply, matching his gesture with practiced ease. "It's a pleasure to have you here."

We settle into our seats around the sleek mahogany table. The polished surface reflects the overhead lights, casting a subtle glow that enhances the room's modern elegance.

"Shall we begin?" Mr. Liang's assistant sets out folders and tablets before us.

I nod, launching into my presentation with precision. "As you'll see in these renderings, we've integrated your feedback to create a design that not only meets your specifications but also harmonizes with Austin's unique landscape."

Their eyes follow my gestures as I point out key elements on the digital display, a blend of steel and glass that rises organically from its surroundings, capturing both innovation and tradition.

I notice Ryan across from me, taking notes and occasionally glancing up to gauge their reactions. His presence is a steady anchor in this sea of corporate expectation.

Mr. Liang studies the designs intently before speaking. "Your vision aligns well with our company's ethos," he says slowly, weighing each word. "But we are curious about the structural integrity of such an ambitious project."

I anticipated this question and prepared for it. "Our engineering team has conducted thorough assessments," I explain confidently, pulling up detailed schematics on my tablet. "Every aspect has been meticulously calculated to ensure both safety and durability."

The tension in the room eases as they review the data. Satisfied nods ripple through the group.

"Impressive," Mr. Liang concedes with a smile that barely reaches his eyes, a man accustomed to getting exactly what he wants.

We continue discussing finer details, material choices, sustainability measures, projected timelines, each point met with approval or constructive critique. The rhythm of negotiation feels like an intricate game of chess.

When the meeting concludes and handshakes are exchanged once more, Mr. Liang pauses at the door.

"Your dedication is evident in your work, Mr. Wolfe," he says appreciatively. "We look forward to seeing this vision come to life."

"Thank you," I respond warmly, maintaining eye contact until they exit the room.

The door closes behind them with a soft click and I exhale quietly, another successful step forward in this grand endeavor.

Ryan stays behind momentarily, tapping his pen against his notebook thoughtfully before speaking up.

"That went well," he observes casually but with genuine satisfaction.

"It did," I agree, though my mind already begins its inevitable drift back toward Iris and the intoxicating puzzle she represents within my otherwise ordered world.

My stomach growls audibly as I round the corner towards my office.

I pause a moment, reconsidering my next step. Maybe now would be a good time for lunch.

I turn around, pressing the button to go down, noticing the elevator has just passed and is headed for the lobby.

Sigh.

This is going to take a minute. I glance over at the stairs, reconsidering my option, but decide I might as well wait, I did already push the button.

As I'm waiting, I hear the familiar sound of Jenna's shoes clacking against the floor.

My eyes go wide, and I freeze absolutely still.

I pause a moment, but the footsteps stop. She must have found someone else to corner and talk to.

Ding.

The elevator arrives and I quickly hop in, hoping to make it down before she changes her mind and catches me alone.

As I turn to press the button, out of the corner of my eye, I see her, Jenna.

I see her approaching and do my best to hide to the side of the elevator.

The doors begin closing. Almost free.

I keep my eyes on the buttons as I see her getting closer.

I begin desperately mashing the close button like a video game controller. The universe can't hold this against me.

It's self-preservation.

I did not see her.

She does not exist.

The doors narrow, cutting me off from the office, blessed relief draws near, four inches, three, two...

"Hold the elevator!"

A hand shoots between the gap. The doors jolt, pausing, then swing open in a betrayal of the highest order.

Jenna bursts in, and with her, that overwhelming high energy and unchecked enthusiasm, like a golden retriever that has just been given espresso.

"Oh my God, Sebastian! What are the odds?"

Not low enough...

I exhale, slipping my hands into my pockets to mask my existential dread. "Jenna."

She pokes the button for the lobby with a "boop", then spins toward me, her hair bouncing like a woman starring in an ad for a shampoo brand I would now boycott on principle.

"So! Lunch plans? I'm going to this amazing poke bowl place, do you like poke bowls? Wait, no, let's start simpler, do you like sushi? Because if not, that's honestly tragic, but also, it makes sense."

I slowly blink, trying to find my footing. "How does that make sense?"

She gasps, her mouth wide, placing her palm on her chest. "Because, Sebastian, you have such haunted Victorian man energy."

I turn my head slightly, staring at the steel panel of the elevator as if it might crack open a hidden escape hatch just for me.

"Do I?"

"Yes! You totally do the whole staring out of windows broodingly thing. You probably own a pocket watch. Do you?"

I exhale sharply, the sound of a man accepting his fate. "No."

"But you want to."

I ignore her comment. I feel like a pilot about to crash his plane into the earth. I need altitude. I need to pull up.

Jenna, completely oblivious to my mental tailspin, snaps her fingers. "Okay! Poke bowls. Come with me. You need omega-3s."

Mayday, mayday!

I stare at my reflection in the steel panel. This is how I die.

The doors chime open at the lobby, and for a split second, I consider making a run for it. Just taking off into the street with no regard for dignity.

Instead, I sigh. "Fine. Poke bowls..."

Jenna grins like she has just won the huge bear at a carnival game. "Sebastian! Socializing! I love this arc for you."

She loops her arm into mine before I'm able to dodge. She proceeds to drag me towards the exit, taking the lead.

I should have taken the stairs.

The doors slide open, releasing us into the harsh glare of midday sun. Jenna maintains her grip on my arm like I'm a flight risk, which, to be fair, I am. I think I understand why coyotes bite off their leg when they're caught in a trap.

"So, the place is called Wow Poke, and it's seriously life changing. I go there like three times a week, and the guy who works there, Mike, he knows my order off by heart now. Is that sad? I don't think it's sad. I think it's efficient."

I open my mouth to respond, but she's already pulling me toward the bus stop.

"We'll take the Number 2. It's way faster than walking, and honestly, in this heat? Your Victorian sensibilities would have you passing out on the sidewalk."

The bus stop is mercifully empty, save for an elderly woman who seems to be having an intense conversation with her handbag. Jenna doesn't notice, or doesn't care, continuing her monologue without pause.

"So, I was telling Brenda from Accounting, you know Brenda, right? Big hair, always wearing those statement necklaces that look like they could double as medieval weapons?"

I nod vaguely, scanning the horizon for the bus.

"Anyway, I told her that the secret to a good poke bowl is the sauce-to-rice ratio. Too much sauce, it's soup. Too little, and you might as well be eating cardboard."

The Number 2 bus arrives with a hydraulic wheeze that I find oddly comforting. We board, Jenna flashing her pass while I fumble for mine. She guides me to seats near the back, her hand still firmly attached to my arm.

"Oh! And they have this spicy mayo that will literally change your life. Not figuratively. Literally. You'll be a different person after tasting it."

The bus lurches forward, and I grip the seat in front of me. Jenna doesn't seem to notice the movement, her body somehow perfectly attuned to the rhythm of public transportation.

"So, what kind of fish do you like? Wait, let me guess. You strike me as a tuna guy. Very classic, very traditional. Am I right?"

I clear my throat. "I don't really have a preference."

Her eyes widen with delight. "A blank slate! This is perfect. I'm going to curate your entire poke experience."

For the next ten minutes, Jenna talks without drawing breath, about poke, about her weekend plans, about a dream she had involving a talking penguin. I nod at appropriate intervals, my mind drifting to Iris as I tune out the conversation. What would she order at a poke place? Would she appreciate the comfort of silence?

The bus stops with another wheeze. "We're here!" Jenna announces, tugging me to my feet.

I pause for a moment gazing at the pinkness of the building in front of us. Such an odd color. What makes it odder is the darker pink tones for the window frames and doors.

"No, not that place, it's just around the corner." Jenna says, continuing to drag me.

As we pass around the corner of the building, a small white food truck can be seen with a small sign labelled "Wow Poke".

"Okay, so for your base, get the half-rice, half-greens. Trust me on this. Then ahi tuna, they get it fresh every morning. Cucumber, edamame, mango, and definitely the crispy onions. For sauce, ponzu and just a touch of that spicy mayo I was telling you about."

I nod, watching through the window as they server assembles my bowl according to Jenna's precise instructions. When it's her turn, she rattles off a complex order without hesitation, punctuating each item with a decisive point.

She leads me to a small picnic table, setting down her tray with a flourish. "Prepare to have your mind blown."

I stare down at my bowl, an artful arrangement of colors and textures that Jenna has orchestrated with the precision of a symphony conductor. She watches me expectantly, eyes wide, fork poised mid-air over her own creation.

"Well?" she prompts, practically vibrating with anticipation. "The first bite is crucial. You need to get a little bit of everything."

I carefully position my chopsticks, making sure to gather rice, tuna, and a hint of that supposedly life-altering spicy mayo she wouldn't shut up about. Her gaze follows my every move like I'm defusing a bomb rather than eating lunch.

"Moment of truth," I mutter, bringing the bite to my mouth.

The flavors blend together nicely, fresh fish, the tang of ponzu, heat from the mayo. It's good. Satisfying, even. But life-changing? Hardly.

Jenna's face splits into a grin as she reads my expression. "Right? RIGHT? I told you!"

Before I can respond, she dives into her own bowl with enthusiasm that borders on aggression, somehow continuing to talk despite her mouth being full.

"I come here all the time," she says between chews. "Mike, the owner, he says I should get a loyalty card or something. I told him, just name a sauce after me instead."

I take another bite, again nodding at appropriate intervals. The food is genuinely tasty, but my mind keeps drifting to the quiet of my office, to the stack of drawings waiting for my attention, to the lingering scent of honey that seems to follow me.

"So," Jenna says, swallowing a massive bite, "what's your deal anyway? Dating anyone?"

I nearly choke on a piece of tuna. "My deal?"

"Yeah! You're always so mysterious. I bet you have women falling all over you with that whole brooding architect thing."

I focus intently on selecting my next bite. "I keep my personal life personal."

"Oh my God, you're totally single," she says, pointing her fork at me accusingly. "I have the perfect friend for you. Her name's Stephanie. She's from Houston, super sweet, studying English literature. You two would be so cute together!"

I take another bite of my poke bowl, chewing slowly to buy time. Jenna stares at me with the intensity of someone watching a lottery drawing, waiting for my answer about this Stephanie person.

"I'll think about it," I finally concede, knowing it's the path of least resistance.

Her face lights up like I've just agreed to donate a kidney. "Oh my God, that's practically a yes from you! This is going to be amazing. Stephanie is literally the sweetest person. She does this thing where she quotes obscure poets at random moments, which sounds annoying but is actually super charming."

I nod vaguely, already regretting my non-committal response. The remainder of my poke bowl suddenly seems endless.

"You two can talk about, I don't know, the symbolism in architecture or whatever. She wrote this paper on the metaphorical significance of staircases in Victorian literature that got published in some journal."

"Fascinating," I mutter, scraping the last bits of rice from my bowl.

Jenna finishes her food with alarming speed, then watches me eat with the patience of a predator. The moment I set down my chopsticks, she springs into action.

"Ready? We should probably head back. I have this call at two, and you probably have important architect things to brood over."

We dispose of our empty bowls, and Jenna continues her monologue as we walk to the bus stop. The Number 2 arrives mercifully quickly, and I settle into a seat by the window, watching Austin blur past while Jenna details Stephanie's entire academic career beside me.

We arrive back at the Sailboat Building and take the elevator together. I keep my eyes fixed on the floor numbers, counting down the seconds until my escape.

"We should do this again!" Jenna declares as the doors open to our floor. "Maybe next time we can try that new Thai place on Sixth Street. Or sushi! Do you like sushi? Of course you do. Everyone likes sushi."

I nod noncommittally, already stepping away. "Have a good afternoon, Jenna."

She waves enthusiastically as I retreat to my office, closing the door behind me with a soft click that sounds like salvation.

I lean against the door, exhaling deeply. The quiet of my space wraps around me like a familiar blanket. I loosen my tie slightly and cross to my desk, settling into my chair, pulling up the renderings on my tablet. Each element speaks of meticulous design, yet now they must evolve further. My fingers move swiftly, altering lines, recalculating angles, ensuring that every modification enhances the integrity without compromising the vision.

The room is silent save for the soft hum of my computer and the occasional rustle of paper.

A sharp knock on my door makes me jump, sending my pen skittering across the page. For a terrible moment, I'm convinced it's Jenna, returned to finish what she started, perhaps with details about Stephanie's dissertation or, God forbid, photos.

Through the frosted glass, I see a silhouette that's mercifully taller and less animated than Jenna's. Ryan Adams peers through the small window panel, eyebrows raised in question.

I wave him in, composing myself as he enters.

"You survived," he says, grinning as he closes the door behind him. "We were taking bets on whether you'd make it back or fake an emergency call halfway through lunch."

I straighten my tie. "Your confidence in me is touching."

"So how was the Jenna Louise Experience?" He leans against my drafting table, arms crossed. "Did she let you get a word in edgewise?"

"I think I managed about seven syllables in total." I turn back to my tablet, swiping through the revised renderings. "Next time, I'm dragging you with me. I need someone else to absorb some of that conversational shrapnel."

Ryan laughs. "Not a chance. I've made that mistake before. Ended up hearing about her cousin's wedding for forty-five minutes. The woman doesn't need oxygen, I swear."

"The food was decent, at least." I pull up the main blueprint on the larger monitor. "Did I miss anything after the meeting?"

Ryan steps closer, scanning the screen. "Hartmann wants the atrium ceiling raised another three feet. Says it feels 'constrained' at the current height."

I zoom in on the section in question. "That'll throw off the proportions of the entire entrance."

"That's what I told him." Ryan points to the eastern corridor. "We'd have to adjust this whole wing to maintain the balance."

We fall into the comfortable rhythm of problem-solving, making adjustments, and calculating structural impacts. Ryan suggests a compromise that might satisfy Hartmann without compromising the design integrity, and I find myself nodding in agreement.

"Not bad, Adams. We might make an architect out of you yet."

"High praise from the great Sebastian Wolfe." He mock-bows. "Almost worth enduring a lunch with Jenna."

My eyes flick to the clock mounted on the wall, 3:47 PM. I have one hour ten minutes before Iris boards the elevator.

I refocus back on the task at hand, tweaking structural elements and fine-tuning details. Mr. Liang's concerns are valid and push me to refine our approach further. The design must be impeccable.

Ryan leans over my shoulder, studying the revised atrium design. "What if we offset the height increase with a graduated ceiling? Start at the original height by the entrance, then slope upward as you move into the main space." His finger traces the path on my tablet. "Gives Hartmann his extra three feet without compromising your proportions."

I consider it, mentally walking through the space. The suggestion has merit, an elegant solution that preserves the essence of my design while accommodating the client's wishes.

"Could work," I concede, making a few quick adjustments to visualize the effect. "We'd need to recalculate the lighting placement."

"Already on it." Ryan pulls out his own tablet, flicking through calculations. "I ran some preliminary numbers during the meeting. The graduated ceiling actually creates an interesting opportunity for natural light if we adjust these skylights."

I glance at him with reluctant appreciation. For all his youthful demeanor, Ryan has sharp instincts. He sees solutions where others see only problems, a quality I value, even if I rarely acknowledge it.

"Send me those calculations," I say, returning to my own screen. "I'll incorporate them into the revised renderings for tomorrow's presentation."

Ryan nods, gathering his things. "Will do. Oh, and Sebastian?" He pauses at the door, a hint of amusement in his expression. "If Jenna corners you about that blind date again, just tell her you're allergic to literature. Works every time."

The door closes behind him before I can respond, leaving me alone with my thoughts and the heavy glow of my computer.

I check the time again, 4:32 PM. I have just under half an hour before Iris takes the elevator down. Just enough time to finish these revisions, prepare for tomorrow, and ensure I'm standing in the right place at the right time.

Another glance at the clock, 4:55 PM. Almost time.

I save my progress and rise from my chair, smoothing out my suit jacket with practiced ease. I exit my office quietly, making my way to the elevator, my pace increasing as my heart begins to hasten in anticipation.

Descending alone in the elevator feels like entering a different world, a place where time stretches and anticipation builds with each passing floor.

The doors open with a soft chime as I step into the lobby, moving to a corner where I can observe without drawing attention. The lobby is a hive of activity at this hour, people coming and going, voices blending into a symphony of urban life.

I make my way to a dark brown leather sofa in the corner of the lobby, the seat partially obscured by the leaves of the fiddle fig tree next to the chair.

I check my watch again as I sit down, 5:02 PM.

Then she appears, Iris Klarelle, gliding through the revolving doors with that same effortless grace that captivates me daily. She pauses briefly to check her phone before continuing toward the exit.

Once Iris vanishes into the thrumming streets of Austin, I linger for a breath, caught in the wake of her presence. Following her movements has become second nature, a ritual that stands in sharp contrast to the rigid framework of my day. Each fleeting glimpse feels like collecting fragments of a puzzle whose solution remains just out of reach.

I retrace my steps to the refuge of my office, the sharp clap of my shoes against the marble floor echoing in time with my pulse.

The door clicks shut behind me, sealing off the chaos outside. Among the blueprints and scaled models of towering structures, a sense of order returns. My drafting table, littered with rulers, graphite-smudged sketches, and stacks of precise calculations, is an anchor. Here, I impose structure, bending disorder to my will through careful lines and deliberate choices.

Sinking into my chair, the familiar weight of responsibility presses down like a second skin. There's work to be done, projects that demand my full focus. Yet, even as I sift through the flood of emails, filtering through proposals and consultations, a part of me remains tethered to her. Thoughts of Iris lurk at the edges of my concentration, an unshakable presence threading through my mind like a melody I can't silence.

The faint trace of her fragrance lingers, whether real or conjured, I can't be sure. A whisper of something elusive drifts through the room, needling at my senses, unsettling in its familiarity. She is a puzzle I have yet to solve, an enigma that refuses to be categorized neatly within the structured order of my world.

With effort, I redirect my focus to the tangible, steel, glass, concrete. The HYTN project demands precision, attention to detail with no margin for error. I meticulously examine the schematics, ensuring every calculation holds, every material choice aligns with both vision and function.

And yet, somewhere in the periphery of my mind, Iris still lingers, unruly, compelling, a disruption I can't seem to reconcile.

I glance up. 10:43 PM. The office is silent, the whisper of the city beyond the glass windows a distant murmur. I exhale, stretching my fingers over the desk. I shake my hands and flex my fingers attempting to dismiss the cramping from the repeated typing and drawing.

I pack my things with practiced efficiency, stacking my tablet and notebooks into my briefcase. The room is left undisturbed, precisely as it should be. Lights off. Door locked.

The corridors of the Sailboat Building are empty at this hour, my footsteps the only sound threading through the stillness. I take the elevator down alone, the descent smooth, seamless.

In the garage, my car waits, a sleek silver machine, pristine, a reflection of careful upkeep. The engine purrs to life, and I navigate the empty streets of Austin with a steady, practiced ease. The city is quieter now, stripped of its daytime urgency. Streetlights paint long shadows across the pavement, the occasional silhouette of a late-night wanderer drifting along the sidewalks.

Home is a fortress of steel and dark wood, a quiet retreat curated to my exacting tastes. I set my briefcase down in the foyer and head to the kitchen. A simple meal awaits, seared steak, wilted greens, a precise arrangement on a white porcelain plate. The meal left and prepared by my cook. The taste barely registers, secondary to the necessity of sustenance.

I retire to my study. The room is hushed, the scent of polished wood, warm pipe tobacco and aged books thick in the air. I pour a measure of whiskey, the amber liquid catching the dim light as it swirls in the glass. Settling into my chair, I let the familiar burn slide down my throat, warmth spreading slow and steady.

Across the room, the photographs wait, my trophies, statuesque and preserved memories of each girl.

I rise, crossing to the built-in shelves where the frames stand in orderly rows. My fingers ghosting over the edges as I take in the images of the statues.

I set the glass down, leaving the study in its perpetual silence.

The bedroom is dark and cool. I undress with precision, pulling back the covers before sliding beneath them. The sheets are crisp, the mattress firm. I close my eyes, letting the weight of the day settle.

As I lie in the solitude of my bedroom, the stillness of the night engulfs me, but it cannot drown out the whispers of her name that echo through my mind, Iris Klarelle. It's a rhythm as persistent as the beat of my own heart, her image a specter that haunts my private quarters as relentlessly as it does my waking hours.

I turn on my side, the soft rustle of the sheets a stark contrast to the cacophony within my chest. Sleep should come easily after such a demanding day, yet it eludes me, a tantalizing mirage just beyond reach. I find myself tracing the contours of her face in the darkness, the curve of her cheek, the arch of her brow, the fullness of her lips, each detail etched into my memory with surgical precision.

I've always prided myself on my ability to compartmentalize, to keep my desires neatly filed away in the appropriate mental drawers. But with Iris, the compartments bleed into one another, her presence seeping through the cracks of my carefully constructed facade.

I rise, the cool air of the room a momentary balm against the restlessness that courses through my veins. I wander to the window, the cityscape stretched out before me. The towering structures, the ordered lines, the controlled chaos of urban planning, it's all a reflection of the discipline I've imposed upon my life.

Yet, as I gaze upon the city, it's not the triumphs of my architectural achievements that hold my attention but the spaces in between, the darkened alleyways, the hidden courtyards, the secluded rooftops. I find myself envisioning her there, in those secret pockets of the city, moving with the same quiet confidence that captivates me daily.

The thought is both exhilarating and unsettling. Iris represents a variable I cannot account for, an unpredictable element that defies calculation. She is a question mark in a world where I have always demanded certainty.

I turn away from the window, my reflection staring back at me, a man of control grappling with the edges of his own restraint. I make my way to my study, the whiskey still where I left it, the amber liquid a silent invitation.

I take a seat, the leather of the chair cool against my skin. The room is a sanctuary of order, every book in its place, every object meticulously arranged. It's a stark contrast to the turmoil that simmers just beneath the surface.

Picking up the glass, I swirl the whiskey idly, the ice clinking against the sides. I take a sip, the warmth spreading through my chest a poor substitute for the fire she ignites within me.

I find myself returning to the photographs, the silent sentinels that bear witness to my hidden truths. Each statue is past work of art, a record of my history that no one else can read. They are my confidants, my silent partners in the dance of control and chaos that defines my existence.

I linger over the images, each one a story of obsession, a study in the beauty of stillness. But as I look upon them tonight, it's not their stoic grace that captivates me but the absence of life, the stark finality of their forms. They are perfect, unchanging, unlike the woman who consumes my thoughts.

The realization strikes me with the clarity of a lightning bolt, Iris Klarelle is not a statue to be possessed, not a story to be interpreted through the lens of my own desires. She is a living, breathing enigma, a force that I cannot shape or mold to fit my narrative.

The truth of it leaves me both humbled and invigorated. She is beyond my grasp, a challenge that I am not sure I can, or even should, overcome. And yet, the very notion of surrender is anathema to my nature.

I set the glass down with a decisive click, the sound echoing in the stillness of the room. I will not be defeated by my own emotions; I will not allow my carefully curated world to crumble under the weight of unfulfilled desire.

I return to bed, the sheets cool and inviting. I close my eyes, willing the image of Iris to recede into the background. Tomorrow is a new day, a day for reasserting control, for reaffirming the boundaries that I have set for myself.

As sleep finally claims me, I hold onto one undeniable truth, I am Sebastian Wolfe, and my will is indomitable.

CHAPTER 3

I sit at my desk, the polished surface reflecting the angular lines of the office, my sanctuary of steel and glass. Plans for today's meetings lay before me, crisp and ordered. I arrange the documents, making sure each page is perfectly organized, labelled, and ready, each file a precise extension of my intent.

My mind wanders, luring me to thoughts of her scent, a reminder of how much I anticipate every encounter with Iris. I've charted her movements like an architect, mapping a blueprint that spans every detailed aspect about her.

Morning coffee run? She takes the stairs, too busy to wait.

Lunchtime stroll? She lingers by the fountain, phone in hand.

Afternoon break? The elevator doors open just as she arrives. Each moment crafted to ensure proximity.

"Sebastian." A voice, light yet filled with potential, pulls at my attention.

I glance up from my notes. Elizabeth's smile breaks across her face, like a flicker of sunlight piercing through clouds. A simple gesture, but in that instant, it's a revelation, a spark igniting something deep within me.

"Ready for the presentation?" She asks, tilting her head slightly.

"Always prepared." I keep my tone steady, masking the exhilaration bubbling beneath my skin.

She nods and turns toward the door, and I fight the urge to follow too closely, I don't mix work with pleasure, but it's hard not to watch how she moves through space as if every step is choreographed for my viewing pleasure.

I walk beside her toward the elevator, captivated by the way her brunette hair sways, how it frames her soft features. The delicate scent of jasmine surrounds her; strong, but not so much as to be offensive. Her buttery smooth brown skin that glisten likes a fountain sculpture in the sunlight.

The doors slide shut behind us, encapsulating us in this fleeting moment of intimacy. I calculate our time together, thirty seconds? More if we pause at each floor.

"Do you ever feel like we're living in a simulation?" She asks suddenly, eyes sparkling with mischief.

"A simulation?" I chuckle lightly. "Why would you think that?"

"I don't know, just a thought," she replies with a playful grin. "Sometimes it seems like there's some grand master controlling it all."

I smile, the conversation pulling me from my admiration of her, trying to redraw the line between reality and fantasy.

"Perhaps we are," I say, playing into the joke, "maybe that's why we call coincidence, fate."

I stand beside Elizabeth Fields in the elevator, ascending to the 30th conference room floor. She taps away at her phone, oblivious to the weight of my gaze. We're off to meet with Smith and Bailey, a formality to push along the zoning permits for our latest project. My mind should be focused on the intricacies of this deal, but it wanders to the soft curves of her neck instead.

We've shared a bed before, Elizabeth and me. A mutually agreeable arrangement, devoid of the messiness of emotions. It's a line I rarely cross, mixing business with pleasure, but with her, it was a physical release, nothing more. She's hinted at wanting more, but I've made it clear that our trysts are mere dalliances. I don't hunt where I feast; I prefer my worlds compartmentalized.

The elevator pings softly, announcing our arrival. We step out into the plush offices of the law firm, our footsteps muffled by the thick carpet. We exchange pleasantries, sign documents, and discuss logistics. Elizabeth is efficient, her attention to detail impeccable. I appreciate that about her, a quality that makes her an excellent secretary but a reminder that our liaison was a deviation from my carefully constructed life.

The meeting wraps up in a symphony of affirmations and approving nods. My presentation, a culmination of weeks of precision and planning, garners the unanimous approval I anticipated. Every word, every gesture, perfectly curated to convey control and command. The room hums with the controlled energy I've crafted, each person a note in my orchestrated composition.

Handshakes and pleasantries follow. Colleagues pat my back, their respect palpable. I gather my materials neatly, keeping everything perfectly aligned and organized. Professional farewells exchanged, but my mind races several steps ahead.

I step into the elevator, the doors closing with a soft whisper. As we descend, I allow myself a rare moment of personal reflection. The day's accomplishments blend seamlessly with lingering thoughts of Iris. Her image flickers in my mind, those delicate features adding complexity to my otherwise straightforward descent.

Back in my office, the atmosphere shifts to one of calculated calm. The minimalist design and faint scent of sandalwood ground me. I place my materials on the espresso-stained oak desk with precision.

The room turns quiet as I refocus on immediate tasks, signing documents, reviewing blueprints. My handwriting etches across the paper, a ritual maintaining the order I so desire.

A glance at my watch, it reveals it's almost 7 PM. An anticipatory shiver runs down my spine as the evening approaches, an echo of the primal hunger meticulously planned to indulge tonight.

Ensuring all project documentation is perfectly aligned on my desk, I listen to the steady ticking of my custom-made clock, the only sound amid silent contemplation of the evening's intentions.

Moving to my office closet, I exchange my tailored suit for something equally refined but darker and more predatory. Each piece chosen with care reflects both sophistication and the darker nature about to be embraced.

I stand before the floor-to-ceiling window, city lights splintered below, each one a potential hiding place. Breathing deeply, I savor anticipation mixed with calculated restraint.

Checking my phone, I dismiss an incoming call, a minor distraction. Focus unwavering, refining tonight's plan with architectural precision.

Pocketing my phone, I exit the office, making my way to the underground parking garage.

As I step into the garage, the click of my shoes announces my presence, echoing against the concrete.

My car, waiting in its designated spot, comes to life as I click the AutoStart. I open the door, sliding into the driver's seat, listening to the rumble of the engine as it purrs, the smooth leather beneath my fingertips.

Downtown is alive with activity, neon lights casting vibrant hues across the pavement. I turn onto 5th Street, my destination already chosen, a sports bar nestled among a row of bustling establishments. The bar's sign flickers with the image of a football helmet, drawing in patrons like moths to a flame.

I park a few blocks away, preferring the anonymity of a short walk, not that I could park on this busy street anyhow. The crowd outside is loud and boisterous, their excitement palpable as they spill into the street. Perfect. The din provides cover, allowing me to blend in without drawing attention.

Inside, the bar is packed. Televisions mounted on every wall display the game in progress, players colliding with brutal force, the crowd's roars punctuating each play. I take a moment to survey my surroundings, eyes scanning for potential targets.

A group of young business types huddle near the bar, their laughter loud and uninhibited. Further back, a couple argues over a spilled drink, their voices rising above the noise. But it's a woman sitting alone at a high-top table that catches my attention. Her posture is relaxed but alert, red hair cascading over one shoulder as she sips her drink.

I order a drink from a waitress that passes by, stopping her with a quick hand gesture, asking for a Whiskey on the rocks.

I continue to keep watch, waiting for my drink and the perfect moment to engage.

The waitress returns quickly, leaving her a $20, telling her to keep the change.

I watch the woman, watching her reaction to the crowd. I see her, wishing to be part of the crowd, see her lack of surety of how to include herself. I get the feeling she doesn't have anyone close to her. And with that reassurance, I make my move.

I approach slowly, methodically weaving through clusters of patrons until I'm close enough to observe without being intrusive. She glances up briefly before returning her gaze to her phone, a calculated move to appear disinterested.

"Mind if I join you?" My voice is calm and measured as I slide into the seat across from her.

She looks up again, eyes narrowing slightly before she nods. "Sure."

I offer a polite smile, keeping my expression neutral yet engaging. "Thank you. It's quite crowded tonight."

"It is," she replies, her tone light but guarded.

"What are you drinking?" she asks, her gaze flickering to the glass in my hand.

"Whiskey," I reply, lifting the glass slightly. "On the rocks."

"Classy choice," she says with a playful smile. "I'm Grace, by the way."

"Sebastian," I respond, returning her smile. Her eyes linger on mine for a moment longer than necessary, a subtle dance of interest and curiosity.

"So, Grace, what brings you here tonight?" I ask, leaning in slightly to close the distance between us.

"I just moved here from Mississippi," she says, her voice carrying a hint of southern charm. "Starting school soon and thought I'd check out the local scene."

"Mississippi?" I echo. "That's quite a change. How are you finding it so far?"

"It's different," she admits, her fingers tracing the rim of her glass. "But I like it. Lots of opportunities here."

"Opportunities?" I raise an eyebrow, intrigued.

"For school," she clarifies. "And... other things." Her smile widens, a hint of mischief dancing in her eyes.

"Well, welcome to the city," I say, raising my glass in a mock toast. "May it bring you everything you're looking for."

She clinks her glass against mine, laughter bubbling from her lips. "Cheers to that."

"Mississippi, huh?" I say, swirling the whiskey in my glass. "I've always been curious about that area of the South. What's it like?"

Grace chuckles, A soft sound that melds into the atmosphere of the bar. "Hot and humid for starters. But it has its charm, friendly people, good food."

"I've heard there are plenty of jokes about Mississippi," I remark, keeping my tone light. "But I imagine it's more than just stereotypes."

She laughs again, this time more freely. "Oh, absolutely. We've got our fair share of jokes, but it's all in good fun."

"Care to share one?" I ask, raising an eyebrow.

She leans back in her chair, eyes twinkling with amusement. "Alright, here's a classic: Why don't Mississippi folks play hide and seek?"

I feign ignorance, shaking my head slightly.

"Because good luck hiding when everyone knows everybody!" she finishes with a grin.

I chuckle appreciatively. "That's clever. I suppose there's some truth to it?"

"Oh definitely," she nods. "It's a small community vibe. Everyone knows your business."

"I can see how that might be both comforting and stifling," I muse aloud.

"Exactly," Grace agrees. "It's nice to have that support system, but sometimes you just want to disappear for a bit."

"I imagine moving here is quite the contrast then," I observe. "The city can be... overwhelming."

"It is," she admits, her gaze momentarily distant before focusing back on me. "But I like the anonymity. It's refreshing."

"To new beginnings then," I say, lifting my glass once more.

"To new beginnings," she echoes, clinking her glass against mine again.

"So, what brought you to school here?" I inquire after a sip of whiskey.

"A change of pace mostly," she explains. "And the program here is top-notch. Couldn't pass up the opportunity."

"What's your story?" She asks with an inquisitive grin.

"I'm an architect," I say simply. "I design buildings."

Her eyebrows lift in genuine interest. "That sounds fascinating. What kind of buildings?"

"All kinds," I reply with a slight smile. "From skyscrapers to small residential projects."

"Wow," she breathes. "You must be very talented."

"I like to think so." My smile widens slightly at her flattery.

Grace leans forward slightly, resting her chin on her hand as she looks at me intently. "So, what brings an architect like you to a place like this?"

I pause for a moment, considering my answer carefully. "Sometimes even architects need a break from designing the perfect structure."

I signal the waitress for another round, and she nods, weaving through the throng of patrons with practiced ease. Grace's eyes follow her for a moment before returning to me, a playful glint in their depths.

"So, Sebastian," she says, leaning in slightly, "do you design anything for fun? Or is it all work and no play?"

I chuckle softly, enjoying the lightness of her question. "A bit of both. Sometimes my work feels like play, especially when I'm creating something new."

"Creating something new," she echoes thoughtfully. "That sounds... exciting."

"It can be," I reply, watching her reaction closely. "But it's also about precision and control. Every detail matters."

"Control, huh?" Her lips curl into a teasing smile. "You seem like someone who enjoys having control."

The waitress returns with our drinks, placing them on the table with a knowing smile before disappearing into the crowd once more. I raise my glass to Grace, savoring the warmth of the whiskey as it slides down my throat.

"I suppose I do," I admit, meeting her gaze head-on. "But sometimes letting go of control has its own rewards."

Her eyebrows lift in mock surprise. "Oh? And what kind of rewards might those be?"

"Depends on the situation," I reply smoothly. "And the company."

She laughs softly, a sound that sends a pleasant shiver down my spine. "Well, tonight's company seems promising."

"I'm glad to hear that," I say, my voice lowering just enough to match the intimacy of our conversation.

Grace takes a sip of her drink, eyes never leaving mine. "So tell me more about this 'letting go' you mentioned."

"It's about trust," I say slowly, choosing my words with care. "Allowing yourself to be vulnerable, at least for a moment."

Her expression softens slightly, curiosity mingling with something deeper. "That sounds... intense."

"It can be," I acknowledge. "But it's also liberating."

She studies me for a moment longer before leaning back in her chair, her posture relaxed yet inviting. "You're an interesting man, Sebastian."

"I try to be," I reply with a slight smile.

I watch as she twirls a strand of hair around her finger, a small gesture of interest.

"Would you like another view of the city?" I ask, letting the question hang in the air between us.

Grace tilts her head slightly, curiosity lighting up her eyes. "What do you mean?"

"There's a place I know," I say, my voice low and inviting. "From my home, actually. The view in the morning is... unparalleled. You can see the city waking up, every light, every shadow. It's something worth experiencing."

She considers this for a moment, her fingers playing with the rim of her glass. "That sounds incredible."

"It is," I assure her, leaning in just enough to convey sincerity. "I'd love to show it to you."

Grace's lips curve into a slow smile, her decision clear in her eyes before she even speaks. "I'd like that," she says softly. "I'd like that a lot."

I return her smile, feeling a surge of satisfaction. "Then let's go," I suggest, standing and offering her my hand.

She takes it without hesitation, her grip warm and firm as she rises from her seat. We weave our way through the bustling bar, the noise and lights fading into the background as we step outside into the cool night air.

As we walk towards my car, Grace falls into step beside me, laughing at the excitement of the moment, probably accentuated by the heavy drinks she just finished. I take advantage of her inebriation, gently sliding her phone out of her pocket.

When we reach my car, I open the door for her, and she slides in gracefully. I make my around, dropping the phone behind my car before opening my door. I slide into my seat, giving her a warm smile, then pressing the button to start the engine. It hums to life and she lets out a giggle, her hands caressing the leather interior of my Aston Martin.

The drive is smooth, punctuated by moments of comfortable silence and bursts of conversation. Grace is animated as she talks about her new life in the city, the excitement of new beginnings mingled with a touch of apprehension.

We arrive at my home, and I lead her inside with an air of familiarity. The elevator ride up to my penthouse is swift, the soft hum of machinery filling the space between us.

When we step into my apartment, Grace pauses to take it all in, the sleek lines of modern furniture, the expansive windows offering a breath-taking view of the cityscape below.

"Wow," she breathes out, turning to me with wide eyes. "This is... amazing."

I smile at her reaction, feeling a sense of pride in my carefully curated space. "Come," I say softly, guiding her towards the floor-to-ceiling windows.

We stand there together in silence for a moment, watching as the city stretches out before us, a sea of lights against the dark sky.

"It's even more beautiful than I imagined," Grace murmurs.

"It has its moments," I reply quietly.

We stay there for a while longer, simply enjoying the view and each other's presence.

"I forget sometimes how great the night view is from up here." I say softly.

"How could you forget a view like this? She asks.

"My job keeps me very busy most of the time, heck, I'm lucky to leave before the sun goes down most days." I answer. "But this, this is nice..."

I look at Grace as she turns back looking up at me. The feeling of her hand slowly, softly touching mine pulls at my attention.

I turn my head towards the sound of her voice, our faces now mere inches apart. My eyes meet hers, and I see the spark of desire dancing in their depths.

"Sometimes we need someone to help us remember," she admits softly, a slight smile playing on her lips.

I reach out slowly, my hand coming to rest on the small of her back. She doesn't flinch away from my touch, instead leaning into it slightly. The warmth of her skin seeps through the fabric of her shirt.

"You're right," I murmur, my voice low and intimate. "Sometimes we do."

Grace's gaze flickers down to my lips before returning to my eyes.

Without another word, I close the distance between us, pressing my lips against hers. It starts as a gentle touch, but soon grows more insistent. She responds eagerly, her mouth moving against mine with growing passion.

My hands slide up her back as we kiss, feeling the smooth skin beneath her shirt. Grace's hands find purchase on my chest, fingers splaying wide over the fabric of my button-down.

She breaks away for a moment, breathless laughter bubbling from her lips. "Sebastian," she whispers, looking up at me through hooded eyes.

I capture her mouth again, our tongues tangling in a dance of desire. She begins to unbutton my shirt with deft fingers, each button releasing with a soft pop. The cool air kisses my skin as she pushes the fabric open.

"Bedroom?" I ask huskily against her lips.

Grace nods wordlessly, already moving in that direction. I guide us there with an arm around her waist.

Once inside my bedroom, she turns to face me fully. Our mouths meet again in a feverish rush of kisses and touches. Clothing falls away piece by piece until we're both bare before each other.

I lay Grace back onto the bed gently, following after her with fluid grace. Her body yields beneath mine as I settle between her thighs.

"You said something about giving up control earlier," I remind her, playfully between kisses along her jawline.

"I did." Her fingers trail down my side teasingly.

"What did you have in mind?" She asks.

There's a beat of hesitation before I continue speaking.

"Perhaps you'd like to be tied up?" The words hang heavy in the air between us.

Her breath hitches audibly at their suggestion.

"Only if you promise not to hurt me."

"No pain," I assure her soothingly. "Just pleasure."

Grace nods slowly.

I move off the bed just long enough to fetch some silk cloth from a drawer.

When I return, Grace looks up at me curiously from where she lies sprawled on top of the covers.

"Lie still while I tie your wrists."

She complies silently so I can begin wrapping one end around each wrist and tying them together behind her back.

Once I finish securely binding Grace's wrists together behind her back, I start trailing soft kisses along her jawline again.

"You are so beautiful," I whisper in Grace's earlobe before trailing further down her neck leaving goose bumps in my wake.

My mouth continues traveling lower - grazing along her collar bone and shoulder blades until reaching her chest.

My face creeps slowly to her breasts, my mouth enveloping her bright pink nipples, licking playfully and caressing over her left breast, then enveloping the other.

I run teeth over flesh delicately tugging almost imperceptibly as my head wanders south toward her thighs.

Her thighs tighten and flex as I reach her hips.

I chuckle lightly knowing exactly what effect my actions are having.

My head dips lower - lavishing attention upon her torso revealing her sensitive spots, once hidden beneath layers clothes, now fully revealed under tender ministrations.

Grace moans deeply as I slowly slide my tongue along her wet folds, revelling in the taste of her desire. Her hips arch up to meet my touch, seeking more of the pleasure only I can give.

I continue my exploration, savoring every inch of her most intimate areas. With a touch, I slide one finger inside her tight entrance, feeling her walls clench around me in response. Slowly, I pump my finger in and out, adding another digit as she grows wetter with each passing moment.

Grace's moans fill the room, the sound chanting me on. I increase my pace slightly as she begins to writhe beneath me.

"Oh god, Sebastian!" Grace cries out.

My mouth finds its way back to her clit as I curl my fingers inside her just right, hitting that sweet spot deep within. Her body tenses suddenly and she bucks against me as wave after wave of orgasm crashes over her, her body tense and shaking.

As Grace comes down from her high, she looks up at me with glazed eyes. "Please," she begs breathlessly, "I want to feel you inside me."

I don't need any further encouragement. Positioning myself between her thighs, I take a moment to admire the sight before me, Grace laid out so vulnerably beneath me, wrists still bound behind her back. The head of my cock nudges at her entrance teasingly before I slowly begin to sink into her.

A groan escapes my lips as inch by inch she takes me in deeper, until finally I'm fully within her tight walls. For a moment we simply breathe together as we savor this feeling.

Grace shifts slightly, urging me on with a roll of her hips.

With a low growl, I start to move within her in slow thrusts, gradually picking up speed. Her legs fall open wider, and I take advantage mounting my legs over hers, pulling her legs together between mine, the sensation causing her to squeeze my cock even tighter within her.

This new angle allows me to slide in at a different angle and I groan at the sensation of being enveloped so snugly within Grace's body.

My hands find purchase on her hips as I begin to thrust into her with more force now, each push hitting her deepest parts and drawing out soft gasps from Grace's throat.

"That feels amazing!" Grace exclaims between breathy moans.

I revel in these little sounds she makes for me alone and use it as encouragement as I search for that spot within her that will make her sing.

Grace arches her back slightly and suddenly cries out sharply, a telltale sign I've found exactly what she craves most.

"Oh yes, right there Sebastian!" Her words end on a particularly high note when my pelvis grinds against her sensitive nub just right sending sparks of pleasure throughout Grace's entire body.

"I'm close," Grace admits through panting breaths.

"Then let go," I urge softly against Grace's lips before claiming them in a searing kiss full of passion and promise.

My thumb parts her mouth, caressing the entrance as I drive into Grace harder still, the sound of our bodies meeting fills the room.

I look down at Grace watching her reaction intently for a sign she might be nearing the edge soon.

I reach up my other hand gently caressing her neck while simultaneously slamming into her body harder still,

"Yes! Yes!" She yells.

Grace's moan is so loud now, it drowns out the sounds of our bodies colliding.

The looks of her clenched face and curling toes tell me she is at the precipice.

It is time.

Slowly my hand begins enveloping part of her neck, and in one swift movement, I collapse my hands around her throat.

Grace's eyes go wide in an utter state of shock.

She writhes on the bed, fighting for another breath, trying to free herself, but it's no use, my grip is too tight.

Her eyes once bright with pleasure, now bloodshot with fear.

Before my eyes, her face shifts.

No longer do I see Grace writhing beneath my hands, her face has been replaced by my ex-fiancé, my first, my Jennifer.

The moment sends me over the edge as I release inside of her every ounce of manhood inside of me.

I moan loudly, as the orgasm builds to its height and I am pushed over the edge, driving my grip around her even tighter.

My body shudders as I cough out a moan, releasing it all in this moment.

Below me, her body finally stills, and I find myself in a state of calm, a tranquillity that follows the storm of my darker desires. I release my hands from around her throat, watching as the last vestiges of life fade from her eyes.

My clean-up is precise, an extension of the control I exert in every facet of my existence.

Donning a painter's suit, I ensure I leave no new trace as I attend to the task at hand, carefully moving her body to the floor. I unroll a black plastic tarp to lay her on, preparing for transport.

I begin with a fresh paintbrush, gently wiping away any stray hairs that might serve as incriminating evidence. A cheap handheld vacuum efficiently collects them, destined for incineration later.

Reaching for my manicure kit, I meticulously clean and trim her nails, filing them down and removing any lingering skin, blood, or other remnants of her final moments. A small trick I've gleaned from watching forensic shows, though I can't recall which one.

From the bottom center drawer of my dresser, I retrieve a new cleaning cloth, placing it on her body. Rising, I head to the kitchen to gather the necessary supplies.

I reach the sink, opening the cabinet door and taking out the large bottle of isopropyl alcohol and its accompanying metal bowl. Returning to the bedroom, I work with haste, ensuring I complete this stage before rigor mortis sets in, preserving her body's flexibility for the final step.

Kneeling beside her, I take the cloth, saturating it with the alcohol, commencing the process of sanitizing her form.

Her body, once a vibrant testament to life, is now a hollow shell, a canvas of ebony.

I place her inside the trunk of my car, transporting her lifeless body to one of my construction sites, to one of the hollow statues I have prepared for just this purpose.

The cool night air brushes against my skin as I exit my car. I open my trunk, picking her up, folding her over my shoulder. I move quickly to maneuver her into the waiting embrace of the statue before her body is too stiff to move. The statue is one of my designs, a sculpture intended to symbolize the resilience and fortitude of the human spirit. How ironic that it will now serve as her tomb, a silent sentinel over her eternal repose.

With careful precision, I pour the cement, watching as it fills the cavity of the statue, encasing her within its unyielding grasp. The cement will harden, solidifying her position in my world, out of sight, but never forgotten.

I depart from the construction site, my mind already drifting towards the morning, towards Iris. Unlike this girl, Iris is no mere shadow, she is an entity unto herself, a siren call to the darkest recesses of my soul.

The game is afoot, and I am more than eager to play.

Chapter 4

I ris stands in the elevator, her presence an intoxicating blend of innocence and allure. Her scent, honey, with a trace of something darker, fills the confined space, invading my senses, clinging to my thoughts. She doesn't notice me, not really, but I see everything. Every detail. Every movement.

This morning is no different. At exactly 8:17 AM, she steps into the elevator. I am already there, waiting. Our daily ritual.

She stands in her usual spot, eyes fixed on her phone, completely unaware of the world around her. Her hair, so soft and luscious, floats on her shoulders like a whisper. It's mesmerizing.

"Good morning," she says, barely glancing up from her screen.

I offer a polite nod, my lips curling into what I hope passes for a casual smile. "Morning."

The doors slide shut with a quiet hiss, sealing us inside this small, intimate world for the briefest of moments. The silence stretches between us, taut and electric.

Her presence is magnetic, drawing me in with a force I can barely comprehend. She shifts slightly, and our arms brush, an innocent touch that sends a jolt through me. She doesn't notice; she's too engrossed in whatever is on her phone.

"You seem deep in thought," I venture, hoping to spark some form of connection.

She looks up, startled for a second before her expression softens into a polite smile. "Just work stuff."

"Ah," I nod knowingly. "The never-ending grind."

"Exactly." Her laugh is light, almost musical.

The elevator dings softly as we reach her floor, and the doors open to release us back into the wider world. Iris steps out first, her perfume lingering like a ghost in the confined space.

"Have a good day," she says over her shoulder as she walks away.

"And you," I murmur to her retreating figure.

I linger for a moment longer, waiting for the elevator doors to close.

Ding.

I reach my floor and step out, my mind already replaying every second of our interaction, analyzing every nuance of her tone and expression.

Her smile was more than just politeness; it was an invitation, a subtle signal that she's beginning to notice me too.

I reach my office door and pause before entering. The memory of Grace's lifeless body flashes briefly before my eyes, a reminder of the duality within me.

But Iris... Iris is not Grace. She's something entirely different.

My hand trembles slightly as I grasp the door handle and step inside my office sanctuary where everything is meticulously placed and ordered to perfection, just like my life, or at least how it appears on the surface.

The gentle silence of my office provides a soothing backdrop as I sift through blueprints and design schematics. The meticulous order of my workspace is a balm to my otherwise chaotic mind.

A faint buzzing sound cuts through the quiet. I pause, checking my phone. Nothing. The sound persists, nagging at the edges of my consciousness.

Ryan enters without knocking, his usual enthusiasm preceding him. "Morning, Sebastian!"

"Morning, Ryan," I respond, my attention still split by the insistent buzz. "Do you hear that?"

He tilts his head, listening. "Yeah, sounds like a phone vibrating."

I check my phone again, more thoroughly this time. Still nothing.

"It's not mine," I say, frustration seeping into my voice.

Ryan moves closer to my desk. "Maybe it fell behind something?"

We begin to search, me with a growing impatience, Ryan with his typical eagerness to help. He checks around the chairs and under the desk while I rummage through drawers and papers.

I move to the bookshelf next. The books are neatly aligned, their spines unbroken by use. I scan the titles quickly, looking for anything out of place.

One title catches my eye: *The Interpretation of Murder* by Jed Rubenfeld. My pulse quickens. I didn't put that there.

"Find something?" Ryan asks, peering over my shoulder.

"This book," I say slowly, pulling it from the shelf.

The buzzing grows louder as I hold it in my hands. My heart races, an unfamiliar feeling of anxiety creeping in.

"Is it in there?" Ryan asks, intrigued.

I open the book carefully, pages fluttering open to reveal a hidden compartment cut into the center of the pages. Nestled inside is a cellphone, the one from last night.

My breath catches in my throat as I stare at it. How did this get here?

"That's...odd," Ryan remarks, leaning closer to see.

"Very," I manage to say, my mind racing with possibilities, none of them good.

I feel exposed, vulnerable in a way I've never experienced before. This was supposed to be a clean break, a memory erased along with Grace's life. But here it is, an echo of last night hidden within these pages.

Ryan looks at me quizzically. "You okay?"

I snap the book shut, forcing calm into my voice. "Fine."

But I'm not fine at all.

My heart races as I stare at the phone, nestled within the book like a macabre bookmark. I feel a sharp pang of discomfort as I realize the implications. This changes things.

"That's quite a title," Ryan observes, eyeing the book with a slight smirk. "Seems like you've got a bit of a murder mystery on your hands."

His casual tone grates on me, pulling me further into the spiralling pit of my own unease. I need to get rid of this, now. "Just some... unusual reading material," I manage, my voice tight as I place the phone on my desk.

"Hey, no judgment," he laughs, holding up his hands. "We all have our quirks."

I force myself to chuckle along, but my eyes remain fixed on the phone, a silent accusation. I walk to the floor-to-ceiling window and gaze down at the city, feeling an acute sense of vulnerability. Someone knows.

Someone planted this here.

My mind reels, suspects already forming, but the why remains elusive. Blackmail? Or is this some twisted game? I shake my head, trying to dislodge the thoughts as if they were physical things lodged in my brain.

"You alright, boss? You look a little..." Ryan trails off, letting the sentence hang meaningfully.

I turn back to him, needing to refocus. "Fine. Just a lot on my mind."

"If you need to talk, I'm here," he offers, his tone sincere.

A part of me wants to confide in him, to unburden myself, but I can't. I've always handled things alone. Besides, what could I possibly say?

Instead, I opt for a vague response, a practiced deflection. "Appreciate it. It's nothing I can't handle."

He nods, seemingly satisfied, though I detect a hint of concern lingering in his eyes. "Well, if you need a break, I could take over that client meeting this afternoon."

"No," I respond more sharply than I intended. "I mean, it's fine. I'll be there."

"Okay, okay," he chuckles, raising his hands defensively. "Just trying to help."

I take a steadying breath, forcing myself to relax. "I know, Ryan. Thank you."

His face softens at my gratitude, and he gives me a quick nod before retreating from my office. I wait until his footsteps fade before moving back to my desk. My eyes fixate on the phone, a silent challenge.

I need to know who sent it.

I approach the phone slowly, as if it might detonate at any moment, blowing my carefully constructed world to pieces. My own personal landmine, buried within the pages of a book.

It's an older model, the kind without fancy fingerprint or facial recognition technology. My mind spins with the possibilities. So many ways it could be traced back to me.

I turn it over in my hands, feeling the cool metal and glass, a stark contrast to the heat of my rising unease. I take a deep breath, steeling myself for what I might find.

I press the unlock button, my thumb hovering over the screen. One touch, that's all it would take.

But I hesitate. This could be a mistake. This could be the moment everything changes.

My thumb hovers for a second longer, and then I press down, watching as the screen illuminates. I half-expect to see a message flashing, some sinister note, but the home screen is empty.

I swipe frantically, scanning the rows of apps. No messages. No emails. Nothing incriminating. The phone is completely wiped clean.

Relief floods through me, but it's short-lived. Who sent this? Was it Ryan? No, that didn't make sense. My eyes narrow. This is a warning. Or a game. My gaze falls on the book, its title now seems like an ominous taunt.

The phone buzzes sharply in my hand, making me jump. A text appears, a single word: Soon.

I freeze, the breath catching in my throat. The phone slips from my fingers, landing on the desk with a soft thud. My heart hammers in my chest as I stare at the screen.

"Sebastian?" Ryan's voice calls from outside my office.

I shake myself from my stupor, quickly grabbing the book and the phone. I rush to the window, considering my options. The phone is too risky to keep.

"Yeah?" My voice is strained, betraying nothing of the turmoil within.

"You still up for lunch? I'm starving."

I gather myself, stepping back from the window. "Sure. Let's go now."

I need to get out of here, if only for a moment. I need to think.

I slip the phone into my pocket, feeling its presence in my pocket. The book, I'll deal with later.

The cool morning air greets us as Ryan and I step out of the office building. I breathe deeply, trying to calm my racing thoughts. The phone in my pocket feels like a ticking time bomb, its presence a constant reminder of the danger lurking beneath my carefully constructed facade.

"Where do you want to go?" Ryan asks, his voice cutting through my internal monologue.

I glance around, suddenly aware of how exposed I feel out here. "Somewhere quiet," I reply, my tone brusque.

Ryan raises an eyebrow but says nothing. We walk in silence for a few minutes before he spots a small cafe tucked away on a side street. "How about this one?" He suggests.

I nod, grateful for the suggestion. We enter the cafe, the aroma of freshly brewed coffee enveloping us. It's nearly empty at this hour, which suits me perfectly.

We settle into a corner booth and peruse the menu. Ryan chatters about a new project he's working on while I listen intently, trying to appear engaged despite the panic raging inside me.

As we wait for our food, my mind drifts back to the phone and book. Who could have sent them? And why? I clench my fist under the table, anger simmering beneath my controlled exterior.

Ryan notices my tension. "Hey, man. You sure everything's alright?"

I force a smile onto my face. "Yeah, I'm fine."

Our food arrives shortly after. Ryan digs in enthusiastically while I pick at mine distractedly.

"You know, Sebastian," he says between bites. "You've been acting pretty strange lately."

My fork stops mid-air. "Strange?"

Ryan nods. "Yeah, you know, like you're carrying around some kind of secret weight."

I laugh it off, but my heart races. Does he suspect something? "Maybe I'm just feeling a little...restless," I say carefully. "I have a lot on my plate at the moment."

Ryan looks skeptical but lets it drop. We finish our meal mostly in silence.

The phone burns in my pocket as we leave the café. Ryan's concern is more dangerous than I initially perceived. He's watching me, picking up on signals of my inner chaos, this requires careful management.

"Thanks for lunch," I say, trying to inject normalcy into my voice. "I needed to clear my head."

"Anytime," Ryan responds, studying my face with uncomfortable scrutiny. "You know, sometimes talking helps. Whatever's bothering you..."

"Nothing's bothering me," I cut him off, perhaps too sharply.

We walk back toward the office in uncomfortable silence. The weight of the phone presses against my thigh with each step, a persistent reminder of my vulnerability. I need to dispose of it, permanently. Not like Grace. That was different. That was... necessary.

As we near the building, I make my decision. "I just remembered something I need to take care of." My voice sounds hollow even to my own ears. "I'll meet you back at the office."

Ryan hesitates, doubt flashing across his features. "Sure, boss. Don't be late for the Madison proposal meeting."

"I won't."

I watch him disappear into the building before turning in the opposite direction. There's a construction site three blocks away, perfect for what I need to do. I walk briskly, scanning my surroundings for observers, cameras, anything that might record my movements.

The site looms ahead, concrete skeleton rising against the sky. I slip past the temporary fencing, using the blind spot I'd noted during a site visit last month. The foundation has been poured, but the basement level remains exposed, a gaping wound in the earth.

I pull out the phone, examining it one last time. The message still glows on the screen: "Soon."

A taunt. A promise.

My hand trembles slightly as I drop the device on the ground. Smacking the pavement in a loud clatter, the screen cracking, but the words still present.

I look around, checking in every direction. "Who sent this, how did they find this phone?"

I have to get rid of it, destroy it, but how? Maybe I can toss it in a dumpster or a storm drain...

Waking back towards the street, I look for the closest storm drain. That will not only destroy the phone but carry it far away as well.

This isn't enough. This is sloppy. Dangerous. The mixer might not destroy it completely, circuits could survive, data could be recovered. The risk is too great.

I reach into the water fountain, my sleeve riding up as I plunge my arm into the cold liquid. My fingers close around the device, still intact, the screen still on. I pull it free, water dripping from my hand, my suit drenched. A small price for certainty.

I move away from the fountain, finding a secluded corner behind a stack of rebar. With trembling hands, I place the phone on the ground and scan the site for a suitable tool. My eyes land on a discarded length of pipe.

Perfect.

The first strike is hesitant, tentative. The second comes harder, the third, I'm consumed by a white-hot rage that burns through my veins.

I bring the pipe down again and again, my breath coming in sharp bursts. The screen shatters, the case splits, the battery dislodges. Still, I continue, smashing the device beyond recognition until it's nothing but fragments and dust.

My shoulders heave as I stare at the electronic carnage at my feet. This isn't like me. This lack of control, this panic, it's foreign and un-settling. I straighten, adjusting my tie with concrete-stained fingers, trying to reclaim my composure.

I gather the destroyed remnants, careful not to leave even the smallest piece behind. As I exit the construction site, I spot a public trash can on the corner. I approach it casually, dropping the shattered phone pieces into its depths, burying them beneath discarded coffee cups and sandwich wrappers.

Walking back toward the office, I try to process what's happening. Someone is playing with me, testing me. But who? And why? The message... "Soon", echoes in my mind like a promise or a threat.

Could it be connected to Grace? Impossible. I was meticulous, as always. No loose ends, no witnesses. Nothing to tie me to her disappearance.

Yet someone knows something. Someone is watching me. My carefully constructed world feels suddenly fragile, like a house of cards caught in a rising breeze.

Back at the office, the air conditioning prickles, dampening my sleeve. A faint water stain spreads along the cuff, darkening the pristine fabric. My reflection in the elevator reveals a stranger, a man rattled, unsettled, the carefully constructed mask shattered. Time to reassemble.

I step out onto the calm hum of the office floor, already feeling a sense of equilibrium return. A pile of proposals sits neatly on my desk, Ryan watching me carefully from across the room.

"Lose something?" He smirks lightly, eyes falling to the dripping sleeve.

"Misplaced my footing," I retort with a forced ease. "A cracked sidewalk. It's nothing."

He nods slowly; doubt stays hidden behind a casual shrug. "Madison meeting is in thirty minutes. Need anything before then?"

"Privacy," I lock eyes with him, smiling without warmth. "And coffee. Black."

The request is clear enough to dismiss him; it gets his attention. Ryan walks away, subdued but suspicious. Once he's gone, I close my office door and allow myself a steadying breath. Through the large, panelled windows, life continues as usual: accountants hovering near desks, architects sketching careful designs, oblivious to my internal fracture. Control returns, cold and reassuring.

A knock interrupts the fragile silence. I glance up sharply, irritation controlled behind a veneer of calm. Iris stands at the threshold of the open door, one hand resting lightly on the frame, an amused curve at the corner of her mouth.

"Delivery," Alexis says as she leans slightly inward, setting a coffee on the edge of my desk with deliberate grace.

"Ryan sent you?" My voice remains level, nonchalant, though my pulse quickens.

Alexis walks in, setting the mug of coffee down on my desk.

"Thank you, Alexis," I offer smoothly, meeting her gaze with practiced warmth as my fingers curl around the steaming cup. The ceramic radiates comfortable heat into my palm, grounding me back in routine, familiarity.

Alexis gives a shy shrug, shifting her weight from one heeled foot to the other. "Of course, Mr. Wolfe. Ryan seemed busy, so I figured..." Another small shrug, eyes dropping briefly before returning carefully to me.

"Kind of you," I say, leaning back casually in the chair. I sip slowly, savoring both the coffee's bitterness and my regained composure. The stain on my sleeve goes ignored, no longer important. "Settling in alright?"

A flush of color blossoms on Alexis's cheeks. "Yes. Everyone's been nice. Really welcoming." Her eyes flick toward Iris, half-visible through the open office door, sharing a hushed conversation with Ryan by the drafting table.

"I've noticed you've gotten acquainted with Iris," I observe, careful to keep my voice innocent, merely curious. Another casual sip conceals contemplation. "She seems rather... difficult to know."

The flush deepens. Alexis twists her hands nervously. "She's lovely. A bit mysterious, maybe, but very nice."

"Nice," I echo, lips curling slightly as my gaze shifts subtly to where Iris leans forward gracefully, smiling at something Ryan says, lost in their private moment. "That's good to hear."

"Yeah," Alexis continues softly, missing my fixation. "She's funny. Really smart, too. Honestly, more approachable than I expected."

"How so?"

Alexis hesitates. "I guess, just, at first glance, she seems elusive. A bit distant, maybe. But, once you talk to her, she's incredibly engaging."

I nod slowly, thoughtfully, adjusting the cuff of my stained sleeve without breaking eye contact. "Interesting insight. I appreciate it."

"Of course, Mr. Wolfe," Alexis replies, relief easing the tension from her slender shoulders.

"Please," I murmur mildly, deflecting the formality of the title, "just Sebastian."

She looks startled at first, then visibly pleased, nodding once. "Sebastian."

My eyes drift idly back to Iris, registering her soft laughter as it drifts casually into my office. Alexis follows my gaze, her voice gaining confidence as she remarks, "If you'd like, I can formally introduce you two."

"No, thank you," I interrupt, maintaining a gentle smile. "I prefer to let these things happen naturally. But thank you, Alexis."

I dismiss Alexis with a gentle nod, then settle back into my chair, knowing I should be immersing myself in the Madison proposal documents. But my attention gravitates toward the hallway where Iris stands waiting for the elevator, her back straight, one foot tapping lightly against the polished floor. I keep my head angled down, allowing only my peripheral vision to track her movements.

She checks her watch, a delicate silver thing that catches the light, and shifts her weight. The way she stands, patient yet somehow restless, reveals a woman accustomed to moving at her own pace. Not rushing, never rushing, but never quite still either.

I shuffle papers deliberately, creating the appearance of productivity while calculating the precise angle needed to maintain my view of her without being obvious. Ryan walks past my office, glancing in with mild curiosity. I respond with a perfunctory nod, my focus never truly leaving her.

The elevator chimes. Iris tucks a strand of hair behind her ear, a gesture I've cataloged dozens of times, yet it never loses its fascination. The doors slide open, and she steps forward, turning slightly as she enters.

Then, unexpectedly, she looks up. Directly at me.

Our eyes lock across the distance. Not a glance, not a passing acknowledgment, but a deliberate, conscious connection. The air seems to compress between us, charged with unspoken recognition.

I jerk my attention back to my desk, suddenly fascinated by the proposal in front of me. My heart hammers like it is hitting my ribs as

I arrange my features into a mask of concentration, squinting slightly at the text that might as well be written in Greek.

When I risk another glance, the elevator doors are sliding closed, taking her with them. But in that final moment before she disappears, I catch something in her expression, something that suggests she was wanting, waiting for me to look at her again.

And then she's gone, leaving me with the sensation that, perhaps, I wasn't the only one watching.

Chapter 5

I stand by my desk, surveying the sketches spread before me, a sea of lines and curves that promise order in a world that seems intent on chaos. The fluorescent lights hum softly overhead, but my thoughts drift, pulling me away from the blueprints. I feel unusually restless, the unease gnawing at the edges of my mind.

The memory of Iris's smile flashes like an image burned into my retina. Just a polite gesture, yet it lingers with a weight I can't shake. I tell myself it's nothing more than a fleeting interaction. Still, it seeps into my thoughts as I flip through the pages.

"Sebastian," David calls from across the office. His voice slices through the haze of distraction.

I glance up. "Yes?"

"We need to finalize the meeting agenda." He leans against my door-frame, arms crossed, a familiar posture that speaks of impatience.

"Of course." My voice remains calm, controlled. I rise and join him at the conference table, trying to push aside thoughts of her.

But it's futile; every moment spent in proximity to Iris rekindles that hunger within me. A quick inhale fills my senses with her lingering scent, honeyed warmth mixed with something elusive that beckons me deeper.

"You alright?" David raises an eyebrow, his tone casual but probing.

"Just considering design elements," I reply smoothly, shifting focus back to the plans laid out before us. "We need to emphasize sustainability in our proposal."

As we discuss timelines and budgets, the words blur together. My mind drifts again to last night, the thrill of pursuit and power as shadows enveloped me in that room. The rush swells like an architect's ambition taking form; precise yet dangerous.

A flicker of movement catches my eye from across the room: Iris enters through the glass doors, oblivious to everything around her. She glides past clusters of coworkers; each lost in their own trivialities.

I can't help but stare as she pauses at the coffee station. Her fingers brush against a mug, a delicate dance I can't resist watching. My heart beats faster, an uninvited rhythm stirring beneath my composed facade.

"Sebastian?" David nudges me again, his annoyance now palpable.

I blink back to reality, forcing myself to focus on him instead of her, the way she moves, how light seems drawn to her presence like moths to flame.

"Are you even listening?" David presses.

"Of course." My response is clipped now; irritation sharpens my tone as I reinstate control over this moment slipping away from me like sand through fingers.

"Let's just finalize this," he mutters under his breath.

But all I can think about is how close she is, how utterly unaware, and how much longer I can keep this hunger at bay while she haunts my thoughts like an architectural flaw begging for resolution.

I inhale deeply, forcing my thoughts back to the blueprints before me. This momentary distraction is unacceptable. I've built my reputation on precision and focus, qualities that have no room for wandering thoughts of honey-scented women in elevators.

"The sustainability features should be highlighted here and here," I tell David, indicating specific sections of the design. My voice is steady now, my attention reclaimed. "Let's emphasize the solar integration. It's what Meridian Construction wanted most."

David nods, seemingly satisfied with my renewed focus. We spend the next hour finalizing our presentation, refining details until every element aligns with my exacting standards.

The conference room fills with clients by two o'clock. I stand at the head of the table, command returning to me like an old friend. As I walk them through our proposal, I notice their eyes light up at the three-dimensional renderings, exactly the reaction I'd anticipated.

"We're impressed with the overall concept," says Thomas Meridian, leaning forward in his chair. "But we'd like to see more green space incorporated into the central atrium."

"And perhaps reconsider the eastern facade," adds his partner. "The afternoon sun might create excessive heat without proper shading."

I smile, not at their suggestions, but at how predictable they are. I'd already prepared alternatives for both concerns. "We've actually explored those very possibilities," I say, smoothly transitioning to my contingency slides.

By 4:53PM, I'm packing my briefcase with deliberate movements. I check my watch, Iris typically leaves at five. I've memorized her pattern over these months, cataloging her habits with the same precision I apply to my architectural measurements.

The elevator arrives precisely when I expect it. I step inside, press the lobby button, and wait. At the third floor, the doors slide open, and there she is, a vision in navy blue today, her scent preceding her into the small space.

"Going down?" I ask, though I know the answer.

She nods, a quick smile that doesn't reach her eyes. The silence between us only heightens my desire. I wonder if she feels the same about these moments.

Iris steps out of the elevator, her heels clicking softly against the marble floor of the lobby. I watch her walk away, each step measured, precise. She doesn't look back. She never does. The scent of honey lingers in the confined space, and I inhale deeply, letting it fill me one last time before the doors close.

I head to my car, parked in its usual spot. Sliding into the driver's seat, I start the engine and ease into the evening traffic. The hum of the city surrounds me, but my thoughts are miles away, lost in the labyrinth of her presence.

As I navigate through downtown streets, a pair of headlights behind me catches my attention. They're too bright, glaring into my rearview mirror like an accusation. I squint, adjusting the mirror to block out the worst of it, but it does little to alleviate my growing annoyance.

The car sticks to me through every turn. Left on Jefferson. Right on Elm. It's still there, a persistent shadow that gnaws at my composure.

My hands tighten around the steering wheel as I make another sharp turn onto Maple Avenue, hoping to lose it in the maze of side streets.

But it follows, relentless.

I feel a prickle of unease creep up my spine. I speed up slightly, weaving through traffic with a precision born from years of meticulous planning and execution.

Just a few blocks before home, the car abruptly turns off onto a side street. My pulse slows as I dismiss it, a coincidence. Nothing more.

I pull into my driveway and cut the engine, silence wrapping around me like an old habit. The house stands as it always does, imposing yet serene, a solemn symbol of order amidst chaos.

Entering through the front door, I lock it behind me with a click that echoes in the stillness. Everything is exactly where it should be; each item placed with deliberate intent. Yet tonight, there's an edge to my thoughts, a whisper of something.

The study beckons, a safe place that offers sanctuary from the day's events. I cross the threshold, setting my bag down, settling into my leather armchair, sinking back as the soft cushion cradles my body. Reaching for my cigar box on the side table, I carefully select one from my collection, a Cuban Robusto that promises a rich, full-bodied flavor.

With precise movements, I pick up the cigar cutter, trimming the end, mouthing the other as I grab my lighter, igniting the cigar with a heavy pull, letting the first wisps of smoke curl around me like familiar company. The smoky scent mingles with the cedar notes from my humidor, creating a heady aroma that tied with the nicotine, provides a rushing calm over me, offering me the opportunity to recalculate my thoughts.

I pour myself a generous measure of scotch from the crystal decanter on my desk and take a slow sip. The amber liquid burns down my throat with a satisfying warmth.

My gaze wanders over the trinkets adorning my shelves, the polished silver pen holder from Barcelona; the crystal paperweight from Milan; each item meticulously selected during my travels and placed with calculated intention.

My eyes land on a small figurine, a delicate bronze statue of Daedalus and Icarus. I recall the myth with its lessons of hubris and caution.

I take another draw from my cigar as I walk over to my bag, the leather soft beneath my fingers. My bag lies where I left it, the weight of its contents feeling lighter than it truly is. I reach into the bag, grabbing the book, exposing it to the smoky air of my study.

I take a moment, just staring at the book, continuing to inhale the cigar, turning the book over, looking for any clues that might help me decipher the purpose of this dangerous tome.

Is the book some kind of warning? Or perhaps a threat?

I put the cigar down on the ash tray momentarily, taking another sip of scotch as I consider the implications. Who could have put it there? And why? The questions swirl in my mind like tendrils of smoke rising from my cigar.

I lean forward slightly, eyes narrowing as I focus on the solution to this riddle.

I place the book on my shelf, not according to my cataloging method, but at the end, just to have a place to store it, just to have it out of my hands, to stop its unease from weighing on me and to give me an opportunity to clear my mind.

I step back; my watchful eye still trained on the book as I take another sip.

The phone on my desk suddenly jolts me back into reality with its sharp ringtone, a sound so unexpected that it makes me nearly drop my drink.

I hesitate for a moment before picking up, cigar held between lips.

"Sebastian Wolfe speaking."

The voice on the other end is smooth, almost melodic. "Sebastian Wolfe," it repeats, "a man who appreciates precision."

My grip tightens on the receiver. "Who is this?"

"Wouldn't you like to know?" the voice purrs, feminine, but rough, with a deep country accent. "Or at least, I hope you do."

I feel a chill run down my spine despite the warmth of my study. "What do you want?" My voice remains steady but there's an edge of annoyance beneath it. I race through my mind, trying to place the voice, if I've ever heard it before, but my mind comes up short, unable to relate it to anyone in recent memory I've spoken with.

"I want to play a game," the caller replies. "A game where perceptions are everything."

I take another drag from my cigar before responding. "And why should I care about your games?"

The caller laughs, a sound like silver on glass. "Because you've already started playing. Whether you realize it or not."

The line goes dead.

I step back, looking around as I connect the book to the phone call like puzzle pieces of the same puzzle, my hand still holding the phone to my ear.

I walk over to my chair, settling in, my heart racing. I close my eyes, taking deep precise breaths to calm myself. I open my eyes, the smoke curling around me once more as I ponder these new developments and their implications to the carefully constructed world I've built.

The scent of smoke mingles with my thoughts, thickening the air with unease. I take another long drag from my cigar, letting the smoke curl around me like a shroud.

A game. A game where perceptions are everything.

I replay the words in my mind, dissecting each syllable for hidden meanings. The voice was unfamiliar, yet it carried an unsettling certainty, as if it knew more about me than I'd ever willingly reveal.

The figurine of Daedalus and Icarus catches my eye again, its bronze sheen glinting in the dim light of the study. Hubris and caution. The myth feels suddenly relevant; a warning etched in metal.

I drain the last of my glass of scotch, savoring the last remnants as it slides down my throat. Who could be behind this? The book on my shelf, the phone call, these are not random acts. Someone is watching, someone who knows too much.

I rise from my chair, the phone still in hand. My mind races through a labyrinth of possibilities, each one more disquieting than the last. The caller knew my name, my reputation for precision. And yet, their identity remains shrouded in mystery.

I return the receiver to its cradle with calculated restraint, refusing to let this unseen adversary see, or rather, sense, my discomfort. I am not easily rattled. I built my empire on the foundations of control and discipline, qualities that do not falter at the whim of an enigmatic stranger.

The scent of my cigar fills the room, a familiar comfort amidst this unexpected intrusion. I draw on it once more, letting the smoke envelop me like armor. I won't be intimidated. I refuse to be drawn into someone else's game without understanding the rules.

I glance back at the bronze figurine of Daedalus and Icarus. The lesson is clear: one must tread carefully at the precipice of ambition. I am no fool; I understand the dangers of flying too close to the sun. And yet, I've always preferred the view from the heights.

The silence of my study feels oppressive now, a stark contrast to the usual hum of productivity and purpose. I need to clear my head, to step away from the confines of these four walls before they close in on me.

I make my way to the large bay window overlooking the manicured lawn. The city lights twinkle in the distance, casting a soft glow over the world I've shaped with my own two hands. It's a view I've come to cherish, a daily reminder of my achievements.

But tonight, it offers little solace. The shadows seem deeper, the lights colder. I can't shake the feeling of being watched, observed by an unseen set of eyes that knows my secrets, or at least, believes it does.

The cell phone incident at work surfaces in my thoughts. It was no mere coincidence, and neither is this call. Someone is toying with me, pushing me to question my own meticulously crafted reality.

I take one last drag from my cigar before extinguishing it in the ashtray on the windowsill. The ember dies with a hiss, leaving behind a tendril of smoke that ascends into the night air.

A sudden compulsion drives me back to the bookshelf. My eyes focused on the title that doesn't belong, *The Interpretation of Murder*. The title alone feels like a taunt.

With a deep breath, I pull it from where I placed it, alongside my carefully curated collection. The cover is smooth beneath my fingertips, the edges sharp and unworn. It's clearly a new copy, something older would have some signs of age or use.

I turn the book over, searching for any clues. I thumb through the pages, releasing a small yellow note onto my floor. Reaching down, I pick up the note, noticing the elegant handwriting on it, almost poetic in the way the letters flourish.

It reads:

"Architects build more than structures; they build worlds within the minds of those who gaze upon their work. But even the most intricate design has its flaws, and it is within these imperfections that truth often lies."

I feel a chill that has nothing to do with the cool night air seeping through the windowpane. The game has begun, whether I like it or not. The question now is who my opponent is and what they hope to achieve by dragging me into this twisted play of perception and control.

I place the book back on my shelf, taking the note with me and walking over to my desk.

I command the computer awake with repeated taps to the space bar, logging in and opening the browser and heading straight to Google to search this phrase written on the note. Maybe it's a famous quote or something that will give me a clue to who has dragged me into this game.

I try multiple combinations of the sentences, but there are no exact matches to this quote, not anything close. A dead end.

Who is this opponent? It must be someone who understands the power of suggestion, the weight of a carefully placed word or object, maybe someone who studied psychology. Like a therapist, or a hypnotist.

Thinking for a long moment, I come up empty, there's no one I can think of that I know who fits the bill.

I slam the laptop shut, frustration coiling in my veins like a serpent. The game, this twisted, unsolicited game, is becoming an obsession of its own, and I refuse to be manipulated.

Standing up, I pace the length of my study, the note crumpled in my fist. Who would dare to challenge me this way? To infiltrate my workspace, my sanctuary? The audacity borders on admirable, if it weren't so infuriating.

I pour another scotch, hoping to ground myself in that perfect state of clarity between sober and intoxicated. The glass catches the light as I swirl the drink, the angular shapes of the glass reflecting like a prism, pulling at my senses, framing and reframing the clues.

The cell phone hidden in the book. The cryptic call. The note with its architectural metaphor. These are calculated moves, designed to unsettle me. To make me question my control.

I take a long sip, letting the scotch coat my throat. There's something almost artistic about this approach, meticulous, measured, much like my own methods. A worthy opponent, perhaps.

But I didn't ask for this game. I didn't consent to these rules.

I cross to the window again, scanning the darkness beyond my property. Is someone out there now, watching? Waiting for my next move? The thought sends a chill through me that has nothing to do with the temperature.

The note feels heavy in my hand, its message both provocative and intimate. Whoever wrote it understands the architect's mind, my mind. They know that we create more than just structures; we shape experiences, perceptions, realities.

And they know about my flaws.

I flatten the note on my desk, studying the elegant script. The flourishes, the pressure points of the pen, these are clues, if only I could decipher them. This handwriting belongs to someone educated, someone with an appreciation for aesthetics.

Someone who thinks they know me better than I know myself.

I stare at the note, my frustration turning to determination. This is a puzzle, and puzzles have solutions. I grab my phone from my pocket and position it over the handwritten message, capturing a clear image of the elegant script. The flourishes and curves mock me from the screen, someone's personal signature of superiority.

Back at my computer, I open the browser again. My initial search for the phrase yielded nothing, as expected. This isn't some famous quote; it's a personal message meant specifically for me. I drum my fingers against the desk, considering my options.

'Handwriting analysis software,' I type into the search bar. Several results appear, forensic tools, personality assessment programs, and pattern recognition applications. I click through several links, scanning for something that might give me an edge.

A web application called ScriptAnalytica catches my attention. 'Upload handwriting samples for comprehensive pattern analysis and demographic probability modeling,' the description reads. Perfect.

I create an account, inputting the bare minimum of information required. The interface is sleek, clearly designed for professionals. I upload the photo of the note and select the 'Full Spectrum Analysis' option.

A loading bar appears on screen: 2% complete.

I lean back in my chair, scotch in hand, watching as the percentage crawls upward. 5%. 7%. The program claims to analyze everything from pressure points to letter formation, potentially identifying education level, geographic influences, and even personality traits.

12%.

My foot taps against the floor. Patience has always been one of my virtues, but tonight it feels like a luxury I can't afford. I take another sip of scotch, feeling the burn spread through my chest.

18%.

Who would go to such lengths? Who would know enough about me to orchestrate this elaborate game? My mind cycles through colleagues, clients, acquaintances, anyone who might have reason to target me.

25%.

The bar inches forward with excruciating slowness. I refresh the page, hoping to speed the process, but it only resets to 23%. Cursing under my breath, I watch the percentage climb again.

30%.

The loading bar inches forward with maddening slowness. 35%. 38%. 42%.

I drum my fingers against the desk, my patience wearing thin. The scotch in my glass has lost its appeal, but I take another sip anyway, letting the burn distract me from the crawling progress on my screen.

56%.

"Come on," I mutter, refreshing the page again only to watch it reset to 53%. A rookie mistake. I won't make it again.

67%. 72%. 80%.

I stand, unable to remain seated any longer. Pacing the length of my study, I keep one eye on the screen as the percentage climbs. 85%. 90%. 95%.

Finally: Analysis Complete.

I'm back in my chair in an instant, eyes scanning the results that fill my screen:

'Handwriting Analysis Report:

- Gender Probability: Inconclusive (51% female, 49% male)

- Education Level: Advanced degree (95% confidence)

- Geographic Influence: Midwestern dialect markers, likely Ohio/Kentucky/Tennessee/Indiana region

- Personality Indicators: Highly intelligent, methodical, calculating

- Additional Notes: Writer displays elegance and control unusual in casual handwriting'

I lean back, processing this information. College educated. Highly intelligent. Calculating. From the Midwest. It's something, but not enough. I run through my mental rolodex of clients, colleagues, acquaintances, anyone who might fit this profile and have reason to target me.

Nothing clicks. No one stands out.

I glance at the clock on my desk: 6:24 PM.

Frustrated by the dead end, I reach for my phone, seeking distraction. I open my notes on Iris, scrolling through the images I've captured of her planner when opportunity allowed. According to her schedule, she should be at the gym right now, Barry's Austin.

I open my browser, searching for the gym. The website loads quickly, showing sleek interiors and fitness enthusiasts with perfect bodies. I scan the class schedule for today, trying to determine what she might be doing.

Today's options include a class in the "Red Room" focused on "Abs & Ass", definitely something I could see her doing. The thought of Iris in form-fitting workout clothes, sweat glistening on her skin as she tones her already perfect ass, sends a pulse of heat through me.

The alternative is a cycle class, which would also maintain that deliciously toned posterior I've come to appreciate.

I check the address, just a three-minute walk from our office building. Convenient. I browse the "First Timers" section, assessing whether

I could observe without drawing attention. Perhaps joining the gym myself wouldn't be too suspicious. People run into colleagues at fitness centers all the time. It would be a natural extension of our elevator encounters.

I set my phone down, decision made. I'll go check out the gym, see what can be seen.

I straighten my tie, smoothing my hand down the front of my shirt. No time to change. I grab my phone and keys from the desk, heading out with purpose in my stride. The need to see her, to observe her in her natural environment pulses through me with each step.

The drive downtown takes precisely seventeen minutes. I find a spot across from Barry's Austin at 6:55 PM, perfect timing. Through the large windows, I can see people milling about in the reception area. I turn off the engine and sit for a moment, collecting myself.

This isn't stalking. This is research. Understanding. I'm merely exploring a gym near my workplace, perfectly reasonable.

I cross the street quickly, but not so quickly as to seem as though I'm in a rush, pushing through the glass door into a blast of air conditioning and pulsing music. The reception area gleams with sharp lines and neon lights on the walls.

"Hi there! Welcome to Barry's." A broad-shouldered man with a staff lanyard approaches. "First time with us?"

"Yes," I smile, relaxed and casual. "I've been looking for a gym close to my office. This location seems convenient."

"Absolutely. I'm John." He extends his hand, grip firm. "Would you like a quick tour?"

"That would be great, thanks."

John leads me down a hallway, pointing out the spacious locker rooms before stopping at a closed door. "This is our Cycle studio. Class is in session, but we can peek in."

He eases the door open, gesturing me inside. The room is bathed in blue light, rows of cyclists moving in unison to thundering beats. Sweat glistens on bare shoulders. I scan the dimly lit faces and figures, but Iris isn't among them.

"Let's check out the Red Room," John suggests, leading me back into the hallway. "We offer a variety of classes, HIIT, full body, upper focus. Monday nights are especially popular."

We approach another door, and immediately I catch the mingled scents of perfume and exertion. John continues talking about membership options as I peer through the window.

And there she is.

Iris moves with the rest of the class, dropping into a perfect squat. Her black hair cascades over her shoulders, swaying with each controlled movement. The spandex clings to every curve, revealing the precise shape of her as she rises and falls in rhythm.

The hunger rises instantly, a physical ache. I watch her muscles flex, the slight sheen of sweat on her exposed shoulders, the concentrated look on her face visible even in profile.

"Sir? Did you have any questions about our class packages?"

I force my eyes away, turning to John with what I hope passes for casual interest. "Sorry, just trying to get a feel for the atmosphere."

Back at reception, John slides a brochure across the counter. "So, interested in signing up today?"

"I should probably think about it," I say, keeping my voice steady despite the heat coursing through me. "Compare a few options."

"Of course. Here's my card when you decide."

I thank him and walk out, my steps quickening as I reach my car. The change in position forces me to adjust myself, the pressure uncomfortable against my pants.

I need release. I need to feed this hunger before it consumes me.

Mayfair. The bar will be crowded enough tonight to find someone suitable. Someone to take the edge off.

I start the car and pull away from the curb, driving toward Mayfair with singular focus.

CHAPTER 6

Mayfair's neon sign bathes the sidewalk in electric blue. A line stretches from the entrance, but I bypass it with a nod to Marcus, the doorman. He knows me or rather, he knows my friend Benjamin Franklin.

He opens the door, the music enveloping me like a heavy curtain as I walk in.

The place is packed, probably well past the fire code, but the people inside couldn't care less. That's why they're here, to give in to their primal urges, to be forced into such close proximity that at any time, you're rubbing against at least two other people.

I can smell it the moment I walk in, sweat, perfume, alcohol. A need for intimacy and a release from the structure of our daily lives.

I weave through the crowd, claiming my usual spot at the bar. The leather stool creaks as I settle in.

"Whiskey. Neat." The bartender doesn't need to ask which brand; he can tell by the way I'm dressed that I want the best. He slides the crystal tumbler across the polished wood, the liquid sloshing lightly.

The glass feels cool against my palm as I survey the scene before me. Bodies twist and writhe on the dance floor, lost in their own worlds. So many possibilities. So many potential indulgences. Yet tonight, something feels different. The usual thrill of the hunt seems hollow, overshadowed by thoughts of her.

I take a slow sip, letting the whiskey burn away these unwanted contemplations. The music pounds louder, drowning out everything but the pulse of bass and the clink of ice against glass.

My eyes scan the room, slow, methodical. The selection process is an art. I don't want the girls in groups, the ones screaming into each other's ears, laughing too loudly, glued to their phones as they document every forgettable moment. No, I look for something different.

Someone alone. Someone not waiting for anyone. Someone present.

A girl at the far end of the bar catches my attention.

The way she moves is like water flowing through the rigid geometry of my designs. Her soft curves, fluid, a contrast to the harsh angles of the city outside. The lights of the club shine against her skin, illuminating the sparkle of her red glittered bikini top. It matches the vibrancy of her smile, electric and contagious, even from a distance.

I step closer, drawn by this unexpected force.

I'm enamored with everything about her. I study her. Her pink hair that spills over her shoulders in loose waves. Her red glittered bikini top that glints in the club's lights, her tight jean shorts that hug her thick thighs perfectly. She's vibrant, electric, perfect.

I can't hear her laugh over the music, but I imagine it as I watch her, bright and carefree. She belongs in this moment, unburdened by the weight of expectations or whatever strife life has thrown at her.

She is the opposite to my own rigidity, a breath of fresh air in a world that has become stale.

I get up, slowly moving closer, drawn to her, like a moth to the flame. I should turn away, someone else knows about me, about my hunger. But there's something about her, an intoxicating mix of innocence and defiance that calls the beast inside me.

She walks over to the bar alone, taking a seat, breathing heavily as she places her order and tries to recuperate. After a very quick vodka shot, she is back on the dancefloor.

As if sensing my gaze, she turns her emerald eyes in my direction. Our eyes meet across the crowded room and for a moment, time seems to stand still. Her lips tilt upwards into a mischievous grin before she returns her attention to her dancing.

I edge closer, weaving through the undulating bodies. The rhythm of the music synchronizes with my pulse, each beat pulling me nearer to her.

She dances, lost in her own world, oblivious to my approach. Her movements are hypnotic, a fluid dance that contrasts with the rigidity I impose upon my own life. She sways, hair shimmering under the lights, her laughter silent but palpable. She finally retires from the dance floor and heads over to the bar, buying herself a drink to gain some energy back. I watch carefully as the bartender slides the drink across the bar to her. She then takes her drink and sits at a lonely table in the corner of the bar.

She is completely alone.

Not looking at her phone, not scanning for someone she knows, just sipping her drink, watching the dance floor with a small, knowing smile. Present.

That smile stirs something in me. The hunger recognizes her before I do.

I let myself watch her for a few moments longer, studying the way she holds her glass. There's confidence in her posture, a quiet awareness of the space she occupies. She's enjoying herself, but not in the way that comes from needing to be seen. That's rare. That's what draws me in.

I rise from my seat, glass in hand, and move toward her with the easy, unhurried gait of a man who belongs here.

She glances up as I approach, her green eyes flicking to mine, sharp, assessing.

"Mind if I join you?" My voice is calm, inviting.

She tilts her head slightly, considering. Then, a slow smile. "Sure."

I take the seat across from her, watching as she crosses one leg over the other, the movement effortless. She's playing along.

"I'm Sebastian."

"Roxy."

Her voice carries above the music, smooth with a hint of playfulness. She extends her hand, and I take it, her fingers warm against mine. Her grip is firm, deliberate. She's testing me.

"Nice to meet you, Roxy."

"You too, Sebastian." She leans forward slightly, resting an elbow on the table. "So, what brings you here tonight?"

I smile, keeping it measured, calculated. "The atmosphere. The people. The occasional good conversation."

She laughs, a bright, uninhibited sound. "You mean the hunt."

I raise a brow. "Excuse me?"

"Oh, come on." She gestures around the club. "Guys like you don't come here for the drinks."

Interesting. She's perceptive.

I chuckle, shaking my head. "Maybe I just enjoy good company."

Roxy smirks but doesn't press further. Instead, she leans back, watching me, letting the silence stretch just long enough to be noticeable. Most people would rush to fill it, but I let it linger, let her sit in the weight of it.

A familiar scent hits my nose, her scent. Faint, but unmistakable. It lingers in the air for half a second before being swallowed by the club's medley of sweat and alcohol. My chest tightens involuntarily.

I turn my head slightly, just enough to scan the crowd. A figure at the edge of the dance floor. Dark hair.

"Iris?" I murmur to myself.

Was that her? Just as quickly as the scent appeared, it is gone, replaced by the acrid tang of spilled drinks and cheap cologne. Maybe it was never there to begin with.

No, she wouldn't come here I tell myself. The lighting makes it hard to discern anyone from a distance, causing shadows to stretch and warp.

My mind is primed to see her because I've trained it to. That's all. Just a trick of the mind.

I refocus my attention to Roxy, hoping she didn't notice my momentary distraction.

"So," I say, leaning in slightly, giving her my full focus once more. "Tell me, Roxy... what do you think guys like me come here for?"

Her smile curves, slow and knowing. "Why don't you show me?"

The hunt is over. I've found my prey.

I signal to the bartender, lifting two fingers. "Another round?" I ask, my eyes never leaving hers.

Roxy tilts her head, considering. "Why not?" she replies, a teasing lilt to her voice.

The bartender sets down fresh drinks on our table, and I slide one toward her. She takes a slow sip, watching me over the rim of her glass. "So, Sebastian," she muses, setting the drink down. "Tell me something about you. Something real."

I smirk. "Now that's an original."

She laughs, a rich, booming sound. "I like to be different."

I swirl my whiskey before answering. "I build things. Design them. Make them exactly as I want them to be."

"Ah, a man who likes control," she teases, leaning closer. "I could've guessed."

I don't deny it. Instead, I watch as she takes another sip, as her fingers tap lightly against the glass in a rhythm that matches the pounding bass.

Then, she reaches for my hand, her fingers wrapping around mine. "Dance with me." She says, not a demand, but a need.

I raise an eyebrow. "Not much of a dancer."

"That sounds like an excuse," she challenges, pulling me toward the dance floor.

I let her. The music swallows us, the beat thrumming in my chest as her body presses close. She moves with easy confidence, her hips rolling against mine, testing the boundaries between play and temptation.

The hunger stirs, stronger now. The scent of her skin, the way she feels against me, it's intoxicating. She tilts her head back slightly, her eyes catching the glow of the lights, lips parted in an unspoken dare.

I tighten my grip at her waist, pulling her just a little closer.

She exhales sharply, a knowing smirk tugging at the corners of her lips. "You're getting the hang of it."

I let my fingers trace the curve of her spine, my voice low. "Maybe I just needed the right partner."

I wrap an arm around her waist, pulling her gently against me. She leans back, her body fitting perfectly into mine, and her eyes close as if surrendering to the moment. My other hand finds hers, our fingers entwining.

The world melts away, the flashing lights, the pulsing crowd. There's only her, and the all-consuming need that threatens to overwhelm me.

A yearning. A hunger.

No, more than that. An obsession.

Our bodies are pressed together, the heat between us building to a fever pitch. Her breath quickens as her eyes flutter open, and I'm unable to breath, consumed with my hunger for her, like falling into an abyss, knowing full well what awaits me at the bottom.

But I can't stop. And I don't want to.

I pull her closer, my lips brushing her ear. "Let's get out of here," I murmur.

Her response is immediate. "I thought you were never going to ask..."

We slip through the crowd, hands still entwined, making our way towards the exit. Desire hangs heavy between us, a shared secret that fuels our haste.

The night air hits us like a cooling breeze as we step outside, the pounding music of the club fading into the distance. I lead her to my car, a sleek Silver Aston Martin, and open the door for her. She slides in, her scent, a heady mix of juniper and spice, filling the cabin as I join her.

We drive through the empty streets, our conversation punctuated by heated glances and stolen touches. I can feel her eyes on me, sizing me up, but I maintain my composure. Tonight is about control, mine.

Finally, we pull up to my home, a modernist masterpiece of glass and steel that juts out over the city like a jagged crystal. She gasps as we step onto the sleek marble foyer, her eyes darting from one polished surface to another.

"It's... breathtaking," she breathes, her voice barely audible in the cavernous space.

"Thank you," I reply with a hint of pride. "Shall we continue this tour upstairs?"

Her response is a coy smile as she follows me up the spiral staircase that winds its way to my sanctuary, my bedroom. The door closes behind us with a soft click, sealing us in our private world of desire and decadence.

The room is dimly lit by flickering candles and the glow of city lights filtering through floor-to-ceiling windows. A four-poster bed dominates one wall upholstered in rich burgundy silk; it beckons like an altar to our impending union. She walks over to it with a slowness that borders on languidity before bouncing on its plush surface with childlike glee...

I stand at the threshold, taking in the scene before me. She's a vision, perched on the edge of my bed, her hair tumbling over her shoulders, eyes shining with amusement. The flickering candlelight casts an ever-changing shape on the walls, enhancing the atmosphere of illicit passion.

"So, what now, mister?" She bites her lower lip, a playful challenge and tease in her eyes. "You gonna just stand there all night?"

I cross the room in a few purposeful strides, closing the distance between us. "Actually, I thought I'd join you."

As I approach, she leans back on her palms, stretching out like a feline ready to play. My heart pounds with a combination of desire and anticipation. This is what I've been craving, what I've needed.

"Well, aren't you going to take off your tie at least?" She grins, her eyes sparking with mischief. "It's a little formal for the occasion, don't you think?"

I chuckle, reaching up to loosen the silk knot. "You have a point."

With a fluid motion, I pull the tie free, letting it fall to the floor. It's a symbolic gesture, shedding the constraints of my daily life, embracing the raw authenticity of this moment. I step closer, and she reaches out, her fingers brushing against the top button of my shirt.

"Let me help you with that." Her voice is husky, filled with promise.

Her fingers work deftly, undoing each button with calculated slowness, exposing more of my chest with each inch of fabric that parts. I breathe deeply, taking in her scent, a heady mixture of sweetness and desire.

My own hands find hers, stilling their motion. "My turn."

I pull her upwards, savoring the feel of her soft frame in my arms. Her laughter rings out, musical and carefree, as I sweep her off her feet. She wraps her arms around my neck, her legs encircling my waist, pressing herself against me.

She looks at me for a moment hungry, needing, and brings her lips to mine. The kiss is fierce and possessive, her tongue gently touching mine, her lips saving as she gently envelops my lower lip with her mouth. She tastes like an intoxicating elixir of coconut and sea water. My hands roam, tracing the contours of her body as I hold her, making my way back towards the bed.

The mattress yields beneath us as we fall together, the beds soft bounce pressing her back into me, our lips still intertwined. I run my hands through her hair, holding her to me as if I could merge our very essences.

Garments are tugged, buttons undone, zippers slid with fevered urgency. The soft fabric of her bikini top gives way, and my mouth finds her skin, tasting the salt of her efforts, reveling in her rapid breaths and the satisfaction that I alone have caused this reaction in her.

My own body is on fire, every nerve ending crying out for more. But there will be time for slow exploration later. For now, only this frenzied joining will suffice.

Her fingers seek the fastening of my trousers, her touch sending sparks along my skin. I arch against her, an animalistic growl rumbling in my throat. With deft fingers, she undoes the button, her touch electric as she slides the zipper down.

The rest of our clothes are quickly removed, falling away like discarded promises. Our bodies press together, skin on skin, no barriers between us. The candlelight casts a soft glow over her curves, accentuating the swell of her breasts, the dip of her waist, the flare of her hips.

With a final fierce kiss, I roll, settling between her thighs. She's breathless, flushed, her eyes shining with desire and a hint of nervousness. I hesitate for a heartbeat, taking in the sight of her, this beautiful stranger who has invaded my world and cast a spell over me.

"Now what, mister?" she teases, her voice laced with anticipation.

I smile, leaning down to whisper against her lips. "Now, we fulfil our desires."

She arches into me, her body a symphony of curves and planes. The heat between us is palpable, a living entity that pulses with its own rhythm. I trace her shape with reverent fingers, soft and strong all at once, learning every contour as if committing it to memory for eternity.

Her skin is smooth beneath my touch, warm from the exertion and flushed from desire. I map her terrain with meticulous care, each dip and hollow receiving equal attention until she's writhing beneath me. Her breaths come in short gasps punctuated by little moans of pleasure.

"I've wanted this," she breathes out between kisses. "All night."

Her confession ignites something primal within me, a hunger that refuses to be satiated by mere words or empty promises. It demands action. Completion.

With one smooth motion, I roll my hips forward. A soft gasp escapes her throat as I fill her completely. Our bodies become one in this intimate dance.

She moves with me, meeting each thrust with an answering roll of her own hips. The rhythm we create is intoxicating, a primal beat that echoes through my very being. Our hearts pound as one, a crescendo of desire building with each passing moment.

Her nails dig into my shoulders, half pleasure, half pain, the sting only fueling my passion further. I bury my face in her neck, tasting her skin, salted with sweat, and breathing in her scent, musky with arousal.

"More," she gasps out between breaths. "Faster."

I oblige willingly, my body responding to her urgings without conscious thought. The bed creaks beneath us as our tempo quickens, a staccato rhythm punctuated by grunts and gasps.

Sweat slicks our skin as we move together, two bodies united in their quest for release. Her legs wrap around my waist drawing me deeper into her core with each thrust. I feel myself slipping closer to the edge, the precipice beyond which there is no return.

"Wait," she gasps out, her voice strained with effort. "I...I need..."

Her words trail off lost in a moan as I hit a particularly sensitive spot within her. Her body arches off the bed, her back bowing beautifully as she surrenders to sensation.

"Let go," I murmur against her ear, my own voice thick with lust. "Give yourself over to it."

My hand finds its way between us seeking out that secret nub hidden within her folds. I stroke it gently at first then more insistently as she writhes beneath me.

"Yes...oh god...yes..." She chants my name like a prayer even as she urges me on.

I can feel the tension building within both of us, the coiling spring that will eventually snap free releasing all its pent-up energy in one explosive climax. My own release draws near, I can feel it building at the base of my spine, a hot molten liquid ready to erupt forth at any moment.

"Don't stop," she pleads, her voice barely above a whisper. "Please don't stop."

As if I could. As if I would dare halt this runaway train barreling towards its final destination.

With one last thrust, the force of which rocks us both, I feel myself tip over the edge into oblivion. A groan tears from my throat as ecstasy crashes over me like a tidal wave sweeping away everything in its path.

In that moment nothing else matters, not past nor present, only this singular perfect union of two bodies joined in their quest for pleasure.

The world narrows to just this one act, a primal joining of flesh and blood and bone.

And when it finally ends, as all things must, we collapse together, spent and sated and boneless as kittens on the floor.

For a long moment we simply lay there catching our breaths, basking in the afterglow of our shared release. Our chests rise and fall in tandem, a synchronized rhythm born of our intimate union.

Slowly, relishing each lingering touch, I pull away from her rolling onto my back beside her on the rumpled sheets.

"That was..." She searches for words but seems unable to find them.

"I know." I finish for her, turning my head on the pillow to regard her.

Her eyes meet mine, soft now rather than blazing with desire, and she smiles languidly stretching out like a cat awakening from a long nap.

"Definitely worth getting out of there for."

Roxy's breath comes in ragged gasps, her chest rising and falling as she turns on her side, facing me. The sight of her naked body is a revelation, a masterpiece of soft curves and supple flesh that seems to glow in the dim light. Her skin, kissed by the sun, bears a light tan that deepens where shadows fall, creating a natural contour that enhances her form. Her hair, a cascade of brunette roots melding into pink strands, spills across the pillow like a vibrant river, framing her face in a way that only adds to her allure.

I can't help but voice what's on my mind. "You're unbelievably gorgeous," I murmur, my gaze tracing the lines of her body. Her smile falters, just for a moment, as if she's unsure whether to believe me. But I mean every word.

She laughs softly, a sound that's both nervous and playful. "You don't have to say that, you know."

I sit up slightly, propping myself on one elbow to better admire her. "I don't *have* to say it. I *want* to. Look at you." My fingers itch to touch her, but I hold back, letting my words do the work. "Every inch of you is perfect."

Her eyebrows arch, and she shifts slightly, as if testing the validity of my claim. "Every inch?"

I double down, my voice steady and sincere. "Your smile, it's warm and genuine, the kind that makes you feel like you're the only person in the room. And your breasts," I pause, letting my eyes linger on the fullness of her chest, the way her nipples tighten at my attention... "they're glorious, so full and inviting, exactly as they should be. No retouching, no pretense."

Her cheeks flush, but she doesn't look away. If anything, she seems to lean into the compliment, her body relaxing into the bed as if allowing herself to be seen, truly seen.

"And your waist," I continue, my gaze moving downward, "those soft, round curves, they're not just beautiful, they're *you*. They tell a story, of confidence and comfort in your own skin. Your hips, the way they flare just so... they drive me mad with desire."

Her smile returns, softer now, as if she's starting to believe me. "You're very persuasive."

"I'm just honest," I reply, my voice low. "Your legs, short and strong, and those feet, small, delicate. They're the perfect finish to the most breathtaking whole."

She laughs again, a sound that's more relaxed now, as if she's let down her guard. "You're making me blush."

"Good," I say, leaning closer, my lips brushing her shoulder. "You should know how incredible you are."

Her response is immediate, her body arching into mine as if she's been longing for this, my lips, my touch, my worship. I kiss my way down her throat, lingering on the hollow where her pulse flutters wildly, before tracing the curve of her collarbone with the tip of my tongue. She shivers beneath me, her breath deepening as I map every inch of her with deliberate slowness.

Her breasts, full and heavy, beckon me next. I take my time, circling the peak with my tongue, savoring her sharp intake of breath. She's soft everywhere, her skin yielding like silk under my hands as I knead and squeeze gently, my fingers tracing the swell of her hips, the dip of her waist.

"Sebastian," she murmurs, her voice thick with need, "I... I want you."

I glance up, meeting her eyes for a moment, before dipping lower still. Her stomach is a smooth plain I explore with reverence, my lips brushing against her skin, my beard scraping lightly, eliciting a gasp. Her hands tangle in my hair, guiding me, urging me onward.

"Again," she whispers, her voice desperate now. "Please, I need you inside me."

I can't resist. Not her. Not this. I slide my knees beneath hers, positioning myself at her entrance, my cock throbbing with anticipation. The head grazes her clit, and she moans, pressing into me, urging me closer.

With a slow, deliberate motion, I slide inside her, inch by inch, our breaths syncing as I fill her completely. Her walls clench around me, warm and tight, a vice I have no desire to escape. My hands grip her waist, pulling her up and into me, our bodies fused as one.

I start slow, each thrust measured, deliberate, savoring the way she feels around me again. Her nails dig into my chest, her head thrown back as she surrenders to the rhythm. I quicken my pace, pressing deeper, harder, our bodies slapping together in a primal cadence.

"Yes," she cries out, her voice raw, "right there, don't stop."

I won't. I can't. Her pleasure is my symphony, her moans my melody. I drive into her with relentless force, chasing that edge, pushing her closer with each thrust. Her walls flutter, her breath coming in sharp gasps as she teeters on the brink.

Her back arches, pushing her breasts up invitingly, and her voice shatters the air with a raw, primal scream.

"Sebastian!" she cries, her voice a desperate plea. "Don't stop, please, I need more!"

Her hands claw at my back, her nails biting into my skin, but I welcome the pain. It fuels the fire burning within me, a hunger that demands satisfaction. I thrust harder, faster, each stroke a ferocious claim. Her screams become a chorus, her name a mantra on my lips.

"Roxy," I growl, my voice hoarse with need. "You feel so good, so tight."

Her moans are incoherent, a language of pleasure that needs no words. Her body shakes, every muscle taut as she teeters on the edge. I lean down, capturing her lips in a fierce kiss, tasting her desperation.

Her response is a keening wail as her body explodes. Her release washes over me, a tidal wave of sensation. Her walls contract, milking me, drawing my own climax closer. I grit my teeth, fighting the urge to follow her over the edge. Not yet. Not until she's wrung dry.

Her screams turn to pleas, her voice hoarse. "Sebastian, please... I can't... I need..."

I don't need her to finish. I know what she needs. I give it to her, my hips snapping relentlessly. Her body is a symphony, every nerve ending singing in harmony. I feel her climax ripple through her, wave after wave, until she's limp beneath me, her body spent.

I bring one of her legs up over my shoulder, adjusting my hips to align perfectly between her thighs. Her body is still trembling from her climax, her muscles pliant and receptive as I slide back inside her. The warmth and wetness envelop me, a welcoming embrace that sends a jolt of anticipation through my veins.

Roxy lets out a slow, moaning growl, "Oh, my god..." Her voice is thick with pleasure, her breath coming in shallow gasps. I can feel the residue of her release coating me, making each movement smoother, more intimate. Her eyes flutter open, meeting mine, and I see a mix of wonder and desperation in them.

I begin to move again, my hips driving deep, deliberate strokes that draw a fresh wave of moans from her lips. Her leg draped over my shoulder gives me leverage, allowing me to angle my thrusts just right, hitting that spot deep within her that makes her gasp and arch. Her hands grip the sheets, her nails digging into the fabric as she braces herself for what's to come.

"Sebastian," she whispers, her voice barely audible over her ragged breaths. "You're, you're everywhere."

I don't reply, focusing instead on the rhythm, the friction, the way her body responds to mine. Her pleasure is already heightened, her nerves raw from her recent orgasm, and I exploit it mercilessly. Each thrust is slower now, more purposeful, wringing every last bit of sensation from her.

"Again," she gasps, her voice a fractured plea. "Don't stop, please... don't stop!"

I don't intend to.

I continue to thrust myself deep, forceful, but not painful. She screams wildly as the pleasure overwhelms her senses, even breathing becomes labored as the ecstasy overtakes her.

I slide my hands up her thighs, my fingers brushing the sensitive skin behind her knees, watching as her legs tremble in response.

"You're not done yet," I murmur, my voice a low rumble.

Her eyes flicker open, her senses clouded. "I... I don't know if I can..."

I smile, a predator's smile, and shift my hips, a slow, deliberate grind that draws a sharp intake of breath from her. "You can. For me."

Her hands find my chest, her nails scratching lightly as she pushes herself up, meeting my gaze. "Then don't stop," she demands, her voice steady despite the hunger in her eyes.

I oblige, my thrusts building in intensity, a steady rhythm that has her gasping anew. Her body responds despite her exhaustion, her muscles clenching, a vice that tightens with each stroke. I lean down, capturing her mouth in a fierce kiss, our breaths mingling as I drive into her.

"Sebastian," she moans against my lips, "I'm..."

I swallow her words with a groan, quickening my pace, my body moving with a primal urgency. Her hands grip my shoulders, her fingers digging in as her pleasure spirals higher.

"Not yet," I growl, my voice hoarse. "Not until I say so."

Her eyes widen, a mix of fear and arousal, as she realizes my intent. I pound into her, relentless, pushing her closer to the edge, her body a taut string ready to snap.

"Please," she begs, her voice a ragged whisper. "I can't..."

Her words are cut off by a sharp cry as her muscles flex and spasm, her release taking all control over her own body. Her muscles contract, milking me, begging for my release.

I slow a moment as I drink her in.

And with a strength born of desire, she pulls me down to the bed, pushing herself up, her hands on my chest, her eyes blazing. "My turn," she says, her voice steady, a promise I have no intention of denying.

She straddles me, her hair a wild halo, her breasts rising and falling with her breath. I watch, mesmerized, as she lowers herself onto me, her hands on my chest, her body controlling the pace.

"Hold on," she murmurs, her lips brushing mine, "this is going to be a wild ride."

Roxy's body moves with a feral grace, her pink-streaked hair bouncing with each powerful thrust as she rides me with a force that leaves me breathless. Her hands grip my chest, her nails digging into my skin, anchoring herself as she uses her legs to propel her up and then slam down, her full weight driving me deep inside her. The sound of skin on skin, the wet slap of our bodies meeting, fills the room, echoing the intensity of the moment.

Her muscles are taut, her thighs trembling with effort, but she doesn't falter. She's relentless, a wild thing unleashed, and I'm helpless to resist her. Her vaginal muscles grips me with purposeful force, the sensation tight and hot, pulling me closer to the edge with each movement. Sweat glistens on her skin, mingling with mine, our bodies slick and slippery as she pistons above me.

"Fuck," she groans, her voice nearly indecipherable as she lets gravity do its work, slamming down with a force that makes the bed creak. "You feel so good, Sebastian. You penetrate so deep."

Her words send a jolt through me, my hands instinctively reaching for her hips, my fingers digging into the soft flesh as I anchor her to me. I can feel her nearing the edge, her body tensing again, her movements becoming more urgent. Her moans grow louder, more desperate, and I know I can't hold back any longer.

I meet her thrusts, pulling her down into me with each upward motion, our bodies colliding with a ferocity that borders on violence. Her skin slides against mine, the friction sending sparks of pleasure through me. I'm close, so close, and I can tell she is too.

"Roxy," I grit out, my voice strained, "I can't take it anymore."

Her eyes flash open, locking onto mine, and her body shudders as she obeys. Her walls clench around me, a tight squeeze that sends me over the edge. Her cries of pleasure fill the room, as she begins her slow surrender, collapsing onto me, her body still trembling from the force of her release.

I hold her there, my hands on her hips, our hearts pounding against one another, the air thick with the scent of sweat and sex.

I hold Roxy against me, our bodies still joined, her weight a pleasant pressure on my chest. Her skin is warm with hues of red blush on her face and chest, her breathing ragged as she collapses onto me. I trace lazy patterns on her back, feeling the rise and fall of her ribs as she struggles to catch her breath.

"Fuck... me..." she finally manages, each word emerging as a labored gasp.

I can't help the low chuckle that escapes me. "I just did. A few times, in fact."

She lifts her head enough to give me a weak slap on the shoulder, her eyes narrowed despite the smile tugging at her lips. "Don't be a smart ass."

"Can't help it," I murmur, brushing a strand of pink-streaked hair from her face. Her makeup is smudged, mascara slightly smeared beneath her eyes. It should look messy, but on her, it's just raw and real.

She shifts, wincing slightly as she disengages from me and rolls to her side, one arm draped across my chest. "Oh, god... I can't remember the last time I had sex this good."

"Must be the architect in me," I say, keeping my voice casual despite the surge of satisfaction her words bring. "I know exactly where to place the support beams."

Roxy bursts into laughter, her body shaking against mine. "That's terrible," she gasps, burying her face in my shoulder. "Like, really, really terrible."

"You laughed," I point out, pulling her closer.

"Yeah, well." She traces a finger along my collarbone, her touch light but deliberate. "Maybe I'm just in a good mood."

Roxy props herself up on one elbow, her hair cascading over her shoulder as she looks at me. Her eyes are soft, the playfulness from earlier replaced by something gentler. She traces a finger along my jaw, her touch light but deliberate.

"Sebastian," she starts, her voice barely above a whisper. I can see the words forming on her lips before she even speaks them. "I think it's time for me to go."

I open my mouth to protest, but she places a finger on my lips, silencing me.

"I had an unbelievable evening," she says, her eyes never leaving mine. "But if I don't go now, I'm going to never want to leave."

I catch her hand, holding it against my chest. "What's wrong with that?" I ask, my voice low.

She smiles, but it's tinged with sadness. "I don't want to get my heart broke, Sebastian. And I'm not sure you can spell monogamy. And that's okay."

I start to speak, but she shakes her head, stopping me.

"I'd rather leave knowing this is the end," she says, her voice steady. "With the memory of our evening together."

She leans down, pressing a soft kiss to my lips, then pulls away, slipping out of the bed. I watch as she gathers her clothes, her movements quick and efficient. She dresses in silence, her back to me, and I can't find the words to stop her.

As she reaches the door, she turns to look at me one last time. "Goodbye, Sebastian," she says, her voice soft. Then she's gone, the door clicking shut behind her.

CHAPTER 7

The first genuine encounter between us feels like fate.

I've fantasized about this interaction and how it might unfold, contemplating what I would say when I felt I'd piqued your interest. I assume it would come as a remark while riding the elevator, or an exchange of looks across the entrance hall, maybe even a brief interaction so minute that you don't realize its significance.

Yet instead, it is here, in this unexpected location, that we have our first genuine encounter as you exit this café and I stroll past it.

In fact, you don't even notice me at first, but I see you. I see how you carry yourself with that perfect grace, I smell that captivating, that maddening and consuming scent as you draw closer.

I watch as you juggle a coffee cup in one hand, your phone in the other, stashing something into your purse as you move toward the streets edge. I'm so consumed in the moment, that I miscalculate, a centimeter astray, a split second of delay.

And suddenly, you bump into me.

Nothing exaggerated. Just the gentle contact of your shoulder against my torso, with a slight catch in your inhale as you halt abruptly.

I watch as you raise your eyes, and in this moment, I sense something transform.

"Oh," Her tone is airy, hardly surprised, more entertained than anything else. "I didn't notice you there."

My grin is already curling like a fox.

"Then I suppose I should be flattered to have caught your attention now."

Her eyes flicker up to mine, dark, assessing, holding the moment.

Then, a smile. Slow, subtle. Coy.

"You move quietly."

I tip my head slightly. "I could say the same about you."

A small pause, a ripple of something unspoken passes between us.

And I take my chance.

"I'm hosting something this weekend," I say, voice casual, as if this invitation wasn't planned, or something I've practiced a thousand times in my head. "A party at my place. You should come."

She doesn't react immediately. She takes a sip of her coffee without saying a word. The moment stretches as every second of silence feels like an hour.

Then, she exhales softly, shaking her head with the faintest smile.

"I don't think so."

It's not a rejection.

Not entirely.

There's something else in the way she says it, not dismissal, but amusement. A playfulness that keeps the door open just enough.

"No?" I echo, curious.

She tilts her head slightly, as if considering. "No," she repeats, but it's almost teasing. "Not this time."

Not this time.

The words slip between my ribs, settle into something deeper.

I watch as she steps away, effortlessly moving back into the rhythm of the morning, disappearing into the stream of people heading toward the office.

I don't follow.

I let the moment stay exactly as it is, untouched.

Her words echo as I continue my walk to the office. Not this time. The implication hangs between us even after she's gone, a thread connecting this moment to some future one. I've waited for this, planned for this, and now it's happened with such natural ease it feels like fate.

The casual collision on a sidewalk. The way her eyes held mine. The promise in her refusal.

I adjust my tie as I enter the lobby, nodding at the security guard. The elevator doors open, and I step inside, breathing in the lingering scent of her perfume. Has she just been here? The thought pleases me. Our orbits drawing closer, intersecting more frequently now.

Not this time suggests there will be another time. Her choice of words were deliberate, I'm certain. She's aware of me in ways I hadn't realized. Perhaps she's been noticing me all along, playing her own game of patience and restraint.

I arrive at my floor and walk to my office with measured steps. The morning light streams through the floor-to-ceiling windows, casting long rays of light onto the blueprints laid out on my desk.

I should be focused on the Morgan project, the client meeting is tomorrow, but my mind keeps returning to her. The slight upturn of her lips when she declined my invitation. The way she sipped her coffee, thoughtful, considering. Not dismissing me outright.

This is progress. A shift in our dynamic.

I reach for my phone, scrolling through my contacts before stopping myself. No. Too eager. Too obvious. The next move must be hers, or at least appear to be.

I settle into my chair, fingers drumming against the desk. The hunger inside me stirs, different from the other hunger, the one I feed in the dark. This one burns slower, more insistent. More dangerous, perhaps.

Not this time.

But soon. I can feel it.

I step into the office, the familiar scent of polished wood and fresh coffee greeting me. The background noise of conversations and the steady rhythm of keystrokes create a comforting backdrop. My presence commands attention, but I wear my charm like an old suit, comfortable, reliable.

"Good morning, everyone," I say, voice warm and inviting. Eyes lift from monitors, smiles forming in response. "I hope you're all ready for a productive day."

I move through the open-plan space with purpose, stopping at each desk to engage in brief but genuine exchanges. My first stop is Meredith, our lead designer, who's engrossed in her latest project.

"Meredith," I start, causing her to look up. "How's the new layout coming along?"

She beams, clearly pleased to have my attention. "It's shaping up nicely, Sebastian. Just finalizing some details."

"Excellent," I reply, nodding approvingly. "By the way, I'm hosting a small gathering at my place this weekend. I'd love for you and your husband to join us."

Her eyes widen with surprise and gratitude. "We'd be delighted. Thank you for the invitation."

I continue on, repeating this ritual with each team member, Brian in accounting, Lucy in marketing, even Charles from IT who rarely leaves his corner of the office.

"Charles," I call out as I approach his cluttered workspace. "How's everything running on your end?"

He pushes his glasses up his nose and looks at me over his screen. "Smooth sailing so far," he says with a hint of pride.

"Glad to hear it," I respond smoothly. "I wanted to extend an invitation to you and your wife for a gathering at my place this weekend."

He blinks, taken aback by the offer. "We'd love that," he finally says.

With each interaction, I reinforce my position, not just as their boss but as someone who values them personally. It's a careful balance of power and connection, one I've mastered over the years.

My final stop is Ryan's office, where he's buried under a pile of blue-prints and proposals.

"Ryan," I call out gently, making him look up from his work.

He stands quickly, offering a polite smile. "Sebastian."

"How's the project coming along?"

"On track," he assures me.

I nod approvingly before extending my hand towards him. "I'm hosting a get-together this weekend at my place," I say smoothly. "You and your wife should join us."

His smile widens just slightly, gratitude mingled with surprise. "We'll be there," he promises.

I make my way to Elizabeth's desk, the epitome of professionalism. Her eyes meet mine with an easy familiarity. "Elizabeth, I'm having a few people over this weekend. I'd be pleased if you'd join us."

She looks surprised but recovers quickly, her smile genuine. "That sounds wonderful, Sebastian. I'd love to come."

With Elizabeth's acceptance in hand, I turn my attention to Alexis Vanderpool, the newest addition to our team. She's young, eager to learn, and there's a certain spark in her that I find intriguing.

I approach her desk, noting the way her eyes brighten at the prospect of being included. "Alexis, I'm hosting a gathering this weekend. It would be a great opportunity for you to meet some of our clients in a more relaxed setting."

She nods enthusiastically; her voice tinged with gratitude. "I'd be honored, Mr. Wolfe. Thank you for the invitation."

Finally, I seek out Rebecca Donovan, my personal assistant. She's the linchpin that keeps my world in order, and I've come to appreciate her efficiency and discretion more than she knows. I find her organizing files in the archive room.

"Rebecca," I begin, and she turns to face me, her movements always so precise and controlled. "I have something for you."

I present her with a garment bag, watching her expression shift from surprise to uncertainty.

"What's this?" she asks, her fingers brushing against the fabric.

"Open it," I urge her gently.

She unzips the bag to reveal the dress I've chosen, a sleek, elegant piece in a deep shade of midnight blue. It's perfect for her, classic with a subtle edge that suits her quiet strength.

"Sebastian, I..." she hesitates, her eyes lifting to meet mine. "This is too much."

I dismiss her hesitation with a shake of my head. "Nonsense. It's a small token of my appreciation for all that you do. I want you to feel as special as you are when you attend the party this weekend."

She holds the dress up to herself, her reflection caught in the polished surface of a filing cabinet. For a moment, she allows herself to imagine it, the fabric against her skin, the way it would move with her.

"I don't know what to say," she admits, her voice soft.

"Just say you'll come," I tell her, my tone earnest. "Your presence would mean a great deal to me."

Rebecca looks at me then, something shifting in her gaze. It's not often that I show my gratitude so openly, and I can see the impact of my words.

"Thank you, Sebastian," she says, and there's a warmth in her voice that wasn't there before. "I'll be there."

I nod, satisfied. The invitations have been extended, the stage set. Now, all that remains is to see how the evening unfolds.

I close the Morgan file precisely at 4:43 PM. Perfect timing. The meeting tomorrow will proceed flawlessly now that I've addressed every potential question, anticipated every concern. I straighten the papers, align them with the edge of my desk, and check my watch.

She leaves at 4:57 PM. Always.

I gather my things methodically, laptop, keys, phone, and make my way toward the elevator bank. Several colleagues call out goodbyes. I acknowledge each with the appropriate level of warmth.

The elevator arrives, doors sliding open with a soft chime. Empty. I step inside, position myself against the back wall, and press the button for the third floor. A calculated detour.

The doors open and there she is, walking toward me, her gaze fixed on her phone. She looks up at the last second, recognition flickering in her eyes.

"Going down?" I ask, holding the door.

She steps inside. "Yes, thank you."

The scent of honey fills the small space between us. I watch her reflection in the polished doors, the way she tucks a strand of hair behind her ear. Our eyes meet briefly in the reflection. She looks away first.

I watch her reflection in the polished elevator doors, tracking every small movement. The air feels charged between us, heavy with unsaid things. We descend in silence, floor numbers ticking down. Three. Two. One.

"I'm sorry for bumping into you today," I remark, voice casual.

Her eyes meet mine in the reflection. "It's okay, it was my fault."

I stare at her as she speaks, watching her large full lips pucker slightly as she apologizes, the look in her dark brown eyes, it's absolutely captivating.

"No, I should have been more careful," I say smoothly.

The elevator slows, then stops. The doors slide open to reveal the marble-floored lobby, busy with the early exodus of workers eager to start their evenings.

She hesitates for a fraction of a second before stepping out. "Have a good evening, Sebastian."

My name in her mouth, it's the first time she's used it. The sound of it lingers in the air between us. I follow her at a measured distance, watching as she moves through the crowd. Her dark hair catches the late afternoon light streaming through the floor-to-ceiling windows. People part for her without seeming to notice they're doing it.

I stand near the revolving doors, observing as she pauses at the security desk to exchange a few words with the guard. He laughs at something she says. She smiles, that same subtle smile she gave me earlier. Not this time.

She walks through the revolving doors and onto the street. I count to thirty before following. By the time I step outside, she's already halfway down the block. I don't pursue her. Instead, I turn toward the parking garage, satisfaction warming me from within.

The encounter was brief, insignificant to most observers. But between us, something has shifted. She acknowledged me directly. Used my name. The distance between us is closing, slowly but surely.

I unlock my car, slide into the driver's seat, and sit for a moment in the dim light of the parking garage. Her scent lingers on me somehow, honey and something deeper. I start the engine and pull out into the evening traffic, already planning tomorrow's movements, calculating how and when our paths will cross next.

Back home, I prepare with deliberate care. Tonight requires precision. I select a charcoal button-down, dark jeans, sophisticated without appearing that I'm trying too hard. I apply cologne with restraint: 1899 Hemingway. Notes of tobacco, spiced wood, and the faintest hint of vanilla. Cultured but understated.

I check my reflection. Control tightens around me like a second skin.

The drive to the club takes exactly thirteen minutes. The Poetry Collective, a dimly lit venue where artistic souls bare themselves through verse and melody. A place where vulnerable prey gather, where people come when they want to be seen and heard.

I park across the street, watching patrons filter in. Young, hopeful faces. Eager to be understood. I wait until the flow of people subsides before making my entrance, the perfect moment to be noticed without appearing desperate for attention.

Inside, a woman with copper hair reads from a worn journal, her voice trembling as she describes love as "a beautiful violence." The crowd snaps their fingers in appreciation. I scan the room, settling into a corner table with clear sightlines to the bar and entrance.

I order a whiskey neat. The bold scent of the drink tickles my nose as I raise the glass to my lips, surveying the hunting grounds with patient focus.

I sip my whiskey, letting the burn anchor me to the present while my mind drifts back to the elevator. The way my name sounded in Iris's mouth, deliberate, measured, as if she'd been practicing it. Sebastian. Not Mr. Wolfe, not a hesitant nod, but my name, spoken with familiarity. Like she's been saying it all along in private conversations we've never had.

Not this time.

The implication of future possibilities lingers, sweet as her honey scent. She's aware of me now, fully, consciously. The careful dance we've been engaged in without speaking is shifting into something more tangible. I imagine her thinking of me after our encounters, perhaps wondering about me as I wonder about her.

My reverie breaks as the emcee announces the next performer. The crowd's polite applause pulls me back to the dimly lit club, to the hunt I came for.

She steps onto the small stage, guitar strap crossed over her chest, dark hair falling in waves past her shoulders. There's something in her posture, a confident vulnerability, that immediately draws my attention. Her fingers adjust the microphone, and she offers a shy smile to the audience.

"This is 'Meant For Me," she says, her voice soft but clear.

The first notes drift across the room with every pick of the strings on her guitar. Then she begins to sing, and the club fades away. Her voice carries both strength and fragility, wrapping around each word like she's sharing a secret.

Halfway through the first verse, her eyes find mine in the darkness. Not by accident, she sought me out, held my gaze with deliberate intent. The corner of her mouth curls slightly, a private acknowledgment between us.

The hunger inside me responds immediately, coiling tight and expectant. She's playing for the room but singing to me. Every note, every word of longing and connection, directed at me alone.

I know then she's the one for tonight. The perfect prey, seeking connection, craving to be truly seen. And I will see her, completely, in that final moment.

I wait until she finishes her set, watching as she accepts the crowd's applause with a modest nod. When she steps off the stage, guitar in hand, I move deliberately toward her, timing my approach so our paths intersect naturally by the bar.

"That was beautiful," I say, my voice pitched just loud enough to carry over the ambient noise. I offer her a warm smile. "Would you let me buy you a drink? Seems like the least I can do after such a moving performance."

She hesitates, studying my face with curious eyes. Her fingers tighten slightly around the neck of her guitar before relaxing again.

"I'd like that," she replies, a cautious smile forming. "Thank you."

I signal the bartender. "What's your poison?"

"Gin and tonic, please."

"A gin and tonic and a whiskey neat," I tell the bartender, then turn back to her. "Would you like to sit? I noticed a table opening up over there."

She nods, following me to the small corner table. I place our drinks down and help her maneuver her guitar case against the wall.

"I just need to put this away," she says, carefully placing her guitar in its case.

I watch her hands, the gentle, reverent way she handles the instrument. The same hands that coaxed such emotion from those strings moments ago.

"I have to confess," I say as she latches the case, "I enjoy singing myself," I offer a self-deprecating smile.

"Oh, do you perform?" She asks.

"Oh no, I keep my singing to the muffled acoustics of my shower, the white noise makes it hard to hear how off key I am." I reply with a smile.

She laughs, a genuine sound that lights up her face. "Well, at least you have an appreciative audience of one."

"Only if you count the rubber duck, and he's a harsh critic." I extend my hand across the table. "I'm Sebastian, by the way. Sebastian Wolfe."

She places her hand in mine, her touch light but not tentative. "Leslie Gonzalez. Nice to meet you, Sebastian."

I hold her gaze across the table, savoring the delicate strength in her hand before releasing it. "That song you performed, did you write it?"

"I did," Leslie nods, her fingers tracing the rim of her glass. "About six months ago, after a particularly bad breakup."

"I could feel that," I tell her, leaning slightly forward. "There's something about pain that creates authenticity in art, don't you think?"

She studies my face, as if searching for signs of insincerity. Finding none, she relaxes. "That's exactly it. When I wrote it, I was trying to make sense of everything, like putting the pieces back together through music."

"The best creative work comes from that place," I say. "When you're standing at the edge between breaking and rebuilding."

Her eyes widen slightly. "That's... yes. That's exactly how it felt."

I take a sip of whiskey, letting the moment breathe between us. "How long have you been performing?"

"Since college, but only seriously for the past two years." Leslie tucks a strand of hair behind her ear, looking down as if to hide her smile and blush. "What about you, Sebastian? What do you do when you're not critiquing shower performances?"

"I'm an architect." I smile, holding her gaze. "I design spaces for people to live in, work in... connect in."

"Like this place?" She gestures to our surroundings.

"Not quite. My work tends to be more... deliberate." I lean closer, as if sharing a secret. "I believe environments shape experiences. The right curve of a wall, the perfect height of a ceiling, they can make people feel things without realizing why."

"That's fascinating," she says, genuinely intrigued. "Do you have a favorite project you've worked on?"

"A private residence overlooking Lake Michigan. I designed every angle to frame the water differently throughout the day." I pause, watching how attentively she listens. "But I'd rather hear more about your music. The way you controlled the room tonight, that's a rare gift."

A blush creeps across her cheeks. "It doesn't always work that way. Tonight felt different somehow." She glances down, then back up through her lashes. "Maybe because of my audience."

I smile, reaching forward to brush my fingers lightly against hers. "I'm glad I was there to hear it."

Leslie's fingers brush mine, and I feel the faintest tremor in her touch. It's a promising sign, she's drawn to me, even if she doesn't fully understand why.

"Your music has a way of making people feel seen," I continue, my voice low and deliberate. "It's a powerful thing, to connect with strangers so intimately."

She smiles, looking down again. Across her face a soft, vulnerable expression hints at the depths of her appreciation for my compliment. She takes a moment, composing herself before lifting her head back up and speaking again. "That's what I love about performing. In that moment, it's like... I'm not alone in my feelings."

I nod, taking a slow sip of my whiskey. "Art has a way of bridging those invisible gaps between us. It's why I'm drawn to architecture, shaping spaces that bring people together, even if they don't realize it."

I trace the rim of my glass, watching the way the dim light catches in the amber liquid. "You know, there's something almost sacred about spaces like this, where people come to be vulnerable together."

"I've never thought about it that way." Leslie tilts her head slightly. "But you're right. It's like... collective permission to feel things."

"Exactly." I lean forward, reducing the space between us by inches. "Though I have to admit, some performances stay with you more than others."

Her eyes meet mine and then she looks away for a moment, her eyes darting, looking back to my eyes, then to my lips and I can feel her accepting the suggestion I've planted. "Like which ones?"

"Like yours." I hold her gaze for three seconds before looking down at my drink with a small smile. "There's an authenticity there that's rare."

Leslie's fingers fidget with her napkin, letting out a subtle giggle.

"That means a lot, especially coming from another artistic person."

"Well, I'm no music critic," I say, my voice lighter now. "The last time I tried to play a guitar, my neighbor thought I was torturing a small animal."

Her laugh bursts forth unexpectedly, genuine, unguarded. The sound transforms her face, softening the careful composure she's maintained. I feel a small thrill at having breached that barrier.

"What happened?" she asks, still smiling.

"She called animal control. I had to explain to a very confused officer why I was attempting to play 'Stairway to Heaven' at midnight." I shake my head ruefully. "Turns out, stairs to heaven sound remarkably like stairs to hell when I play them."

Another laugh, deeper this time. Her shoulders relax further.

"So I stick to appreciating rather than creating," I continue, letting my fingers brush against hers as I reach for my drink. The contact is brief, deliberate, a test she doesn't pull away from. "Though I do sometimes wonder what it feels like, to move people the way you just did."

"It's... hard to describe." Her eyes drop to where our hands nearly touch. "When you're performing and you can feel the audience with you, it's like time stops for a moment."

"Like perfect alignment," I murmur, holding her gaze. "When everything unnecessary falls away."

She nods slowly, something shifting in her expression, recognition, perhaps. Of being understood.

I smile, letting a hint of shyness show through my usual composure. "Sorry if that sounds pretentious. Hazard of the profession, we architects tend to wax philosophical after a good whiskey."

"No, it's not pretentious at all," she says softly. "It's exactly how it feels."

"So, Leslie," I say, leaning back slightly in my chair, creating an illusion of casualness. "What brings a talented singer like you to a place like this?"

She smiles, tucking a strand of hair behind her ear. "Just trying to get my name out there, you know? Hoping someone might hear something they like."

"I think they did," I reply, holding her gaze. "Your performance was captivating. The way you commanded the room, it was impressive."

A blush creeps across her cheeks. "Thank you. It's not always easy to get up there and bare your soul."

"But you do it beautifully," I say, my voice softening. I reach out, gently touching her hand. "It takes courage to be vulnerable like that."

She looks down at our hands, then back up at me. "You seem to know a lot about being vulnerable, Sebastian."

I chuckle, a self-deprecating sound. "Only from observation. I'm not much of a performer myself."

"Could have fooled me," she says, her eyes sparkling with amusement. "You have a certain... presence."

"Is that a compliment?" I ask, raising an eyebrow.

"Definitely," she laughs. The sound is genuine, warm. I've breached another barrier.

"Well, in that case, thank you," I say, smiling. "Though I must admit, I'm much more comfortable behind the scenes. Shaping the stage rather than standing on it."

"There's something to be said for that too," Leslie says, her fingers tracing the rim of her glass. "Creating the space for others to shine."

"Exactly," I agree, leaning forward. "It's all about setting the right mood, the right atmosphere. Making people feel something without them even realizing why."

She nods, her eyes never leaving mine. "Like what you're doing now?"

I pause, caught off guard. Then I smile, a slow, genuine smile. "Maybe," I admit. "But only because you're worth setting the stage for."

Her breath hitches slightly, a barely noticeable intake of air. She's affected, drawn in. I can see it in the way her pupils dilate, the way her body language shifts subtly towards me.

"You're quite the charmer, Sebastian Wolfe," she says, her voice soft.

"Only when inspired," I reply, holding her gaze. I let the moment stretch; the silence filled with unspoken tension. Then I break it with a gentle laugh, leaning back again. "But seriously, Leslie, your talent is rare. You deserve to be heard."

She smiles with a soft expression. "Thank you, Sebastian. That means a lot."

I reach out, tucking a strand of hair behind her ear. A intimate gesture, familiar but not invasive. She leans into the touch slightly, her eyes fluttering closed for a moment. When she opens them again, there's a new warmth in her gaze.

"You know," I say, my voice low. "I have a friend who owns a small music venue downtown. He's always looking for new talent. Maybe I could introduce you sometime?"

Her eyes widen, hope sparking in their depths. "Really? That would be amazing, Sebastian."

"Consider it done," I say, smiling. "Anything to help a talented artist like you."

She beams at me, her defenses lowered, her trust gained. I've played this game well, each move calculated, each word designed to draw her in. And now, she's exactly where I want her.

I lean in closer, watching the subtle shifts in Leslie's expression as she speaks about her music. The air between us feels charged, intimate in a way that transforms this crowded bar into our private world.

"You know what I find fascinating about songwriters?" I ask, my voice low enough that she has to lean forward to catch my words. "The way you translate emotion into something tangible. Taking what most people can barely articulate and turning it into art."

"It's not always easy," she admits, fingertips tapping lightly against her glass. "Sometimes the feelings are too big for the words."

"Yet you found them tonight," I say. "That last verse about 'shadows stretching between heartbeats', that stayed with me."

Surprise flickers across her face. "You really were listening."

"To every word." I hold her gaze, allowing genuine appreciation to show. "How could I not?"

The flush that spreads across her cheeks isn't from the gin anymore. She takes a sip of her drink, using the moment to collect herself.

"What about you?" she asks. "Do your buildings tell stories too?"

"They do, but in a different language. Glass and steel instead of notes and lyrics." I trace a pattern on the table between us. "I design spaces that make people feel protected yet free. There's an intimacy to architecture that most never notice."

"Like what?" Her curiosity is genuine now; her body angled toward mine.

"Like the way ceiling height affects conversation. Lower ceilings create closeness, they make voices softer, more confidential." I gesture slightly to the space above us. "This height, for instance, invites sharing secrets."

She glances up, then back at me with a small smile. "Is that why I'm telling you things I don't usually share with strangers?"

"Are we still strangers, Leslie?" I ask softly.

Her smile deepens, reaching her eyes. "No, I don't think we are."

"I had no idea it was so late," she says, looking around at the thinning crowd.

"Time has a way of disappearing in good company," I reply, finishing my drink. "I've enjoyed tonight more than I expected I would."

She gathers her guitar case, pausing briefly in her movement. "Me too. It's been... refreshing."

I follow Leslie, holding the door for her as she steps out into the night. Leslie shivers as the night air blows, goosebumps start forming on her bare arms.

"My place isn't far from here," I say, the words casual, unrushed. "I have a collection of rare acoustic guitars that might interest you. A 1967 Martin that would sound incredible with your voice."

Her hesitation is brief but noticeable, a moment of internal debate playing across her features.

"Just for a nightcap," I add, giving her the space to decide. "And maybe you could play something on a guitar worthy of your talent."

Leslie studies my face, her dark eyes thoughtful. Then that slow smile returns, the one that transforms her entire countenance.

"I'd like that," she says. "I've never played a vintage Martin before."

Leslie shivers again, her arms crossing over her chest. Without hesitation, I slip off my jacket and drape it over her shoulders.

"Here," I say, my voice gentle. "The night air has a bite to it."

"Thanks." She pulls the jacket closer, her small frame nearly swallowed by the tailored wool. The sight stirs something in me, possession, perhaps. My clothes on her body.

"Let me take that." I reach for her purse, leaving her hands free for the guitar case. "You've got enough to carry."

She relinquishes it with a grateful smile. "Chivalry isn't dead after all."

"Just dormant in most men." I guide her with the lightest touch at the small of her back. "My car's just around the corner."

We walk in comfortable silence, her heels clicking against the pavement. When we reach the Aston Martin, I enjoy the widening of her eyes.

"This is yours?" she asks, running her fingers lightly over the metallic silver finish.

"One of my few indulgences." I press the key fob, watching the lights flash in response. Opening the passenger door, I hold it for her. "After you."

Leslie slides in, the leather seats embracing her. I carefully place her guitar in the trunk, then her purse, before joining her in the car. The engine rumbles to life, a sound that never fails to please me.

"This feels surreal," she admits as we pull away from the curb. "I wasn't expecting my night to end like this."

"The best nights rarely follow expectations." I navigate through the quiet streets, streetlights casting rhythmic patterns across her face. "Music, conversation, spontaneity, these are the elements of a perfect evening."

Her fingers trace patterns on the leather armrest. "And expensive cars, apparently."

I laugh, the sound genuine. "The car is just transportation. The company is what matters."

The drive to my home passes quickly, our conversation flowing easily between music theory and architectural influences. I pull into my driveway, the security lights illuminating automatically as we approach.

"This is where you live?" Leslie stares up at the modern structure of glass and steel, its clean lines cutting against the night sky.

"Home sweet home." I retrieve her belongings from the trunk, then lead her to the front door. The house responds to my presence, lights warming to a soft amber glow as we enter.

Leslie steps inside, her eyes taking in the open concept living area, the floating staircase, the carefully curated art pieces.

"It's beautiful," she breathes, turning slowly. "Like something from a magazine."

"I designed it myself." I set her guitar down carefully. "Would you like the tour?"

She nods, still absorbing the details. I lead her through the main floor, enjoying her reactions to each thoughtful element. Finally, we reach my study.

"This is where the magic happens," I say, opening the double doors.

Leslie steps inside, drawn immediately to the architectural blueprints mounted on the walls. "These are incredible. So detailed."

"Architecture is all about the details." I watch her move around the room, fingers hovering just above the surface of my drafting table. "And speaking of details..." I gesture to the vintage Martin propped on a stand beside one of the bookcases. "As promised."

Her face lights up. "It's gorgeous."

"Can I offer you a drink?" I move to the small bar cart in the corner. "Whiskey, wine, something else?"

"Wine would be nice," she says, still examining the guitar with reverent hands.

I pour myself two fingers of whiskey, then select a rich cabernet for her. "I think you'll appreciate this one. It has depth, like your music."

Leslie's fingers hover over the vintage Martin, her touch feather-light, almost reverent. "I'm afraid to play it," she admits, her voice barely above a whisper. "It's such a piece of art, in perfect condition. I wouldn't want to..."

"It's deserving of a proper artist to play it," I interject, my voice firm with conviction. "Instruments like this are meant to be brought to life, not just admired from afar."

She looks at me, her eyes reflecting the soft light of the study. "But what if I..."

"You won't," I assure her, taking a step closer. "You have a gift, Leslie. This guitar deserves to be played by someone who can do it justice."

Her fingers finally make contact with the strings, a tentative brush that sends a resonating echo through the room. The sound is rich, full-bodied, and Leslie's eyes widen in surprise and delight.

"It's incredible," she breathes, her fingers pressing down more firmly now, exploring the chords. The guitar responds beautifully, its voice filling the space between us, wrapping around us like a warm embrace.

Leslie's hesitation melts away as she begins to play, her fingers dancing over the strings with a grace that comes from years of practice. The melody she weaves is intricate, emotional, a reflection of the depth she carries within her.

I watch her, the way her eyes close as she loses herself in the music, the way her body sways gently to the rhythm. There's a joy in her expression, a pure, unadulterated happiness that's infectious. I find myself smiling, not just with my lips, but with my eyes, with my entire being.

Leslie's fingers dance over the strings, her voice filling the room with a warmth that seeps into my bones. Each note resonates, stoking a hunger deep within me. This isn't just about tonight, about a fleeting moment of passion. No, this is about possession, about making her a permanent part of my collection.

I inch closer, drawn to her like a moth to a flame. Her voice is intoxicating, her presence a drug I can't resist. She's mine, she just doesn't know it yet. The thought sends a shiver of anticipation down my spine.

"That's incredible, Leslie," I murmur, my voice low, almost a growl. I position myself closer, under the guise of being captivated by her music. My eyes flutter closed, as if I'm lost in the melody, but every sense is heightened, attuned to her.

She laughs softly, a sound that's music in itself. "You're too kind, Sebastian."

"I'm just honest." I open my eyes, meeting her gaze. There's a warmth there, an invitation. She's lowering her defenses, letting me in. I lean in slightly, my body language open, non-threatening. Just a man entranced by a woman's talent.

Her fingers never stop their dance over the strings, but her eyes stay locked on mine. She's searching, trying to read me. I give her a small smile, a hint of vulnerability. The coy boy, captivated by her song. It's a role I play well.

"You have such a gift," I say, my voice barely above a whisper. I'm close now, close enough to feel her breath on my skin. Close enough for her to kiss me, if she just leaned in a little.

Her eyes flicker down to my lips, then back up to my eyes. She's considering it, I can see the thought flitting across her features. I hold my breath, waiting, the predator in me still, patient.

"Thank you, Sebastian," she whispers, her voice barely audible over the sound of the guitar. She leans in, just a fraction, her eyes never leaving mine. I can feel the heat of her, the promise of her.

And I wait, the hunger inside me growing, gnawing. Soon, I promise myself. Soon, she'll be mine. Completely, utterly mine.

Leslie leans in, her eyes fluttering closed as she closes the distance between us. She hesitates for a heartbeat, a moment of delicious anticipation that sends electricity coursing through my veins. Then her lips touch mine, soft and tentative. The guitar between us creates a barrier, but somehow makes this moment more intimate, as if we're stealing something forbidden.

I return the kiss with careful restraint, matching her gentleness. Though every instinct urges me to devour, to claim, I hold back. This dance requires patience. The perfect hunt always does.

She pulls away first, her bottom lip caught between her teeth. Her eyes meet mine, dark and questioning, before dropping to my mouth again. The flush on her cheeks has deepened, and her breathing has quickened ever so slightly. The guitar rests against her, forgotten now, though her fingers still touch the strings.

"I don't usually do this," she whispers, vulnerability threading through her voice.

"Neither do I," I lie, the words falling easily from my lips. "There's something about you, Leslie."

She searches my face, looking for deception, for the warning signs women are taught to recognize. I offer only sincerity, my expression open, my eyes warm. I've perfected this mask, the thoughtful architect, the appreciative listener, the man worth trusting.

Her gaze lingers on my lips, desire warring with caution. I can almost hear her thoughts, the internal debate. Should she stay? Should she go?

Leslie carefully sets down the guitar, her fingers lingering on the polished wood for a moment. The reverence in her touch stirs something in me, appreciation, perhaps, for someone who understands the value of beautiful things.

I move toward her slowly, confidently, making sure not to startle her. Taking the Martin from its resting place, I feel its weight in my hands, substantial yet balanced, like all perfect instruments.

"I want you to have it," I say, the words leaving my mouth before I've fully considered them.

Her eyes widen, confusion replacing the warmth that had been there moments before. "What? No, Sebastian, I couldn't possibly..."

"You can," I interrupt, my voice soft but firm. "A guitar as lovely as this needs to be in the hands of an equally lovely and talented musician."

Leslie shakes her head, her lips parting as she struggles to find the right response. "That's incredibly generous, but it's too much. We barely know each other."

"Sometimes recognition happens in an instant." I hold the guitar out to her, watching her internal struggle play across her features. "I've owned this guitar for years, but I've never heard it sing the way it did in your hands."

Her resistance wavers. I can see it in the softening of her expression, the slight trembling of her fingers as they reach tentatively toward the instrument. She relents, her hands moving to grasp the bottom and the neck of the guitar.

As her fingers wrap around the neck, they brush against mine. She doesn't pull away. Instead, her eyes lift to meet mine, and what I see there is captivating, that exquisite moment of surrender, like the look before a leap into the unknown.

Time suspends between us. Her pulse is visible at her throat, quickening. My own heart responding in kind.

Leslie leans in, crossing the final distance between us. This kiss is different, deeper, hungrier. Her free hand moves to my chest, fingers curling into the fabric of my shirt. The guitar presses between us, a witness to this moment of connection.

I taste the wine on her lips, feel the heat of her breath mingling with mine. My hand finds the small of her back, drawing her closer, claiming her. The hunger inside me sharpens, focusing to a fine point.

I gently take the Martin from Leslie's hands, our fingers brushing against each other in the exchange. The connection consuming me with immediate need, like being hit by a bolt of lightning. With reverent care, I return the guitar to its stand, positioning it just so.

When I turn back, Leslie is there, closer than before. Her eyes hold mine, dark and wanting. She moves toward me with newfound confidence, closing the distance between us. Her lips find mine, no hesitation this time. The kiss is deeper, hungrier, her body pressing against mine with unmistakable intent.

I respond in kind, one hand cupping the back of her neck, the other at her waist, pulling her closer. The taste of her floods my senses. Her hands explore my chest, fingers working at my shirt buttons with growing urgency.

"Sebastian," she breathes against my mouth, the sound of my name on her lips feeding that primal hunger within me.

I guide her backward, our bodies still connected, mouths still hungry for each other. Her back meets the wall, and she gasps, a sound that sends heat coursing through me. My hands find their way under her blouse, fingertips tracing the warm skin beneath.

"Is this okay?" I ask, my voice rough with restraint.

Her answer comes in the form of her hands tugging my shirt free, pulling it from my shoulders. I mirror her actions, lifting her blouse over her head, revealing smooth skin that begs to be touched. My fingers trace the delicate lace of her bra, appreciating the artistry of her form.

We move through the hallway, shedding layers like barriers between us. Each article of clothing marks our path, my shirt by the study door, her blouse near the guest room, shoes abandoned without care.

I steer her toward my bedroom, our progress slowed by lingering kisses and exploring hands. The hunger inside me grows with each step, with each new inch of her skin revealed to me. By the time we reach my door, we're both breathing heavily, desire evident in every touch.

Leslie pulls back slightly, her eyes meeting mine. There's trust there, alongside the want, a surrender that feeds the predator in me.

"I want this," she whispers, answering the question I already answered.

I guide her backward toward my bedroom, our mouths still hungry for each other, eager for more. The need in my blood demands satisfaction, and I crave to possess, to explore every inch of her.

She leans back onto my bed, her eyes never leaving mine.

I crawl toward her, delighting in the sight of her sprawled across my bed, her hair spilling across my pillows, her skin gleaming in the muted city light filtering through the hazy window shade. Her beauty calls to me.

Moving closer, I claim her lips, tasting the sweetness of her mouth, the hint of wine still lingering. My hands find her waist, then move upward, caressing the smooth skin of her sides, my thumbs grazing the underside of her breasts.

She arches into my touch, a silent invitation to explore further. My lips trail along her jawline, down to the hollow of her throat, tasting the delicate skin there. My tongue teases the sensitive spot just below her ear, and I feel her shiver in response.

With deliberate slowness, I continue my path downward, my lips and tongue leaving a trail of heat along her collarbone. Her pulse flutters like a trapped bird beneath my kisses, and I wonder if it's excitement or uncertainty that quickens her heartbeat.

My knee presses into the soft space between her thighs, a bold statement of my desire. I savor her gasp, the way she instinctively presses back against me, inviting more. With a gentle rhythm, I begin to massage her core with my leg, a slow torture that builds anticipation.

Her kisses grow more frantic, her hands tangling in my hair, urging me closer. I let my hand wander, teasing the delicate lace of her bra, my thumb finding the taut bud of her nipple beneath the fabric.

She moans, her hips pressing against my leg in silent request for more pressure. I grant her wish, increasing the intensity of my touch, my hand moving in time with the movements of my thigh. Her body responds instinctually.

With gentle precision, I unclasp her bra, baring her breasts to my hungry gaze. The sight of her, naked and vulnerable, sends a surge of possessiveness through me.

I drink in the sight of her, her tan skin glowing softly, her breasts rising and falling with her quickening breath. My lips find her nipple, kissing, sucking, my tongue teasing the sensitive peak.

Her moans fuel my desire, each sound a drop of sugar that feeds the hunger inside me. My mouth moves to her other breast, lavishing attention, sucking gently as my hand explores the curves of her body.

Her hands grasp my shoulders, her nails digging into my skin as she arches into my touch. I savor her responses, the way her body moves in sync with mine, the soft sounds of pleasure she can't contain.

Her moans fill the room with desire that strokes the flames of my own need. My hand moves downward, tracing the curve of her waist, the gentle swell of her hip. With each touch, each kiss, I claim another piece of her as my own.

She shifts restlessly beneath me, her breath coming in shallow as I continue my exploration. I feel her pulse quickening, the dampness between her legs, soaking through her pants.

Leslie's breath hitches, her chest rising and falling rapidly beneath my lips. I press my knee firmer against her, feeling the heat of her through the fabric of her pants. My hand grips her hip, holding her steady as I move, a slow, deliberate rhythm that mirrors the dance of our bodies.

Her fingers find the waistband of my pants, hesitating for a moment before dipping lower. She traces the length of me, her touch gentle yet firm, sending a jolt of desire coursing through my veins. I groan against her skin, my lips never leaving her neck, her collarbone, her chest.

Her breath comes faster now, shallow pants that match the pace of my movements. I can feel her heart racing, her pulse fluttering beneath my lips. Her hips move in sync with mine, her body instinctively seeking more pressure, more friction.

I oblige, my hips thrusting forward, increasing the intensity. Her grip on me tightens, her fingers stroking, exploring. The sensation is exquisite, a mix of pleasure and pain that feeds the hunger inside me.

Her moans grow louder, more insistent. She's close, I can feel it. Her body tenses, her nails digging into my shoulder as she clings to me. I keep my rhythm steady, my mouth on her skin, my body pressed against hers.

"Sebastian," she gasps, her voice a ragged plea. Her hips buck against mine, her body convulsing as she reaches her peak. Her grip on my shoulder tightens, her nails biting into my flesh, her breath hot and desperate against my ear.

I don't stop, don't slow. I keep moving, keep pressing, keep pushing her over the edge. Her moans fill the room. I can feel my control slipping, the hunger inside me growing, demanding more.

Leslie's screams fill the room, ragged and desperate. It's almost unbearable not to lose myself in this moment, in her raw need. I slow my movements, easing the pressure, drawing out her pleasure.

She's hungry for me, pulling off her pants quickly, throwing them to the floor. Her panties slide over her soft legs, over her feet with a quick flick. Her eyes never leave mine, dark with desire.

Her hands find my pants, pulling them off quickly. My manhood emerges through my boxers, slick with desire. She takes me in her hand, grasping with a hungry smile. Her lips taste me, her tongue rolling across the tip. The sensation sends a jolt through me, and for a moment, I feel myself losing my grip on control.

Leslie lays back, her hand still on my cock, pulling me closer to her. I follow, grabbing my waistband, pulling my boxers down, off of me. She releases me just long enough for me to discard them.

I move over her, my manhood firm with need and desire. Lifting her legs, I pull them over mine as I sit, my legs towards her, my shaft between her lips, begging for entry. I take myself in hand, massaging against her clit.

Leslie lets out a deep moan, her eyes fluttering closed as she surrenders to the sensation. I rotate my hips, letting my shaft drop down towards her entrance, then back to her clit, lubricating the path further with each movement. She lays there, enjoying the sensation, her moans like a cat's purr.

I resist the urge to plunge into her, to end the exquisite torture. She shifts beneath me, pressing herself against my tip, seeking more.

Her fingers thread through my hair, pulling me down until our lips meet. The kiss is passionate, needy. She tastes of salt and wine, a combination that ignites my hunger further. I feel her tongue against mine, tempting me to deepen the kiss, but I pull away, needing to keep a semblance of control.

I watch her face as I slowly push into her, savoring the way her eyes flutter closed, her lips parting on a soft gasp. I pause for a moment, giving her time to adjust to the sensation, then gently push further, feeling the warmth of her envelop me.

"Oh, God," she breathes, her back arching slightly as I seat myself fully inside her.

Her nails dig into my shoulders, her hips instinctively moving to meet mine. I resist the temptation to thrust wildly, to take what I crave with abandon. Instead, I force myself to move slowly, carefully, keeping a measured pace despite the growing hunger that threatens to consume me.

My hands find her hips, guiding our movements in a steady rhythm. Her body moves with mine, her breaths quickening as our dance becomes more frantic. I feel the tension building within her, the way her body responds to mine, and I know she's close.

Withdrawing almost completely, I thrust forward again, moving with more force this time. A moan, almost a whimper, escapes her lips, a sound of unadulterated pleasure that sends a jolt of satisfaction through me. I repeat the motion, my pace quickening, my control threatening to slip.

"Harder," she begs, her voice thick with desire.

I answer her plea, driving into her with increased force. Our bodies collide, the sound of flesh meeting flesh filling the room. Her nails scratch down my back, a sensation that only fuels my hunger.

"Yes, yes, harder," she urges me on, her voice hoarse with need.

Her words push me further, the pressure building inside me until I feel like I might splinter. I lose myself in the motion, slamming into her with abandon, my hips colliding with hers.

She cries out, her body convulsing as she rides the wave of her release. The sound of her pleasure sends me careening toward my own edge. I lean forward, bracing myself on my hands, using her body as leverage to thrust deeper.

Her legs wrap around my waist, pulling me closer, her body clinging to mine. I can feel her heart racing against my chest, her breath hot on my neck. I savor the sensation, the way her body grips mine as if she can't get close enough.

She begins to scream, her voice raw with ecstasy. I feel her peaking, and something feral stirs within me. I lean back, changing the angle, driving into her with a new intensity.

"Choke me," she says, her voice trembling.

I freeze, my eyes searching hers, unsure if I heard her correctly. I see the request in the dark depths of her eyes, and something within me stirs in recognition.

My hand moves to her throat, gently at first, my thumb caressing her soft skin as my fingers find purchase. I feel the pulse beneath my fingertips, steady and strong.

She bucks her hips against mine, urging me on. I tighten my grip, applying just enough pressure to elicit a soft cough. Her eyes glaze over with pleasure, and she arches her back, pressing herself against me.

I lose myself in the moment, my body moving instinctually, my need for release overpowering. I drive into her with desperation, my knees sinking into the mattress on both sides of her.

I look down at her, and in that moment, I see Jennifer's face above my hands. My grip tightens unconsciously, my knuckles whitening as I squeeze harder. Her hands grasp at my arms, a strangled gasp escaping her throat.

I watch, transfixed, as her legs begin to kick, her body responding to the friction between us. Her touch is like fire against my skin, burning away the last vestiges of control. I continue to drive into her, my movements frantic, driven by the need for release.

Her eyes are wide, her lips parted as she struggles for breath. My orgasm rises within me, a tsunami of sensation that threatens to consume me. I squeeze tighter, my fingers digging into her delicate throat.

The world narrows to this moment, to the feel of her body beneath mine, the heat of her skin, the taste of her moans in the air. I surrender to the pleasure, letting it wash over me, through me, my body moving of its own accord.

I release her throat, my hands falling to her sides as I collapse onto her, spent. My breaths come in shallow pants, my heart pounding in my chest. I feel her body beneath me, soft and still.

I look up, my gaze taking in the perfection of her in this moment, her skin aglow, her expression peaceful, her lips parted just so. My eyes trace the graceful curve of her throat, the delicate shape of her windpipe, now free of my restraint.

I feel for a pulse, my fingertips pressing gently against her neck. There's no response, no flicker of movement beneath my touch. I release her, stepping back to take in the sight of her one last time.

She lays there, beautiful and unmoving, the only sign of our encounter the slight dishevelment of her clothing and the flush on her skin. I relish the image, the perfection of her in this fleeting moment, before it's disturbed once again.

Retreating from the room, I leave behind this work of art, a masterpiece that only I will appreciate.

Pulling myself away from Leslie's still form, my heart rate gradually slows as I step onto the cold tile floor. The bathroom light flickers on, its harsh fluorescence revealing the evidence of our encounter on my skin, the faint scratches on my shoulders, the lingering scent of her perfume.

The shower hisses to life and I step under the spray, letting the hot water cascade over me. I wash thoroughly, scrubbing every inch of skin, paying special attention to my hands and under my fingernails. The soap creates a thick lather that spirals down the drain, carrying away all physical traces of Leslie that might remain on me.

I dry myself with a fresh towel, wrapping it around my waist as I return to the bedroom. Leslie remains exactly as I left her, beautiful in her stillness. I dress quickly in clean clothes I'd set aside earlier, then turn my attention to her.

The room must be pristine. I pull on latex gloves with a snap and begin the familiar process. First, I check for any trace evidence that might connect me to this moment. Cleaning away any hair, fibers, fingerprints, body fluid. All of which must be eliminated and sterilized.

I clean her body with warm water and a soft cloth, gentle as I give her this last right. There's an artistry to this part, a reverence. I dress her carefully in the clothes she arrived in, smoothing wrinkles, adjusting fabric until everything looks natural.

The sheets come next. I strip the bed efficiently, bundling everything into a plastic bag that will later be disposed of at one of my construction sites. I remake the bed with fresh linens from the closet, hospital corners and precisely folded edges.

I move through the room methodically, wiping down surfaces, erasing our presence. The glasses she drank from, the doorknobs we touched, all receive my attention. Nothing is overlooked. Nothing is left to chance.

When I finish, the room bears no evidence of what transpired. It's as if Leslie and I were never here together, as if this perfect moment existed only in my mind. I gather my supplies and the plastic bags, checking the room one final time before I prepare to move her.

I wrap Leslie carefully in a plastic sheet, securing it with tape. Her body feels light in my arms as I carry her through the house and into the garage. My car waits, trunk already open, a space cleared specifically for her.

My Aston Martin's trunk is surprisingly spacious, a feature I considered when purchasing it. I place her inside, arranging her limbs with care. Next to her lies her purse, sealed in a specially designed bag that blocks all signals. No GPS tracking, no cell phone pings. Nothing to connect her to this place or to me.

I close the trunk with a soft thud, the sound final and somehow satisfying. Sliding into the driver's seat, I feel the leather cool against my back. The engine purrs to life with the press of a button, a sound that always soothes me. I press the garage door opener and wait for it to rise completely before easing the car forward.

The drive to my construction warehouse takes exactly twenty-three minutes at this time of night. The roads are empty, streetlights casting rhythmic patterns across my windshield. I drive precisely at the speed limit, my hands at ten and two on the wheel. No reason to attract attention.

The warehouse comes into view, a hulking shadow against the night sky. I pull up to the gate, entering the code on the keypad. The chain-link fence slides open with a metallic rattle. Once inside, I exit the car briefly to secure the padlock, ensuring no one can follow.

I drive to the warehouse entrance, park, and step out. The key turns easily in the lock, and I push open the heavy door. The space inside is cavernous, filled with half-finished projects and construction materials. Perfect for my needs.

Back at the car, I open the trunk. Leslie looks peaceful, almost as if she's sleeping. I lift her, carrying her to where the statue waits, a hollow concrete form, designed by my own hand for this exact purpose. I lower her inside carefully, making sure she fits properly within the mold.

Her purse follows, tucked in beside her. All evidence of Leslie, contained in one neat package. I step back, admiring the composition for a moment before pressing the button on the mixer. Concrete begins to flow, gray and thick, filling the spaces around her. I watch as it rises, slowly covering her, erasing her from the world.

When the statue is filled completely, I seal it with a plank of plywood, covering her exit from this world, leaving the statue to set over the next two days. I begin to gather my tools, cleaning remnants of the wet concrete from the mixer, leaving no signs I was here tonight. When I am finished, the warehouse looks undisturbed, as if nothing happened here tonight.

I lock up behind me, the Aston Martin's engine cutting through the silence as I head home, another perfect moment preserved forever in concrete.

CHAPTER 8

I wake beneath silk sheets, fragments of her still clinging to my consciousness. The dream dissipates like vapor, but the sensations remain, her fingertips tracing patterns across my chest, her breath warm against my neck. Iris. Even in sleep, she's found her way to me.

The morning light filters through the blinds I never fully close, the first signs of the sun waking to greet me. My body feels heavy, reluctant to leave the phantom intimacy of the dream where she was finally mine.

In this liminal space between sleep and wakefulness, I can still taste her, honey-sweet with that deeper note I cannot place. I can feel the weight of her body against mine, the way her hair fell across my chest as she leaned over me.

I stare at the ceiling, allowing myself to linger in this fabricated memory. How she looked at me with those knowing eyes. How she smiled, not the polite one she offers in the elevator, but something more private. Something meant only for me.

"Not this time," she'd said on the street, her voice carrying a promise I intend to collect.

I run my hand across the empty space beside me. The sheets are cool, undisturbed. Perfect. I've never liked the disorder another body brings, the scattered possessions, the unpredictable sounds, the lingering presence that disrupts my careful routine.

But Iris... I imagine she would fit here seamlessly. She would understand the importance of order, of control. She wouldn't disrupt; she would enhance.

I rise from my bed and move to the window. The city sprawls below, still waking. Saturday morning quiet. Usually, I appreciate this silence, this solitude. Today it feels hollow.

The dream has left me unsettled, hungry in a way that's becoming familiar. I press my palm against the cool glass, steadying myself against the intensity of my own want. It's unlike me to be so affected. I've always been able to compartmentalize, to channel my desires into appropriate outlets.

But she's different. She's becoming necessary, like the precise measurements in my architectural designs. Without her, the structure feels unstable, incomplete.

I leave the window and move to the bathroom, turning the shower to precisely 105 degrees, hot enough to stimulate, not so hot it leaves my skin red. The water pressure hits with perfect consistency. This is what I need. Structure. Routine. Control.

Water cascades over my shoulders, washing away the last remnants of sleep, of that dream. I close my eyes, focusing on the sensation. Clean. Precise. Under control.

I step onto the heated marble floor, wrapping a towel around my waist. The mirror has fogged, I wipe it clear with one smooth motion. My reflection emerges, familiar yet somehow changed. The hunger that's been growing leaves subtle marks only I can see.

I dry methodically, each movement deliberate. My hair requires attention, not too much product, just enough to maintain the perfect balance between professional and effortless. I trim my beard with surgical precision, evening the edges to the millimeter. Even alone, these standards matter.

The cologne comes next, three precise spritzes. Neck, wrists. Not overpowering, just present enough to create an impression. Something memorable but subtle. Professional but masculine.

My closet presents orderly rows of garments arranged by color, then by material. Weekend attire occupies its own section, still impeccable, but less formal than my workweek wardrobe. I select dark jeans, a cashmere sweater in deep navy. The weight of the fabric feels reassuring against my skin.

In the kitchen, my espresso machine waits. I measure the beans to the gram before grinding them. The ritual soothes me, the aroma filling the kitchen, the slight resistance of the tamper, the rich scent intensifying as water filters through compressed grounds.

The machine whistles to life as I watch the dark liquid stream into the cup, crema forming a perfect layer on top. No sugar. No milk. Nothing to dilute the experience.

I raise the cup to my lips, breathe in the bitter perfume before taking the first sip. The coffee is strong, almost harsh. It anchors me to the present, washing away the last traces of my dream.

I sip my espresso and open my laptop, pulling up the event planning document I've been refining for weeks. The party requires perfection, every element a reflection of my standards, my control. I scroll through the catering contract from Elysium, the most exclusive service in the city. I've selected a menu that balances sophistication with accessibility, delicate canapés, seasonal offerings prepared with molecular precision, nothing that could disintegrate and create mess.

The waitstaff will arrive two hours early. Six of them, dressed in black, trained to move through crowds like shadows, to anticipate needs before they're expressed. The bartender, Alessandra, comes highly recommended for both her mixology skills and discretion. I've commissioned three signature cocktails for the evening, each reflecting architectural principles: structure, balance, innovation.

My finger hovers over the confirmed guest list. Thirty-seven names. Influential clients, respected colleagues, carefully selected acquaintances. Names that matter.

The only name that matters isn't there.

"Not this time," she'd said, as if there would be other times. As if declining was temporary, not final.

What did she mean? The question circles my mind like a persistent melody. Was it a challenge? An invitation to persuade her? Or merely polite deflection?

I close my eyes, replay the moment on the sidewalk. The soft collision of her body against mine. The way her eyes widened in recognition. That smile, playful, knowing. There was something there, beneath the surface. A current between us that she must have felt too.

Perhaps she's cautious. Professional. Avoiding complications in a workplace context. Understandable, even admirable. But unnecessary. We're both adults capable of discretion.

What would convince her? A formal invitation might feel impersonal after our encounter. A handwritten note, too forward, too revealing. Perhaps an approach through mutual connections? Ryan knows her department, he could mention the event casually.

No. Too indirect. Too passive. She deserves my direct attention.

I could find her at lunch, suggest we discuss the party further. Frame it as an opportunity to network, to meet influential people who could advance her career. But that feels manipulative, reducing what I'm offering to mere professional advantage.

The truth is simpler, more compelling. I want her there. Her presence would transform the evening from mere social obligation to something meaningful. I want to see her move through my space, observe her reaction to the design choices I've made, the life I've constructed.

I need her to say yes.

The weight of my espresso cup feels reassuring in my hand, a tactile reminder of the precision and control that define my existence. Iris's refusal to attend the party has left a fracture in my carefully constructed day. The more I think about it, the more the uncertainty grates. I've always appreciated certainty, the solidity of knowing, of being in control. But with her, I find myself on unstable ground.

I set the cup down, the porcelain kissing the coaster with a muted click. My thoughts return to Iris, to the softness of her voice, the way she'd said, "Not this time." There was a playfulness to her tone that I couldn't quite decipher. Was it genuine amusement or a gentle way to keep me at a distance?

I rise from my desk, pacing the length of my living room. The floor-to-ceiling windows offer a panoramic view of the city, but I hardly notice the skyline. My mind is a maze, each thought leading back to her. I've always prided myself on my ability to read people, to anticipate their moves, but Iris... she remains an enigma.

I stop mid-pace, transfixed by an idea so perfect it steals my breath. Of course. *Of course.* What better way to capture her, to preserve what she makes me feel, than through my art?

My fingers itch for a pencil. I move to my drafting table with renewed purpose, pulling out the pristine sketchbook I reserve for my most personal inspirations. The page is blank, a canvas waiting for her.

The pencil flies across the paper without hesitation. First, the foundation, strong, uncompromising. Then sweeping curves that echo her movements, the way she carries herself through space. I incorporate golden ratios, sacred geometry, mathematical perfection that mirrors what I see in her.

This building will be unlike anything in my portfolio. More fluid, more daring. The structure emerges on the page, glass and steel intertwining like lovers, creating spaces of light and shadow. The central atrium soars upward, a cathedral to beauty and permanence.

And at its heart... her. A statue.

My hand slows as I sketch her form. This requires precision, reverence. I capture the tilt of her chin, the subtle curve of her neck, the way she holds herself with that quiet confidence. In bronze and marble, she'll stand at the center of my creation. Timeless. Untouchable. Mine in a way she cannot refuse.

I lean back, studying what I've created. The statue will join my private collection, the others I've made, each marking a special indulgence, each preserving a moment of perfect release. But hers will be different. Superior. A masterpiece among lesser works.

In this form, she'll never leave. Never refuse. She'll endure as I've designed her, the heart of something magnificent that bears my name, my vision. My signature on her permanence.

My hands darken as I work, graphite and charcoal smudging across my skin like shadows. I don't notice at first, I'm too consumed by the vision pouring from my mind onto the page. It's only when I reach for my eraser that I see how the darkness has spread, coating my fingers, embedding itself in the lines of my palms.

I don't stop to clean them. The mess is necessary, part of the process. I can't interrupt the flow, not when she's coming to life before me.

The building takes shape, a temple of glass and steel rising from the page, catching light in ways that defy conventional architecture. I've never designed anything this fluid, this daring. The usual constraints I work within, budgets, structural limitations, client preferences, have fallen away. This is pure creation, unfettered by anything but my vision.

When the building is complete, I turn to a fresh page. This requires a different approach, a more intimate touch. I select softer charcoal, something that will capture the subtleties of form. My blackened fingertips hover over the pristine white, the moment of anticipation almost unbearably sweet.

Then I begin.

Her statue emerges stroke by stroke. Not merely human, but transcendent, an angel with wings that spread like protective shadows. Her face holds that expression I've glimpsed in our fleeting moments, knowing, slightly amused, eternally beyond reach. But here, in my creation, she is captured, preserved.

I work with religious intensity, shading the curve of her neck, the elegant line of her collarbone. The wings extend from her shoulder blades, powerful yet delicate, casting her in divine light. In her hands, she holds a pitcher, tilted as if in offering, the source from which milk and honey will eternally flow.

My fingers are nearly black now, the charcoal ground into my skin like a stain that marks me as her creator. I don't mind. This transformation seems appropriate, necessary, my hands darkening as I craft her into perfection.

When I complete the final stroke, I sit back, studying what I've created. This will be her eternal resting place, more beautiful than anything earthly constraints could produce. In this form, she'll never refuse me. Never leave. She'll simply exist, perfect and mine, the center of my greatest work.

I set my charcoal down, mesmerized by what I've created. The design will remain private for now, a promise I'm making to both of us. When the time is right, when she's fully mine, I'll reveal it to her. A gift. A declaration.

It's not a matter of if, but when.

She said, "Not this time," which means there will be another time. A next time. Her words weren't rejection but postponement. She's being careful, deliberate. I respect that. Patience has always been my virtue.

I run my blackened fingers over the curve of her wing on the page. The charcoal smudges slightly, creating a shadow that only enhances her form. Even in this imperfection, she's magnificent. Just as she will be when she finally surrenders.

And she will.

I've never been wrong about these things. I know the signs, the subtle tells that reveal desire beneath polite refusal. The way her eyes lingered on mine for a fraction longer than necessary. The slight flush that colored her cheeks when our bodies connected on the sidewalk. The music in her voice when she said my name.

When she is mine, wholly, completely mine... I'll show her pleasures she's never imagined. I'll worship every inch of her body, memorize every sound she makes. I'll bring her to the edge and hold her there, suspended in that perfect moment between anticipation and release. Then I'll capture it, that exquisite instant of pure, unfiltered ecstasy. Preserve it. Make it eternal.

She'll be different from the others. Special. The culmination of everything I've been searching for. The others were merely practice, pale imitations preparing me for her. Those encounters helped me refine my technique, taught me patience, control. How to extend that golden moment to its absolute limit.

But with Iris, it will be transcendent. She'll be my masterpiece, my magnum opus. The perfect indulgence that will satisfy this hunger that's been building inside me for so long.

Chapter 9

The sound of the espresso machine's last remnants of steam fades into the background as I finish my cup.

My phone buzzes, breaking the tranquillity of the morning. A message from Ryan: "Site inspection at 10."

I reply with a simple "On my way," and pocket the phone. Work is a sanctuary of sorts, a place where every variable can be controlled, every element meticulously planned. It's where I can escape the gnawing hunger Iris has awakened in me.

The drive to the construction site is uneventful, the city passing by in a blur of steel and glass. I arrive with time to spare, stepping out of the car and taking in the skeletal framework of what will soon be a new high-rise. It's an extension of myself, every beam, every joint, precisely where it should be.

Ryan approaches, hard hat in hand. "Morning, Sebastian. Everything looks on track."

"Good," I say, taking the hard hat and securing it. "Let's go over the structural integrity reports."

We walk through the site, discussing load-bearing walls and foundation depths. The familiar terminology and calculations ground me, provide a respite from the invasive thoughts of Iris.

As we near the center of the site, Ryan pauses. "There's something you should see." He gestures towards a tarp-covered object.

"What is it?" I ask, my curiosity piqued.

I pull back the tarp, bracing myself for what lies beneath.

A man's body lies curdled upon the concrete, limbs arranged in unnatural stillness. His face is taught, eyes closed, his body in a tight fetal position, like he was trying to protect himself. There are no signs that accompany a violent death. No blood. No visible wounds. Just the hollow absence of life.

My shoulders release tension as I exhale in relief. This isn't connected to me. This isn't one of mine.

"Jesus Christ," Ryan whispers, stepping back. The other workers gather, their faces turning pale at the sight.

I crouch down, careful not to touch anything. The man is wearing a fine suit, Armani most likely, not just some bum on the street. No wallet visible. No identification. Nothing to indicate why he ended up here, on my site.

"Call the police," I say, my voice steady despite the twist of unease in my gut. "Everyone clear the area. This is now a crime scene."

The workers scatter, mumbling among themselves. Ryan stays beside me, phone already pressed to his ear.

"We need to contact Marsden," I tell him, referring to our project manager. "This will push back our timeline. I'll handle the board, explain the situation."

"You think he just... died here?" Ryan asks, voice hushed.

"That's for the police to determine." I replace the tarp, covering the vacant eyes that seem to follow me. "I'm heading back to the office. Keep me updated."

The drive back gives me time to think. Who was he? Why our construction site? The questions fade to background noise as my mind turns to Iris. I think I have just enough time to catch Iris for coffee. Perhaps today is the day she'll finally say yes.

I park in my reserved space, straighten my tie in the rearview mirror, and head into the building. The elevator is waiting, a good sign. I press the button for my floor, then on impulse, press 3 as well.

The doors slide closed. I take a deep breath, rearranging my features into professional concern rather than the anticipation pulsing beneath my skin.

The elevator opens on 3, then closes as the elevator and I continue to my office floor.

I step into my office, settling into my organized workspace to make the necessary calls this setback requires.

I reach for my phone, dialing the number of our project manager first.

"Marsden. We have a situation at the Hawthorne site."

I explain the discovery in clinical terms, stripping away emotion, reducing a man's death to a logistical problem. Marsden curses under his breath.

"How long do you think this will delay us?"

"At minimum, a week. Possibly more. The police will need to investigate, determine the cause of death."

"The board won't be happy."

"I'll handle the board," I say, already mapping out the conversation in my head. "Just ensure everyone understands the site is off-limits until further notice."

I hang up and dial the chairman next. I've always had a good relationship with Thompson, he trusts my judgment, values my precision. Today is no different. He receives the news with stoic practicality.

"These things happen, Sebastian. Not your fault. Keep me updated on the timeline adjustments."

Three more calls and my immediate responsibilities are handled. I step out of my office to find Ryan and two other senior architects waiting for me, their faces etched with concern.

"The police are at the site now," Ryan reports. "They're saying they need statements from everyone who was there."

"Expected. Cooper, can you compile a list of all personnel on site this morning? And reschedule today's client meetings."

Cooper nods, already pulling out his tablet.

"Martin, I need you to contact suppliers. Our delivery schedule needs to be adjusted."

"What about the Richardson presentation next week?" Martin asks.

"Proceed as planned. This doesn't affect that project."

They disperse, leaving only Ryan lingering in the doorway.

"They're saying it looks suspicious," he says quietly. "The body. The police think..."

"It's not our concern what they think," I cut him off. "Our job is to minimize disruption to our work."

Ryan hesitates, then nods. "Right. I'll be in my office if you need anything else."

I watch him go, my mind already shifting back to thoughts of Iris. Perhaps this disruption is an opportunity, a chance meeting in the aftermath of chaos.

I check my watch. 2:17 PM. According to my observations, she takes her afternoon coffee break now, alone, at the small café on the third floor. I've watched her routine for weeks, the way she stirs her coffee three times counterclockwise, the corner table she prefers with its view of the courtyard, how she always brings a book but rarely opens it.

The elevator doors slide open on three, and I step out, adjusting my cufflinks. I see her immediately, black shiny- hair catching the afternoon light, fingers wrapped around a white ceramic mug, her profile a study in quiet contemplation.

I approach with controlled steps, not too eager, not too hesitant. Control in all things.

"Iris." Her name feels heavy on my tongue.

She looks up, surprise flickering briefly across her face before settling into that same knowing smile. "Sebastian."

"May I join you?" I ask, already pulling out the chair across from her.

"Of course." She gestures to the empty seat, watching me with those unreadable eyes.

I sit, leaning forward slightly. "I wanted to ask you again about my gathering this weekend. I think you'd enjoy it."

"I'd have to know more about it first," Iris says, lifting her cup to her lips. The ceramic rim touches her mouth, leaving a faint smudge of lipstick, pale pink, not her usual color. "What kind of gathering are we talking about?"

"Small, intimate. Just a few colleagues and clients. Good wine, better conversation." I lean back, affecting casualness while studying her reaction. "My home overlooks the river. The view alone is worth experiencing."

Iris tilts her head, sunlight catching in her hair. "And who's on this exclusive guest list?"

"People worth knowing. Martin Hayes from the city planning commission. The Crawfords, they're funding the new cultural center downtown. A few architects from the Berlin office." I pause, allowing my next words their proper weight. "People who could be useful to someone with your talents."

Her eyes widen slightly, interest, finally, before narrowing again into that maddening expression of hers that reveals nothing. "Sounds impressively curated."

"I'm selective about who I surround myself with." I hold her gaze, making sure she understands the compliment.

"I bet you are." She smiles, running her finger around the rim of her cup. "I might be able to stop by."

Might. Not a yes, not a commitment. The ambiguity grates against my nerves like sandpaper.

"It would be a shame if you didn't," I say, voice carefully modulated. "I've reserved a particularly interesting Bordeaux I think you'd appreciate."

"How did you know I like wine?" Her question carries an edge, sharp enough to cut.

I hadn't known. A lucky guess, or an inevitability. People like her always appreciate fine things.

"Just an instinct," I reply smoothly. "Was I wrong?"

"No." She laughs, the sound light but somehow not reaching her eyes. "Your instincts seem quite... developed."

"I pay attention," I say, dropping my voice slightly. "To things that matter."

Iris takes another sip, considering me over the rim of her cup. "I'll think about your party, Sebastian. That's the best I can offer right now."

The silence between us stretches. Her face reveals nothing while mine struggles to maintain its practiced composure. A group of interns pass by, their chatter fading as they notice me sitting with her.

"What are you reading?" I gesture to the book beside her cup.

She places her hand on it, fingers splayed protectively. "Just something to pass the time."

I glimpse the title: *Bluebeard's Egg* by Margaret Atwood.

"Interesting choice," I manage.

"Have you read it?" Her eyes fix on mine, searching.

"I haven't," I admit. "Though I appreciate Atwood's architectural use of language."

Iris's finger traces the book's spine, a gesture both casual and deliberate. "It's about a collection of stories, this particular one follows a man who believes he understands the woman he desires. He's quite convinced he knows who she is."

"And does he?" I ask, voice steady despite the strange prickling at the back of my neck.

"No." She looks up, meeting my gaze directly. "He never really sees her at all. Just his own reflection."

I'm caught off-guard by her words, feeling strangely exposed under her steady gaze. A sudden flash of uncertainty, not a feeling I'm accustomed to, makes me adjust my position.

"An interesting interpretation," I say, recovering quickly. "Though fiction rarely captures the complexity of real understanding between people."

"Doesn't it?" Iris closes the book, her fingers lingering on the cover. "I find fiction often reveals more truth than we're comfortable admitting."

Her phone buzzes. She glances at it, then back at me with what appears to be genuine regret. "I need to get back. Meeting with our PR team."

"Of course," I say, rising as she does. "About Saturday... "

"I'll let you know," she cuts in, gathering her things. "Tomorrow, perhaps."

She leaves with a small wave, her scent, honey and something I can't quite place, lingering in the air. I remain standing, watching her retreat, feeling off-balance in a way that both disturbs and intrigues me.

He never really sees her at all. Just his own reflection.

I stand motionless as Iris disappears around the corner, her words lingering like smoke. *He never really sees her at all. Just his own reflection.*

These literary observations might apply to Atwood's fictional character, some hapless man blinded by his own desires, but they don't apply to me. I understand Iris in ways others never could. I've studied her, her movements, her preferences, the subtle changes in her expression when she's pleased or bored. I know her in a way that transcends conventional interaction.

The afternoon light shifts through the windows as I return to my seat, absently touching the place where her book rested. Unlike Atwood's deluded character, I see Iris clearly. I notice the details others miss, how she holds her coffee mug with both hands when she's thinking deeply, the slight furrow that appears between her brows when she's skeptical, the precise shade of her lipstick today (lighter than usual, a subtle change that speaks to a different mood).

This isn't self-delusion. This is observation, careful and meticulous. I'm an architect; I understand how to read structures, to see beyond facades to the essential framework beneath. People are no different, patterns revealed to those who know how to look.

Her reluctance to accept my invitation is merely part of the dance. "I might be able to stop by," she'd said. The ambiguity is deliberate, designed to maintain the tension between us. She knows what she's doing, creating a space where desire can grow. It's calculated, and I respect the strategy.

Still, her offhand literary reference nags at me. The suggestion that I'm somehow blind to her true self is absurd. If anything, I see parts of Iris that she herself may not recognize, the potential between us, the perfect alignment of our sensibilities that she hasn't fully acknowledged yet.

No, I'm nothing like the man in her book. I see her completely, in totality. I've cataloged every detail, mapped every gesture. In time, she'll understand this. She'll recognize that I've already seen through to the essence of who she is.

She just doesn't know it yet.

I return to my office, the conversation with Iris replaying in my mind. Her words, that line about a man seeing only his reflection, gnaw at me. She's wrong. I know she is. I understand her better than anyone else could.

My phone rings, pulling me from my thoughts.

"Sebastian Wolfe."

"Mr. Wolfe, this is Detective Harmon with Metro Police." The voice is clipped, professional. "I need to speak with you regarding the body found at your construction site."

"Of course. How can I help?"

"We'd prefer to have this conversation in person. Would you be available to come down to the station this afternoon?"

A request, not a demand, yet... "I have meetings scheduled until four. I could come by after that."

"That works. Ask for me at the front desk." He pauses. "And Mr. Wolfe? We've identified the deceased. Thomas Grayson. Does that name mean anything to you?"

I search my memory. Thomas Grayson. The name is vaguely familiar, but I can't place it.

"I don't believe so," I answer carefully. "Should it?"

"That's what we're trying to determine. See you at four."

The line goes dead. I set the phone down, my mind working to place the name. Thomas Grayson. Where have I heard it before?

I open my laptop and type the name into the search bar. Several results appear, a LinkedIn profile for a Thomas Grayson who works as a private investigator, a few social media accounts, an obituary from three years ago for a different Thomas Grayson.

The private investigator catches my attention. I click on his profile, studying the photo. A man in his fifties, graying at the temples, serious expression. Not someone I recognize. But a private investigator found dead at my construction site, that can't be coincidence.

Who hired him? What was he investigating?

I close the laptop, a cold sensation spreading through my chest. This complicates things. A dead body is one problem. A dead investigator is something else entirely.

The quarterly review meeting drags into its final hour, my attention split between budget projections and the approaching police interview. Martin drones on about material costs while I nod at appropriate intervals, my mind elsewhere. Thomas Grayson. Private investigator. Found dead at my site.

"Sebastian? Your thoughts on the revised timeline?"

I blink, refocusing on the conference room. "The adjustments are reasonable. Let's proceed with Martin's proposal."

The meeting concludes at 3:47. Perfect timing. I gather my things, offering brief goodbyes before heading to the parking garage and departing.

I'm greeted at the police station by smells of industrial cleaner and stale coffee. I approach the front desk, straightening my tie.

"Sebastian Wolfe for Detective Harmon."

The officer nods, picks up a phone, and mutters something I can't quite catch. Minutes later, a man appears, mid-forties, rumpled suit, tired eyes that miss nothing.

"Mr. Wolfe. Thank you for coming." His handshake is firm. "This way."

He leads me not to an office but to a small room with a table, three chairs, and a mirror I immediately recognize as two-way glass. An interview room, not a conversation space.

"Can I get you anything? Water?" Harmon asks, gesturing to a chair.

"No, thank you." I sit, maintaining perfect posture. "I'm eager to help however I can."

Harmon takes the seat across from me, placing a folder on the table. "Tell me about your movements yesterday evening."

The question catches me off-guard. "My movements?"

"Where were you between 8pm and midnight?"

"At home," I answer, keeping my voice even. "I had dinner, reviewed some blueprints, then went to bed early. I had an early meeting scheduled."

"Anyone who can verify that?"

"I live alone."

Harmon nods, making a note. "And how would you characterize your relationship with Thomas Grayson?"

"As I mentioned on the phone, I don't believe I knew him."

"Yet his body was found at your construction site."

"A site accessible to the public despite our security measures," I counter. "We've had issues with trespassers before."

"When was the last time you visited the Hawthorne site yourself?"

"Three days ago. For a scheduled inspection."

"And you've never hired Mr. Grayson's services?"

"No."

"Has anyone in your firm?"

"Not to my knowledge."

Harmon studies me, his expression unreadable. "Do you know anyone who might want to harm you, Mr. Wolfe?"

The question hangs between us. My pulse quickens slightly.

"I don't appreciate the direction of these questions," I say, voice hardening. "I came here voluntarily to assist your investigation. Now I feel as though I'm being treated as a suspect."

"Just standard procedure."

"Is it standard procedure to ask if someone has enemies when a stranger is found dead?"

Harmon sighs, then opens the folder. He slides a phone across the table, a black smartphone in an evidence bag.

"This belonged to Mr. Grayson." He taps the screen, navigating to the photo gallery. "Care to explain why a private investigator who you claim not to know had dozens of photographs of you?"

I stare at the screen, my body frozen while my mind races. Dozens of photographs of me. Dozens. Grayson had been following me. Watching me. Documenting me.

"Mr. Wolfe?" Detective Harmon prompts.

I force myself to lean forward, examining the images with what I hope appears to be detached curiosity rather than mounting horror. There I am entering my building. Walking to my car. At dinner with clients.

"I have no idea why this man would be photographing me," I say, my voice steady despite the cold sweat breaking out along my spine. "I'm a relatively prominent architect. Perhaps he was investigating something related to one of my projects?"

Harmon swipes through more images. Me at the construction site. Me at the coffee shop. Me entering and exiting a bar with one of my last... indulgences.

"These don't look like professional inquiries," Harmon says. "They look like surveillance."

"I can't explain it." I straighten my posture, channeling indignation to mask my growing panic. "But I can tell you I never met this man, never hired him, and had no knowledge I was being followed."

"Then you'll have no objection to us examining your phone records? Your financial statements?"

"Not without a warrant," I say automatically. "Not because I have anything to hide, Detective, but because I value my privacy, especially now that I know it's already been violated by a stranger."

Harmon continues quietly studying me, his constant stare unnerving me. "Grayson was a former cop. Kept meticulous records. If someone hired him to follow you, we'll find out who."

"Please do," I say, forcing confidence into my voice. "I'd like to know who's invading my privacy as well."

But my mind is elsewhere, calculating rapidly. Someone knows. Someone has been watching me. And now they've left a dead investigator at my doorstep like a calling card.

CHAPTER 10

I wake with exact precision at 5:00 AM, no alarm necessary. My body knows the rhythm I've set for it over the years. By 5:45, I'm seated in my study, the mahogany desk arranged just as it should be, laptop centered, notepad aligned to its right, fountain pen placed perpendicular to the notepad's edge.

Morning light filters through the blinds in measured strips. I prefer the controlled illumination, no harsh glare to disrupt concentration, just clean lines of light against shadow. I open my laptop, the whir of the cooling fan indicating signs of life.

First, client emails. I respond to each with appropriate authority and restraint, scheduling meetings for the Hayes Tower revisions and answering questions about the Waterfront Project's sustainable materials. Then, internal correspondence, Ryan's updates on permits, Anna's design modifications. Each requires specific responses, tailored with precision.

I shift to my calendar, adjusting Thursday's meeting from 2:00 PM to 3:30 PM to accommodate the zoning committee's delays. The symmetry pleases me, my week balanced between design work and client interactions, no day overloaded or empty.

A new email notification appears. Subject line: "Open Me." No sender name.

I pause, finger hovering over the trackpad. This doesn't fit. Anonymous emails don't arrive in my inbox, my assistant filters spam, and my security protocols are thorough. Yet here it sits, an aberration in my ordered morning.

I should delete it. That would be the rational response to an unknown sender.

Instead, curiosity or paranoia get the best of me, I click.

The email contains only a link, no text, no signature. Just a blue hyperlink against white space.

My finger taps twice on the trackpad before I can reconsider. The link opens to a video player, black screen waiting. I adjust the volume down, a precaution, and press play.

It's camera footage.

The footage is grainy, filmed in low light. Dark shadows stretch across a familiar sidewalk, the area outside Meridian, that upscale cocktail bar downtown. The timestamp reads 11:42 PM.

My throat tightens as I recognize myself walking into frame. My posture straight, confident, the tailored Brioni suit I wore three nights ago. Beside me walks a woman, her auburn hair catching in the subtle glow of streetlights. Her body tilts toward mine as we walk, our shoulders nearly touching. Her name escapes me momentarily. Cassandra? Caitlin? It doesn't matter. What matters is that she should be nothing now. A memory. Dissolved.

Yet here she is, preserved in pixels, her hand brushing against mine as we pause at the curb. The camera follows us, slightly shaking, handheld, not professional surveillance. The angle shifts, adjusting as we move toward my car. My Aston Martin appears at the edge of frame, sleek and dark against the night.

I watch myself open the passenger door for her. She smiles, that exact smile I'd catalogued during our conversation at the bar. The genuine one, reaching her eyes, crinkling the corners. Not the polite smile she'd given the bartender. The one she'd reserved for me.

My chest constricts. My lungs seem to collapse, refusing to expand properly. I try to inhale but can't seem to draw enough air. The room narrows around me, walls pressing closer.

I lean forward, gripping the edge of my desk. My breaths come in short, painful gasps. Sweat beads along my hairline despite the controlled 68-degree temperature of my study.

The video continues. We drive away, taillights fading into the darkness. Then the camera turns, capturing the reflection of whoever filmed us in the side mirror of their parked car. Just a shadow, indistinct. Anonymous.

The video ends. Loops back to the beginning.

Someone was there. Someone was watching.

I slam the laptop shut and surge to my feet, knocking my chair back. The precise thud of its legs against the carpet feels distant, everything feels distant except the thundering in my chest. My lungs burn, constricting with each shallow breath, as if the air itself has grown thick and hostile.

This isn't happening. This can't be happening.

My fingers claw at my collar, loosening the tie that suddenly feels like a noose. Sweat breaks across my forehead, trickling down my temples.

I stagger across my study, my usual measured stride abandoned as I reach for the door.

Someone knows. Someone was there. Someone has been in my home.

I move through my house like a man possessed, checking each lock, each window. Front door: locked, deadbolt engaged. Kitchen door to the patio: locked. Sliding glass doors to the garden: locked, security bar in place. I tug on each handle twice, three times, testing, confirming.

The living room curtains hang slightly askew. Did I leave them that way? I never leave them that way. I straighten them with trembling hands, then pause, fingers still clutching the fabric. Slowly, I part the curtains just enough to peer outside.

A car sits across the street, dark sedan, nondescript. Windows tinted. Have I seen this car before? It doesn't belong to any of my neighbors, it's too basic to be one of theirs.

I gasp for air as I drop the curtain and move quickly to the security panel in the hallway. I put in my code, frantically typing in my code... I enter the wrong code, my fingers slipping. I try again...

UGHHHH! I scream out in a huff, hitting the wall next to the panel.

I shake my hands, wiping my sweaty palms on the side of my shirt and type in my code again, this time the screen illuminates, showing feeds from each camera around my property.

Front door: clear. Backyard: empty. Driveway: my car, perfectly parked. Side of the house: nothing unusual.

I cycle through the feeds again, stopping at the street view. There it is... the sedan, partially visible at the edge of the frame. I zoom in but can't make out the license plate. It's angled perfectly to see my house while remaining mostly obscured from my cameras.

"Coincidence?" I mutter, but the word rings hollow, unconvincing even to my own ears.

I move to the kitchen window, using the edge of the blinds to shield myself as I look out again. The car is still there. Still waiting.

I stand frozen at my kitchen window, sweat cooling against my neck as I stare at the sedan. Someone is watching me. Someone knows.

This can't continue. I won't be observed, analyzed, manipulated, not when I'm the one who should be in control.

I stride to my foyer, yank open my front door, and step outside without pausing to consider consequences. The morning air hits my face, cooler than expected. I'm still in my dress shirt and slacks, no jacket, no watch, my feet in leather shoes with no socks. Incomplete. Unprepared. But it doesn't matter now.

The sedan sits there, engine silent, windows like black mirrors reflecting morning light. I can't see inside, can't tell if there's one person or two. Can't see if there's a camera pointed at me.

My concrete walkway feels unusually hard beneath my feet as I move with deliberate steps. A neighbor's sprinkler system hisses to life two doors down, the rhythm of water hitting grass creating an absurd backdrop to this confrontation.

"Who are you?" I mutter under my breath, quickening my pace. "What do you want?"

I reach the end of my walkway, feet touching the public sidewalk. My heartbeat thundering.

Ten yards separate me from the car.

Eight.

Six.

The engine springs to life.

My pace increases, hand raising as if to command them to stay. "Wait..."

Tires spin against asphalt. The sedan lurches forward, gaining speed with startling efficiency. No squealing tires, no dramatic peeling out, just smooth, practiced acceleration.

I break into a run after the car, but it's pointless. The car turns at the corner, disappearing from view without revealing its license plate.

I stand in the street, caved over, chest heaving, sweat darkening my shirt beneath the arms. A passing jogger gives me a curious glance, then averts her eyes.

The street looks normal, peaceful, trees swaying gently, sprinklers running, birds calling. Nothing to suggest the violation I've just experienced. Nothing to confirm I'm not losing my mind.

Nothing except the certainty settling in my gut like ice.

My hands clench as I force myself to contain the frustration, to avoid screaming in public and making myself look crazy to any neighbors who may be watching.

Because I know for sure now, someone is watching.

I straighten slowly, fingers flexing at my sides. My heart rate steadies as I draw in a deeper breath. Losing composure serves no purpose; I need control, not panic.

Inside, I glance at the wall clock, 7:52. Later than I'd like. I stride to my bedroom, quickly stripping off my sweat-dampened shirt and slacks. After a swift cold shower to shake off the morning's unease, I dress meticulously, a fresh shirt, navy suit, tailored yet understated; cufflinks secured; shoes polished as though nothing is wrong. Appearances matter.

By 8:01, I'm sliding behind the wheel of my Aston Martin, fingers tightening around cold leather. The engine roars to life, the sound growing louder as I race along familiar streets. My glance flickers impatiently to the dashboard clock with each red light. At one intersection, I ease to a stop, but impatience overtakes me. Checking the street ahead for patrol cars, pedestrians, anything, I punch the accelerator, tires gripping the asphalt as I surge through the solid red. No consequences. Today, luck accommodates urgency.

8:15 exactly as I pull into the parking space. Quickening my stride, I enter the building's lobby, stepping inside the familiar polished-metal elevator at 8:16. I exhale slowly, pulse steadying at last. My reflection smoothes back at me from the shining steel.

At 8:17 precisely, the elevator doors whisper open again, Iris gliding in. Her presence floods the confined space, warm honey scent once more brushing softly at my senses. She turns, acknowledging me without hesitation, offering a joyful, unguarded smile.

"Good morning," she says warmly. "You look a little out of breath."

"Maybe a little," I reply evenly, holding her gaze a moment too long. "I had a rough morning jog."

She laughs lightly, tilting her head, eyes glinting in a curious and longing gaze. "Do you jog to workout often?"

Something in the ease of her voice teases me, wiping away my worries of this morning encounter and I feel amusement rise unbidden. "Jogging isn't my typical form of working out." I reply.

"What is then?" She asks.

She raises one elegant shoulder, casual yet intentional.

I give her a look, raising my eyebrow, hoping my face implies my response.

"Oh..." She replies, her cheeks redden as she blushes and gives me a smile that implies she understands, but also, maybe she would like to know more.

The digital numbers flick upward quietly. Second floor. Third floor approaching. She turns briefly, her gaze flickering to the doors, then back to me. "Have a good day, Sebastian."

"You too, Iris."

When the elevator pauses at three, the door slides open, and she steps gracefully away without looking back, leaving in her wake only the lingering warmth of her presence.

The elevator doors close, and for a moment, I stand alone in the perfect quiet of the ascending car. Her scent defies logic, lingering after her departure, honey notes suspended in the filtered air. My pulse steadies, finding its natural rhythm again.

This is what matters. This fleeting encounter burns brighter than the morning's disturbance.

I savor what just happened between us. The way she asked about my workout routine. The blush spreading across her cheeks when she understood my implication. This was no passing pleasantry. This was different.

The heat of her reaction stays with me. Her eyes held mine longer today, curious, inviting, interested. Not the polite, empty gaze she offers strangers. Not the dismissive glance she gives others in the building.

For a man who notices everything, these distinctions matter.

The elevator stops at my floor, and I step into the familiar corridor. My momentary alarm about the sedan, the video, the invasion fades, not gone but properly recontextualized. Nothing I can't handle. Nothing I can't control.

Ryan nods as I pass his desk. "Morning, Sebastian. The Peterson clients called again, they've got questions about the north facade materials."

"I'll handle it," I answer, voice measured, calm. Only I know the storm that churned inside me less than an hour ago. Only I understand how Iris's presence silenced it.

In my office, I place my briefcase precisely on the credenza, hang my jacket on its designated hook. I drop into my chair and consider the morning's events with new clarity.

Someone is watching me. Someone knows about my indulgences. These facts remain unchanged.

But Iris looked at me today. Really looked at me. Her eyes curious, her smile genuine. That warmth in her cheeks as she caught my meaning about "workouts." Progress. Connection. A transaction of mutual interest, not just the fantasy I've been cultivating.

I need to be more careful, yes. More vigilant. They haven't contacted the police, so I merely need to understand how to play this game.

I sit at my desk, fingers interlaced, pressing against my chin as I mentally arrange what I know. Someone is watching me, recording me, studying me. They've been inside my home multiple times. The pieces are scattered, but a pattern is emerging.

First, the cell phone. Hidden in a book I never purchased, a book about murder.

Now this video. The timing, the angles, this wasn't opportunistic surveillance. They knew where I would be. They followed me.

But why not go to the police? Why this game of cat and mouse?

I pull a notepad toward me, scrawling the facts in my precise handwriting. Three incidents, escalating in intimacy. Invasion. Objects moved. The phone hidden. The video sent directly to my email.

Each intrusion more personal than the last. Each designed to provoke a reaction.

This isn't random. This isn't a concerned citizen gathering evidence. This is... intimate. They want me to know they're watching. They want me to feel exposed, vulnerable, hunted.

They're mirroring what I do to my indulgences.

My pen stills against the paper.

Is this someone I've hunted? No, impossible. No one survives. No one escapes.

A flash of insight strikes me. I reach for my laptop, fingers flying across the keyboard as I access the building's directory. The third floor houses three companies, a marketing firm, a financial analytics group, and a private investigator's office.

PI. Of course.

But who would hire them? Who would care enough?

I think of Jennifer, my fiancée. The way she looked at me when I ended things. The rage beneath her hurt.

I run through the list of my indulgences, matching faces to timelines. Could one of them have been investigated by family? By a concerned spouse?

Another possibility emerges, more unsettling.

What if this isn't about punishment or justice? What if this is about something else entirely?

I lean back in my chair, staring at the ceiling. The smooth lines of the crown molding draw my eye, perfect angles, meticulous craftsmanship. Order among chaos. I need to think clearly.

What is their endgame? What do they want from me?

If it were blackmail, they would have made demands by now. If it were entrapment, police would be at my door. This is something else, something more personal, more deliberate. This is about control.

My fingers drum against the leather armrest. They want me unbalanced, uncertain. They're trying to strip away my control, to make me feel what my indulgences feel in those final moments. They want me vulnerable.

But why? What comes after I'm destabilized?

The answer hits me with startling clarity. They're not trying to expose me. They're trying to understand me. To connect with me.

This isn't a hunter tracking prey, this is a mirror reflecting back my own methods. They're courting me.

A strange calm settles over me as I consider this possibility. Someone is playing my game, using my rules. Instead of some nebulous threat, I'm facing an equal, or someone who believes themselves to be one.

I need to regain control, shift the dynamic. If they're watching, studying, analyzing, then I need to give them something unexpected. I need to change the script.

If I retreat, grow more cautious, more paranoid, I play into their hands. If I lash out, become erratic, I give them what they want. The power to affect me, to make me dance to their tune.

No. I need to turn this around.

I straighten in my chair, mind already formulating the plan. If they want to watch me, let them watch. But I'll control what they see. I'll provide a performance so compelling they'll eventually reveal themselves. I'll create a narrative they can't resist participating in.

And Iris, she's already part of the equation. Our exchange this morning confirms it. Whoever is watching me knows about my fixation. They'll expect me to pursue her more aggressively now.

Instead, I'll pull back. Show restraint. Demonstrate control where they expect weakness. They'll wonder why, start questioning their assumptions. They'll need to get closer to understand.

And when they do, I'll be waiting.

The predator becomes prey only until the trap is sprung.

I take a measured sip of coffee, watching the computer screen as I finalize the last details of the Peterson project. The office has emptied gradually, Ryan departed an hour ago with a casual wave, the cleaning staff making their rounds with practiced efficiency.

I've remained precisely on schedule all day. No rushed decisions, no visible anxiety. If they're watching, and I'm certain they are, they'll see nothing but Sebastian Wolfe, consummate professional, unaffected by their little games.

My phone buzzes. A text from an unknown number: *Leaving early tonight?*

I smile faintly at the screen, refusing to give them the reaction they want. No tracing the number, no alarmed expression. I simply set the phone down, face up, letting them see I'm unbothered.

At exactly 6:47, I save my work, shut down my computer, and gather my belongings with deliberate care. Briefcase, jacket, phone. I straighten my desk, aligning the pens in their holder, a final check that everything is in place.

The elevator arrives with a soft chime. Empty. I step inside, press the button for the lobby, and stand centered, hands relaxed at my sides. The doors close and I brace myself for the eventual shift.

The elevator continues down, without stopping, but as I reach the 3rd floor, the elevator stops.

The door opens to no one waiting for the elevator.

Guess they decided to take the stairs.

As the doors begin to close, and just before they clasp together, a slender arm shoots between them.

The sensors trigger, doors sliding open again to reveal Iris. She's slightly breathless, as though she hurried to catch the elevator. Her hair falls in soft waves around her face, cheeks flushed with exertion.

"Thanks for waiting," she says, though I made no effort to hold the doors.

"Of course," I answer smoothly, stepping slightly to the side.

She enters the small space, standing closer than necessary given the emptiness of the elevator. Her scent envelops me, stronger tonight, warmer. I resist the urge to inhale deeply.

The doors close. We descend in silence.

I feel her eyes on me, not directly, but in glances. When I turn slightly, her gaze slides away, but there's something in her expression. Not the casual warmth of this morning, something else, something more playful. The corner of her mouth curves up almost imperceptibly.

Her fingers brush against mine as the elevator reaches the lobby, so subtle it could be accidental. But her eyes meet mine as the doors open, and the look she gives me isn't innocent at all.

I don't react, don't pursue. Let her walk ahead, creating distance between us.

Today, restraint is my weapon of choice.

I watch Iris glide away through the lobby, taking her time, aware of my eyes on her. She never turns back, doesn't need to. She knows I'm watching.

The game shifts beneath my feet again, rules rewriting themselves. I wait a calculated thirty seconds before following her path toward the parking garage, maintaining distance. My footsteps echo against polished marble, then concrete.

The parking garage smells of exhaust and cold stone. I scan the shadowed corners as I walk, alert for any movement, any sign of surveillance. Nothing obvious presents itself, but they've grown skilled at hiding. I no longer trust empty spaces.

My car waits in its assigned spot. I circle it once, checking underneath, examining the door seals for tampering. Nothing appears disturbed. I slide behind the wheel, start the engine, and pull out slowly.

At the exit, I catch a glimpse at Iris's car turning onto the main road, a sleek silver Lexus. There's a certain symmetry in watching her drive away while someone else, invisible, watches me.

The drive home feels longer tonight. My eyes flick constantly to the rearview mirror, tracking headlights, noting which cars maintain my pace, which turn away. One sedan follows for three miles before turning, coincidence, or something more deliberate? Impossible to know.

My house stands quiet upon my arrival, its clean lines and large windows now vulnerabilities rather than aesthetics. I check each room methodically, noting the position of objects, running my fingers along shelves, looking for disturbances in the dust. Nothing seems changed. No new gifts left on display. No messages hidden in plain sight.

Still, sleep will not come easily tonight.

I prepare for bed with the same precise ritual, shower, teeth, glass of water on the nightstand. I dim the lights but leave the bathroom illuminated, casting a faint glow across the bedroom floor. Not because

I fear the dark, but because I need to see if shadows move where they shouldn't.

Under the cool sheets, I stare at the ceiling. My mind catalogs the day's events, analyzing, dissecting. Iris's playful glances. The anonymous text.

Sleep tugs at my consciousness, but I resist. In vulnerability, there is danger. In unconsciousness, exposure.

Yet eventually, fatigue wins. My eyes grow heavy, thoughts scattered.

Against all better judgment, and I surrender to sleep.

CHAPTER 11

I wake at precisely 5:00 AM, eyes opening to darkness just seconds before my alarm sounds. I silence it with a practiced motion, already fully alert. There's comfort in routine, the same movements, same timing, same results. Control begins here, in these quiet morning moments.

The shower runs at exactly 103 degrees. I count each stroke as I brush my teeth. My razor glides in perfect, measured strokes. The ritual calms me, centers me after a night of fitful sleep and half-remembered dreams.

I select a charcoal suit today, white shirt, burgundy tie. Professional, commanding, but not overly aggressive. My reflection shows nothing of last night's unease. Good. I've learned to compartmentalize, to separate the parts of myself that shouldn't mix.

Traffic reports show a minor accident on my usual route. I adjust, taking the longer way that adds seven minutes to my commute. No matter. I've built this buffer into my schedule precisely for such contingencies. Nothing will prevent me from being in that lobby at 8:15.

I arrive with three minutes to spare. The security guard nods as I pass. I position myself near the potted Ficus, angled to appear occupied with my phone while maintaining clear sightlines to the entrance.

She enters at 8:17, exactly as expected. Today she wears a cream blouse, navy skirt, hair swept up to expose the delicate curve of her neck. I begin my approach, timing my steps to intercept her path to the elevator.

Before I'm halfway there, it hits me. Her scent, that delicious essence of sweet honey. It floats toward me, wrapping around my senses, pulling me forward. The world narrows, sounds fading to background static. My steps quicken involuntarily.

The scent intensifies as I draw closer. My head feels light, my focus absolute. I've never understood those cartoon characters, floating helplessly toward a pie cooling on a windowsill, but now I do. Her fragrance is a physical force, a current I willingly surrender to.

I slide into the elevator behind her, positioning myself in the back corner. The mirrored walls reflect her profile from multiple angles, a kaleidoscope of Iris that I drink in without seeming to look directly at her. Years of practice have taught me how to observe without being observed.

Three other people crowd the small space, creating a natural barrier between us. Perfect. Too obvious an approach would spoil the delicate dance we're engaged in, whether she realizes it or not.

She presses the button for the third floor. I already knew that's where she works, of course, but watching her slender finger extend to touch the illuminated circle sends an electric current through me. Such a mundane action transformed into something intimate by her performance of it.

"Excuse me," a man mumbles, shifting to make room for a late arrival. The movement presses Iris slightly in my direction. She adjusts her stance, the back of her head now just inches from my chest. If I inhaled deeply enough, I could draw her scent directly into me.

I resist. Patience has its rewards.

The elevator ascends with mechanical precision. First floor... second... The space grows quieter, that peculiar hush that falls when strangers are forced into proximity. I use the silence to my advantage, studying her reflection in the brushed steel doors.

She checks her watch, a delicate timepiece with a thin leather band. Her nails are unpainted today, natural. She shifts her weight from one foot to another, creating a subtle sway that draws my eye to the curve of her hip.

The elevator chimes for the third floor. She moves forward, and I allow my gaze to drop to the floor, a perfect image of disinterest. As she steps out, I glance up just enough to catch her profile once more, a casual, accidental look that no one would question.

Our eyes meet for the briefest moment. She doesn't smile, doesn't nod, but there's recognition there. She knows I exist. It's enough for now.

The doors close, and I exhale slowly, savoring the lingering traces of honey in the air.

I watch the elevator doors close, cutting off my view of Iris. The honey scent lingers, trapped in this small space with me, growing fainter with each floor we ascend. By the time I reach my office, it's almost completely dissipated. The thought irritates me.

"Morning, Sebastian." Ryan steps into the elevator at the fifth floor, clutching his usual oversized coffee. "Ready for the McKinley presentation?"

I nod, not bothering with pleasantries. Ryan knows me well enough to understand my morning silence isn't personal. My mind is still processing, cataloging every detail of our brief encounter. The way her hair fell against her neck. The subtle shift of her weight. The barely perceptible recognition in her eyes.

The elevator arrives at our floor, and I step out first, Ryan trailing behind me. The office is already humming with activity, phones ringing, keyboards clicking, the soft murmur of voices discussing projects and deadlines. I move through it all with purpose, nodding at employees who greet me, but never slowing my stride.

My office door closes behind me with a satisfying click. I settle into my chair, turning to face the floor-to-ceiling windows that showcase the city below. From this height, people look like insects, scurrying along predetermined paths. Predictable. Controllable.

Unlike my current situation.

I pull out my phone, checking for new messages. Nothing from unknown numbers. No suspicious emails. The silence is almost more unnerving than another threat would be.

Who is watching me?

I turn to my computer, pushing thoughts of Iris aside. The McKinley presentation demands my full attention, it's a $40 million project that could redefine the city skyline. I pull up the rendering files, scrolling through the 3D models we've spent months perfecting.

"Ryan," I call through the intercom. "Bring the McKinley files in."

He appears moments later, arms loaded with presentation boards and material samples.

"I've got the revised cost projections," Ryan says, spreading documents across my conference table. "And the sustainability metrics you wanted highlighted."

I nod, examining each board with critical precision. "The shadow studies for the east elevation?"

"Right here." He slides a folder toward me. "I also included the alternative glazing options they mentioned last time."

We work methodically, arranging everything in presentation order. Ryan's attention to detail is why I keep him on my key projects. He anticipates needs before I voice them.

"The zoning variance documentation?" I ask.

"Filed and approved. Got the final sign-off yesterday."

My phone rings, interrupting our workflow. Unknown number. I consider letting it go to voicemail, but something, intuition, perhaps, makes me answer.

"Sebastian Wolfe."

"Mr. Wolfe, this is Detective Mercer with Metro Police." The voice is deep, authoritative. "I was hoping you might have time to come down to the station for a conversation."

My pulse quickens, but my voice remains steady. "May I ask what this is regarding?"

"Just some questions we'd like to clear up. Nothing to worry about." His casual tone doesn't match the request.

"I have an important client meeting at eleven."

"This shouldn't take long. The sooner we can chat, the sooner you can get back to your day."

I weigh up my options. Refusing would look suspicious. "I'll be there within the hour."

I hang up and turn to Ryan, who's watching me with curious eyes.

"I need you to contact McKinley and reschedule for tomorrow. Same time."

"Everything okay?"

"Police want to 'chat.' Probably about that break-in at the Riverside site." The lie comes easily. "Handle McKinley personally, apologize for the short notice, offer lunch at Le Bernardin on the firm."

Ryan nods, already reaching for his phone. "Want me to come with you?"

"No. Hold things down here. I'll be back as soon as I can."

I gather my coat and keys, mind racing through possibilities. What do they know? What evidence could they possibly have? I've been careful, meticulous, even.

As I head toward the elevator, I school my features into a mask of mild inconvenience. Just a busy executive interrupted by bureaucracy. Nothing more.

I park in the police station lot, allowing myself a moment to collect my thoughts. My reflection in the rearview mirror shows nothing, no fear, no guilt, just the mild annoyance of a successful man whose day has been interrupted. Perfect.

Inside, the station buzzes with activity. Officers move between desks, phones ring constantly, and the air smells of burnt coffee and industrial cleaner. I approach the front desk, stating my business with practiced confidence.

"Mr. Wolfe." Detective Mercer appears from a hallway, extending his hand. "Appreciate you coming in."

I note immediately that we're not heading toward the interrogation rooms in the back. Instead, he gestures to a small conference room near the front, glass walls, door left open. Less formal. Less threatening. Interesting.

"Can I get you something? Coffee? Water?" he asks, unusually hospitable.

"Water is fine." I take the seat facing the door, maintaining sightlines to the rest of the station.

Mercer returns with two water bottles, settling across from me. "I wanted to follow up on our conversation about the Riverside site."

"Of course. Has there been a development?"

"We visited Mr. Grayson's residence and place of business, and there's no record of him officially being hired to investigate you."

I take a measured sip of water. "That's disturbing news."

"Here's the thing, Mr. Wolfe." Mercer leans forward. "I checked with my colleagues. Despite what you may have gathered from our previous conversation, there's no active file on you. You weren't under investigation."

I allow a slight frown. "I'm not sure I understand."

"That's what's strange." He opens the folder now, revealing not crime scene photos but a single photograph, Iris and me outside the coffee shop last week. The moment she bumped into me, her hand resting briefly on my arm to steady herself.

"We work in the same building," I say evenly. "Different companies. We occasionally see each other in the elevator or around the neighborhood."

Mercer nods slowly. "I want to be clear, Mr. Wolfe. You're not a suspect in our homicide investigation. But I would classify you as a person of significant interest."

"What about Ms. Klarelle?" I keep my expression neutral, betraying nothing despite the sudden tightness in my chest. "Is there a file on her?"

Mercer shakes his head. "No active investigation involving Ms. Klarelle either." He taps the photo. "We're simply trying to establish connections between various individuals."

I lean back slightly, letting my shoulders relax. "We're barely acquaintances. As I said, we work in the same building. Different companies."

"Would you characterize your relationship as friendly?"

"Professional," I correct. "Cordial. We exchange pleasantries in the elevator. That's the extent of it."

He studies me for a moment, eyes searching for something. I maintain steady eye contact, not challenging, not defensive, just the calm confidence of a man with nothing to hide.

"I'm happy to help in whatever way I can, Detective." I spread my hands slightly. "If there's anything specific you need to know, just ask."

The phone once held in my jacket pocket makes me uneasy, it's almost like I can feel it vibrating in the place it once occupied. I could tell him about it, about the book, about the car watching my house. I could lay it all out, someone is stalking me.

But then questions would follow. Why target you, Mr. Wolfe? Any enemies? Anyone who might want to hurt you? And inevitably: What exactly would they have against someone like you?

No. Better to say nothing. Keep my secrets close.

"Ever heard the name Mary Kate Conley?" He asks.

"No, should I?"

"Not necessarily. The last entry in his journal was a phone call from Tennessee, from a Mary Kate Conley, asking about help with a missing person."

"No, it doesn't ring any bells at all."

"I appreciate your cooperation," Mercer says, closing the folder. "If you think of anything that might be relevant, here's my card."

I take it, slipping it into my wallet. "Of course. And if there's anything else you need, don't hesitate to call."

We stand, shake hands. His grip is firm, professional. Nothing in it suggests suspicion.

"I'll walk you out," he offers.

We make small talk as we head toward the exit, the weather, the city's new development plans. Normal, mundane topics that have nothing to do with missing women or planted evidence.

At the door, he pauses. "Drive safe, Mr. Wolfe."

I nod, thanking him, and walk to my car. Not too fast, not too slow, in case he's watching. Just another busy professional, eager to return to his day.

Once inside, I lock the doors and exhale deeply, the tension flooding out of me in a rush. My hands tremble slightly on the steering wheel, the first physical manifestation of the fear I've been suppressing.

I return to the office, my mind cycling through every detail of the conversation with Detective Mercer. The photograph of Iris and me, innocent enough on the surface, yet somehow weaponized in his hands. The careful way he watched my reactions. The deliberate casualness of it all.

Ryan intercepts me the moment I step off the elevator, coffee in hand and concern etched across his face.

"How'd it go? What did they want?"

I gesture for him to follow me to my office, waiting until the door closes behind us before responding.

"Nothing substantial. They have no real leads and were hoping I could help shed some light on the situation." I remove my jacket, draping it precisely over the back of my chair. "They don't have a file on me or anyone else at the firm. So Mr. Grayson's dead body at our site and the fact he had pictures of me are little to go on."

Ryan's eyebrows lift. "Pictures of you? That's... unsettling."

"Apparently he was posing as a private investigator." I settle into my chair, reclaiming my territory, my control. "But there's no record of him being hired officially."

"That's odd." Ryan leans against the conference table, arms folded. "Though construction sites can be dangerous places, especially when it's dark. Anyone could access them if they're determined enough."

"True." I pull up the McKinley presentation on my computer, signaling a return to business. "Did you manage to reschedule?"

"Tomorrow at eleven. They were understanding, actually seemed relieved to have an extra day to prepare their questions."

I nod, satisfied. "Good. Let's use the time to strengthen our case for the east tower modifications."

Ryan hesitates, clearly wanting to ask more about the police, but reading my body language well enough to know the subject is closed. He shifts gears smoothly.

"I'll get the revised renderings from Graphics."

After Ryan leaves, I sit alone in my office, staring at the city sprawled beneath me. The conversation with Detective Mercer replays in my mind, each word and gesture analyzed for hidden meaning. The name Mary Kate Conley lingers. Someone from Tennessee looking for a missing person. The connection eludes me, but instinct tells me it's significant.

I turn to my computer and type her name into a search engine. Thousands of results appear, social media profiles, news articles, public records. I narrow the search to Tennessee, adding "missing person" to the parameters.

A news article from eight months ago catches my attention: "Kentucky Woman Seeks Answers in Husband's Disappearance." The thumbnail shows a woman with honey-blonde hair standing before a podium, microphones thrust toward her face. Mary Kate Conley, 34, pleading for information about her husband, Joseph James Conley, last seen in Nashville.

I click the article, scanning for details. Joseph Conley, 38, musician, disappeared after a business trip to Nashville. No signs of foul play. No body recovered. The case went cold.

I lean back, processing this information. A private investigator with photos of me is found dead at my construction site. He had contact with a woman searching for her missing husband. Now someone is leaving me messages, planting evidence.

The connections are forming, but the picture remains incomplete.

My phone buzzes, a text from an unknown number:

"Enjoying your day, Sebastian?"

I stare at the screen, thumb hovering over the delete button. Instead, I take a screenshot and save it. Evidence. For what, I'm not yet sure.

The intercom buzzes. "Mr. Wolfe, your twelve o'clock is here."

I straighten my tie, close the browser windows. Whatever game is being played, I won't be rattled.

"Send them in," I respond, voice as steady as steel.

I rise from my desk as Walter Kingsley enters my office, his imposing frame filling the doorway. Despite being in his sixties, he moves with the confident stride of a much younger man. Old money has that effect, it preserves, protects, creates an illusion of immortality.

"Sebastian." He extends his hand, grip firm and dry. "Appreciate you making time on short notice."

"Of course. Your projects are always a priority for us." I gesture toward the conference area where Ryan has already arranged water, coffee, and the preliminary site analyses.

Kingsley settles into a chair, immediately leaning forward with the eagerness of a man half his age. "Let's not waste time. The waterfront property, I want something revolutionary."

I take out my notebook, pen poised. "Tell me your vision for the space. What purpose do you see it serving beyond the obvious commercial functions?"

"I want it to be a destination," he says, eyes bright with ambition. "Not just another shopping center. Something that draws people to the waterfront at all hours."

"Mixed use, then? Retail, dining, perhaps residential components?"

He nods. "All of that, but with something special. Something iconic that becomes synonymous with the city skyline."

"What aesthetic are you drawn to?" I ask, sketching a rough outline of the waterfront property. "Contemporary glass and steel? Something that references the city's industrial past? Or perhaps something entirely unexpected?"

"I've always admired your Helix Tower in Chicago," he says. "The way it seems to twist toward the sky yet remains grounded. Organic but disciplined."

I nod, making notes. "And regarding sustainability requirements? The waterfront location presents both challenges and opportunities."

"I want it green, not just for show, but genuinely efficient. Solar, rainwater collection, living walls. Whatever makes sense without compromising the design."

"Budget parameters?" I ask, though I already know the answer.

Kingsley smiles. "Let's design it right first, then we'll talk numbers."

I appreciate his approach. It's refreshing to work with clients who understand that vision should precede budget constraints.

"Any specific requirements for public spaces? The relationship between the development and the waterfront itself?"

"I want people to engage with the water," he says. "Terraced approaches, maybe floating platforms."

As Walter Kingsley rattles off his vision for the waterfront property, I find myself becoming more and more engaged in the project. The challenge of creating something iconic, yet functional, is invigorating. I jot down notes and rough sketches on my notepad, my mind already racing with ideas.

"...make the river part of the experience, not just a view," Kingsley concludes.

I look up from my notes, mentally filing away his last request. "Mr. Kingsley, if you'll give me a moment, I'd like to share a preliminary concept."

He nods his approval as I quickly transfer my rough sketch onto a clean sheet of paper. The outline of the building takes shape, a sinuous form that twists organically from the ground upward, like a helix reaching for the sky. I shade in areas for greenery and open spaces, incorporating terraces and floating platforms that blur the line between land and water.

"Here," I say, sliding the drawing across the table. "This is just a rough draft, but it captures some of your requirements."

Kingsley leans in to study the sketch, his eyes widening with interest. "I like it," he says after a moment's silence. "The way it curves around the river... it's as if it's embracing it." He taps his finger on one of the terraces jutting out over the water. "This is exactly what I had in mind."

"Thank you," I say with a slight bow of my head. "We can refine these details further once we've completed our due diligence on zoning regulations and environmental impact studies."

"Of course," he agrees distractedly, still absorbed in my drawing. "I want you to lead this project personally, Sebastian." His gaze meets mine across the table, resolute and unyielding. "I won't settle for anyone else."

I smile, a confident air surrounding me. "Thank you, Mr. Kingsley. I'm honored by your trust in my expertise."

"Please," he says with a wave of his hand. "Call me Walter."

"Walter," I correct with a nod.

He stands up abruptly after glancing at his watch.

"Is it one thirty already?" I ask, double-checking the time myself even though the antique clock on my wall reads just past one twenty-nine. "It seems meetings always run longer than we anticipate."

Walter Kingsley lets out a small chuckle, placing his hand on the table. "Time has a way of sneaking up on us, don't it? I wish time ran towards us as eagerly as it runs away from us."

"That would make life predictable," I say. "But not necessarily enjoyable."

Walter smiles at that and points his head toward the door. "I think it's time for me to go."

I rise up from my chair as well. "It was good seeing you, Walter."

Walter nods as he leaves my office.

I head downstairs to the sandwich shop on the first floor; a quaint little place tucked between the bank and a florist. The lunch rush has mostly subsided, leaving only a few stragglers waiting for their orders. I nod at the owner, a middle-aged man who knows my usual without asking, and collect my sandwich wrapped in crisp white paper.

"Turkey club on rye, light mayo, no tomato," he confirms, sliding it across the counter.

"Perfect as always, Tony." I leave a generous tip in the jar.

The elevator ride back up is mercifully empty, giving me a moment to breathe, to reset. The conversation with Detective Mercer still lingers in the back of my mind, but I push it aside. Work is my sanctuary, the place where everything makes sense.

I head toward our office lounge, a bright, airy space with floor-to-ceiling windows overlooking the city. As I push open the glass door, the animated conversation inside abruptly halts. Alexis, Maria, and Elizabeth are seated around the round table, half-eaten salads and sandwiches in front of them. Their heads turn toward me, and Elizabeth quickly leans in to whisper something to the others.

I raise an eyebrow as I make my way to the coffee machine, unwrapping my sandwich.

"Don't let me interrupt the secret meeting of the office illuminati," I say dryly, pouring myself a cup of coffee.

Their stifled giggles only confirm my suspicion. Maria covers her mouth, eyes darting to Alexis, who seems to be struggling to maintain her composure.

"Seriously, what's so amusing?" I ask, taking a seat at the adjacent table. "Did Ryan finally wear matching socks today?"

Elizabeth shakes her head, another round of whispers passing between them.

"Alright, I give up." I bite into my sandwich. "What's the joke I'm missing?"

Maria finally speaks up, her voice lilting with barely contained amusement. "We were just discussing your lunch date with Jenna yesterday."

"Lunch date?" I repeat, genuinely confused.

"She's been telling everyone how you're such a, what did she call it, Alexis?" Elizabeth turns to her younger colleague.

"A 'brooding Victorian man,'" Alexis supplies, her eyes dancing with mischief. "Apparently, you have the 'dark, tortured soul of a Brontë hero.'"

"It wasn't a date," I say, setting my coffee down with more force than intended. "She cornered me in the elevator. I simply didn't have the energy to refuse."

Maria snorts, nearly choking on her salad. "That sounds about right. Jenna's like a heat-seeking missile once she's locked onto a target."

"She spent twenty minutes talking about her cat's dietary restrictions before getting to the point," I continue, shaking my head at the memory. "Apparently, she has this friend who would be 'perfect' for me."

Elizabeth's eyebrows shoot up. "Oh? Do tell."

"A yoga instructor who's 'really into mindfulness and clean eating.'" I take another bite of my sandwich. "Because clearly, that's what I'm looking for in a partner, someone to lecture me about the spiritual benefits of kale."

The women burst into laughter, Alexis nearly spitting out her drink.

"I can just picture it," Maria says between giggles. "You are sitting in lotus position, trying not to check your watch while someone explains the proper alignment of your chakras."

"Maybe she could design you a Zen Garden for your office," Elizabeth suggests, eyes twinkling. "Replace all those architectural models with little rakes and pebbles."

I roll my eyes but can't help smiling. "If Jenna asks, tell her I've taken a vow of celibacy. It seems less complicated."

This sends them into another fit of laughter, and for a moment I forget about the detective, the text, the phone, all of it.

I finish my sandwich, crumpling the wrapper into a tight ball. "Well, ladies, it's been enlightening as always, but I should get back to actual work. Some of us don't have time to gossip about fictional romance novels."

"Oh please," Elizabeth says, waving her hand dismissively. "We all know you're secretly reading Jane Eyre under your desk when no one's looking."

"You caught me," I deadpan. "I keep a dog-eared copy next to my building codes and zoning regulations."

Maria nearly chokes on her water. "I can just picture you sighing dramatically over Mr. Rochester."

"If I ever start wandering the office hallways muttering about voices on the wind, please have me committed." I stand, straightening my tie. "Enjoy the rest of your lunch, ladies."

"We'll keep you posted if Jenna has any more spiritual matches for you," Alexis calls after me.

I give them a smile, genuine, despite myself and head back to my office. Their laughter follows me down the hallway, and I chuckle a laugh.

Back at my desk, I pull up the waterfront project files, losing myself in the work. Walter Kingsley's vision is ambitious but not impossible. I sketch several variations of the concept I showed him, refining the curves, adjusting the relationship between the structure and the river. The work calms me, centers me. Here, in the clean lines and precise measurements, everything makes sense.

After an hour of focused work, I send a message to Ryan, Elizabeth, and Maria, asking them to join me to discuss tomorrow's presentation.

Within minutes, they file into my office, notepads in hand, all traces of lunchtime levity replaced by professional focus.

"Let's go through the McKinley proposal one more time," I say, pulling up the presentation on the conference screen. "I want us all aligned on our approach for tomorrow."

I bring up the presentation on the conference screen, leaning forward in my chair as the others settle around the table. The McKinley proposal is one of our larger projects this quarter, a mixed-use development that could transform the downtown area if executed properly.

"Let's start with the introduction," I say, clicking through to the first slide. "Elizabeth, you'll cover the overview and market analysis. I've made some adjustments to the economic impact projections based on the latest data."

Elizabeth nods, making notes. "I noticed that. The numbers look more conservative than our initial estimates."

"Better to under-promise and over-deliver," I reply. "Especially with the city council members in attendance. Ryan, you're handling the technical specifications and timeline, correct?"

Ryan flips through his notebook. "Yes, I've got the construction phases mapped out, including contingencies for weather delays. Did we get confirmation on the soil testing permits?"

"They came through yesterday," Maria interjects. "I've added them to the appendix and included a summary of the findings on slide twenty-three."

I make a note to review that section. "Good. What about the community impact statement? That's likely to draw the most questions."

"I've prepared responses to the potential concerns raised during the town hall," Elizabeth says. "Traffic flow, noise pollution during construction, shadow studies for the adjacent park."

"The shadow studies are particularly important," I remind them. "The last thing we need is another Park Plaza situation where we had to redesign mid-construction."

Maria pulls up the environmental impact report on her tablet. "All the necessary signatures are here. Department of Environmental Protection, Historical Preservation Committee, even that wildlife conservation group that was concerned about the migratory birds."

"Perfect." I move to the next slide. "Now, for the visual presentation. Ryan, did you finalize the 3D renderings?"

"Completed last night," he confirms. "The walkthrough animation is rendering now, should be ready by the end of day."

"And the physical model?" I ask.

"In the presentation room, covered and ready," Elizabeth assures me. "I triple-checked the lighting this morning."

I nod, satisfied. "Maria, you'll handle questions about zoning and permit processes?"

"Already prepared. I've compiled one-sheet with all the approved permits and pending applications with their expected approval dates."

I lean back in my chair, a sense of satisfaction settling over me. "Well, I'd say we're in exceptional shape for tomorrow. Everything appears to be in order, which naturally means something catastrophic is about to happen."

Elizabeth laughs. "Don't jinx us, Sebastian."

"I'm simply acknowledging Murphy's Law," I reply, straightening a stack of papers on my desk. "The universe has a perverse way of punishing overconfidence."

"If anything goes wrong, we'll handle it," Maria says with her typical pragmatism. "We always do."

Ryan glances at his watch. "It's 4:32. Should we wrap this up?"

My pulse quickens slightly at the time. Perfect. "Yes, I think we've covered everything essential. Let's reconvene tomorrow at eight to run through the presentation once more before the clients arrive."

As they gather their materials and file out of my office, I begin methodically organizing my desk. Each document returns to its proper folder, each pen aligned in the leather holder, computer shut down with precision. The ritual calms me, prepares me for what's next.

At 4:45, I slip my laptop into my briefcase, adjust my tie in the reflection of the window, and lock my office door. The timing must be perfect. Too early, and I might miss her. Too late, and the opportunity vanishes.

I make my way toward the elevator bank, maintaining a casual pace. No need to appear eager. No need to reveal that this moment, this brief, fleeting interaction, has been calculated down to the minute.

I press the down button and wait for the elevator to arrive, feeling a slight tingle of anticipation. The doors slide open with a soft ding, and I step inside, positioning myself in the back corner, my usual spot as I press the lobby button. She should be boarding exactly as we reach her floor.

The elevator descends smoothly but stops at the fifth floor. I maintain my neutral expression as the doors open, though irritation flickers through me. A balding man in an ill-fitting suit steps in, nodding vaguely in my direction before turning to face the doors. I offer a perfunctory nod in return, though my mind is elsewhere.

An intruder in my carefully orchestrated moment.

The elevator continues its descent, and I find myself willing it to move faster. The man shifts his weight from one foot to the other and checks his watch. Each movement grates on my nerves.

When we reach the third floor, I straighten almost imperceptibly. The doors slide open, and there she is.

Iris steps into the elevator with her usual grace, but today something is different. As she enters, her eyes meet mine briefly, and her lips curve into a small, coy smile. My breath catches in my throat, not just the polite acknowledgment she sometimes offers, but something more deliberate. More intimate.

She takes her position near the front, facing forward as always. The balding man seems oblivious to the charged atmosphere that now fills the small space.

I watch her reflection in the polished steel walls, studying the curve of her neck, the way her fingers lightly grip her purse. Then I notice something that makes my pulse quicken. In the reflection of the reflection, I can see her eyes. They're not fixed forward as I'd always assumed.

They're watching me.

For a fleeting moment, our gazes meet in this double reflection. Does she observe me as carefully as I observe her? Has she been aware all along? The possibility sends an unexpected thrill through me.

The thought is intoxicating. Has she been watching me all this time? Playing her own version of the game I thought was mine alone? The possibility sends heat coursing through my veins. Perhaps she's been studying me with the same intensity, the same hunger.

In this small metal box, suspended between floors, our eyes meet in the layered reflections. A secret conversation without words. The balding man shifts his weight again, completely unaware of the electric current passing through the air around him.

I adjust my stance slightly, straightening my shoulders. If she's watching, I want her to see me at my best. Controlled. Poised. A man worthy of her attention.

Her perfume fills the small space, honey and something deeper, more primal. I inhale slowly, savoring it. The scent of her has become a fixation, one I recreate in my mind during the hours between our encounters.

She tucks a strand of hair behind her ear, a gesture I've seen countless times before. But now it feels different. Deliberate. Is it meant for me? A silent acknowledgment of our shared secret?

The elevator slows, announcing our arrival with an audible ding.

Iris steps out first, her movements fluid and unhurried. I pause for a moment, allowing her the space to move ahead while I remain close enough to stay within the cloud of her scent. It draws me forward like an invisible thread connecting us.

I follow at a measured distance, watching the gentle sway of her hips, the confident rhythm of her steps across the lobby. She knows I'm behind her, I'm certain of it now. The slight tilt of her head, the deliberate pace of her walk, these aren't coincidences.

My heart pounds against my ribs as I maintain the perfect distance between us. Not too close to appear threatening, not too far to lose the delicate trail of her perfume. The dance continues, unacknowledged but unmistakable.

I follow her out of the building, watching as she turns left toward the parking garage while I head right to my car. The evening air carries a hint of autumn, crisp and full of possibility.

As I drive home, my mind replays our silent exchange in the elevator. That look in the reflection wasn't my imagination, right? Of course I'm right, she sees me. Maybe she wants my attention as much as I want hers...

Tomorrow will be different. I'll speak to her properly, not the accidental collision we had before, but something deliberate. I'll invite her to my gathering again, and this time, I'll ensure she accepts. Perhaps I'll mention the art collection she seemed interested in during our brief conversation. Or the view from my terrace that overlooks the city lights, women always appreciate thoughtful details like that.

I pull into my driveway, the security lights illuminating automatically. My home welcomes me with its clean lines and perfect order. Inside, I pour myself two fingers of whiskey and settle into my chair, surveying my domain. Everything in its place. Everything under control.

The party this weekend will be perfect. I've already arranged for the catering, nothing ostentatious, just elegant hors d'oeuvres and a carefully curated wine selection. The guest list includes the right balance of colleagues and acquaintances, creating the ideal backdrop for Iris to feel both comfortable and impressed.

I imagine her here, moving through these rooms, her scent mingling with the space I've created. Perhaps she'll linger after the others have gone. Perhaps we'll share a final drink on the terrace, the city spread below us like a carpet of stars.

Yes, tomorrow I'll make sure she says yes. And then, who knows what might follow?

CHAPTER 12

I wake to the familiar chime of my alarm at 5:00 AM, precisely. No need to hit snooze. My body knows the routine, moving with practiced efficiency before my mind fully engages. Cold water on my face. Coffee brewing while I shower. Everything in its place, every task being completed in order according to my routine.

The morning light cracks through my blinds as I dress, selecting a charcoal suit with subtle pinstripes. Power without ostentation. Control without arrogance. I adjust my tie in the mirror, Windsor knot, perfectly centered.

My kitchen gleams under the recessed lighting as I prepare breakfast. Two eggs, scrambled. Whole grain toast. Black coffee. I eat standing at the counter, scrolling through emails, mentally arranging my day into neat compartments of time.

The drive to work follows the usual pattern, light traffic, the same NPR segment, the same parking spot waiting for me in the garage. I'm early, as always. Precisely seventeen minutes before I need to be at my desk. Enough time to prepare for her.

I take my position in the lobby, pretending to check my phone while watching the entrance from my peripheral vision. The security guard nods at me, we've established this as a morning ritual by this point. I return the gesture without breaking my rhythm.

At 8:15, I make my way to the elevator bank. Not too eager, not too casual. I time it perfectly, stepping into the car just as the doors begin to close, ensuring I'll be heading up when she arrives.

The elevator descends back to the lobby. My heart rate increases slightly, a physiological response I've come to anticipate. The doors slide open, and there she is.

Iris.

Today she wears a navy dress that accentuates the curve of her waist, her hair pulled back in a loose knot that reveals the elegant line of her neck. She steps inside, that familiar sweet scent of honey filling the small space between us.

I position myself at the perfect angle, close enough to observe her reflection in the polished doors, far enough to appear disinterested.

I focus on Iris's reflection in the elevator doors hoping to get another glance of her looking back at me.

We're alone.

Just the two of us in this perfect, contained space. Today feels different. Today feels like an opportunity.

She hasn't acknowledged me yet, but that's our dance. I've learned to read the subtle tells in her body language, the way she stands slightly angled toward me, the occasional glance from the corner of her eye. She knows I'm here. She's waiting for me to make the first move.

I clear my throat softly. "I've been meaning to..."

The elevator dings. The doors start to close, then suddenly bounce back open as a hand jams between them.

"Hold it! Hold it! I'm here!"

Jenna Louise bursts into our sanctuary, her oversized tote bag swinging wildly, nearly colliding with my ribs. Her presence instantly transforms the space, from intimate to chaotic in a heartbeat.

"Morning, Sebastian! Morning!" Jenna's voice bounces off the walls, too loud for the confined space. "Can you believe the traffic today? I told my roommate, I said, 'mark my words, that construction on Seventh is going to make everyone late,' but did he listen? No! And then my coffee maker decided today was the day to just give up on life..."

I take a measured breath, watching as my carefully orchestrated moment dissolves. Iris shifts slightly, putting more distance between herself and Jenna's animated gestures. The corner of her mouth twitches, amusement or annoyance, I can't tell.

"And then the bus driver looked at me like I was crazy when I asked if he could just go around the backup, which is a completely reasonable request if you ask me, because there's that side street that nobody ever uses..."

Jenna continues without pausing for breath, her words filling every molecule of air between us. I catch Iris's eyes in the reflection. For a split second, we share something, a mutual acknowledgment of this intrusion. It's the most genuine connection we've had.

Then the moment passes. Iris returns to her phone. My opportunity evaporates.

The elevator begins its ascent. My hand instinctively grips the brass railing, a reflex born from an irrational but persistent fear. Despite designing buildings with elevators far more complex than this one, I've never fully trusted the mechanisms. Too many variables. Too many potential points of failure.

"...and then my neighbor's dog, you know, the one I told you about the last time we spoke, the one with the weird bark that sounds like it's saying 'hello'? ...well, he got into my recycling again and..."

Jenna's voice becomes white noise as I focus on Iris. She stands perfectly still, eyes fixed on her phone, seemingly unbothered by Jenna's verbal assault. I study the way her fingers tap rhythmically against her screen. What is she reading? Who is she messaging? The questions burn in my mind.

The floor numbers illuminate in sequence. One. Two. The elevator climbs too quickly, each second with Iris is precious, yet paradoxically too slow, trapped in this metal box with Jenna's incessant chatter.

"...which is totally ridiculous because who puts pineapple on a pizza and then claims it's a cultural tradition? I mean, I looked it up, and Hawaii doesn't even..."

The elevator lurches violently. My body tenses as the car shudders to a halt between floors. The lights flicker once, twice, then stabilize. The sudden silence is deafening.

"Oh my God! Are we stuck? We're stuck! This is exactly what happened to my cousin in Seattle, and she was trapped for six hours! SIX HOURS!" Jenna's voice rises an octave, her hands fluttering like panicked birds.

I straighten my tie, forcing my breathing to remain even. This disruption wasn't part of my plan. The confined space suddenly feels smaller, the air thicker. Iris looks up from her phone, her expression unreadable as her eyes meet mine for the first time today.

"I should call someone! Who do we call? Is there an emergency button? There's always an emergency button in movies!" Jenna lunges toward the control panel, nearly colliding with me.

"Don't touch anything," I say, my voice sharper than intended.

Jenna's breathing grows increasingly erratic, her eyes darting around the elevator like a trapped animal. She wraps her arms tightly around herself, rocking slightly.

"What if we run out of air? Can we run out of air? I read about this guy who..." Her words tumble out faster than before, pitch rising with each syllable.

"We have plenty of air," I say, keeping my voice deliberately steady. I pull my phone from my pocket, grateful for the signal. "I'm going to call my office, let them know we're delayed."

Ryan answers on the second ring. "Sebastian? A few of McKinley's team just arrived in the conference room."

"I'm stuck in the elevator," I say, watching Jenna pace the small space available. "Between floors. Tell them I'll be there as soon as possible."

"Stuck? With who?" Ryan sounds almost amused.

"Jenna from accounting. And..." I glance at Iris, lowering my voice slightly, "someone from the third floor."

"Ah." Ryan's tone shifts, knowing exactly who I mean. "Want me to stall or reschedule?"

"Stall. I shouldn't be long." I end the call, turning my attention back to Jenna, who's now pressing random buttons on the control panel.

"Jenna." I step toward her, gently placing my hand over hers to stop the frantic button-pushing. "Take a deep breath. These systems have multiple redundancies. We're perfectly safe."

Her eyes, wide with panic, lock onto mine. "But what if..."

"The emergency protocols are already activated," I explain, guiding her away from the panel. "Pressing more buttons won't help. Let's just stay calm and wait."

From the corner, I hear Iris's voice, soft but clear as she ends a call.

"Security is aware of the situation," she says, slipping her phone into her purse. "They've called the maintenance team. Should be about fifteen minutes."

Jenna whimpers. "Fifteen minutes? I can't, I can't breathe in here for fifteen minutes."

I place my hand lightly on her shoulder, feeling her trembling beneath my touch. "You're doing fine. Just focus on your breathing. In through your nose, out through your mouth."

She follows my instruction, her breath hitching slightly.

"That's it," I continue, my voice calm and measured. "Now again. Slower this time."

Gradually, her breathing steadies. The wild look in her eyes begins to fade.

"Thank you," she whispers, visibly embarrassed by her outburst. "I'm not usually... I mean, small spaces aren't normally..."

"It's a perfectly natural response," I assure her. "The brain's fight-or-flight mechanism doesn't always distinguish between real and perceived threats."

I catch Iris watching me, her head tilted slightly, a new curiosity in her expression. For once, I'm not performing for her benefit.

The minutes crawl by, each one stretching longer than the last. I check my watch, we've been trapped for nearly twenty minutes now. The maintenance team should have had us out five minutes ago.

"It's been more than fifteen minutes," Jenna says, her voice rising again. She presses herself against the wall, fingers digging into her palms. "Why aren't we moving? Something's wrong."

"These things often take longer than estimated," I tell her, keeping my voice level. "The important thing is that they know we're here."

But even I'm beginning to feel the first flickers of unease. Not fear, I don't allow myself that luxury, but a growing irritation at this disruption to my carefully planned day. The McKinley meeting is important; I can't afford to miss it.

Jenna's breathing quickens again, shallow and rapid. "I can't, I can't do this. The air feels thin. Is it getting thinner?"

"The air is fine," I say firmly, moving closer to her. "Look at me, Jenna. Focus on my voice. We're going to count together, alright? One, two, three..."

She nods frantically, trying to follow along. Her eyes dart to Iris, who stands calmly in the corner, watching us with that same unreadable expression.

"Four, five, six..." I continue, guiding Jenna through the breathing exercise. Gradually, her shoulders relax slightly, though her hands still tremble.

Iris's phone rings, cutting through the silence. She answers immediately, her voice low and controlled as she listens.

"I see," she says after a moment. "And how long will that take?" Another pause. "Understood. Thank you."

She ends the call, looking up at us. "That was security. Apparently, their override key isn't working, something about a system malfunction. They've called the fire department for assistance."

Jenna makes a strangled sound, somewhere between a gasp and a sob. "The fire department? Oh God, this is serious. We're going to be stuck for hours!"

"Not hours," I say, shooting Iris a look that silently asks for clarification.

"They didn't give an exact timeframe," Iris replies, her voice calm, likely to keep from exciting Jenna again. "But they assured me it's a standard procedure when the override fails."

I place my hand gently on Jenna's shoulder again. "See? Standard procedure. The professionals are handling it."

Jenna's breathing gradually steadies as I continue counting with her. The panic that had contorted her features begins to recede, replaced by a flush of embarrassment.

"I'm sorry," she mumbles, straightening her blouse with trembling fingers. "I don't usually... I mean, I'm not normally like this."

"It happens to the best of us," I assure her, stepping back to give her space. "Confined spaces can trigger unexpected responses."

Jenna nods gratefully, retreating to the corner of the elevator to collect herself. She pulls out her phone, fingers tapping rapidly, probably texting someone about our predicament.

My phone rings.

"Sebastian," I say.

"Hey, are you going to make it, everyone's here for the meetings, except you." Ryan replies.

"They have the fire department coming, they said it could be a couple of hours, but we aren't sure," I continue. "Ask if there's any way we can reschedule due to unforeseen circumstances, I don't want to just leave them waiting."

"I'll... see what I can do." Ryan drolls.

I hang up my phone, placing it back in my pocket.

In the sudden quiet, I become acutely aware of Iris. She stands opposite me, one shoulder leaning against the wall, watching our interaction with that same inscrutable expression. When our eyes meet, she doesn't look away. For once, there's no pretense of disinterest, no quick aversion of her gaze.

I hold her stare, feeling a current of something pass between us. Is this recognition? Curiosity? I can't read her.

"You handled that well," she says, her voice low enough that Jenna can't hear. "The panic attack."

"Architecture isn't just about buildings," I reply, matching her tone. "It's about understanding how spaces affect people."

The corner of her mouth lifts slightly, not quite a smile, but close. "Is that what you tell yourself when you're designing those glass towers? That you're considering human psychology?"

There's a challenge in her voice, playful but pointed. This isn't the passive Iris I've observed in the elevator all these months. This woman is engaged, present.

"Among other things," I say, stepping slightly closer. "Though I admit, being trapped in an elevator wasn't part of today's plan."

"No?" Her eyebrow arches.

"I plan most things carefully," I admit, studying the way her dark hair catches the dim emergency lighting. "But sometimes... disruptions happen."

"And how do you feel about disruptions, Sebastian?" she asks, my name on her lips sending an unexpected jolt through me.

I consider her question, aware that this is the longest conversation we've ever had. "They're necessary sometimes. They break patterns, force new perspectives."

"Is that what you're doing on the elevator every morning at precisely 8:17?" Her eyes hold mine steadily. "Breaking patterns?"

The directness of her question catches me off-guard. She's been aware of me all along, not just peripherally, but deliberately. The realization shifts something fundamental between us.

"You noticed," I say, neither confirming nor denying.

"It would be difficult not to," she replies, her voice carrying a hint of amusement. "You're not exactly subtle."

Jenna's head swivels between Iris and me, her eyes narrowing with sudden interest. The panic that had consumed her moments ago seems to evaporate, replaced by a gleam of curiosity that makes my jaw tighten. I've seen that look before, the look of someone who believes they've stumbled upon a secret.

"Wait a minute," she says, her voice rising with each word. "Do you two know each other?"

I maintain my composure, careful not to react. "We work in the same building."

Jenna's eyes widen, her mouth forming a perfect 'O'. "Oh my God. Oh. My. God." She bounces on her toes, the previous claustrophobia apparently forgotten. "You're totally into each other, aren't you? I can feel it! The tension in here isn't just from being stuck!"

I feel a muscle in my jaw twitch. "Jenna..."

"Are you guys like, star-crossed lovers or something?" She clutches her chest dramatically. "Forbidden office romance? Different departments, stolen glances across the lobby?" Her words tumble out faster now, gaining momentum. "It's like that movie... what was it called? The one with the guy and the girl who worked in the same building but didn't know they were emailing each other? Except you obviously know who each other are because you're making those eyes right now."

Iris shifts her weight, her expression unreadable. I can't tell if she's amused or annoyed by Jenna's performance.

"We're not..." I begin, but Jenna cuts me off again.

"Don't even try to deny it! I have like, a sixth sense for these things. My roommate says I should've been a matchmaker instead of an accountant. I can spot chemistry from a mile away." She turns to Iris, lowering her voice to what she probably thinks is a whisper but is still perfectly audible. "He's quite a catch, you know. Half the women in the building have tried to get his attention."

I feel heat rising up my neck, not embarrassment, but irritation at having my carefully constructed narrative hijacked by Jenna's juvenile romanticism. This isn't how I wanted my conversation with Iris to unfold. This isn't part of my plan. But maybe it can still work.

I take a breath, feeling the tension between irritation and opportunity. Jenna's interruption has thrown me off balance, but perhaps I can redirect this unwanted energy. If Iris won't acknowledge our connection directly, maybe Jenna's misplaced enthusiasm can serve my purpose.

"Actually," I say, my voice measured, casual, "I have been trying to convince Iris to attend a gathering at my home tomorrow evening."

Jenna gasps, her eyes widening with delight. "I knew it! I totally called it!"

Iris's expression shifts subtly, surprise, then something more guarded. I hold her gaze, silently challenging her to contradict me.

"It's just a small party," I continue, addressing Jenna but watching Iris. "Nothing elaborate. A few colleagues, some friends from the industry. I've extended the invitation several times, but..."

I trail off deliberately, allowing a hint of wistfulness to color my tone. Jenna takes the bait immediately.

"And she won't say yes?" Jenna looks scandalized, turning to Iris. "Why not? Is it because of office politics? Or do you have a boyfriend? Or..."

"I haven't said no," Iris interjects smoothly, her eyes never leaving mine. "I simply haven't committed either way."

"She keeps her options open," I explain, a slight smile playing at the corners of my mouth. "Every time I ask, she finds a new way to sidestep the question. 'Perhaps.' 'We'll see.' 'Not this time.'"

"Playing hard to get!" Jenna claps her hands together. "That's so classic! And obviously working."

I shrug, affecting nonchalance. "I appreciate someone who knows their own mind. Though I admit, a clear answer would be refreshing."

Iris tilts her head, studying me with that same unreadable expression. "Would it? I rather thought you enjoyed the chase."

The directness of her response catches me off guard. There's something in her tone, a knowing quality that makes me wonder, just for a moment, if she sees more than I want her to.

Jenna's enthusiasm builds with each passing minute, her earlier panic completely forgotten. She's positioned herself between Iris and me like some self-appointed matchmaker, her eyes darting back and forth as if watching a tennis match.

"So what's the theme of this party?" she asks, practically bouncing. "Is it formal? Semi-formal? Costume? I love costume parties, but Sebastian doesn't strike me as the costume type. Too dignified."

I resist the urge to check my watch. The McKinley meeting is undoubtedly lost, but strangely, I find myself less concerned about that than I should be.

"Just cocktails," I answer, my eyes finding Iris's over Jenna's shoulder. "Nothing elaborate."

"Cocktails!" Jenna squeals. "That's perfect. Iris, you have to go. Have to. When was the last time you went to a good cocktail party?"

Iris's lips curve into a slight smile. "I don't typically discuss my social calendar with strangers."

"We're not strangers anymore!" Jenna protests. "We're elevator survival buddies. That's like, a bond for life."

"Is it?" Iris raises an eyebrow, her gaze sliding from Jenna to me. "I wasn't aware we were forming lifelong connections here."

"You never know what connections might form in unexpected places," I say, holding her gaze. "Sometimes the most significant relationships begin in the most ordinary circumstances."

"Or perhaps they never begin at all," Iris counters, her voice soft but challenging. "Just because paths cross doesn't mean they're meant to intertwine."

Jenna gasps. "Oh my god, that was so poetic. You two are killing me right now." She turns to me. "Sebastian, you need to try harder. What kind of cocktails will you have at this party? Iris looks like a gin girl to me. Am I right?"

"Actually," Iris says before I can answer, "I prefer martinis."

"Shaken, not stirred?" I interject, giving my best Sean Connery James Bond impression.

"Actually, I just like them dirty," she replies with a smile.

I swallow deeply.

"How dirty?" I reply, raising one eyebrow, my face forming a grin.

"The dirtier, the better." Iris says, returning my look.

I watch Iris's lips form the words "the dirtier, the better," and something shifts in the air between us. She's not talking about just martinis.

For a moment, I forget about the stalled elevator, the missed meeting, even Jenna's presence. There's only Iris and the unmistakable challenge in her eyes.

"Oh my GOD!" Jenna practically shrieks, breaking the tension. "Did you hear that, Sebastian? She likes them dirty!" She fans herself dramatically. "The chemistry in here is palpable. I'm getting hot flashes just watching you two."

"So when is this party again? Tomorrow? Iris, you have to go. Have to. I've never seen Sebastian look at anyone like this before, and I've been watching."

I raise an eyebrow at that last comment, but Jenna barrels on, oblivious.

"What are you going to wear, Iris? Something red, I bet. You look like you'd kill in red. Or maybe black? Ooh, a little black dress is always sexy but sophisticated, right Sebastian?"

"I think Iris is capable of choosing her own attire," I say, not taking my eyes off Iris.

"But you haven't said yes yet!" Jenna exclaims, turning to Iris with an expression of genuine distress. "Why haven't you said yes? Is it because you're playing hard to get? Because let me tell you, that's working beautifully, but there comes a point where you have to seal the deal."

Iris's mouth curves into that enigmatic smile that's haunted my thoughts for months. "Perhaps I'm waiting for the right moment."

"This is the right moment!" Jenna practically shouts, throwing her hands up. "Trapped in an elevator, forced proximity, sexual tension you could cut with a knife! It's like the universe is literally giving you a sign!"

I can't help but laugh at Jenna's theatrical interpretation of our situation. It's absurd, this whole scenario, being trapped here with the woman who's occupied my thoughts for months and the most talkative person in the building playing amateur matchmaker.

"So what's it going to be, Iris?" Jenna presses, leaning forward eagerly. "Are you going to put Sebastian out of his misery and say yes to his party?"

A moment of silence falls over the elevator. I watch Iris, wondering what's going through her mind. Her expression gives nothing away, that same unreadable quality that's drawn me to her from the beginning. The quiet stretches between us, charged with possibility.

Jenna, predictably, can't bear the tension. She claps her hands together like a game show host. "Time's up! The suspense is killing me, Iris. You have to answer!"

I say nothing, letting Jenna's enthusiasm work in my favor. Her persistence might accomplish what my careful approaches haven't.

Iris tilts her head, considering. "What exactly would I be saying yes to? I don't recall hearing many details about this gathering."

"It's tomorrow evening," I explain, keeping my voice casual. "Eight o'clock. Nothing too formal, cocktails, hors d'oeuvres, conversation. A few colleagues, some friends from the industry."

"And will Jenna be attending?" Iris asks, her eyes sparkling with something I can't quite place.

The question catches me off guard. I hadn't considered including Jenna in my plans, she wasn't part of the narrative I'd constructed. But I recover quickly.

"Jenna is welcome to join, of course," I say smoothly. "If she'd like to come."

"Me?" Jenna's eyes widen comically. "Oh my God, I would LOVE to come! Are you kidding? I've never been to your place, Sebastian. I bet it's amazing. Is it one of those minimalist bachelor pads? All chrome and leather?"

I smile tightly. "Something like that."

"So it's settled then," Jenna declares, turning back to Iris. "We're both going to Sebastian's party tomorrow night. Right, Iris? Say yes. Say it. Say. Yes."

Iris laughs, a genuine sound that echoes in the small space. "You're very persistent, Jenna."

"It's one of my best qualities," Jenna agrees without a hint of irony. "So? What's your answer? The suspense is literally killing me."

Iris holds my gaze for a long moment, her expression inscrutable. Then her lips curve into a smile that sends a current through me.

"Yes," she says simply. "I'll come."

The single word echoes in the small space, landing with more impact than I'd anticipated. Something shifts in my chest, a tightening of anticipation, a rush of satisfaction. I've been planning this moment for weeks, imagining how it would unfold, but the reality is sweeter than my projections.

Jenna erupts beside us, her excitement physical and immediate. She literally jumps, her hands flailing as she lets out a squeal that reverberates off the elevator walls.

"Oh my GOD! Yes! This is happening!" She grabs Iris's arm, shaking it. "You won't regret it! Sebastian throws the best parties, I mean, I've never actually been to one, but I just know they're amazing because look at him!" She gestures wildly in my direction. "He's like, sophistication personified!"

I maintain my composure, allowing only a measured smile to surface despite the triumph surging through me. Carefully, I school my features into pleasant interest rather than the hunger I feel building.

"I'm glad you changed your mind," I tell Iris, my voice steady despite the quickening of my pulse. "Eight o'clock tomorrow. I'll text you the address."

"I don't recall giving you my number," Iris says, that enigmatic smile still playing at her lips.

"You haven't," I acknowledge. "Yet."

Jenna bounces between us, practically vibrating with excitement. "Exchange numbers! Do it now! This is like watching a real-life romantic comedy unfold before my eyes!"

Iris pulls her phone from her pocket, eyes dancing with amusement. "I suppose I should give you my number, since I've committed to this party now."

I retrieve my phone with deliberate calm, though inside I'm experiencing a rush unlike anything I've felt in months. This moment, her number in my phone, represents more than just digital information. It's the first tangible connection between us, something real I can hold onto.

"Don't worry," Iris says as she takes my phone, her fingers brushing against mine. "I won't give you a fake number. Though I did consider it."

"I'd expect nothing less," I reply, watching as she types her information. Her fingers move quickly, confidently across the screen. I wonder what else those hands are capable of.

Jenna practically vibrates beside us, her excitement reaching fever pitch. "This is seriously the most romantic thing I've ever witnessed! Two beautiful people meeting in an elevator, exchanging numbers, it's like fate brought us all together today!"

"I wouldn't call a malfunctioning elevator 'fate,'" I say dryly, but can't help the smile that forms. Jenna's enthusiasm is irritating but oddly useful. Her presence has somehow made Iris more receptive, not less.

"Oh, it's totally fate," Jenna insists, clutching her chest dramatically. "I mean, what are the odds? If this elevator hadn't broken down, Sebastian might never have gotten your number, Iris! And I would never have witnessed the beginning of what's clearly going to be an epic love story!"

Iris hands my phone back, her expression unreadable. "I wouldn't get ahead of yourself, Jenna. It's just a party."

"Just a party," Jenna repeats, rolling her eyes. "Right. And the Titanic was just a boat."

"That's not the most encouraging comparison," I point out, pocketing my phone. Iris's number is now mine, a small victory, but significant.

"You know what I mean!" Jenna waves dismissively. "I'm just so excited for both of you! Sebastian, you must be over the moon right now. I can tell you've been into her for ages."

I maintain my composure, though I feel a muscle in my jaw twitch. Jenna's perception is more than accurate. "I'm simply looking forward to having both of you at my gathering tomorrow." I reply, giving them both an honest smile.

The elevator lurches suddenly, as if waking from sleep. The lights flicker once, twice, then steady.

"Oh thank God!" Jenna exclaims. "I was starting to think we'd be stuck here forever!"

I feel a vibration in my pocket, my phone. Expecting it to be Ryan with an update on the McKinley meeting, I pull it out casually. The screen shows an unknown number, not Ryan's.

I swipe to unlock the screen and open the message. My pulse quickens as I read:

"You think you have control, but control is an illusion. See you soon."

The words are a punch to the gut. My mind races through possibilities.

My fingers tighten around the phone. The air in the elevator suddenly feels thin, insufficient. I can feel sweat forming at my hairline.

"Sebastian?" Iris's voice cuts through the fog of panic. "Is everything alright?"

I lock my phone screen immediately, forcing my features into a mask of mild annoyance rather than the cold dread coursing through me.

"Just work," I say, the lie coming easily. "They've had to cancel and reschedule the McKinley meeting I was headed to. Unfortunate timing."

"Ugh, don't you hate when that happens?" Jenna commiserates. "Like, you psych yourself up for a big meeting and then, poof... canceled. Such a waste of mental energy."

I nod, pocketing my phone with a deliberate casualness that takes all my control to maintain. Who is watching me? Who knows? The questions hammer against my skull, but externally, I maintain my composure.

"These things happen," I say, rolling my shoulders slightly as if shaking off minor irritation. "It'll give me more time to prepare, at least."

Iris studies me, her gaze more penetrating than Jenna's. "You seemed quite startled for a simple rescheduling."

"Did I?" I laugh lightly, meeting her eyes with practiced ease. "I suppose I was just thinking about the cascading effect on my schedule. I'm rather particular about my time."

The elevator begins its descent again, and relief washes through me. Just a few more moments and I can escape, can think, can plan.

"Well, at least our little impromptu elevator party had a happy ending!" Jenna chirps. "Iris is coming to your cocktail soiree, and I got invited too! Silver linings, right?"

"Indeed," I agree, my mind already racing ahead, calculating risks, identifying threats. "Silver linings."

The elevator doors slide open on the third floor, flooding the small space with light from the hallway. Relief washes over me, not just from escaping the confined space, but from the temporary reprieve from whoever sent that message.

"This is me," Iris says, stepping out with that effortless grace that's become so familiar. She turns back, her eyes meeting mine. "I'll see you tomorrow night, Sebastian. Looking forward to those dirty martinis."

"Eight o'clock," I remind her, maintaining my composure despite the chaos churning inside me. "Don't be late."

"I'm never late," she replies with that enigmatic smile. "I always arrive precisely when I mean to."

She walks away, the gentle sway of her movements drawing my gaze until she disappears around a corner.

"I need to take the stairs," I announce abruptly, stepping out of the elevator before the doors can close. "After being trapped, I need the space."

"Oh my God, same!" Jenna exclaims, following me out. "Elevators are basically coffins with cables when you think about it. Totally get the claustrophobia."

I push through the door to the stairwell, not bothering to correct her assumption. The cool, concrete space feels safer somehow, no cameras, no electronic systems that can be hacked or monitored.

"Eleven flights is quite the climb," I warn her, hoping she'll reconsider.

"Please," Jenna scoffs, falling into step beside me. "I do SoulCycle three times a week. This is nothing."

As we begin our ascent, Jenna launches into a detailed analysis of what just happened in the elevator, her voice echoing in the stairwell.

"I mean, did you see how she looked at you? That was not a 'just friends' look. That was a 'I'm imagining you naked' look. Trust me, I know these things."

Normally, Jenna's constant chatter would irritate me, but right now, her presence is oddly comforting. With her beside me, talking about trivial matters, I'm less alone with my thoughts, less vulnerable to whoever is watching me.

"And the way she said 'dirty martinis'? Come on! That was practically foreplay!"

I tune out Jenna's endless prattle as we climb the stairs, my mind racing through possibilities. Who sent that message? How much do they know? The phone from my last indulgence appearing in my office, the car outside my house, and now this text, the pieces connect in a pattern I can't quite decipher.

"...and did you notice how she touched her hair when she was talking to you? Classic flirting signal!"

"Mmm," I respond absently, my thoughts elsewhere.

By the sixth floor, Jenna's breathing has grown heavier, her commentary punctuated by gasps. "Okay, maybe... eleven flights... is more than... I thought."

"You're welcome to take the elevator the rest of the way," I state teasing.

"No way!" she protests, though her face has reddened considerably. "I'm... committed now."

By the tenth floor, Jenna's enthusiasm has completely evaporated. "Maybe... I'll take... the elevator... from here," she wheezes, leaning against the wall.

"No, come on Jenna, you got this, you've made it this far, we're almost there." I reply.

We finally reach the 14th floor, Jenna practically crawling up the last few steps. Her face is flushed red, hair sticking to her forehead with sweat. She collapses against the wall, dramatically clutching her chest.

"I think... I'm dying," she gasps. "Tell my mother... I loved her... and that she was right about those platform shoes."

I can't help but smile despite the anxiety still coiled inside me. "You made it, Jenna. Quite impressive."

She straightens up, trying to compose herself though her breathing remains labored. "Yeah, well... I'm full of surprises."

"Speaking of surprises," I say, my voice dropping to a more sincere tone, "I want to thank you. For what happened in the elevator with Iris."

"What? Why?" She looks genuinely confused.

"You helped make her comfortable. She might not have agreed to come tomorrow if you hadn't been there."

Jenna's eyes widen. "Oh my God, are you saying I'm like your... wing woman? That's the coolest thing anyone's ever said to me!"

"Something like that," I admit.

Without thinking, I step forward and pull her into a hug. Her body stiffens with surprise before she relaxes, returning the embrace with enthusiasm.

"Oh! Okay, we're hugging now. This is happening," she says, her voice muffled against my shoulder.

I release her quickly, maintaining my professional demeanor. "I appreciate your help. That's all."

She beams at me, practically bouncing on her toes despite her earlier exhaustion. "This is going to be so amazing! You and Iris are going to hit it off, I just know it. And I'll be there to witness it all! Should I wear something fancy? Is it cocktail attire? Or more casual chic?"

"Whatever you're comfortable in," I reply, already stepping away. "I need to get back to work now."

"Right, right! Me too. So much to do!" She walks backward, still talking. "Tomorrow night is going to be epic. Just epic! You'll see!"

I watch her leave, her excitement creating a wake of energy behind her. Once she's gone, I turn walking down the hall to my space of solitude.

Inside my office, I close the door firmly behind me and lean against it, finally allowing myself to breathe, to process everything that just happened.

CHAPTER 13

I settle at my desk, trying to force my focus back to the McKinley project. The blueprints blur before my eyes. My fingers tap an uneven rhythm against the mahogany, a betrayal of my usual composure. The text message replays in my mind like a skipping record.

"You think you have control, but control is an illusion. See you soon."

"See you soon." See me where? At my party? At my office?

Three simple words that claw at my sanity. Direct. Devastating.

And now Iris is coming to my home. Tomorrow night. The thought sends electricity through my veins, anticipation mixed with something darker. Something hungry.

I pull up my email, composing a message to the McKinley team with apologies for my absence. I offer to review their materials personally this evening and schedule a one-on-one with their lead developer Monday morning. Maintaining the professional and precise demeanor I always do, maintaining the façade as if my world isn't fracturing beneath me.

My stomach tightens. Not from hunger for food, but from that other appetite. The one I've kept caged and fed on schedule. The one now clawing at me, demanding release.

I check my watch: 4:37 PM.

Perfect timing.

Almost time to see her again, that is if she decides to take the elevator again after today's earlier fiasco. I should take the elevator just in-case.

The thought of seeing her, even briefly, calms the storm in my head like a long inhale from a cigarette.

I gather my things methodically, sliding papers into my leather portfolio with practiced precision. My movements betray none of the chaos inside me. Control. Always control.

The walk to the elevator feels longer today. Each step hammering to the beat of the ticking of my watch. 4:46 PM. I press the down button and wait, straightening my tie, adjusting my cuffs. Everything in its place.

The elevator arrives empty. I step inside, positioning myself in the back corner, casual but calculated. Third floor next. Her floor.

The elevator stops at the third floor. The doors slide open, and there she is.

Iris steps inside, a wisp of honey-scented air following her. She glances up, recognition flickering across her face when she sees me.

"We meet again," I say, my voice lighter than I feel. "Twice in one day. Must be fate."

Her lips curve upward, not quite a smile but something close. "Or maybe it was intentional."

She stands beside me, closer than necessary given the empty space. I can almost feel the heat radiating from her skin. My fingers itch to touch her, to confirm she's real and not some figment conjured by my unraveling mind.

"I wasn't sure you'd risk the elevator again after our little adventure this morning," I say. "Most people would take the stairs after being trapped."

"I'm not most people." She glances at me, something playful dancing in her eyes. "Besides, the odds of getting stuck twice in one day seem astronomical."

"Never tell me the odds," I quip. "I'm an architect. We specialize in defying probability."

A soft laugh escapes her, genuine and unguarded. The sound ripples through me, settling somewhere deep and dangerous.

"How's your day been?" I ask, desperate to keep her talking, to hold her here in this moment.

"Better now," she says, then adds, "Almost over."

The elevator chimes as we reach the lobby. The doors open too soon.

"Looking forward to tomorrow night," I say as she steps forward.

She turns, walking backward for a moment. "We'll see if it lives up to expectations."

And then she's gone, moving through the lobby with that same effortless grace that first caught my eye.

I breathe in deeply, catching the last traces of her scent before stepping out myself.

I walk to my car with my pulse hammering in my throat. The hunger claws inside me, demanding attention. It's been building for days now, intensified by Iris's proximity, by the surveillance, by the feeling of losing control. I need to regain equilibrium. I need to feed.

Not the usual places tonight. I need somewhere fresh, somewhere I haven't been marked or noticed. Somewhere less conspicuous.

I open my phone, looking at the map for the wider area, a place where I can find the type of woman I need to satiate this desire. Somewhere where we can meet one on one, somewhere I can keep a look out for anyone following me or keeping tabs on me.

My first thought is a coffee shop of some kind, but that presents challenges, maybe somewhere that serves coffee, but as a secondary thing, like a bookstore.

I search around on the map until I find something that catches my eye.

BookPeople. A quiet bookstore downtown, large, but not too big, with an interesting old school theatre appeal. The perfect hunting grounds.

I drive downtown, my thoughts considering, plotting conversations to lead conversations, to draw the prey into my net. The bookstore sits nestled between a coffee shop and a vintage clothing store, its windows contrasting with the darkening sky.

Inside, the scent of old paper and coffee wraps around me. I move through the shelves with casual purpose, fingertips grazing spines, eyes scanning for potential. I settle in the literature section, close enough to romance to observe but not so close as to seem obvious.

I drift through the aisles, a predator in search of prey. The romantasy section proves fruitful, women often browse alone here, lost in fantasies of dark heroes and forbidden desires. How fitting.

A brunette catches my eye first. She stands with one hip cocked, finger tracing the spine of a book with a bare-chested man on the cover. Her nails are bitten down to the quick, cuticles ragged. Too nervous. Too unpredictable. A woman who can't control her own anxieties would make for messy work.

I move on.

Near the new releases, a blonde in a crisp business suit flips through pages with methodical precision. Professional, controlled, promising. Then her phone rings. She answers loudly, discussing dinner plans with "the kids." The maternal edge in her voice sets off warning bells. Children mean complications, questions, investigations that dig deeper.

Not her.

A redhead browses nearby, her posture almost mirroring mine, careful, calculated. She selects a book, examines the back cover, then replaces it exactly as she found it. Promising. I drift closer, positioning myself to "accidentally" reach for the same title.

As I approach, I notice her eyes darting around the store, checking exits, scanning faces. She touches her purse with the same awareness I touch my knife with. She's hunting too, though for what, I can't say. Our eyes meet briefly. Recognition flashes between predators. We both retreat.

A woman with a messy bun sits cross-legged on the floor, completely absorbed in a thick paperback. No wedding ring. No nervous habits. Perfect isolation. I move toward her, selecting a book from a nearby shelf.

She glances up, offering a distracted smile before returning to her page. But something stops me. A small tattoo peeks from beneath her sleeve, a semicolon. The survivor's mark. She's already faced darkness and lived to tell the tale. Her senses would be heightened, her survival instincts sharp.

Too risky.

I continue my circuit, growing increasingly frustrated. Every potential target reveals some fatal flaw, too attentive, too connected, too likely to be missed. The hunger grows sharper, more demanding.

That's when I see her, a young redhead with curves that strain against her sundress. She moves with unselfconscious grace, fingers trailing along book spines, her full bright red lips moving silently as she reads titles. Something in her posture speaks of longing, of hunger not unlike my own, though infinitely more innocent.

She picks up "Butcher and Blackbird," studying the cover with obvious interest. Her teeth catch her bottom lip as she reads the back.

"That one's quite the ride," I say, keeping my voice soft, non-threatening. "Though it depends on what you're looking for in a story."

She looks up, startled but not displeased. Her eyes, green with flecks of gold, widen slightly.

"I'm looking for something... intense," she says, a blush creeping across her cheeks. "Something that doesn't hold back."

"Melissa," her name tag reads. Perfect.

"The protagonist in that one certainly doesn't hold back," I say, stepping closer. "He takes what he wants. No apologies."

"That's... exactly what I'm looking for." Her voice drops, becomes more intimate. "I'm tired of stories where everyone's so... careful. So restrained."

"Most people are afraid of their own desires," I say, letting my gaze hold hers. "They never experience the freedom that comes with surrender."

I watch her fingers tighten around the book, her pulse visibly quickening at the base of her throat.

"What is it you really want, Melissa?" I step closer, my voice dropping to a whisper that forces her to lean in. "In these books. What are you searching for?"

Her eyes dart around the store before returning to mine, magnetized. "I..." She stops, swallows. "I like when the male characters are... assertive."

"Assertive," I repeat, letting the word roll off my tongue like velvet. "That's a careful word for what you mean, isn't it?"

Her chest rises and falls more rapidly now. I can almost hear her heart racing beneath that thin fabric.

"Tell me," I continue, moving close enough that my breath stirs the hair at her temple. "What happens in the scenes that make you read them twice?"

She clutches the book tighter, knuckles whitening. "When he takes control," she whispers, the words tumbling out. "When he doesn't ask for permission."

"And that excites you." Not a question.

"Yes." Her voice is barely audible.

I reach out, brushing my fingers against hers as I take the book from her hands. "Fiction is safe," I say, examining the cover before meeting her eyes again. "But reality can be so much more... satisfying."

Her lip's part, trembling slightly. "What do you mean?"

"I mean that some men don't just write about taking what they want." I let my gaze travel slowly down her body, then back to her eyes. "Some men know exactly how to give a woman what she craves, even when she can't bring herself to ask for it."

She doesn't step away. Doesn't break eye contact.

"I could show you," I say, my voice like gravel. "Everything you've read about, everything you've imagined late at night when you're alone. I could make it real for you, Melissa."

Her name in my mouth makes her shiver. I can see her mind racing behind those wide eyes, desire warring with caution, hunger with fear.

I watch the internal struggle play across Melissa's face, desire fighting caution, curiosity battling fear. Her inner conflict only heightens my anticipation. I lean closer, my voice dropping to a silken whisper.

"What is it you are thinking about, Melissa? When you're alone at night?" I run my finger along the spine of the book still in my hand. "These stories must inspire such... vivid thoughts."

She swallows hard, her eyes darting around before settling back on mine. "I shouldn't... we're in public."

"That's not what I asked." I take a half-step closer, not touching her but close enough that she can feel my presence. "Tell me what you imagine. The parts you read over and over."

Her breathing quickens. "I like when... when the man takes charge completely."

"Takes charge how?" I press, tilting my head slightly. "Be specific. Say it out loud."

"When he..." she lowers her voice to barely a whisper, "when he pins her down. When he doesn't ask permission."

I smile slowly. "Good girl. And what else?"

"When he knows what she needs before she does." Her words come faster now, tumbling out. "When he makes her beg for it."

"And is that what you want, Melissa? To beg?" I let my gaze drift to her lips, then back to her eyes. "To surrender completely to someone who knows exactly how to handle you?"

She nods, almost imperceptibly.

"Say it," I command softly. "I want to hear you say what you need."

"I want..." she starts, her voice trembling. "I want someone to take control. To not be gentle. To make me..." she falters.

"Make you what?"

"Make me feel everything. Push me past what I think I can handle." Her eyes are locked on mine now, pupils dilated. "I'm tired of being treated like I'll break."

"And what if I told you I could give you exactly that?" I brush my fingers against her wrist, feeling her pulse jump beneath my touch. "What if I promised to show you just how much you can really take?"

"Is that what you want, Melissa?" I ask, my voice low and controlled despite the thundering in my chest. "Someone who won't hold back. Who'll push you beyond what you think you can handle?"

She wets her lips, the pink tip of her tongue darting out nervously. Her eyes lock onto mine, then drift to my mouth as if mesmerized by each word forming there. Her breathing comes shallow and quick, the rise and fall of her chest betraying her excitement.

"Yes," she whispers, the single syllable trembling in the air between us. "That's... that's exactly what I want."

I place my hand at the small of her back, applying gentle but firm pressure. "Then let's not waste any more time here."

I guide her through the store, past the curious glances of other patrons. Outside, the evening air hits us, cooler now. She shivers, though not from cold.

In my car, she sits with her hands folded in her lap, knuckles white. I start the engine but don't pull away immediately. Instead, I reach over, brushing my fingers along her bare knee.

"You're trembling," I observe, tracing small circles on her skin. "Nervous?"

She nods, eyes wide. "A little."

"Good." I let my hand drift higher, just an inch. "Anticipation heightens everything."

I drive with one hand, the other resting possessively on her thigh. At each stoplight, I move my fingers higher, drawing small patterns on her skin. By the time we reach my neighborhood, her breathing has grown ragged, her thighs parting slightly beneath my touch.

"Almost there," I murmur, squeezing gently. "You've been so good, waiting patiently."

I pull into my driveway, kill the engine, and turn to her. "When we go inside, you'll do exactly as I say. No questions, no hesitation. Do you understand?"

"Yes," she breathes, eyes dilated with desire.

I lead her to my front door, unlocking it with steady hands despite the hunger clawing inside me. Once inside, I close the door behind us, shutting out the world.

"Take off your shoes," I command softly. "Then wait for me in the living room. Don't sit. Stand in the center of the room until I come for you."

She complies immediately, slipping off her sandals and padding barefoot into my living room. I watch her position herself exactly as instructed, her hands clasped in front of her, waiting.

Perfect. So perfectly compliant.

I step back into the living room, savoring the sight of her, so obedient, so still. She stands exactly where I left her, hands clasped in front of her, eyes following my every movement. The hunger inside me pulses with anticipation.

"Follow me," I command softly, extending my hand.

"I didn't catch your name..."

"Sebastian."

Her fingers tremble slightly as they meet my outstretched hand. I lead her down the hallway toward my bedroom, feeling her pulse quicken through our connected hands. The darkness within me surges with each beat.

My bedroom door opens silently. I guide her inside, watching as her eyes widen, taking in the minimalist design, the platform bed with its crisp white sheets, the absence of clutter, the perfect order.

"Sit," I instruct, gesturing to the edge of the bed.

She complies immediately, perching on the edge, her hands now resting on either side of her, fingers curling into the sheets. I circle behind her, my footsteps silent on the hardwood floor. From my dresser drawer, I retrieve a black silk blindfold.

"Trust requires surrender," I whisper, my breath stirring the fine hairs at the nape of her neck. "Do you trust me, Melissa?"

She nods, her voice barely audible. "Yes."

I slip the blindfold over her eyes, tying it securely at the back of her head. Her breathing changes immediately deeper, more rapid. The loss of sight heightens everything else, touch, sound, anticipation. I run my fingers lightly down her arms, feeling goosebumps rise in their wake.

I move around to stand before her, studying her blindfolded face, the parted lips, the flush spreading across her cheeks. Gently, I press against her shoulders, guiding her onto her back. She follows my direction without resistance, lying back on my bed, her hair spreading across my sheets like fire.

Kneeling, I reach beneath the bed, extracting what I need, the Hitachi wand, its weight substantial in my hand. I set it beside her on the bed.

I begin with my hands, tracing patterns up her calves, watching her reaction to each touch. My fingers find the sensitive spot behind her knee, causing her to take a quick breath. I note this, returning to it, circling the area with my thumb. Her response is immediate, a soft gasp, her back arching slightly.

My lips follow the path my hands have taken, pressing against her ankles, her calves, the inside of her knees. I move higher, my mouth tracing the contours of her thighs, my hands spreading her legs wider. Each time she responds with particular intensity, I repeat the touch, building a map of her pleasure, memorizing what makes her breath quicken, what draws those delicious sounds from her throat.

I slip my hands beneath the hem of her dress, fingers trailing up her thighs. Her skin feels impossibly soft, like velvet warmed by sunlight. Each inch I explore draws a new sound from her, little gasps and sighs that feed the darkness coiling inside me.

"You're so responsive," I murmur against her inner thigh, my breath hot against her skin. "So beautifully sensitive."

I push her dress higher, exposing more of her to my hungry gaze. The blindfold has heightened her other senses, each touch makes her jolt; each kiss draws a deeper moan. I trace patterns on her stomach with my tongue, tasting salt and sweetness, feeling her muscles contract beneath my mouth.

"Please," she whispers, her hips rising slightly.

"Please what?" I ask, my hands moving to the buttons of her dress. "Tell me exactly what you want."

"Touch me," she breathes. "Everywhere."

I unbutton her dress slowly, deliberately, revealing her inch by inch. When I push the fabric aside, her breasts spill free, pale as moonlight against the darkness of my room, nipples a delicate pink, hardened with anticipation. The sight of her sends a jolt of hunger through me so intense I have to pause, regain control.

"Beautiful," I whisper, running my fingertips around her areolas, watching them tighten further.

She arches toward my touch, seeking more pressure. I lean down, letting my breath ghost over one nipple before taking it between my lips. Her reaction is immediate, a sharp cry, her back arching off the bed. I suck harder, flicking my tongue against the sensitive peak while my hand finds her other breast, squeezing, teasing.

With my free hand, I reach for the Hitachi, flicking it on to its lowest setting. The sound of the motors reciprocation fills the room, and Melissa tenses, recognizing the sound.

"What, what is that?" she asks, her voice tight with anticipation.

Instead of answering, I press the vibrating head against her inner thigh. Her response is visceral, a deep, guttural moan, her entire body shuddering. I continue to suck at her breast, moving the vibrator higher, watching her come undone beneath my calculated touch.

I watch her writhe beneath my touch, memorizing each gasp, each shudder. The Hitachi vibrates against her inner thigh as I trace it slowly upward, never quite reaching where she wants it most. Her hips rise instinctively, seeking contact.

"Patience," I whisper against her breast, my tongue circling her nipple before taking it between my teeth. The gentle bite draws a sharp cry from her lips, a sound that sends electricity down my spine.

I slide my free hand down her stomach, fingers slipping beneath the waistband of her panties. They're soaked through, the thin fabric clinging to her like a second skin. The evidence of her arousal feeds the darkness inside me, makes it swell and pulse with anticipation.

"You're drenched," I murmur, pressing my palm against her through the fabric. "So responsive to my touch."

Her breath catches as I apply pressure, rubbing slow circles. Her thighs tremble, spreading wider. I hook my fingers into the waistband of her panties, dragging them down her legs with deliberate slowness. She lifts her hips to help, eager to be bare beneath my hands.

"I want to hear you," I tell her, moving the vibrator closer to her center. "I want you to come undone for me, Melissa. Don't hold anything back."

I press the Hitachi directly against her, watching her body bow off the bed, a strangled cry tearing from her throat.

"That's it," I encourage, adjusting the angle to hit exactly where she needs it most. "Scream for me. Show me how much you want this"

Her hands fist in the sheets as pleasure overtakes her, her cries growing louder, more desperate. I slide my finger inside of her, keeping the vibrator at her clit, a deep unquenched gasp for air releases from her lips. I explore with my finger as it pumps in and out of her.

When I find a particularly sensitive spot, her entire body recoils, her muscles tightening, a guttural moan escaping her lips.

"Yes," I breathe, focusing on that spot, watching her unravel. "Let me hear how good it feels. Don't hold back. Scream to your heart's content."

Her screams fill my bedroom, echoing off the walls like music. Each cry more desperate than the last as I curl my finger inside her, pressing against that perfect spot that makes her whole body convulse. The Hitachi vibrates relentlessly against her clit, its buzz nearly drowned out by her frantic moans.

"That's it," I whisper, watching her writhe beneath me. "Cum for me Melissa."

I maintain a perfect rhythm, finger beckoning inside her, the vibrator pressing harder against her swollen flesh. Her thighs tremble violently on either side of my arm, muscles tightening as she climbs higher.

"Sebastian," she gasps, my name breaking into fragments as it leaves her lips. "Oh god... I can't... it's too much..."

"You can take more," I tell her, increasing the pressure. "I know you can."

Her back arches off the bed, her blindfolded face contorted in exquisite agony. The sounds tearing from her throat are primal, uninhibited, exactly what I want to hear. Her hands scramble for purchase, finding nothing but sheets to grip as I drive her relentlessly toward the edge.

I slide a second finger inside her, stretching her, feeling her inner walls clench around me. The response is immediate, a scream so raw it seems to tear from the very center of her. Her entire body shakes, helpless against the pleasure I'm forcing upon her.

"Don't fight it," I command, curling my fingers more deliberately, finding that spot that makes her sob. "You want this."

I watch her come undone beneath my touch, her body convulsing with pleasure so intense it seems to consume her entirely. Her orgasm rips through her like a storm, violent, uncontrolled, magnificent. Her back arches off the bed, her neck straining, veins standing out as she screams my name, the sound tearing from her throat raw and primal.

"That's it," I whisper, maintaining the perfect pressure, the perfect rhythm. "Let go completely."

Her inner walls clamp down on my fingers with astonishing strength, pulsing and gripping as waves of pleasure crash through her. I can feel every contraction, every spasm. The power I hold in this moment, the ability to reduce this woman to nothing but sensation and sound, feeds the dark hunger inside me, even if it just a small taste.

Her hips buck wildly against my hand, demanding more even as she's overwhelmed by what I'm already giving her. I press the vibrator more firmly against her swollen clit, watching her reaction with clinical precision. Her screams grow louder, if I didn't know better, I might worry she would bring the walls down crumbling around us.

"More," she gasps between screams, the word barely recognizable. "Please... more..."

I press the button on the Hitachi, increasing the intensity, continuing to slide my two fingers inside her, curling upward to stroke that perfect spot that makes her sob with pleasure. Her thighs clamp around my wrist, her entire body shuddering violently.

"Look at you," I murmur, a smile spreading across my face as I watch her writhe. "Taking everything, I give you. Wanting more."

Her blindfolded face contorts in ecstasy, mouth open in a continuous scream. Sweat gleams on her skin, her chest heaving with desperate breaths between cries. She's beautiful like this, completely undone, completely at my mercy.

The darkness inside me pulses with satisfaction as I watch her climax extend.

I watch in fascination as her pleasure builds to something even more intense. Her body begins to tremble differently now, not just the shaking of orgasm but something deeper, more primal. Her thighs quiver uncontrollably around my hand, her stomach muscles tightening visibly beneath her skin.

"Oh god... something's happening... I can't..." Her words dissolve into incoherent sounds as her back arches impossibly higher off the bed.

Then it happens, her body releases completely, a gush of warm wetness flooding over my hand, soaking the sheets beneath us. The sound she makes is unlike anything I've heard from her yet, a piercing scream almost a blood curdling scream of pleasure. Her entire body convulses with the force of it, her hands clawing desperately at her own body, at me, and the sheets.

I ease the pressure slightly but don't stop, watching in awe as she squirts again, her body surrendering completely to the sensation. The sight of her, blindfolded, writhing, completely undone, feeds something primal within me.

"You did good," I murmur, my voice thick with appreciation. "You're absolutely exquisite when you let yourself be who you need to be."

Her chest heaves with ragged breaths, her skin flushed and glistening with sweat. The sheets beneath her are soaked, evidence of her complete surrender.

"Gorgeous," I whisper, slowly withdrawing my fingers from inside her. "Absolutely delicious."

I move down her body, positioning myself between her trembling thighs. The scent of her arousal is intoxicating, musky and sweet and undeniably feminine. I lower my head, my breath ghosting over her swollen flesh.

"I'm not done with you yet," I tell her, my voice a low rumble against her inner thigh. "There's still more."

Her body tenses in anticipation, a whimper escaping her lips. Even after that release, she's still hungry, still wanting. Perfect.

I bring my face closer to her wet lips, breathing in her scent. The first taste of her sends electricity through me, tangy, sweet, primal. I moan against her, the vibration of my lips making her hips jerk upward, pressing into my mouth.

"Sebastian," she gasps, her voice ragged, desperate.

I linger, savoring the taste of her on my tongue. My hands grip her thighs, holding them apart as I explore her with deliberate slowness. Each stroke of my tongue draws a new sound from her throat, whimpers, gasps, broken pleas.

The wetness coating my lips and chin is intoxicating. I press my tongue flat against her, dragging it upward with firm pressure before circling her swollen clit. Her hips buck against my face, seeking more contact, more pressure.

"You taste divine," I murmur against her, the words sending vibrations through her sensitive flesh. "I could feast on you for hours."

Her fingers find my hair, tangling in it, pulling me closer. The slight pain only heightens my focus, my determination to reduce her to nothing but sensation once more.

I slip my tongue inside her, tasting her from within, feeling her inner walls clench around the intrusion. Her thighs grip around my head, her heels digging into my back as she tries to pull me closer, deeper.

I slide my tongue deeper inside her, savoring the way her body quivers around me. The taste of her sweet, tangy, and heavenly.

"Oh god," she gasps, her fingers tightening in my hair, pulling me closer.

I alternate between thrusting my tongue inside her and sucking gently on her swollen clit. Her hips rise to meet my mouth, desperate for more contact. I hold her firmly in place with my hands on her thighs, maintaining control even as I give her pleasure.

"You taste so amazing," I murmur against her wet flesh.

Her legs wrap around my shoulders, heels digging into my back as she pulls me closer. The desperation in her movements, the unrestrained need in her cries, it's intoxicating. I circle her clit with the tip of my tongue, watching her stomach muscles tighten, her calve muscle taught and she pulls me in harder.

"Please don't stop," she begs, her voice breaking. "Please, Sebastian..."

I have no intention of stopping. The taste of her is too addictive, the power I hold in this moment too seductive. I suck her clit between my lips, applying just enough pressure to make her cry out, her thighs trembling against my cheeks.

"That's it," I encourage, my breath hot against her sensitive flesh. "Let me hear how good it feels."

Her moans grow louder, more frantic as I increase the pressure, alternating between broad strokes of my tongue and focused attention on her most sensitive spots.

The wetness coating my chin, the scent of her arousal filling my lungs.

I can't help but let out an audible moan myself.

I devour her with growing intensity, my own desire building with each taste, my hands singing into her thighs and ass as I squeeze her into me.

I can feel it, the moment she's teetering on the edge, her body trembling beneath my touch. Her breaths come in short, ragged gasps, her hips bucking against my face in desperate circles. The wetness coating my chin and her thighs is a testament to her arousal, and I know she's close, so close.

"Sebastian," she moans, her voice a desperate plea. "Oh god, I'm so close."

I look up at her through hooded lids, gauging her. Noting the blindfold is no longer covering her eyes, it is now resting across her neck, pushed down from the constant motion.

I release her hips with one arm, sliding my finger inside of her again.

"That's it," I purr against her swollen clit. "Cum for me, Melissa. Show me how much you want this."

Her fingers desperate grasp for anything to grab, anything to help her push into me harder. Her thighs quiver around my head as she pulls at my hair, her fingers collapsing around the hair in tight fists, urging me onward with every fiber of her being.

"Yes," I growl against her wetness. "Cum for me, Melissa. Let go of that control you always cling to and cum for me."

It's as if my words are the key to unlocking something within her; with a strangled cry, she shatters apart in my arms. Her body convulses around my tongue and fingers, milking them both as wave after wave of pleasure courses through her trembling form. The sight of her, eyes squeezed shut, lips parted in ecstasy, is almost enough to send me over the edge myself. But not yet... not just yet...

I continue to stroke and suckle at her sensitive spots until the last tremor leaves her body; only then do I reluctantly pull away from between her legs and rise to sit on my heels between them...

I rise to my knees, allowing Melissa a moment to catch her breath as she quivers and shakes on the bed. I take this opportunity to admire the beauty of her flushed, sweat-soaked body laid out before me. Her chest heaves with each ragged breath, her thighs still trembling from the force of her orgasm. Her swollen lips glisten in the dim light, and a smirk curls my lips.

After a moment, I stand up, towering over her like a colossus. I unbutton my trousers, letting them pool at my ankles alongside my boxers. My erection springs free, hard and throbbing with need. I step closer to the bed, positioning myself between her spread thighs.

Without warning, I trace the tip of my cock between her wet folds, teasingly brushing against her entrance before moving upward to circle her swollen clit. Melissa's eyes fly open, and she moans in desperation as she feels the heat of my arousal against her slickness. Her legs involuntarily wrap around me in invitation, or perhaps desperation, begging me for more friction, more contact.

"Please," she whimpers between pants. "Sebastian... don't tease me... I can't... take it..."

I can't take it any longer. The sight of her, the way she trembles beneath me, her needy moans filling the air... it's too much. I give in to my own primal urges, sliding my hard cock inside her tight, wet heat. Her walls clench around me like a vice grip, welcoming me in with a mixture of eagerness and resistance that only fans the flames of my desire.

"Oh fuck," I groan as I bottom out, our hips pressed together. Her tightness is almost too much to bear, but I know she can take it, she needs it.

Her nails dig into my back as she arches her hips upward, begging for more. "Yes," she moans. "More... don't stop."

I pull back slowly, savoring the sensation of her wetness around my cock before sliding all the way back in again. Her moans spur me on, and soon we find ourselves caught in a primal rhythm: thrust and counterthrust, our bodies moving together as one. My hands roam her body, squeezing her breasts, tracing along her sides, anything to enhance the pleasure coursing through both of us.

"Fuck me like you mean it!" she cries out as our pace quickens further still. It's all the encouragement I need; I drop my hips slightly lower and begin to grind against her most sensitive spot with each thrust. Her cries escalate with each rotation of my hips; she's close again, I can feel it in every fiber of my being.

"That's it," I growl against her ear before biting down gently on her earlobe.

I grip Melissa's hair, pulling her head back to expose the delicate line of her throat. Her eyes widen; pupils dilated with a mixture of fear and arousal. Perfect.

"Not yet," I command, my voice rough with exertion. "Stay right on the edge for me."

She whimpers, her inner walls clenching around me as she struggles to obey. The power of holding her pleasure in my hands, of deciding when she falls, sends electricity down my spine.

"Please," she gasps, her body trembling beneath mine. "I can't..."

"You can," I growl, thrusting deeper. "And you will."

I release her hair, bringing my hand to her face. My thumb traces the outline of her lips, feeling their softness, their vulnerability. She kisses it gently, then takes it into her mouth, sucking with surprising strength. The wet heat of her mouth mirrors the tight heat gripping my cock, and I groan at the dual sensation.

My thrusts grow more forceful, more demanding. The bed frame creaks beneath us, protesting the violence of our movements. Sweat slicks our bodies, the sound of skin against skin filling the room alongside our ragged breathing.

My hand slides down to her throat, fingers splaying across the delicate skin. I feel her pulse racing beneath my palm, the fragility of her life force pounding against my fingertips.

"Sebastian," she whispers, uncertainty coloring her voice.

I apply pressure, not enough to cut off her air, but enough to slow the blood flow to her brain. Her eyes dart around in panic, her hands flying to my wrist.

"Shh," I soothe, maintaining the rhythm of my hips. "Trust me. It'll make it better."

Her fingers loosen around my wrist as she surrenders to the sensation. I watch her face carefully, monitoring the flush spreading across her cheeks, the dilation of her pupils.

I'm close, so close, the familiar tightening at the base of my spine signaling my approaching release, the feeding of my deep hunger.

I expect to see Jennifer's face, the way I always do at this moment, but instead...

Iris.

Her gorgeous smile, her sweet dark eyes, they flash before me with such clarity that I jerk back my hand, releasing Melissa's throat entirely.

No longer am I looking at Melissa, instead, it's Iris. It is Iris who is below me, slamming her hips into me, the thing I've dreamed of for months, happening. I quickly resume thrusting my hips into her, my body a hair trigger from the cliffs edge.

My hips slamming forward with force, chasing the fantasy with desperate abandon. Melissa, no, Iris, cries out beneath me as the sudden rush of blood to her brain sends her into a violent, uncontrollable orgasm. Wetness gushes between her legs, soaking us both as her inner walls clamp down around me with bruising force.

As I come undone, my body shuddering with the force of my orgasm, I cry out, not her name, but the name of the woman who haunts my every waking thought: Iris. The sensation is more pleasurable than any feeding I've ever experienced before. It's like a drug, coursing through my veins, setting every nerve ending ablaze with pleasure. My body spasms, shuddering from the sensation.

I continue to thrust my cock into her as it empties itself inside her tight heat. Her walls clench around me, milking every last drop from me, and for one last fleeting moment, I see Iris's face, wrought with ecstasy, her face smiling back at me.

But as quickly as the fantasy consumes me, it dissipates like smoke in the wind. Reality crashes down around me like a ton of bricks: I'm in my bed with a girl who isn't her.

Withdrawing from her still quivering body, I stand and reach for my boxers, tugging them on without so much as a backward glance. The adrenaline high fades as quickly as it came, leaving only emptiness in its wake.

Walking to the bathroom, I turn back to look at her one last time hoping to see Iris, but no, it's still Melissa, her chest heaving with each ragged breath she takes. Her eyes are glazed over with lust and something else... something that looks dangerously close to obsession.

"Next time," she pants out between gasps, "you can call me by my real name."

I chuckle a laugh, playing off the moment as some sex charged accident.

I splash cold water on my face, staring at my reflection in the bathroom mirror. The man looking back at me seems different somehow, hungrier, less controlled. I grip the edge of the sink, steadying myself. Iris's face flashing through my mind during sex with Melissa wasn't part of the plan. It wasn't supposed to happen like that.

After drying my face, I return to the bedroom where Melissa lies sprawled across my sheets, her body still flushed from our encounter. I sit on the edge of the bed beside her, my weight causing the mattress to dip slightly.

"You know," Melissa says, a lazy smile spreading across her face, "for sex like that, you can do or call me whatever you like." She stretches like a satisfied cat, completely unbothered by my slip. "Or whoever you like."

I laugh, the sound coming easier than expected. "Is that so?" I run my fingers lightly along her thigh, watching goosebumps rise in their wake. "So I delivered on what was promised, then?" I already know the answer, her multiple orgasms and the current state of my sheets are evidence enough.

Melissa lets out a rough, labored breath, her eyes rolling back slightly at the memory. "God, Sebastian. That was..." She pauses, searching for words. "Better than anything I've ever read. Better than anything I could have imagined." Her hand finds mine, squeezing it with surprising strength. "Those romance novels I read? They don't even come close to what you just did to me."

Her honesty is disarming. For a moment, I almost feel something like tenderness toward her, this woman who gave herself so completely to me, who accepted my domination without question.

"The way you just... took control," she continues, her voice dropping to a whisper. "Like you knew exactly what I needed before I did."

I run my fingers through my hair, the satisfaction I usually feel after a feeding conspicuously absent. Something has changed, shifted inside me. The hunger that normally subsides after these encounters still gnaws at my insides, unsatisfied.

"You're incredible," I tell her, my charm sliding back into place like a well-worn mask. But behind the mask, my mind races.

Melissa stretches languorously across my sheets, her body bearing the marks of our encounter. She looks thoroughly pleased, utterly spent, almost lifeless as she lays there, but she isn't, I can still hear the sounds of her breaths reminding me of how I was unable to finish. Inside, a hollow feeling grows with every passing moment.

"Will I see you again?" she asks, her voice still husky.

I smile, noncommittal. "We'll see."

Standing at my bedroom window, I stare out at the city lights. This pattern has sustained me for years, the hunt, the seduction, the feeding. It's been methodical, controlled. But now? Calling out Iris's name, seeing her face at that crucial moment, it changes everything. It's dangerous.

The hunger has changed. Evolved. Or perhaps it's always been this way, and I've only now recognized its true nature. These women, these substitutes, they no longer satisfy. They're pale imitations of what I truly crave.

Iris.

The realization settles over me with terrifying clarity. My carefully constructed system is failing because I'm feeding it the wrong fuel. These women aren't Jennifer. They aren't Iris. They're shadows, placeholders.

I glance back at Melissa, who watches me with adoring eyes. She thinks she knows me, thinks she's experienced something special. She has no idea how close she was to being just another pawn in a much larger game.

"What are you thinking about?" she asks, propping herself up on one elbow.

"Just appreciating the view," I lie smoothly, turning back to her with a practiced smile.

But inside, I'm calculating. Recalibrating. If ordinary women can no longer satisfy this hunger, then perhaps it's time to pursue what I truly want. Not another substitute. Not another temporary fix.

Iris is the answer. She has to be.

I watch as Melissa struggles to her feet, her legs visibly trembling. She reaches for the edge of the nightstand to steady herself, nearly knocking over a lamp in the process. Her movements are uncoordinated, almost comical, like a newborn deer finding its footing.

"Having some trouble there?" I ask, unable to suppress a smirk. "You look like you're walking on a ship during a storm."

She shoots me a playful glare, tugging her dress back into place. "Very funny. This..." she gestures down at her wobbly legs, "...is entirely your fault, Sebastian."

"My fault?" I raise an eyebrow, crossing my arms over my chest. "I believe you specifically asked for someone to take control and 'ravage you beyond your limits.' Your words, not mine." The memory of her confession at the book store earlier tonight flashes through my mind. "I merely delivered what you needed."

Her cheeks flush, but she doesn't deny it. "Fair enough." She glances up at the clock on my wall, her eyes widening. "Is that really the time? It's later than I thought."

She begins rummaging through her purse, emptying its contents onto my bed with increasing frustration. Lipstick, wallet, keys, but no phone.

"I can't find my phone," she says, panic edging into her voice. "I know I had it earlier."

Of course she can't find it. It's sitting on a bookshelf at the bookstore, where I left it after our encounter.

"You can use mine," I offer, handing her my phone. She takes it gratefully, dialing her number.

No answer.

She opens a website, logging in to find the location of her phone.

After a moment, relief washes over her face. "It's at the bookstore. They probably found it and put it behind the counter." She hands my phone back. "I'll have to get it tomorrow."

She looks at me through her lashes, a coy smile playing on her lips. "So... should I stay the night? Or would you rather take me home?"

I consider her for a moment. The hunger inside me is still unsatisfied, but not in a way she can help with. My mind is elsewhere, on Iris, on the shifting nature of my desires, on the growing complications in my carefully ordered life.

"I'd love to have you stay," I lie smoothly, "but I have an incredibly busy day tomorrow. Wouldn't want to leave you stranded here alone or have to wake you at dawn." I touch her cheek gently. "Better if I take you home tonight," I flash a cheesy grin. "I think you could do with as much sleep as you can get."

"I suppose I should get dressed then," she says, fighting her body to comply. "Have you seen my panties?" She asks, looking around, unable to locate them.

Melissa gets on her hands and knees, peering under the bed. I take a moment to admire the view before joining her in the search. After a few moments of fruitless searching, she sits up with an exasperated sigh.

"I give up," she says dramatically. "You can keep them as a souvenir... or something to remember me by." She winks at me before planting a lingering kiss on my lips.

Raising an eyebrow, I give her a sweet smile. "I'll be sure to think of you... fondly."

I escort her to my car, opening the door for her like a gentleman before getting in myself. Once inside, I start the engine and ask for her address. She rattles off an address across town, and we're off into the night.

The drive is uneventful; soft music playing in the background as we share small talk about work and life outside of our shared... encounter.

We pull up outside her building, and she turns to me, giving me that same almost obsessive look.

She leans in, placing a full wet kiss on my lips again.

"Sebastian," she purrs, turning her body to face me with that almost desperate look in her eyes. "I... I just wanted to say... that was... incredible."

"I'm glad you enjoyed yourself," I reply smoothly, feigning more interest than I feel. "I aim to please."

She blushes and fiddles with the hem of her dress before continuing.
"Listen... I know this might sound forward, but... would you be interested in doing this again sometime?" She bites her bottom lip and
waits expectantly for my response.

"Of course," I say without hesitation, plastering on my most charming
grin. "You know where to find me." It's a half-truth at best; while it's
true that she could likely track me down at work or the usual haunts
we frequent, there's no guarantee I'll be there when she comes calling.

"Great!" Her face lights up with relief and something else... Hope?
Desire? Whatever it is, it doesn't last long as reality sets in. "Oh!
Almost forgot." She rummages through her purse and produces a
scrap of paper with her number scrawled on it. "Here," she says shyly,
pressing it into my hand. "In case you ever want to... you know..." Her
voice trails off suggestively as she exits my car, closing the door behind
her as she walks away.

Chapter 14

I wake with a jolt, heart pounding against my ribs. The room is still dark, but my mind is already racing, cataloging the day ahead. I check my watch, 6:17 AM. Not enough sleep, but I can't afford to waste time today.

The party. My home will be filled with people and I can't take any chances. Everything must be perfect.

I drag myself to the shower, letting scalding water chase away the fog of exhaustion. As steam fills the bathroom, fragments of last night invade my thoughts, Melissa's eager touch, the pleasure I felt seeing Iris's face as I came in a way that puts all other ecstasy to shame. Then, there's the hunger I couldn't satisfy, the one that even now I feel roaring inside me, forcing me to have to purposefully focus my mind for even menial tasks.

In my office, I open my laptop while the coffee brews. The familiar scent fills the air as I scan through emails, client updates, RSVPs for tonight, mundane correspondence. Nothing suspicious. No taunting messages. No evidence someone is watching me.

I return to the kitchen, pouring the coffee into my mug, and drink it down without pausing. The heat burns my throat, but I welcome the sensation.

Another cup. Black and bitter.

My mind drifts back to Melissa and then Iris. Melissa, available, willing, eager to please. And yet, when I had her beneath me, all I could see was Iris. Iris, who remains just beyond my reach. Iris, whose face replaced Melissa's at the moment when I should have been consumed by pleasure.

The hunger gnaws at me again. Unquenched. Unsatisfied.

I drain my second cup and check my watch again. Almost time.

At precisely 9:58 AM, the doorbell rings. The catering service. I straighten my shoulders and put on the mask I wear for the world, confident, controlled, commanding.

"Good morning," I say, opening the door to a team of professionally dressed staff. "Everything should be set up in the main living area and extending to the terrace."

I lead them through the house, pointing out where the bar should be positioned, how the lighting should be arranged, where to place the serving stations.

"The ambiance needs to be sophisticated but not stuffy," I explain, gesturing to the space. "I want guests to feel both impressed and comfortable."

I stand in my polished kitchen, checking my phone for the twelfth time in an hour, like a high school girl waiting for a boy.

The marble countertop gleams under strategic lighting; each element of my home designed for both beauty and impact. The soft jazz I've selected fills the space with just the right atmosphere: sophisticated without trying, intimate without presuming.

Everything is perfect. Everything is ready.

I adjust a napkin that doesn't need adjusting, align a fork that's already precisely placed. The spread I've prepared sits untouched, small plates arranged with mathematical precision, wine breathing at exactly the right temperature. I've created a sequence, a careful choreography for the evening ahead.

I check my watch, 2:47PM. Just before three.

I begin thinking of Iris again. Will she really come? When I first invited her, her smile held that teasing edge, that infuriating blend of interest and distance. But yesterday, when we were stuck in the elevator, something shifted, and she let me in.

"I'll be there," she said, those three words hanging between us like a promise.

I check the room again, finding it near perfect, but lacking. Something's missing. Something that speaks directly to her.

Flowers. Not just any flowers, irises. The thought strikes me with such clarity that I'm already grabbing my keys.

"I'll be back in thirty," I tell the caterer, who nods without looking up from her meticulous arrangement of canapés.

I drive fast but controlled, parking outside Botanica, the high-end florist downtown. The bell chimes as I enter, and the scent of fresh blooms envelops me.

"I need irises," I tell the woman behind the counter. "The finest you have."

She raises an eyebrow. "Special occasion?"

"A party," I reply, offering nothing more.

She leads me to a selection of purple, blue, and white irises. I study them with the same intensity I bring to examining architectural plans. Each petal, each stem must be perfect.

"These," I point to a collection of deep purple blooms with delicate white centers. "A dozen."

While she wraps them, I imagine Iris's face when she sees them. Will she understand the significance? Will she recognize herself in their elegant lines?

Back home, I select a crystal vase, tall, slender, with clean lines that complement rather than compete with the flowers. I arrange them myself, refusing the caterer's offer to help. This is personal. This needs to be from me.

I place the vase at the center of the main table, where it can't be missed. The irises stand tall and proud, commanding attention just as she does.

Yes. Perfect. Now everything is perfect.

The doorbell chimes, a crisp, clear note that cuts through the soft jazz filling my home. I straighten my already perfect tie and stride to the door, ready to begin the performance.

William and Claire stand on my doorstep, Claire radiant in a midnight blue dress, William looking sharp in his tailored suit.

"There he is! The man who thinks concrete can float," William laughs, clasping my hand.

"Only when I design it." I pull him in for a brief embrace, then turn to Claire. "You look stunning, as always. William, how do you keep convincing her to stay with you?"

Claire rolls her eyes but smiles. "Someone has to keep him in line."

I usher them inside, pointing toward the bar. "Make yourselves at home."

The doorbell rings again. Ryan stands there, looking more polished than usual, with a willowy blonde on his arm.

"Ryan, good to see you. And who is this vision?" I extend my hand to his date.

"Sebastian, meet Vanessa. Vanessa, the infamous Sebastian Wolfe."

"Infamous? I'm wounded." I smile at her, warm but not too warm. "Pleasure to meet you, Vanessa."

From across the room, William calls out, "Ryan! Get over here and tell me if this scotch is as good as Wolfe claims it is!"

I guide them toward the bar with a few pats on Ryan's shoulder.

The next arrivals are business connections, David Henderson from city planning, Adam Michaels from the investment group, Jacob Peterson from the foundation board. I greet each ensuring they feel both welcomed and important.

"So nice to see each of you," Shaking each hand as they enter. "Please, help yourself to a drink." I say directing them to the bar.

Rebecca and Maria arrive together; both transformed from their office personas. Rebecca in a sleek red dress, Maria in something flowing and emerald.

"Ladies, you're making me reconsider the decor. I should have designed the entire evening around you both." My eyes linger just long enough to be flattering but not inappropriate.

Rebecca laughs. "Save it for someone who hasn't seen you charm city officials out of building codes."

Elizabeth and Alexis follow with their dates, both looking radiant. I compliment them both, careful to include their companions in my welcome.

At the bar, I order a whiskey neat, savoring the momentary quiet as I slide between Ryan and William.

"How's the Peterson project?" William asks, swirling his drink.

Before I can answer, the doorbell rings again. More business associates, the Thompsons, the Harrises, faces I know from boardroom meetings.

Then Jenna appears, transformed from the office chatterbox into something elegant and surprising. Her usual frenetic energy is contained within a silver dress that catches the light.

"Jenna, you look absolutely stunning." My surprise is genuine.

Her cheeks flush. "You think? The makeup artist said this shade might be too bold, but I said sometimes bold is exactly what you need, right? And the traffic was terrible, there was an accident on Fifth, so I had to detour through downtown, which actually worked out because I remembered this shortcut from when I dated that guy who lived near the park..."

I smile, letting her speak to her hearts content.

I peer around, checking to see if Iris came with her, or maybe somewhere to be seen. But no, no sign of Iris.

I return my attention to Jenna, who is still in the middle of her story about the accident on Fifth Avenue and the shortcut she took. I nod and smile at the appropriate moments, guiding her towards the bar as she speaks.

"...so I just knew that this dress would be perfect for tonight," Jenna finishes, her eyes shining with excitement.

"It's stunning on you," I say sincerely, signaling the bartender for a refill on my whiskey. "White wine?" I ask her.

"Oh, yes please! And could I also get a club soda with lime?" she adds, turning to me with an apologetic grin. "I know, boring right? But I'm trying to cut back."

"No judgments here," I assure her as we wait for our drinks. "To moderation." We clink glasses before she downs half of her wine in one gulp.

Rebecca approaches us then, saving me from a night of Jenna's non-stop chattering.

"Jenna! You look gorgeous! Girl, where did you get that dress?" The two of them are soon engrossed in their own conversation about designers and sales, giving me an opportunity to mingle.

I take the moment to slip away from Jenna and Rebecca, spotting Ryan across the room with Henderson and Michaels. They're laughing, drinks in hand, relaxed in a way that only comes after the second or third glass. Perfect. Maybe I can pre-grease the wheels ahead of time with Henderson from city planning and Michaels from the investment group, make the Riverfront project a little easier to get approved.

I approach, catching the tail end of Ryan's story.

"...and Sebastian walks in, looks at the model for maybe thirty seconds, then just picks up a pencil and starts sketching right on top of the blueprints!" Ryan gestures wildly, nearly spilling his drink. "We're all thinking he's lost his mind. Two months of work, and he's scribbling all over it!"

Henderson chuckles, his substantial frame shaking. "Let me guess, it worked?"

"Better than worked," Ryan continues. "He completely flipped the orientation of the central atrium, added these cantilevered walkways that shouldn't have been structurally possible, but were, and suddenly the whole flow made sense. The client went from ready to walk to signing that afternoon."

Michaels raises his glass. "That's why he's our favorite boy."

I step into their circle, clinking my glass against Michaels'. "I haven't been a boy for quite some time, gentlemen. When I started? Sure. Fresh-faced, eager to please. But I've grown up." I turn to Ryan with a smirk. "This one, though, he's the new boy in town. Still gets excited about concrete samples."

Ryan rolls his eyes but grins. "Only the expensive ones."

Henderson claps me on the shoulder, his grip firm. "Grown up or not, you still pull rabbits out of hats, Wolfe. The council's impressed with the preliminary plans for the Riverfront."

"Speaking of which," Michaels leans in, lowering his voice, "we should talk about the funding structure before the next phase."

I laugh, raising my glass toward Michaels. "Gentlemen, tonight is strictly for pleasure, not business. We have enough meetings scheduled to last us through the next quarter."

Michaels' eyes crinkle at the corners as he takes another sip of his scotch. "Well, it certainly pleases me when I'm making money. And your designs, Wolfe... they make me very pleased indeed."

"The highest compliment from a man who measures worth in dollar signs," I reply, clinking my glass against his. Henderson and Ryan chuckle.

"Speaking of pleasure," I say, glancing around the room, noticing a few new arrivals at the door, "I should attend to my other guests. The burden of being a good host."

"Go, go," Henderson waves me off. "We'll be right here bleeding your bar dry."

"Help yourselves," I say, stepping back from their circle. "Ryan, make sure they try that Japanese whiskey in the square bottle. Cost more than your first car."

Ryan's eyes widen slightly. "The Yamazaki?"

I nod, already turning away. "Consider it market research for our Tokyo project."

As I move through the crowd, I scan each new face, searching for the one that matters most. Still no sign of Iris.

I glide through the crowd, scanning faces for Iris. A sharp knock at the door draws my attention, must be the valet letting me know more guests have arrived. I check my watch: 8:17PM. She should be here by now.

Opening the door, I find Gerald Harrington and Thomas Webber, two senior board members from Wolfe & Hart, accompanied by their wives. Gerald's silver hair is perfectly coiffed as always, his wife Diane resplendent in pearls and navy silk. Thomas stands with his usual military posture, Patricia on his arm in a conservative black dress that probably cost more than most people's monthly salary.

"Sebastian," Gerald extends his hand, his grip firm but not challenging. "Magnificent to see you boy."

"Gerald, Diane," I nod to each in turn. "Thomas, Patricia. I'm delighted you could make it."

"Wouldn't miss it," Thomas says, his voice carrying the clipped precision of his former military career. "The firm's been buzzing about your Riverfront presentation all week."

I usher them inside, taking Diane's wrap and Patricia's light coat. "I hope we can avoid shop talk for at least the first hour. The bar is fully stocked, and I have that Bordeaux you enjoyed at the Christmas party, Thomas."

Patricia's eyes sweep the room with the practiced assessment of someone who has spent decades judging other people's homes. "You've outdone yourself, Sebastian. Particularly those." She nods toward the irises.

"Thank you," I say, not elaborating on their significance. "Thomas, I believe William was just saying something about drinking you under the table or something. I also believe he said something about Marines eating crayons, but I can't be certain." His face turns to a determined scowl. I point over to the side wall showing him where to locate his target. "He's by the fireplace."

"William, what is this I hear you saying?" He booms, his voice barely fading as he gets further away.

I laugh heartily, watching William's face contort in confusion and maybe a little fear.

I linger by the door for a moment longer, eyes fixed on the entrance, checking my watch, 8:47PM. Where is she? Did something happen? Or worse, did she change her mind?

I take a deep breath, to steady myself, forcing my hand to close the and return to my guests, to put on the display of the perfect host even though my mind remains fixed on the door and who isn't walking through it.

I move back through the crowd, nodding and smiling at conversations that drift past me.

At the bar, I signal for another whiskey. I take the glass, feeling its weight, the cool crystal against my fingertips.

"Sebastian!" William calls from across the room. "Come settle this debate about the Richardson project!"

I raise my glass in acknowledgment but don't move. Just one moment of quiet. One moment to recalibrate.

I bring the glass to my lips, ready to take that first sip when it hits me, sweet honey and something deeper, something primal. That scent. Her scent.

I freeze, the rim of the glass barely touching my mouth. My nostrils flare slightly, drawing in more of that intoxicating aroma. It fills my lungs, spreads through my chest, awakening that hunger that has been lying in waiting.

The room seems to narrow, conversations fading into a distant background noise. I lower my glass slowly, not trusting my suddenly unsteady hand. The scent grows stronger, more insistent.

I turn, scanning the crowd with new intensity. Where is she? The scent is unmistakable, I've memorized it from those brief elevator moments, cataloged it among my most precious sensory experiences.

She's here. Somewhere in my home, Iris is here.

The scent intensifies, that strong scent of honey that fills my lungs and ignites a fire in my veins. Where is she?

I move through the crowd, weaving between clusters of guests with practiced grace, all while straining my senses for another trace of that intoxicating aroma. It's everywhere and nowhere at once, teasing me with its presence without revealing its source.

I pause near the windows, scanning the faces reflected in the glass - no Iris. A glance toward the balcony shows only shadowed silhouettes against the city lights below - not her either.

Panic begins to creep under my carefully maintained veneer of calm as I turn back to face the room. She has to be here. That scent - it's unmistakable, seared into my memory from those fleeting elevator encounters. But now it seems to have vanished like a ghost.

I make another pass through the crowd, this time pausing by each woman I pass to breathe in subtly, hoping to catch her unique fragrance again. But everyone smells different - perfume layered over soap over sweat over... but never her.

A bead of sweat trickles down my spine beneath my crisp shirt as I force myself not to rush, not to look too eager or desperate as I hunt for Iris among these people who are meant to be here celebrating *my* achievement.

Where is she? Has she decided not to come after all? The thought claws at me with razor-sharp talons. No, no - she'd never do that without warning me first. We had an arrangement...

But where?

Another circuit through the partygoers yields nothing but increasingly worried looks from William and Ryan across the room as they try to get my attention with drinks and conversation starters that fall flat on their way to me through the air.

I scan the room once more, desperately seeking that flash of her smile, the silhouette I've memorized from our elevator rides. Nothing. My pulse quickens, and a cold sweat breaks across my forehead.

Is this happening again? Like last night with Melissa, when I swore I saw Iris's face instead of hers? When my mind played tricks on me, transforming another woman into the object of my fixation?

I take another large gulp of whiskey, taking it all down in one gulp, the liquid burning down my throat. The room suddenly feels too warm, too crowded. Faces blur together, smiling, laughing, talking, but none of them hers.

What if I imagined her scent? What if my obsession has reached the point where I'm manufacturing her presence out of thin air?

William catches my eye from across the room, his brow furrowed with concern. Ryan stands beside him, mid-conversation but watching me with equal parts curiosity and worry.

I raise my glass in acknowledgment, forcing a smile that doesn't reach my eyes. "Gentlemen, excuse me for a moment," I call out, my voice steadier than I feel. "I'll be right back."

I set my glass down on a nearby table and make my way toward the hallway, forcing myself to maintain my composure until I'm out of sight.

Once around the corner, I quicken my pace to the bathroom, shutting the door behind me, and locking it.

The silence is immediate and welcoming, the cold of the room soothing my hot skin. I grip the edges of the marble sink, staring at my reflection in the mirror.

My eyes look like I haven't slept in a week. I barely recognize myself.

"Get it together," I mutter, turning on the cold water. I splash my face once, twice, three times, letting the shock of it pull me back to reality. Water drips from my chin onto my shirt collar.

I breathe deeply, counting each inhale and exhale. One. Two. Three. Four.

She's not here. She was never here. It was just my mind playing tricks on me, just like with Melissa.

More than worrying about her not coming, I'm worried I'm losing control, and that thought terrifies me more than anything else.

I need to just forget it, forget her.

I need to focus on my guests and the party.

I splash my face with water again, the coldness stinging my skin and helping to clear my mind. I grab a towel from the rack, dabbing it against my face and neck before crumpling it in my fist. Taking a deep breath, I force out my anxiety with the exhale.

I straighten my shirt and smooth back my hair in the mirror.

I grip the doorknob, unlocking it, then taking another breath, steeling myself and exiting the bathroom, walking down the hallway, determined to rejoin my guests and forget about Iris.

As I pass by my study, something catches my eye. The door is cracked open ever so slightly. Forcing me to stop in my tracks. I'm certain I had closed it earlier and locked the door.

Heart pounding in my chest, I approach the door cautiously, as if it were a live wire that might shock me if touched incorrectly. My study is supposed to be a sanctuary, my own personal Fort Knox where no one but me is allowed entry without express permission. The idea that someone might have been rifling through my things sends a shiver of unease down my spine.

I reach out with trembling fingers to push the door open...

CHAPTER 15

I push the door open wider, and my breath catches in my throat.

Iris.

She's here. In my study.

The soft glow of my wall lamp catches in her hair, creating a halo effect that makes her look almost ethereal. She's wearing a low-cut black top, her mid drift slightly exposed, a black skirt cut just above the knee. It clings to her body in a way that makes my mouth go dry.

Her fingers trail lightly over the framed blueprint on the wall. My blueprint.

Or rather, H.H. Holmes' blueprint.

For a moment, I wonder if I'm hallucinating again. If my obsession has finally manifested itself into a full-blown delusion. But the scent, honey and something deeper, is unmistakable. Too real to be imagined.

My hands clench at my sides, unable to determine if its unease or desire that's washing over me. This is my private space. My sanctuary. No one enters without my permission. Yet here she is, making herself at home as if she belongs here.

"Hello, Sebastian," she says without turning around, her voice like warm honey, seductive and sweet. The sound of it sends a jolt through my system, confirming what I already know, this is real. She's real.

I stand frozen in the doorway, unable to move forward or retreat. My carefully constructed composure crumbles like sand between my fingers.

"How did you..." The words die in my throat. I clear it and try again. "I didn't see you arrive."

She still hasn't turned to face me.

As her fingers continue to trace the lines on the blueprint, she tilts her head as she studies it reminding me of an artist examining another's brushstrokes, looking beyond the lines, searching for the mind behind the design.

She doesn't turn back as I approach. She lingers.

I watch her as I approach, studying her. Waiting until I'm just a few feet away before speaking again. "Find something interesting?" I ask.

Iris doesn't startle by my close presence. She doesn't glance at me right away. Instead, she runs a slow fingertip across one last architectural line before finally looking over her shoulder.

A smirk tugs at the corner of her lips. "Your taste is... unexpected."

She turns fully now, facing me.

I take a step forward, slow, deliberate.

"I like to collect unique pieces," I say smoothly, keeping my voice even.

She studies me, then the blueprint again. "Unique is one word for it."

Her fingers skim lower, trailing toward the bottom of the frame. Toward the name.

She sees it. I can tell the moment she does.

H.H. Holmes.

The flicker of recognition is small, most people wouldn't notice.

But I do.

She knows.

I keep my expression neutral, my pulse steady. I watch for any shift in her demeanor, discomfort, unease, curiosity.

But there's none of that.

Instead, her lips part slightly, as if she's tasting the weight of the knowledge.

"Chicago," she muses, thoughtful. "The World's Fair. The infamous 'Murder Castle.'"

She tilts her head slightly, slow, deliberate. "Interesting choice."

There is a moment of pause, as if she's measuring the silence between us.

Then I chuckle lightly, stepping closer to the blueprint. Not too close, but just enough to make my presence more dominant.

"An architectural marvel," I say, keeping my voice casual. "Innovative for its time... It had an unconventional layout. Hidden passages. It's a truly remarkable study in design."

Iris's gaze flickers to mine, holding long enough to show a spark of amusement behind her dark eyes.

"Of course," she murmurs, nodding slowly. "Purely, architectural."

The way she says it... it's teasing. Playful.

But not mocking.

She isn't uncomfortable. She isn't backing away.

She's intrigued, genuinely intrigued, in me, or the blueprint.

And then she moves.

Not toward the door. Not away from me.

Toward the blueprint. Towards me. Closer.

Her image reflects back from against the glass, mingling with the structure itself.

She leans in slightly, close enough that if I moved, just a fraction, the space between us would shift into something more.

I consider it. Just for a moment.

Mirroring her. Closing the gap between us.

But I don't.

I remain composed. Still. In control.

I let her come to me.

The tension is not in words but in placement, in the deliberate nature of the moment.

She exhales softly, then steps back.

"Well," she says, her voice smooth as she turns away from the blue-print. "I'll let you get back to your party."

She holds my gaze for a breath, staring into my eyes, almost like playing a game of chicken. Then she breaks eye contact, walking past me, out of the study, leaving behind only the faint scent of honey.

I remain in the study for a moment longer, staring at the closed door she left behind.

She didn't startle.

She didn't reject me.

She didn't ask why I had the blueprint, why I kept it in my private space, why a respected architect would display the plans for a building designed for death.

She had looked at it, at me, and smiled. She saw me and didn't run away.

She just played along.

Most people, if they were to recognize what she was looking at, would have laughed nervously, changed the subject, maybe even excused themselves altogether. But not Iris.

She lingered here.

Iris leaned in, her reflection merging with the glass. Almost enough to feel.

For a moment, it almost felt like it may have been an invitation.

I exhale slowly, forcing myself to move, to let go of the moment, to shake the way it coils around me. As I step away from the blueprint, the scent of her presence remains, like a haunting ghost.

I open the door to the study, taking one last moment to absorb this memory of Iris, then step out, closing the door behind me.

I rejoin the party, following a ways behind Iris. Everyone in the room seems to be unable to look away from her, even those with their spouses present.

It's like she's a magnetic force and there's nothing any of them can do to look away.

The sudden silence she's created with her presence is quickly broken as Jenna sees Iris walking into the room.

I watch as Iris makes her way through the crowd, drawing attention like a comet with its own gravitational pull.

I see Jenna spot Iris from across the room as her face lights up like a child on Christmas morning.

"IRIS!" Jenna squeals, loud enough to turn a few heads.

Before Iris can respond, Jenna darts through the crowd, grabbing Iris by the arm, dragging her towards the bar.

Iris turns back, giving me one last glance, her face alight with a genuine smile. But maybe just a hint of a plea for help in her eyes before she looks away.

"My elevator bestie!" Jenna announces to anyone within earshot. "What are you drinking? Sebastian has everything. And I mean every-thing."

Iris laughs, a sound I've rarely heard, and it hits me like a physical force. Her shoulders relax as Jenna continues chattering, pulling bottles from behind the bar like a kid in a candy store.

"Sebastian."

I turn to find Ryan and William flanking me, both nursing drinks, both staring in the same direction I was.

"Quite the turnout," William says, though his eyes never leave Iris. "That's a smoking hot fox you've got over there. Where'd you find her?"

I feel my jaw tighten. Even though William is married, his words still grate my nerves, my possessive jealousy wining over.

"She works in our building," I say flatly.

Ryan nudges me with his elbow, a knowing smirk on his face. "Is she the reason you've been so distracted lately?"

Ryan lets out a quiet exhaling whistle.

I maintain my composure, though something cold slithers through my chest.

"We're acquaintances," I say carefully.

Both men continue to stare at Iris, who's now the center of my attention.

I watch her from across the room, unable to look away. Iris is... perfection. She's always been beautiful, but tonight, she's exceptional. Her thick curves, usually hinted at beneath her work attire, are now on display, hugged by the fabric of her skirt. Her calves, muscular and toned, are exposed, a sight I've never seen before. They flex as she shifts her weight, and I can't help but imagine how they'd feel under my hands.

Her top, low cut and black, showcases her chest, leaving just enough to the imagination to make my mouth water. And her midriff, sexy and exposed, showing off just a sliver of skin that makes my pulse quicken. It's not vulgar, not too much. It's just enough to leave you wanting more. To leave me wanting more.

She laughs at something Jenna says, her head tilting back slightly, exposing the elegant line of her throat. I want to trace that line with my fingers, with my lips. I want to feel the vibration of her laughter against my skin.

I take a sip of my drink, trying to distract myself, but my eyes never leave her. I can't look away. I don't want to. She's captivating, enchanting. She's everything I've ever wanted, everything I've ever desired. And she's right here, in my home, at my party.

But she's not mine. Not yet.

I watch as she moves, her body fluid and graceful. She's not self-conscious, not trying to impress. She's just... Iris. Unapologetic, unreadable, exceptional.

I want her. I want her more than I've ever wanted anything in my life. And I always get what I want.

But Iris... she's different. She's not like the others. She's not a game, not a conquest. She's a challenge, a mystery. And I love a good mystery.

I take another sip of my drink, my eyes still on her. I can feel the hunger growing inside me, the need to possess her, to make her mine. But I push it down, control it. I can't rush this, can't force it. I have to be patient, have to be smart.

And I will be. Because Iris Klarelle is worth the wait. She's worth the chase.

She's worth everything.

I inhale deeply, drawing in her scent, letting it envelop me, distracting me from everything else around me.

An elbow nudging me repeatedly pulls me from my trance. I look to my side noticing William and Ryan's eyes locked onto Iris like moths drawn to a flame.

"Introduce us," Ryan murmurs, his voice barely audible over the hum of the party.

I brush him off, but I'm met with another nudge, this time from William. "Yeah, introduce us Sebastian."

I huff a sigh, knowing they aren't going to let this go, stepping forward, I close the distance between us and Iris.

She turns, her eyes meeting mine, and a smile plays at the corners of her lips. It's not the warm, inviting smile she gave Jenna. It's something else, the kind you give to your opponent during chess when you have checkmate in two moves.

"Iris," I say, my voice steady despite the storm raging inside me. "I'd like you to meet Ryan Adams and William Freed. They're architects at my firm."

Iris extends a hand, first to Ryan, then to William. Her grip is firm, confident. "A pleasure to meet you both," she says, her voice smooth as velvet.

William clears his throat, his eyes never leaving Iris. "So, Iris, what do you do?"

She tilts her head slightly, a small smirk playing on her lips. "I'm in charge of PR," she says, her tone playful yet assertive.

Jenna, who's been hovering nearby, jumps in, her voice loud and eager. "I bet you are amazing at that job! She's so good with people. And I bet you can charm anyone, seriously..."

Jenna's voice fades into the background. I barely register her words, my focus entirely on Iris. Her presence commands the space, drawing us in like gravity. Ryan and William are transfixed, their eyes following her every movement.

Iris handles Jenna's interruption with grace, her smile never wavering. She doesn't try to steer the conversation back to herself or cut Jenna off. Instead, she lets Jenna ramble, her gaze flicking between the three of us, amusement sparkling in her eyes.

She knows the power she holds. She knows we're hanging on her every word, every gesture. And she revels in it, playing us like a virtuoso plays an instrument.

The tension builds, the air thick with unspoken desire and competition. But Iris remains unruffled, her composure unbreakable. She's not a prize to be won, not a trophy to be claimed. She's a queen, and we're her subjects, vying for her attention, her favor.

And I'm the fool who believes he can win her, who believes she's playing his game. But is she? Or is she playing her own game, by her own rules? And I'm just a piece on her board?

The air crackles with tension, a silent battle waging between Ryan, William, and me. Iris standing at the center, her smile enigmatic, her eyes reflecting the dance of candlelight. She's unfazed by the undercurrents, a queen holding court amidst her subjects.

"Sebastian, who is this charming creature?" A voice cuts through the tension, sharp and possessive. Claire, William's wife, loops her arm through his, staking her claim. Her eyes, cold and assessing, flick over Iris.

Iris doesn't flinch under the scrutiny. Instead, she turns to Claire, her smile warm and genuine. "Iris Klarelle," she introduces herself, extending a hand. "A pleasure to meet you."

Claire takes her hand, her grip tight, her smile brittle. "Claire Freed. I see you've met my husband."

Iris's laughter is soft, melodic. "Guilty as charged. He was just telling me about your recent trip to Italy. It sounds divine."

Claire's expression softens, surprised. "It was. William, darling, you didn't tell me you were sharing our travel stories."

William shrugs, a faint blush creeping up his neck. "You know how these things go, dear. Small talk."

Ryan's date, the petite blonde with too much makeup and too little dress, chooses that moment to chime in. "And who might you be?" she asks, her voice a high-pitched giggle as she clings to Ryan's arm.

Iris turns to her, her smile unwavering. "Iris. And you are?"

"Chelsea," she replies, extending a limp hand. Iris takes it, her grip firm but gentle.

"A pleasure, Chelsea. Ryan, she's lovely." Iris's compliment is smooth, effortless, but there's a hint of amusement in her eyes, a spark that tells me she sees right through Chelsea's facade.

Chelsea preens under the praise, giggling again. "Thank you. Ryan and I have been dating for a few weeks now." She leans into him, her message clear. He's taken.

Iris nods, her expression neutral. "How wonderful to meet you both." Her eyes flick to mine, a brief, barely-there glance that I don't quite understand. Is she telling them I'm hers, or is this some other game?

Claire watches the exchange, her eyes narrowing. "And how do you know Sebastian, Iris?"

Iris's smile widens, her eyes dancing with mischief. "Oh, we're just elevator buddies. Isn't that right, Sebastian?"

I nod, my mouth dry. "Yes, that's right."

Claire's eyebrows arch, disbelief clear on her face. "Elevator buddies? How quaint."

Iris laughs. "Well, it's been a pleasure meeting you both. If you'll excuse me, I think I'll mingle a bit more." She says raising her martini glass in a toasting salute.

She steps away, leaving each of us staring after her as we watch her go.

Claire's eyes narrow as she watches Iris walk away. "I don't like her," she declares, her voice sharp enough to cut glass.

Chelsea nods in agreement, her lips pursed in a disapproving pout. "Me neither. There's something... off about her."

Jenna, who's been quietly sipping her drink, suddenly chimes in. "I like her. She's nice. Maybe you guys just feel threatened."

Mid swallow, I choke on my whiskey, some of it reaching my nostrils as I try not to laugh at Jenna's retort. The burn in my sinuses makes my eyes water and I struggle not to laugh. Jenna's not wrong, there's an edge to Claire and Chelsea's dislike that reeks of jealousy.

Claire scoffs, her gaze flicking back to me. "Threatened? Please. She's just... too much. Too confident, too forward."

Chelsea nods again, eager to agree. "Exactly. She's probably one of those girls who thinks she's better than everyone else."

Jenna rolls her eyes, her voice taking on a sarcastic edge. "Right, because God forbid a woman be confident and friendly. How dare she not be a wallflower?"

I cough again, trying to clear my throat and regain my composure. Jenna's bluntness is refreshing, a stark contrast to the veiled barbs Claire and Chelsea are throwing.

Claire's expression sours, her lips pressing into a thin line. "You wouldn't understand, Jenna. You're too... different."

Jenna just smiles, seemingly unfazed by the insult. "Different is good, Claire. Boring is bad." She takes a sip of her drink, her eyes meeting mine over the rim of her glass. There's a spark of amusement in them, a silent laughter that we share.

I raise my glass to her, a small smirk playing on my lips. Jenna might be socially awkward, but she's perceptive. She can clearly see the jealousy written all over Claire and Chelsea's face. And she's not afraid to call them out on it.

I step away from the group, my gaze lingering on Iris for a moment longer before I turn to Jenna. "Can I speak to you for a moment?"

Jenna looks at me, her eyes wide with surprise, but she nods, following me to the other side of the room. The noise of the party dissipates as we step away, the clinking of glasses and the murmur of conversation blending into a single, indistinct sound.

I turn to face Jenna, my expression serious. "I wanted to thank you, Jenna. Really."

She blinks, taken aback. "For what?"

"For helping me with Iris. If it wasn't for you, I don't think she would have come tonight."

Jenna's face breaks into a wide, genuine smile. "Of course she would have. She was just playing the long game, making you work for it." She nudges me playfully with her elbow. "You know how it is. Some people just like the chase."

I let out a soft laugh, shaking my head. "Maybe you're right. But still, I appreciate it. You've been a great help and you're a great friend."

Jenna's smile softens, her eyes shining with unshed tears. "That means a lot, Sebastian. Really."

I give her an honest smile, a rare gesture of genuine gratitude. Then, without a second thought, I pull her into a hug. Jenna stiffens for a moment, surprised, before melting into the embrace. She wraps her arms around me, squeezing tightly.

"Thank you, Jenna," I murmur, my voice barely audible over the rest of the party.

As we pull away, Jenna's face is flushed, her eyes bright. "Anytime, Sebastian. Really." She gives me a small, grateful smile, her hands still resting on my arms. "I'm always here to help."

I stride to the bar, signaling the bartender for another whiskey. "No, not that one, The Dalmore, the 45 year please." The copper like liquid sloshes into the glass, reflecting the dim lights overhead. I take a sip, relishing the taste of such an amazing, but also quite expensive single malt.

I turn, facing the crowd. With a flick of my wrist, I clink the spoon against the crystal, the sharp ring cutting through the chatter. Heads turn, eyes landing on me, a sea of expectant faces.

"I must say," I begin, a smirk playing on my lips, "when I envisioned this party, I didn't expect to see so many of you here. I thought I was more... tolerated than liked." A chuckle ripples through the crowd, the tension breaking. "But it seems I underestimated my charm."

The laughter grows, a warm, collective sound that fills the room.

"In all seriousness," I continue, my voice steadying, "I want to thank each of you for being here tonight. You're not just colleagues or ac-quaintances. You're the people who make my life... something special." I pause, my gaze sweeping over the crowd. "You challenge me, inspire me, and sometimes," I chuckle, "drive me to the brink of insanity. But I wouldn't have it any other way."

I raise my glass, a silent salute. "To each of you. Thank you for the part you play in my life." The room echoes with the clink of glasses, a chorus of cheers.

But as the noise swells, my eyes search the crowd, landing on the one person who makes me feel anything but balanced. Iris stands at the edge of the group, her glass raised, her eyes locked onto mine. There's a hint of a smile on her lips, that sharp curve that sends a shiver down my spine.

It's a game now, a dance of gazes, a conversation without words. She sips her drink, her lips curving into a soft smile, a challenge. I lean against the bar, my own glass in hand, my eyes never leaving hers.

We're speaking volumes in this silence. Questions, answers, dares. She tilts her head, a small gesture, but it's a taunt. A tease. A promise. I raise my eyebrow, a silent acceptance of her challenge. She laughs, a soft, melodic sound that cuts through the haze of the party.

But the game is interrupted as guests begin to approach, their voices cutting through our silent conversation.

"Sebastian, thank you for a wonderful evening." A hand clasps my shoulder; a voice murmurs in my ear. I turn, my smile automatic, my eyes never truly leaving Iris.

"A pleasure, thank you for coming." I shake hands, accept hugs, kisses on the cheek. The crowd thins, the room empties, but she remains.

The goodbyes continue, a steady stream of thanks and see you soon. I nod, I smile, I play the gracious host. But my focus is elsewhere.

And then, there's just three of us. Iris, Jenna, and me.

Jenna looks around, her eyes widening as she realizes she's the last guest remaining. She turns to me, her face breaking into a wide grin.

"Sebastian, this was amazing. Really. Thank you so much." She pulls me into a tight hug, her body warm and inviting. I hug her back, my eyes meeting Iris's over Jenna's shoulder.

Jenna pulls away, her hands still on my arms. She winks, a small, conspiratorial gesture. "Good luck," she whispers, her voice barely audible. And then, she's gone, the door clicking shut behind her.

And it's just us. Iris and me.

I approach Iris, my heart pounding in my chest like a drumbeat. She watches me, her eyes reflecting the soft glow of the dimmed lights. I stop a few feet away, close enough to be fully immersed in that honey that's uniquely hers.

"So, Iris," I begin, my voice steady despite the storm inside me. "How did you find the evening?"

She tilts her head, a small smile playing on her lips. "I quite enjoyed it, Sebastian. Your parties are as impressive as your designs."

I chuckle, taking a step closer. "Well, I'm glad you approve. I must admit, though, I've been waiting all night to talk to you."

Her eyebrow arches, a playful challenge. "Is that so? And why is that?"

I mirror her expression, a smirk tugging at my lips. "Because you're the most interesting person here. And I think you know that."

She laughs, a soft, airy sound. "Do I? Or are you just trying to flatter me?"

I shake my head, my eyes locked onto hers. "I don't flatter, Iris. I state facts."

She holds my gaze for a moment, her expression unreadable. Then, she breaks the connection, glancing at her watch. "Well, as much as I'd love to stay, I should get going. Busy day tomorrow."

I nod, trying to hide my disappointment. "Are you sure you won't join me for another drink before you go?"

She shakes her head, her smile softening. "No, thank you. I really should be going."

I take a deep breath, my heart pounding in my chest. "Iris," I say, my voice low. "Would you like to have dinner with me tomorrow? Or maybe just a drink?"

She looks at me, her eyes searching mine. For a moment, I think she's going to say no. But then, she smiles, a slow, full smile formed with her full red lips. "Ask me tomorrow, Sebastian. Maybe I'll say yes."

And with that, she turns and walks away, her heels clicking on the hardwood floor. I watch her go, my heart throbbing, my mind racing. She reaches the door, her hand on the knob. She looks back at me, one last smile, one move.

"Goodnight, Sebastian," she says, her voice soft.

"Goodnight, Iris," I reply, my voice barely audible.

And then, she's gone, the door clicking shut behind her. But even her closing that door behind her, I get the feeling that she's left a door open. A chance. A possibility. And I'm determined to take full advantage of it.

CHAPTER 16

I wake to the familiar filtered noise of the city, the sun casting sharp shadows through the blinds. My routine is normally exact, each step a dance of precision. But today, I linger. Today, I take my time. I trim my beard, the clippers buzzing like a hive of bees. I adjust my tie, the silk cool against my fingers. I brew my coffee, the aroma rich and dark. All the while, her words echo in my mind. *Ask me tomorrow, Sebastian.*

The elevator doors slide open, and I step inside. The scent hits me first, a warmth that fills the small space. Iris stands closer today, her shoulder almost brushing mine. I can see the faint pulse at the base of her neck, the soft rhythm a silent invitation. I grip the railing behind me, the metal cool and grounding. My hunger stirs, a beast roused from sleep, but I hold it back. I leash it, for now.

The floors tick by, each one testing my resolve. I can feel her eyes on me, a gentle gaze that lingers just a moment too long. I want to reach out, to trace the line of her jaw, to feel the perfection that is her skin. But I don't. I stand still, my body tense, my heart pounding.

Ding!

The elevator pauses, the doors opening.

Her floor.

She steps out, her heels clicking on the tiles. I open my mouth to speak, but she's already gone, swallowed by the conversations of the office. The doors close, and I'm left alone the scent of her lingering like a promise.

I curse under my breath, the word sharp and bitter. I'll have to catch her this evening. This game we're playing, it's not over. It's only just begun.

The elevator doors close, sealing me in with the echo of her scent. I press the button for my floor, the whir of the machine a dull drone in the silence. The numbers tick upward, each one a step closer to the controlled chaos of my day.

The doors open to the familiar space of my firm. Alexis looks up from her desk, her eyes bright. "Morning, Sebastian. Great party last night."

William echoes her sentiment from his doorway, "Yes, quite the soirée. Claire couldn't stop talking about it."

I nod, an acknowledgment that's more automatic than genuine. "Glad you both enjoyed it."

Ryan strolls by, his usually sharp demeanor slightly rumpled. He offers a half-smile, "Morning, Sebastian. Quite the night, huh?" His eyes are a little too bright, his movements a touch too careful.

"Indeed," I reply, my voice clipped. I don't have time for small talk, not with the hours ticking away, each one bringing me closer to her.

I sink into my chair, the leather cool against my back. Work is a welcome distraction, a way to keep my mind occupied until the elevator ride. I hammer away at emails, review blueprints, and approve designs. The clock ticks steadily, each second a heartbeat counting down to her.

The morning bleeds into afternoon. I barely notice the comings and goings around me, the conversations, the ringing of phones. My focus is singular, my patience wearing thin. I check my watch, the hands moving too slowly.

Finally, the hour arrives. I save my work, close my laptop, and stand. My heart thumps in my chest, a steady drumbeat of anticipation. I straighten my tie and step out of my office.

The elevator waits, its doors opening like an invitation. I step inside alone, feeling the walls close in as the doors close behind me.

I press the button for her floor, the numbers lighting up one by one. The descent begins, each floor a step closer to her, to the moment I've been waiting for.

The doors open, and there she is, standing with her back to me, her hair a cascade of dark curls down her back. She turns, her eyes meeting mine.

She steps in, turning towards the door, standing there, just waiting.

The elevator hums, descending with a smoothness that belies the chaos inside me. Iris stands close, her scent filling the air, a sweetness that's both intoxicating and maddening. I can't take it anymore. I need to know. I need to ask.

"Iris." Her name escapes my lips; a secret whispered into her ear. She turns, her eyes meeting mine, a soft smile playing on her lips.

"Yes, Sebastian?" Her voice is a melody, a sweet siren's song that only I can hear.

"Would you like to have dinner with me tonight? Or perhaps a drink?" The words hang in the air, a question that feels heavier than they ever have.

She looks at me, her eyes unreadable. Then, she smiles, a slow, teasing curve of her lips. "Not tonight, Sebastian."

The words hit me like a punch to the gut. I struggle to keep my composure, to keep the frustration from showing on my face.

I open my mouth to ask why, to demand an explanation. But before I can form the words, she speaks again.

"I'm performing tonight, Sebastian. Singing. And I'd like you to come." Her eyes sparkle with an invitation that's hard to resist. "There will be food and drinks. You can wait for me, and we can share that drink after my performance."

"Ok." I reply, just the words, Ok.

She looks at me for a moment, possibly understanding I'm still a little confused. "Meet me at The Symphony Club downtown, I start at 8 o'clock, so arrive early."

When the doors finally open to the lobby, I gesture for her to exit first. "Ladies first."

"Such a gentleman," she teases, her eyes sparkling with mischief.

"So, I'll see you at eight?" I ask, already knowing the answer, but making sure what I know is real.

"I'll see you at eight," She replies, giving me a wink, "don't be late."

I watch her walk away, the gentle sway of her hips like a metronome measuring the seconds of my anticipation. The lobby's harsh fluorescent light catches in her dark hair, transforming ordinary space into something transcendent. People move around her, faceless suits with mundane concerns, but she parts them like water, unaware or perhaps uncaring of how they turn to look.

A cabaret singer. I roll the thought around in my mind, examining it from all angles. It fits her in ways I hadn't considered before. I've watched her enter the Westbrook Music Academy every Wednesday at 6:15, violin case in hand, even seen her attend her music lessons. I've heard her hum to herself in the elevator when she thinks no one is listening. But cabaret, that suggests something more complex, more seductive than just singing. The realization slides into place with satisfying precision. Of course, she would be drawn to cabaret, that delicious blend of vulnerability and control, of artifice and raw emotion. The stage allows for both exposure and concealment. You reveal only what you choose to reveal.

I exit the building and slide into my car, already mentally cataloging what I'll wear tonight. The Symphony Club is like old San Francisco, dark wood, brass fixtures, and cocktails that haven't changed since prohibition. It demands respect.

At home, I take my time. Shower first, water as hot as I can stand it. I select my navy Tom Ford suit, not the charcoal gray I wear for clients, too formal; not the black, too severe. The navy suggests appreciation without desperation. I pair it with a crisp white shirt, a well-chosen silk tie. The top button undone.

The Cologne is critical, Creed Aventus, applied sparingly to pulse points. Enough to be noticed only when I'm close enough to touch. I check my watch: 7:30. Time to leave, allowing for traffic and finding the perfect seat, close enough to see every expression across her face, but not so close that she feels my observation.

I straighten my cuffs; I notice my hands are steady. Good. Tonight is important, another piece of Iris revealed, another layer of understanding between us. I need to see her in this new context, to add it to my collection of observations.

The Symphony Club emerges from the night like a well-preserved secret, a dark brick facade softened by warm light spilling from lead-paned windows. I park my car and walk towards the entrance, the polished wooden door gleaming under the antique brass lamp above it. The doorman nods discreetly as I approach, his eyes flickering over me before opening the door with a small bow.

Inside, the club is everything I remember and more. Dark wood paneling lines the walls, punctuated by floor lamps that cast pools of warm light. The air vibrates with conversation and laughter, but there's a hush that speaks to respect for tradition. A maître d' in impeccable black tie greets me.

"Name please?" He kindly request.

"Sebastian Wolfe," I reply.

The maître d' looks down a moment, his finger tracking the line of names, "Yes, Mr. Wolfe, right this way please."

He leads me through the dining area, a space that seems frozen in time with its crisp tablecloths and heavy silverware, towards the stage. The tables around me are filled a considerable number of men from local politics and corporations, men in tailored suits paired with women whose designer dresses shimmer in the dim light.

My escort stops at a table centered near the front of the stage and pulls out my chair. "Your table, sir." He hands me a menu and bows slightly before turning to greet another guest.

I take in my surroundings while pretending to study the menu. The room seems packed, much busier than I would have anticipated a place like this to be. I didn't realize Cabaret had revived such popularity. In front of me stands an elevated stage framed by heavy velvet curtains in burgundy red.

The lights dim subtly, signaling the start of the show. Conversations fade as everyone's attention shifts towards the stage. I set down my menu and straighten in my seat.

A figure emerges from between the curtains, a slender silhouette outlined by spotlights that cast shadows deep enough to obscure details but not quite enough to conceal identity entirely.

The orchestra begins its warm-up notes, a violin quietly playing smooth practice notes, a large base beside it.

The slender woman on stage welcomes everyone with a warm, inviting smile that spreads across her face like the lights above her. Her voice is smooth, practiced, and full of the confidence that only comes from countless nights in front of expectant audiences.

"Good evening, ladies and gentlemen," she begins. "Welcome to The Symphony Club. Please enjoy our fine orchestra, your exquisite meals, and the finest drinks."

The crowd responds with polite applause and murmurs of appreciation.

"And I know you're all excited to hear the enchanting voice of Iris tonight," she continues, a knowing smile curling her lips.

At the mention of Iris's name, the room erupts into cheers and whistles. It reminds me of that old cartoon, the one with the wolf whistling and losing his mind every time a beautiful woman appeared on stage.

I can almost feel my own control slipping, the anticipation clawing at me from within.

A server approaches my table, setting down a plate in front of me. Prime rib, medium rare, garlic mashed potatoes, roasted carrots, each element meticulously arranged.

"I didn't order this," I remark, looking up at the server.

"Mr. Wolfe," he says with a slight bow. "The meal was picked and prepared especially for you."

The server begins pouring wine into my glass, a deep red that catches the low light perfectly. He finishes with a flourish and steps back.

I lift the glass to my nose first, inhaling deeply. Notes of pepper, berries, tobacco, and smoke fill my senses. It's a Syrah, a full-bodied wine chosen for its complexity and richness. I take a sip, savoring how it pairs with the flavors in front of me.

"An excellent year," I murmur to myself as I take another sip.

The orchestra begins their first piece, a haunting melody that sets the mood for the evening. I glance around the room, seeing other patrons equally engrossed in their meals or conversations. But my mind is on Iris...wondering how she'll look under those spotlights when she finally takes the stage.

As I cut into the prime rib, the tender meat practically melts under my knife. The first bite is exquisite, the flavors perfectly balanced by the garlic mashed potatoes and roasted carrots. Each element seems to heighten my anticipation further.

Tonight is going to be memorable, one way or another.

The orchestra shifts, the final notes of the previous melody fading into expectant silence. A single spotlight flickers on, catching the silhouette of a woman as she steps onto the stage. The room stills. The anticipation is palpable, a collective inhale held tight in every chest.

Iris.

She doesn't rush. Her presence commands attention without asking for it. The deep burgundy of her gown clings to her frame, the shimmering fabric reflecting the light.

She reaches the microphone, fingers trailing along the metal stand in a slow, absent caress. Her gaze sweeps the room, not searching, but claiming.

Then, she sings.

"Come closer love, don't be afraid...

You've already lost the game you played..."

Her voice is low, smooth, each note sliding like silk through the air. The melody winds through the club, slow and deliberate, curling around the audience like invisible hands. I feel like she's looking at me as her finger curves in a come-hither gesture.

"Didn't you know? Didn't you see?

No one walks away from me..."

Her lips curve, not quite a smile. A look of joy and amusement hidden beneath the lull of the song. Her hand drifts over her shoulder, fingers skimming skin before falling away. The movement is unhurried, calculated, as if testing the restraint in the room.

Then she steps down.

A ripple of reaction, barely a murmur, passes through the crowd as she moves through the tables. She doesn't acknowledge it. She doesn't need to. The space shifts around her, parting as if the song itself is leading the way.

"Your hands are shaking, your breath runs tight,

Still you beg me, 'Stay the night...'"

She is close. The candlelight catches in her eyes as she reaches my table. I can't move. I'm utterly under her spell.

She circles behind me, the scent of honey threading through the air. Her voice is quieter now, meant only for me.

"Your hands are shaking, your breath runs tight,

Still, you beg me, Stay the night.

But darling, love is a crimson tide

You dive too deep, you're swept inside..."

Fingers ghost along the back of my chair. Then across my shoulder. Barely there. A whisper of contact.

"Oh, drown for me, sink so slow,

Let the waves pull, let the tides take hold.

Is this heaven? Is this sin?

Either way, I'll pull you in."

She leans in.

Close enough that I feel her breath, that I can see the flicker of amusement in her half-lidded eyes. The next words fall from her lips like a slow-moving current, as her gloved hand slides across my face, departing from my lips as she continues to sing.

"You taste the danger sweet as wine,

But sip too long and you are mine..."

Her mouth is a breath away from mine, the heat of her presence unbearable. The song is still playing, the world around us still watching, but this moment belongs to neither the music nor the crowd. Just us as she whispers the words into my ear.

"I never push, I never fight

I only whisper, and you comply."

Then, just as smoothly as she came, she withdraws, her silk-gloved fingers grazing the line of my jaw, the barest touch, an afterthought, a ghost.

Iris continues singing as she makes her way through the tables around the room.

"Oh, drown for me, sink so slow,

Let the waves pull, let the tides take hold.

Is this heaven? Is this sin?

Either way, I'll pull you in."

My eyes stay locked on her, unable to look away as she continues her siren's song.

"Don't you struggle, don't you pray,

No god can hear you anyway.

You should have left, you should have run

But you love the dark and what I've done."

She moves, stepping onto my chair, one foot placed between my legs, not touching, but close enough that the space between us is almost nothing. The hem of her gown brushes against my knees.

"Don't you struggle, don't you pray,

No god can hear you anyway."

Her finger caresses my lips in a hushing gesture, exactly in sync with the symbolic words.

"You should have left, you should have run"

She pushes me back slightly, sinking me into the chair as she leans forward into me.

But you love the dark and what I've done."

Iris grabs my tie, pulling me into her knee, resting against my chest.

She lets go as she transitions to the chorus again, pushing me down into my chair again, walking back to the stage.

"Oh, drown for me, sink so slow,

Let the waves pull, let the tides take hold.

Is this heaven? Is this sin?

Either way, I'll pull you in."

The last words of the song come slow. She's no longer just looking at the crowd, she's looking right at me.

"So take my hand, don't make a sound,

To a place no one is found

That this was never meant to be...

 Here you are, drowning for me."

Chills run through me as she finishes the song. The room erupts into applause, whistles, hollers, and one table is practically beating their table to death in excitement.

Iris thanks the audience, her smile genuine yet somehow distant. She retreats from the stage, the spotlight fading with her exit, leaving the room in a hushed anticipation.

I wait, fingers tapping against the tablecloth, each second stretching into eternity. My gaze is fixed on the stage, willing her to reappear. The room buzzes around me, conversations picking up, but I hear none of it. I'm a statue amidst the living, frozen in my seat, awaiting her return.

A few moments later, she's there, slipping into the chair across from me. Her presence is like a shockwave, jolting me back to life. She leans in, chin propped on her hand, eyes sparkling with amusement. "So, Sebastian, how was your meal?"

I swallow, trying to find my voice. "The best I've ever had." It's not a lie. I can barely remember tasting it, but with her here, everything is amplified, intensified.

"And the performance?" she asks, her voice a gentle purr.

"Indescribable," I manage to say, my heart pounding in my chest. "You were... breath taking."

She smiles, a slow, knowing curve of her lips. "I'm glad you enjoyed it."

I grasp for something to say, something to keep her here. "Would you like a drink?"

Iris leans back, her eyes never leaving mine. "How about we just get out of here?" She asks.

With barely a breath between thoughts, I'm wiping my face, standing up and straightening my tie. I step behind her, taking her seat to let her stand.

I reach out my arm to take Iris's, escorting her towards the exit as we leave The Symphony Club headed to my car.

I stop at the passenger door, unlocking my car and opening the door for her to have a seat first.

I practically stumble over my feet as I hurriedly run around the car to my side. I hop in, sinking into my seat, giving Iris a smile, then pressing the start button, my cars engine roaring to life.

I tear off from the parking spot, flying both of us towards my home as fast as my car will allow...

CHAPTER 17

Dinner was pleasant, a careful indulgence, a dance of words, of glances, of the space between us thinning with every passing moment. Now, she is here, in my home, moving through it with the same quiet confidence that has unraveled me from the beginning.

I watch her fingers drift over the polished surface of my coffee table, the rim of the wine glass she still holds. She moves without hesitation, without doubt. As if this was always meant to happen.

The air between us is warm, thick with something I can't quite name. She has barely touched me, and yet I feel the weight of her presence against my skin.

"I should pour us another drink," I say, my voice steady.

She doesn't respond right away. Instead, her gaze lingers on me, assessing. A slow, unreadable shift in her expression.

"Are you nervous?" she asks.

I let out a quiet chuckle, controlled, effortless. The answer is no. The answer is yes. The answer is that I don't know how to name what she is doing to me.

"Should I be?" I counter, stepping toward her.

She doesn't step back.

Instead, she leans against the arm of my sofa, stretching one leg out, her bare foot resting lightly against the floor. A single, fluid motion. Unstudied, unforced.

Heat coils low in my stomach, sharp and immediate.

I lift my hand toward her, fingers reaching, drawn to her, to the undeniable tension thickening in the air.

And then, she stops me.

Not with her hands. Not with words.

With the lightest pressure of her foot against my lips.

The world contracts to a single, unbearable point of contact.

I go still.

Not out of hesitation. Not out of restraint.

Out of something deeper. Something visceral.

Her touch, barely there, featherlight, and yet so deliberate, thrums through me like a live wire.

She is in my home. She is touching me. She is dictating how.

A slow, deliberate pulse of heat spreads through my chest.

Then, her voice, soft, measured, undeniably in control.

"No," she murmurs. "You can only touch me with your mouth."

A sharp inhale. A flicker of something dark, something electric, twisting through me.

She doesn't move.

She doesn't pull away.

She only watches. Waiting. Expecting compliance.

My lips part slightly, leaving a breath against her skin, a silent acknowledgment.

She does not react.

She does not break the moment.

She only holds it. Holds me.

And I realize, with absolute certainty, this is not the game I thought we were playing.

I concede my obedience with a blink.

A quick smile on her face acknowledging my surrender, and with her legs, she pulls me toward her.

Her now open skirt revealing her supple mound of perfection.

My mouth begins to water as I grow closer.

I taste her.

My mouth enveloping her.

My tongue lapping against her.

I struggle to contain my hunger.

My hunger for her. With every taste of her like a freshly bitten peach, smooth, wet, and sweet.

Her hips begin to grind into me as I taste her.

I feel a slap at my hands wrapped around her thighs. Unconsciously I must have reached out to pull her closer to me.

Returning my hands to my sides, I resume tasting her, devouring her.

I lose myself in her, the way my mouth glides over her soft skin, each kiss igniting a fire that burns hotter with every flick of my tongue. She tastes like honey, that intoxicating sweetness mixing with something deeper, something I can't name. I pull back for a moment, just long enough to catch her gaze, the flicker of delight and mischief dances in her eyes.

"You're enjoying this," she teases, her voice a soft whisper wrapped in velvet.

The urge to answer is there, but it dissipates into the air around us. Instead, I dive back in, pressing my lips against her warmth again. Her body arches toward me as if it knows my intent better than I do. She pulls at me, a magnet drawing me closer, as if she understands the gravity of this moment more than I could ever admit.

Her breath hitches, a delightful sound that reverberates through me. I dive deeper, anchoring myself to this paradise as I taste her essence, a heady mix of lust and an ache for something far more primal.

"Sebastian," she breathes out, each syllable a plea or a command; it's hard to decipher which when every ounce of my focus narrows onto her.

The world outside fades away, the ticking clock no longer matters; the shadows in the corners of the room dissolve into obscurity. All that exists is this moment: my mouth on her body, our connection tightening like a drawn bowstring.

Her fingers weave through my hair, tugging gently, guiding me where she wants me to go. With every gentle pull, she makes it clear how much power she holds over me; and yet here I am, willingly surrendering to that control.

I trace the line of her body with my mouth, a delicate path from her navel to the smooth curve of her hips. The scent lingers still, the sweet notes of honey mixed with the urgency rising within me.

"More," she demands softly.

I obey without hesitation. I descend deeper, savoring the taste of her, so rich, so alive. She wraps her legs around me, pulling me closer, anchoring me to this paradise we've crafted together. I feel consumed by the moment and yet aware of how dangerously close we tread into uncharted territory.

With every movement, every gasp that escapes her lips, I'm reminded of how much I crave this intimacy, the thrill of being completely lost in another person. Her fingers tangle in my hair, guiding me as if she knows precisely how to wield control over this exquisite dance.

But it's more than mere pleasure; it's a tether that pulls at something inside me, a hunger I can no longer ignore. My mind races through tangled thoughts: Is this truly just physical? Or has she breached a wall I carefully constructed?

A growling moan escapes from Iris, an invitation or a challenge? Perhaps both.

"You're so good at this," she teases again, a playful edge lacing her words that sends heat rushing through me.

Her voice is like music to my ears, each note heightening the tension building between us until it feels almost unbearable. I pull back slightly to drink in the sight of her, the glimmer in her eyes and the way her lips part ever so slightly as if waiting for more.

And in that moment, everything shifts within me, the perfect balance teetering on a knife's edge.

I sit back, tearing at my belt, desperate to undress, standing to drop my trousers to the floor. Ripping off my shirt and throwing it away.

Crawling up towards Iris, nude, ready to feel myself inside of her.

I am pushed down again by her as she sits up.

"No." She says calmly.

"No?" I ask.

"Don't worry, I won't leave you wanting, but you have to do as I say." She replies softly.

"Sit." She commands softly.

With desperate obedience, I sit down, obeying her.

"Hands to your sides." She follows.

Again, I follow her instructions.

"You have been a good boy, Sebastian." She purrs. "Now, I'm going to reward you."

As I sit there, I am struck with shock, excitement, and pleasure as her feet reach down and begin stroking my cock. I shudder from the inexplicable ecstasy of it.

She squeezes my shaft as she grips it tightly between her soft, small, manicured toes, stroking it up and down. The feeling is indescribable, more pleasurable than any experience with any other woman, better than the feeling of release as I orgasm while taking a life in the same moment.

Her touch sends jolts through me, each stroke igniting a fire I didn't know I could feel. The sensation of her feet gripping my shaft is overwhelming, both delicate and demanding.

I gasp, the breath caught in my throat, fighting to maintain some semblance of control. But how can I when she commands every part of me with just her feet? The heat radiates from her as she leans closer, her lips curving into a satisfied smile that drives me wild.

"Good boy," she whispers, the words curling around my mind like smoke. "Now just enjoy."

I nod, willing to surrender completely. My hands twitch at my sides, an instinctual urge to reach for her, but I hold myself back. Each time I resist the urge to touch her, the tension coils tighter within me.

She begins to quicken the pace, her toes flicking and teasing with an expert precision that feels utterly divine. I feel myself swelling further under her skillful manipulation. My heart races; desire pulses through my veins like a raging river.

"You like this?" she asks playfully, tilting her head to watch my face closely.

I nod again, unable to form words, only breathless gasps escape as my body betrays me.

"Tell me," she commands softly.

"Y-yees-sss," I manage to choke out, the word drawn out, dripping with need.

She responds with a wicked smile, and in that moment, something shifts between us, an unspoken understanding that teeters on the edge of pleasure and power.

With each stroke of her feet against me, I find myself slipping further into a haze, a euphoric surrender where all thoughts about control fade away into the background. All that matters is this moment, the electric connection pulsing between us and the way she manipulates my pleasure as if it's a work of art.

Her laughter dances around us like music; it's intoxicating.

The heat builds inside me as she keeps working me over with that delightful rhythm; the world outside fades into nothingness. I can't help but wonder how this simple act, this exquisite display of dominance, has shattered everything I thought about desire and control.

Each flick of her toes draws out a moan from deep within me; the sound feels foreign yet exhilarating, my body responding to her in ways I've never allowed before.

I'm acutely aware of the way my body responds to her; each stroke is electric, a tantalizing blend of pleasure and control that pulls me deeper into her web. The room feels smaller as the air thickens around us, charged with an energy I've never experienced before.

"I knew you'd enjoy this," she teases, her voice laced with a playfulness that makes my heart race.

I can't reply; words escape me like whispers lost in the night. My breath hitches as she tightens her grip with those delicate toes. It's a delicate dance of power, one I never anticipated but now crave with a hunger I didn't know existed.

"Good," she says softly, almost conspiratorially. "Now let go."

Her words send ripples through my mind. Let go? Of what? Control? Reality? For the first time in years, it feels both terrifying and liberating.

With every flick of her foot, the tension builds within me, a raw, primal need that pushes against every carefully constructed wall I've built around myself. I want to surrender completely; to be consumed by this moment.

But part of me resists, something in me whispers reminders of precision and restraint. Yet here I am, in this beautiful chaos, willing to abandon all reason for the sake of pleasure.

Her laughter bubbles up again, light and teasing as if she senses my internal struggle.

"Sebastian," she purrs, leaning closer until I can smell the honey on her skin mingling with something deeper, something intoxicating that lures me further down this rabbit hole.

I focus on her eyes, those captivating pools where mischief dances just beneath the surface.

"You know what you need to do," she instructs gently.

I hold still as her feet glide over me, each stroke a reminder of how little control I have left.

The moment stretches out, a suspended reality where all I can think about is how much I crave more of this intimacy. Each touch sends heat spiraling through me; each second drags on longer than the last.

With every flick and caress, my world narrows down to just us, an exquisite tunnel vision honing in on nothing but Iris and this unfathomable pleasure.

I give in, conceding it all, everything, power, control, my entire life. I want this, need this!

My body can take it no longer and I begin to cum, I scream out a booming moan of pure pleasure. The moment prolongs as she continues stroking me, egging me to keep going. The moment seems to last minutes as I release it all.

Iris lets out a knowing laugh, looking at me and what she has done. It echoes through the room, a sweet melody that vibrates against my skin. Her eyes gleam with mischief, sparkling like shards of glass catching the light.

"You didn't expect that, did you?" she teases, her voice dripping with satisfaction.

I can't respond, words feel foreign now, lost in the haze of ecstasy that still lingers around me. Every nerve ending tingles; my body convulses with residual pleasure, leaving me raw and exposed.

She watches me, her expression playful yet contemplative, as if she's just unraveled a great mystery hidden within my carefully constructed facade. I sit there, panting, trying to collect myself while my mind races in circles.

"I told you I wouldn't leave you wanting.," she continues, leaning back on her elbows as if basking in the aftermath of our encounter. Her confidence radiates from her like heat off asphalt; it pulls at something primal deep within me.

My pulse thrums in my ears, a frantic rhythm fueled by more than just pleasure; it's an undercurrent of vulnerability mixed with exhilaration.

I should reclaim control, remind her of who I am, but the words die on my lips. Instead, I find myself drawn into her gaze; the way it pierces through layers of pretense and scrutiny until nothing is left but an honest need for connection.

"You look... unsteady," she observes with that same teasing lilt. Her foot glides lightly across my thigh, a reminder of what just transpired between us.

Heat rushes to my cheeks, an unusual sensation when I've spent so long mastering every aspect of my life. The image of her laughter dances in my mind, free and unencumbered, as if she's unleashed something hidden inside me.

I watch her, utterly entranced, as she lounges back, the weight of our encounter settling between us like a thick fog. Every inch of me feels electrified, and yet I'm painfully aware of how exposed I am.

Her foot glides along my thigh again, teasingly slow. Each stroke ignites a new wave of warmth that spreads through me. She leans closer, and her honeyed scent wraps around me like a soft embrace, almost suffocating in its allure.

"You seem to enjoy relinquishing control," she muses, tilting her head to study me. That playful glint in her eyes hints at the depths of her understanding, far beyond what I ever anticipated from her.

The heat radiates from where she touches me; it's intoxicating. I find myself captivated by the confidence radiating off her, mingling with my own desires. But this is dangerous territory, allowing anyone into my world means relinquishing the careful precision I've honed for years.

"It's... different," I admit finally, forcing myself to hold her gaze instead of succumbing to the swirling thoughts racing through my mind.

Her smile widens at my confession, a victorious spark that sends a shiver down my spine.

"Good different or bad different?"

The question hangs in the air like a challenge, and I can't help but marvel at how effortlessly she navigates our shifting dynamic. Does she even realize the precarious edge we dance upon?

I clear my throat; words spill out before I can think better of them. "It's not often I allow myself such... indulgence."

Her laughter bubbles up again, a sound that dances around us and fills the space with warmth.

"And here you are," she says lightly, "indulging more than you expected."

My heart races anew as I grapple with this new reality: she has slipped beneath my defenses in ways no one else ever has. A part of me wants to pull away, to remind myself who I am, the architect of my own life, and yet another part relishes this thrill.

But what comes next? What happens when we're done playing this game? The hunger still coils tightly within me, a need that gnaws deeper than mere pleasure.

I watch as Iris rises, her silhouette shifting against the moonlight spilling from the window. The way she moves is effortless, a fluidity that captivates me. I catch my breath, still reeling from our encounter, as she walks toward the bathroom.

"I'll be quick," she calls over her shoulder, a playful smile lingering on her lips.

The door clicks shut behind her, and I'm left in silence, the air heavy with remnants of what just transpired. My heart races, not just from the pleasure but from the undeniable shift between us. This feels different.

I run my fingers through my hair, still buzzing with sensation. Every inch of me feels alive; it's unsettling yet intoxicating. I sit on the edge of the bed, trying to gather my thoughts amidst the chaos swirling in my mind.

Time drags on until I hear water running, a gentle cascade that invites my thoughts to drift. I'm reminded of her laughter, how it danced through the air like music. I replay every moment we shared; how her touch ignited something inside me that I thought long buried.

Minutes slip by before I finally push myself up to stand, needing to wash away this overwhelming mixture of sweat and desire.

I walk to the guest room, and into the spare bathroom, stepping into the shower. I turn the water to cold, the sudden stream jolting me from my desires, allowing my thoughts to focus on cleaning alone, removing any lingering signs of my arousal.

I close my eyes, allowing myself to truly feel each drop as it cascades over me. It's meditative, this act of cleansing, but it also churns deeper reflections within me: What does this mean? What am I willing to risk for this woman who has so easily unraveled me?

I linger under the stream longer than necessary, lost in contemplation as heat wraps around me like a cocoon. My thoughts spiral between control and indulgence, two forces at war within me.

Finally, after what feels like an eternity, I step out of the shower and towel off. The cool air bites against my skin; I pull on fresh clothes, a tailored shirt that fits just right and dark trousers that speak of precision.

As I finish dressing, Iris emerges from the bathroom, a plush towel wrapped snugly around her body, droplets still clinging to her skin like tiny jewels.

"I see you showered already," she comments casually, tilting her head slightly as if appraising me anew.

Her gaze holds mine with an intensity that reinvigorates that need rushing through me again. I take a deep breath, working to regain my composure.

Once I've composed myself fully and re-established some semblance of control, she asks casually, "Could you give me a ride home?"

The request hangs in the air between us, a simple question with an undercurrent that leaves my pulse racing once more.

I glance at Iris, her eyes sparkling with mischief as she leans casually against the doorframe. The towel clings to her skin, a delicate reminder of our shared moment, and I feel my heart quicken. She's a siren in this space, drawing me in even as I grapple with the chaos of my own mind.

"Of course," I reply, my voice steadier than I feel. It's a simple request, yet it sends a rush of electricity through me. Each interaction with her pulls at something primal, something that whispers promises of indulgence and danger.

I retrieve my jacket from the chair, fingers brushing against the cool fabric as I contemplate the night ahead. The thrill of her presence fills the room like a fine wine, intoxicating and dangerous all at once.

Iris watches me intently as I slip on my shoes. Her gaze is unyielding, searching for cracks in my carefully constructed facade. It's unnerving yet exhilarating; she sees beyond the polished exterior I present to the world.

As we step outside into the crisp night air, the streetlights illuminate the ground around us, creating silhouettes that seem to dance with every movement. I offer her my arm instinctively, and she accepts it with an amused smile, a gesture that feels almost intimate.

The drive is quiet, tension crackling between us like static electricity. I focus on the road ahead, but Iris occupies every corner of my mind. The way she spoke earlier, her laughter lingering like honey, echoes in my thoughts.

"Tonight was... interesting," she says finally, breaking the silence.

I turn to her briefly before shifting my focus back to navigating through the streets. I respond, striving for casual nonchalance while wrestling with the deeper implications of her words.

"Is that how you see it?" she muses, tilting her head slightly as if trying to peel back layers of my carefully constructed identity.

I suppress a smile; she has no idea how much intrigue simmers beneath my surface, how every calculated move masks an underlying hunger for something far beyond mere architecture or control.

"Interesting can be exhilarating," I reply cryptically, keeping my tone light while my heart races beneath that veneer.

Her gaze sharpens; I can sense her curiosity deepening like a well-crafted design revealing its hidden intricacies.

As we drive through the quiet streets, a subtle shift occurs in our dynamic. The air no longer crackles with tension; instead, it's infused with a newfound lightness, a delicate dance of anticipation and understanding.

"So," Iris begins, her voice soft yet tinged with mischief, "did you have a good time?"

The question catches me off guard; it's an invitation to be honest, to shed the layers of precision I've honed for so long. I glance at her briefly before turning back to focus on the road ahead.

"I... I did," I admit reluctantly. My heart races as the words leave my lips, an admission that feels both dangerous and exhilarating.

Iris lets out a subtle laugh, a high pitch nasally sound that fills the space around us. It's contagious, and before I realize it, a smile tugs at the corners of my mouth.

"Maybe we can explore this further sometime," she suggests playfully. Her tone is laced with promise, a hint of adventures yet to come.

As we round another corner, her house comes into view, its outline illuminated by streetlights that cast shadows across its facade. She shifts slightly in her seat as if preparing herself for departure.

When we pull up to her driveway, she turns to me with an expression that holds equal parts curiosity and satisfaction. Our eyes meet for a brief moment, a connection that sends warmth spiraling through me once more.

"Thank you for tonight," she says as she reaches for the door handle. "It was certainly interesting."

Her choice of word echoes back to me, interesting, and something in my chest tightens at its implication.

Before I can respond or even think about it further, she slips out of the car with grace, a fluid movement that catches my eye once more.

As she walks toward her front door, I feel an overwhelming urge to call out to her, a desire for one last moment of connection.

But Iris pauses before reaching the door, glancing back at me over her shoulder.

Her expression holds a knowing glint, a playful challenge wrapped in an air of mystery.

"Goodnight," she says, her voice trailing off. "And thank you again."

The words hang in the air between us, unspoken promises mingling with unmet desires.

As Iris disappears into the shadows of her house,

I feel my heart pounding against my rib cage, a reminder of how much she affects me.

I sit in silence for a moment after she's gone, the weight of our encounter still pressing down on me like a heavy blanket.

Slowly, I ease the car forward, the sound of the engine breaking through the quiet of the night air.

As I drive home, my mind replays every moment we shared, the laughter,

the teasing, and most poignantly, the way she unraveled me so effortlessly.

Each memory feels like a delicate brushstroke on canvas, coloring in shades I never knew existed within my carefully constructed world.

I think about our conversation, her questions probing deeper than any others have dared to go.

She saw past my precision, past the controlled exterior that has served as armor for so long.

And yet, she didn't recoil or judge; instead, she seemed intrigued by what lay beneath.

The drive passes in a blur, as thoughts swirl through my mind, each one painting new possibilities onto an ever-shifting canvas.

When I finally pull into my driveway, a sense of unease settles over me, a mix of anticipation and uncertainty.

What does this mean?

What am I willing to risk?

These questions linger, as I step out into the cool night air, questions without clear answers but filled with potential none-the-less.

With every step toward my front door,

I feel myself slipping further away from control, toward something wilder,

something I want more than anything, something I didn't know I needed.

I unlock the door, push it open wide, and step inside.

CHAPTER 18

I jolt awake, my head throbbing with an unforgiving ache. The clock on my nightstand blinks 12:00 PM, its red digits taunting me. Impossible. I never oversleep. I rip the clock from the outlet, but the cord is intact, the batteries fresh.

I snatch my phone. 8:37 AM.

A guttural sound escapes me as I hurl the clock across the room. I scramble for my clothes, yanking a shirt over my head without a second thought to its state. My fingers fumble with the buttons, misaligning them, and I have to start over. The tie I grab clashes horribly with my suit, but I knot it, putting it on anyway.

No time for coffee. No time to align the items on my nightstand just so. No time to double-check the locks.

The drive to work becomes a blur of honking horns and glaring red lights. My knuckles whiten as I grip the steering wheel, tension coiling within me.

9:18 AM. I've never been this late. Not in fifteen years.

The elevator doors part on my floor, and I step into the office, jaw clenched. Ryan spots me immediately, his face shifting from surprise to worry.

"Hey, Sebastian! We were starting to worry. Everything okay?"

I brush past him, his voice grating like sandpaper.

"Sebastian?" He tails me down the hallway. "The McKinley presentation got moved up. They want to see preliminary designs by Thursday instead of next week."

"Handle it," I bark, not breaking stride.

"But they specifically asked for..."

I spin around. "I said handle it."

Ryan's face falls as he stops dead in his tracks, falling behind me.

My office door slams shut behind me, closing me off from the world, offering a brief illusion of sanctuary. I let my briefcase fall to the floor in reckless abandon.

Emma, my assistant, knocks timidly, a stack of messages in her hand.

I look up, but I dismiss her with a silent wave of my hand.

The blueprints on my desk call for my attention, but I can't, not now. Focus slips through my grasp. All I see is Iris. Iris smiling. Iris challenging. Iris walking away.

Another knock disrupts the fragile silence. Claire from Accounting, armed with budget questions.

"Not now," I say, my voice a flat line.

"But we need to..."

"I said not now." I reply, this time more assertive.

I power on my computer, the tactile feeling of the cool keys providing a familiar comfort. But as I enter my credentials, my fingers hesitate, betraying my lack of focus. The screen flickers to life, revealing the chaos of my digital world, emails demanding replies, calendar reminders blinking incessantly, project deadlines looming.

I click on my calendar, the grid of appointments and meetings, all color coded, categorized, and painstakingly ordered. Yet, as my eyes scan the entries, they fail to register. My mind is ensnared by a different image: Iris, her lips curling into a subtle, knowing smile.

I lean back in my chair, the leather creaking beneath me. My thoughts drift back to our evening together. The way she took control, the precise, yet gentle command in her voice as she whispered, "No, you can only touch me with your mouth." It was a role reversal I had never anticipated, never experienced. And the pleasure... exquisite, maddening, had consumed me in a way that left me both sated and desperate for more.

I should be repulsed by the loss of control, but instead, I find myself craving it. The memory of her, the sensation of her silken skin against my lips, the power she held over me in those moments, it's intoxicating. I had begged, not with words, but with my body, for release. For her to bring the sweet agony to an end. The recollection sends a shiver down my spine, and I realize how much I enjoyed it, the act of surrender, the ecstasy of it.

But the enjoyment is laced with a gnawing hunger for more, a need that has taken root deep within me. It's a craving that I'm familiar with, one that I've always been able to satiate on my own terms. Yet, with Iris, it's different. The control she wields over my desire, it's unnerving and exhilarating in equal measure.

I shake my head, trying to clear the fog of longing. I need to focus on work, on the tangible results of my labor. Mckinley's design won't blueprint itself. But as I turn my attention back to the screen, the lines of the blueprint blur into the contours of Iris's face, her form superimposed upon the architecture.

A knock at the door jars me from my reverie. Emma peeks in, her expression a mix of concern and caution.

"Sebastian, the team is waiting for your input on the McKinley project."

I nod, acknowledging her without words. She retreats, leaving me once again with the ghost of Iris and the echo of her command.

I stand, pacing the length of my office. My thoughts are scattered, fragmented by the memory of Iris's touch, her assertion of control, a control I willingly yielded. The realization is both unsettling and arousing.

I stop at the window, gazing out at the cityscape below. The towering structures I've designed rise like monoliths against the sky, crafted with precision and discipline. But even as I survey my kingdom of steel and glass, I can't escape the hold Iris has over me.

The intercom buzzes, Ryan's voice cutting through my thoughts. "Sebastian, we need you in the conference room. It's urgent."

I take a deep breath, steeling myself to face the day. I have to regain control, to compartmentalize my desire for Iris.

As I step out of my office, the taste of her still lingers on my lips, a sweet hunger that refuses to be quelled.

I walk down the hallway toward the conference room, my head swirling with two poisons: Iris and my own carelessness. Morning fog still lingers in my mind, though thoughts of her begin to evaporate as I approach the glass doors.

Ryan stands at the head of the table, his usual chipper demeanor replaced with something taut and severe. Around him sits Marcus, our structural lead with his perpetually loosened tie; Diane, head of materials procurement, her silver-streaked hair pulled into a tight bun; and Thomas, our legal counsel whose presence alone tells me this isn't a standard project review.

"Sebastian." Thomas nods, gesturing to the empty chair.

Ryan clears his throat. "McKinley pulled out this morning."

The words hang in the air. McKinley Tower was to be our flagship project this quarter, twenty-seven stories of sustainable luxury that would define the city skyline for generations.

"They felt we weren't giving their project adequate attention," Marcus adds, sliding a folder toward me. "Three missed deadlines in the preliminary phase. The last one was today's presentation that got rescheduled."

I remember dismissing Ryan's urgent message about the presentation when I arrived. My stomach tightens.

"That's not all," Thomas interjects, his voice carrying the weight of graver news. "We've been served. The Westfield Complex, those condominiums from last year? The foundation is showing critical structural failure. Concrete cancer throughout the southern wing."

"Impossible." The word escapes me before I can stop it. "We specified specialized mix ratios specifically to prevent alkaline-silica reaction."

Diane slides photographs across the table. "Tell that to the three-inch cracks forming in the basement levels. The residents have filed a class action."

"We've already reached out to Hannover Construction," Ryan says, "but they've declared bankruptcy. Convenient timing."

My mind races through the Westfield specs, every calculation, every material choice. I designed that foundation system myself.

"The liability falls to us," Thomas says quietly. "Unless we can prove contractor negligence, which will be difficult with Hannover's records now scattered to the wind."

The room spins slightly. I grip the edge of the table to steady myself.

"How bad?" I ask.

"Eight figures, potentially," Thomas replies. "And that's before we factor in reputational damage."

"Fuck me!" I reply.

I can't believe this is happening. McKinley Tower, our most prestigious project this quarter, gone. And now, the Westfield Complex, my baby, my pride and joy, falling apart literally and figuratively. Concrete cancer? How? I designed that foundation system myself.

"We need to get our hands on those construction records," I say through gritted teeth. "There must be something we missed."

Ryan nods in agreement. "I've already put a team on it, but with Hannover folding so suddenly..." he trails off, leaving the rest unsaid.

Thomas clears his throat, his expression grim. "Sebastian, there's more."

Of course there's more. Nothing can go right today. "What now?" I ask wearily.

"The board... they're calling an emergency meeting this afternoon." Thomas pauses before dropping the bombshell: "They're considering your position as lead architect."

The room goes silent as the implications of his words sink in. My position, my life's work, hanging by a thread because of one mistake I didn't even make? It's not fair! The blood in my veins boils with fury and indignation. This can't be happening to me, Sebastian Wolfe! The man who single-handedly turned this firm into what it is today!

"This is bullshit!" I slam my fist on the table, rattling the photographs of the crumbling foundation before me. "I won't let my reputation be tarnished by someone else's incompetence!"

Diane places a calming hand on my arm, her eyes filled with empathy and understanding. "We know you didn't do this intentionally, Sebastian," she says calmly. "We all have faith in your abilities." Her words do little to quell the rage coursing through me like molten lava, but I know lashing out at my team won't solve anything right now...

The rest of the meeting is a blur. Voices swirl around me, discussing damage control and contingency plans, but my mind is elsewhere. My entire world has come crashing down around me, and all I can think about is how to rebuild it.

As soon as the meeting adjourns, I retreat to my office and slam the door shut. I pace back and forth across the room, my thoughts racing as fast as my heartbeat. McKinley Tower gone, Westfield Complex crumbling before my very eyes... and now this, my position on the line. No, I won't let this happen. I won't allow one mistake, a mistake not even of my making, to bring me down.

I reach for my phone and begin dialing numbers, one after another: former clients, industry contacts, anyone who might have insight into Hannover's sudden downfall or a lead on their missing records. The hours blur together as I leave voicemail after voicemail, sending emails and text messages in between calls.

By lunchtime, my stomach growls in protest but I ignore it; there's no time for distractions when everything I've worked for hangs by a thread. Instead, I rifle through stacks of paperwork on my desk, contracts, blueprints, anything that might hold a clue to what went wrong at Westfield Complex or assuage McKinley's concerns about our commitment to their project.

Ryan pokes his head in around 2:00 PM with a concerned look on his face and a Styrofoam container in hand. "Sebastian," he says cautiously, "you haven't eaten all day."

I barely register him entering as he sets the food down on my desk and retreats just as quickly. Only when hunger pangs gnaw at me do I even notice the sandwich he brought me: turkey on rye with mustard, my usual order from Mike's Deli downstairs. It tastes like cardboard in my mouth, but I force myself to chew mechanically while scanning through more documents with bleary eyes...

A knock at the door jolts me from my haze. I glance at the half-eaten sandwich, now cold and unappetizing.

"What?" I snap, not bothering to hide my irritation.

Emma stands in the doorway, her usual composure replaced with hesitation. "The board meeting has been moved up. They're waiting for you in the main conference room."

"Now?" The word comes out sharper than intended. Emma nods, a quick, nervous gesture that speaks volumes.

I straighten my tie, run a hand through my hair, and gather the Westfield documents. My reflection in the glass wall shows a man I barely recognize, disheveled, worn, the carefully cultivated image of control beginning to crack.

The walk to the conference room feels like a march to the gallows. Each step echoes in my ears, matching the pounding of my heart. I pause outside the door, drawing a deep breath. I've faced challenges before. I've overcome every obstacle in my path. This is just another test.

I push open the door.

Twelve faces turn toward me, the full board, plus Thomas and Ryan. The CEO, Harrison Wolfe (no relation, despite sharing a surname), sits at the head of the table, his expression unreadable.

"Sebastian," he says, gesturing to the empty chair at the opposite end. "Please join us."

I take my seat, acutely aware of every eye on me. The room smells of expensive cologne and tension.

"We've been discussing the Westfield situation," Harrison continues, his voice measured. "And the loss of the McKinley account."

I open my mouth to defend myself, but he raises a hand, silencing me.

"The board has concerns about recent developments. We've invested considerable resources in your vision for this firm, Sebastian. The results have been... impressive, until now."

"Harrison," I begin, fighting to keep my voice steady, "the Westfield issue is a contractor failure, not a design flaw. As for McKinley..."

"It's not just about Westfield or McKinley," he interrupts. "It's about a pattern of... distraction that's been noticed recently."

I feel my throat constrict at Harrison's words. Distraction? The accusation lands like a physical blow. I've never been distracted a day in my professional life. My designs are immaculate. My work ethic unimpeachable. My...

"Sebastian, when was the last time you personally reviewed the Westfield weekly reports?" Board member Janet Chen's voice cuts through my thoughts.

"I delegated those to my team," I reply automatically.

"And the McKinley presentation?" Harrison presses. "The one you rescheduled three times?"

The room swims before me. I straighten my spine, refusing to show weakness.

"The board has voted," Harrison continues after my silence stretches too long. "We recognize your contributions to Wolfe & Hart. Your designs have put us on the map. But recent events cannot be ignored."

My mouth goes dry. This is it. They're going to remove me. Everything I've built, everything I am, gone in an instant.

"We've decided to retain you as lead architect," Harrison says.

Relief floods through me, but his expression remains grave.

"However," he continues, "you'll be placed on a three-month probationary period. Ryan will co-sign all major decisions. Weekly progress reports delivered personally by you to the board. And a complete audit of your current projects."

The relief evaporates, replaced by indignation. "Co-sign? With Ryan?" The words escape before I can stop them.

Ryan shifts uncomfortably in his chair, avoiding my gaze.

"This isn't a punishment, Sebastian," Harrison says, though his tone suggests otherwise. "It's a chance to regroup, to refocus. We need the Sebastian Wolfe who built this firm's reputation, not..." he gestures vaguely at me, "whatever's been happening lately."

I swallow my pride. Three months of Ryan looking over my shoulder. Three months of weekly interrogations disguised as progress reports. Three months to prove myself all over again.

"I understand," I manage to say, the words tasting bitter on my tongue. "I appreciate the board's confidence."

Harrison nods, satisfied with my capitulation. "Good. We expect to see immediate improvement."

The meeting concludes with a few more pointed questions, each one driving the knife deeper. I remain outwardly composed, offering reasonable responses despite the hurricane raging within me. When Harrison finally dismisses us, I stand with practiced dignity, though my legs feel wooden beneath me.

Ryan and I walk silently down the corridor, the tension between us thick enough to cut with a blade. He follows me into my office like an unwelcome shadow. The door clicks shut behind us, sealing us in a vacuum of awkward silence.

"This isn't as bad as it seems," Ryan ventures, his voice too cheerful, too optimistic. "Three months will fly by."

I turn to face him. His youthful features hold an earnestness that makes my head ache.

"We can use this as an opportunity," he continues, oblivious to the danger. "Streamline some processes, maybe redistribute some of your workload..."

"Redistribute?" I say, almost choking on my words.

Ryan shifts his weight. "Just the routine stuff. Free you up for the creative work you excel at and reviewing reports so nothing is missed."

My hands clench and unclench at my sides. The hunger that's been simmering since this morning roars to life, a beast awakening from slumber. It claws at my insides, demanding release, demanding blood.

I imagine how easy it would be to reach out, to wrap my fingers around his throat, to watch the light fade from those earnest blue eyes. The hunger pulls at me like I'm tied to a moving train, dragging me toward the precipice of violence.

I turn away before he can see the truth in my face. Three deep breaths. Control. I must maintain control.

"We'll discuss the review process later," I say, keeping my voice neutral as I straighten papers on my desk. "I need some time to process this."

"Of course." Ryan hesitates at the door, radiating concern. "For what it's worth, I didn't know about this until right before the meeting started. I would have given you a heads-up."

"I appreciate that." The words taste like ash. "We'll talk tomorrow."

When the door finally closes behind him, I sink into my chair, the beast still prowling beneath my skin, hungry and restless.

I check my watch, 7:13 PM. The day has bled into evening without my notice. My office, usually a sanctuary of order, now feels like a prison cell. The walls press in, reminders of failure etched into every corner.

With mechanical movements, I straighten the papers on my desk, aligning edges that don't need aligning. The familiar ritual offers no comfort tonight. Nothing feels right in my hands, not my expensive pen, not the leather portfolio, not the architectural model I spent weeks perfecting.

I grab my coat and briefcase, not bothering to shut down my computer properly. Let it run all night, what difference does it make? Three months of Ryan Adams breathing down my neck. Three months of proving myself to men who should be thanking me for their success.

The elevator ride down is mercifully empty. No small talk, no awkward glances from colleagues who've already heard about my professional crucifixion. The parking garage is quiet too, most sensible people having left hours ago.

My car purrs to life beneath me, German engineering responding to my touch with more loyalty than any human has shown today. I pull out onto the street with no destination in mind. Not home, I can't face those walls tonight, can't stomach the emptiness waiting there.

I drive aimlessly through downtown, the city lights blurring into streaks of neon and shadow. Traffic moves around me like water around a stone. I'm barely conscious of the turns I make, the streets I pass.

At a red light, my gaze drifts to a bar on the corner, The Last Call. Not my usual type of establishment. No carefully curated wine list or designer cocktails here. Just glass bottles and promises of temporary oblivion.

The light turns green. My hands turn the wheel.

I find a spot half a block down and sit for a moment, engine idling. What am I doing here? This isn't me. I don't drown my problems in cheap liquor. I solve them, dominate them, bend them to my will.

But tonight, the hunger inside me needs quieting, and I'm too exhausted to fight it the usual way.

I kill the engine and step out into the night.

I step into The Last Call, leaving behind the crisp night air for the warm haze of cheap liquor and disappointment. The bar is exactly what I expected, dark wood worn smooth by countless elbows, neon beer signs casting sickly blue and red shadows across uneven walls. A handful of patrons dot the space, each isolated in their private misery.

I choose a stool at the far end of the bar, away from the others. The leather seat creaks beneath me as I set my briefcase on the floor.

The bartender, a heavyset man with arms covered in faded tattoos, makes his way over, wiping his hands on a rag that's seen better days.

"What can I get you?"

"Whiskey neat. Macallan 18, if you have it." The words come automatically. Even here, I can't lower my standards.

He snorts, not unkindly. "Sorry, friend. We're not that kind of establishment. Got Jim Beam or Wild Turkey."

Of course they don't have Macallan. Nothing about this day could possibly go right.

"Wild Turkey, then." I loosen my tie, suddenly feeling the constriction around my throat.

The bartender nods, returning moments later with the bottle, a sorry excuse for Whiskey. It's not enough, not nearly enough to silence the storm in my head.

"Leave the bottle," I say, sliding over my credit card.

He hesitates, probably wondering if he should cut me off before I've even started, then shrugs and places the bottle next to my glass. "Rough day?"

I don't answer, just pour myself a generous measure and down it in one burning swallow. The whiskey hits my empty stomach like liquid fire, spreading outward through my limbs. I pour another, and another, each glass emptied as quickly as the last. The burn lessens with each drink, turning from pain to warmth to numbness.

Five drinks in rapid succession, and I haven't even settled into my seat. The bartender raises an eyebrow but says nothing. Smart man.

The bottle in front of me has dwindled significantly, though I've lost track of exactly how much I've consumed. I check my watch, 10:07 PM. I've been here nearly three hours, though it feels both longer and shorter simultaneously.

The door to the bar swings open, letting in a gust of cool night air and with it, a wave of noise. College students, laughing too loudly, their voices carrying the invincibility of youth. They flood into the space like water finding its level, filling empty tables and crowding the bar.

Their energy is almost offensive, how dare they be so carefree when my world is crumbling?

I pour another drink, watching with the concentration of a hawk focused on its next meal, as it fills my glass. The whiskey has done its job; the sharp edges of my humiliation have dulled to a manageable ache. Even the hunger that's been clawing at my insides has retreated to a distant rumble.

"Hey, buddy." The bartender leans across the counter toward me. "End of my shift. Gotta close you out."

I reach for my wallet, movements sluggish but still precise. I pull out a hundred-dollar bill and slide it across the sticky wood.

"Keep the tab open," I say, my words clear despite the alcohol. "This is for you."

He looks at the bill, then at me, surprise flashing across his face before he tucks it into his pocket.

"Thanks, man. Appreciate it." He hesitates. "You good to drive later?"

I wave away his concern. "I'll call a car."

He nods, seemingly satisfied, and moves down the bar to brief his replacement. I watch as she emerges from the back room, mid-thirties perhaps, with a confident stride and curves that draw the eye. Her dark hair falls in a sleek curtain to her shoulders, and her features suggest Asian heritage, Japanese maybe, or Hawaiian. Something about her catches my attention in a way nothing else in this bar has tonight.

She notices my gaze and approaches, her smile professional but warm.

"Taking over your tab," she says, glancing at the bottle. "Can I get you anything else?"

I study her face, feeling the pleasant haze of alcohol softening my edges. Something about her, her smile, perhaps, makes me want to keep talking.

"You wouldn't happen to have anything stronger than this, would you?" I tap the bottle with my finger. "Something that fixes professional humiliation and wounded pride?"

She laughs, a genuine sound that cuts through the bar noise. "Sorry, we're fresh out of miracle cures. Though I hear the pretzels help with the hangover you're building."

"Hangover implies I plan to stop drinking." I offer a smile that feels foreign on my face. "The way I see it, if I stay drunk, I never have to face tomorrow."

"Sound logic. Terrible liver strategy." She slides a glass of water next to my whiskey. "I'm Aimi, by the way."

"Sebastian." I extend my hand, noting how it doesn't quite shake despite everything I've consumed. "Currently failing architect and newly appointed disappointment to the firm I helped build."

Aimi shakes my hand, her grip firm and warm. "Failed architect? That's a new one. Usually get stockbrokers or lawyers in here having meltdowns."

"I'm innovating in the field of professional self-destruction." I drain the water she provided in one long swallow. "Ten years of perfect designs, and suddenly I'm being babysat by a kid who still gets ID'd buying lottery tickets."

"Sounds like you've earned that bottle." She refills my water without asking. "Though in my experience, the world usually looks different in the morning."

"That's what I'm afraid of." I pour another whiskey, this one smaller than the last. "It might look worse."

"What could be worse?" Aimi leans against the counter, arms crossed. "Let's see... you could wake up and discover you've drunk-texted your boss a resignation letter in emojis. Or maybe you'll realize that fancy architect brain of yours designed a building that looks suspiciously like a giant..."

"Please don't finish that sentence," I interrupt, feeling an unexpected laugh rise in my throat.

"Or," she continues, undeterred, "you could wake up and realize that after all your professional humiliation, you spent the night crying to a bartender about how your protractor collection just doesn't understand you."

Despite everything, the board meeting, Ryan's promotion, the whiskey burning a hole in my stomach, I crack a smile. It feels strange on my face, like exercising a muscle long neglected.

Aimi returns the smile, genuine and warm. There's something disarming about her, no pretense, no hidden agenda. Just a woman doing her job, finding humor in the wreckage of my day.

"For what it's worth," she says, filling another glass of water and sliding it toward me, "most people who come in here claiming their careers are over usually show up a week later celebrating some unexpected victory. Funny how that works."

I take the water, our fingers brushing briefly. "And if that doesn't happen?"

"Then you come back, and I'll save you a seat at the bar for your regularly scheduled breakdown." She winks. "We offer a loyalty program, five existential crises get you a free basket of wings."

Our fingers touch for only a moment, but it's enough. A small grumble stirs in my stomach, a familiar hunger awakening despite the whiskey's numbing effect. I study her face as she moves down the bar to serve another customer, the smooth curve of her cheek catching the dim light, the slight upturn of her lips even when she's not actively smiling. Her body moves with effortless grace as she reaches for bottles, the fabric of her shirt pulling tight across smooth curves.

The hunger whispers to me, reminding me of its presence. It's different from what I feel for Iris, less consuming, more immediate. More... manageable.

Aimi returns, catching me watching her. She doesn't seem uncomfortable with my gaze, meeting it with that same warm smile that somehow cuts through my carefully constructed walls.

"Still with us?" she asks, tapping the counter near my hand. "You looked like you were a million miles away."

I clear my throat, regaining my composure. "Just contemplating the wisdom of bartenders. Surprisingly profound for someone who serves liquid bad decisions for a living."

"Bartending is just architecture with alcohol," she replies. "We both create spaces for people to exist in. Yours are just more permanent."

The hunger stirs again, more insistent this time. I wonder what she'd look like in my space, my control, as a part of my collection. I wonder if she'd still smile that way if she knew what I was thinking.

I push the thought away. Not here. Not her.

She's not my usual prey, she's too integrated into the community, she would be noticed immediately if she went missing. Someone might recognize her talking with me, especially with my car sitting here overnight.

I study Aimi, the hunger shifting from something predatory to a more mundane sensation. My stomach growls audibly, reminding me I haven't eaten since morning.

Not unless you count that sandwich that gave only the fulfilling sensation of eating cardboard.

"These wings from your loyalty program," I say, leaning forward slightly. "Any chance I could order some now without waiting for my other four existential crises? I'm suddenly realizing whiskey on an empty stomach might not have been my wisest architectural decision today."

Aimi's laugh is warm and genuine. "I wouldn't recommend the wings unless you're truly desperate. Between us?" She leans in conspiratorially. "They come frozen in a bag with a brand name I'm not legally allowed to pronounce in this establishment."

"That bad?"

"Let's just say they're not winning any culinary awards." She taps her fingers against the bar top. "But our burgers and fries? Those are to die for. Eddie in the back used to work at some fancy steakhouse before he decided cooking pretentious food for pretentious people wasn't worth the stress."

The phrase "to die for" tickles something dark inside me, and I can't help but smile at the irony.

"Well, I'd hate to die on an empty stomach," I say, the double meaning dancing on my tongue. "I'll take the burger and fries, then. Medium rare, if Eddie can manage it."

"Coming right up." She scribbles the order on a pad. "And I'm adding extra fries because, frankly, you look like you could use the carbs to soak up that bottle you've been nursing."

I chuckle, offering Aimi a genuine smile, one I rarely give to anyone. "Thank you. I think you've already saved me from myself tonight, or at least from the worst hangover of my architectural career."

I down the third glass of water in long, grateful gulps. The cool liquid cuts through the whiskey haze, bringing a moment of clarity I'm not entirely sure I wanted. The bar continues its loud chatter, college students and regulars creating a tapestry of noise that somehow feels comforting in its anonymity.

Aimi moves away to help other patrons, expertly mixing drinks and making conversation. I watch her work, appreciating how well the mix glasses spin in her hands She has her own architecture, the way she builds relationships with customers, structures conversations, designs experiences with each pour and smile.

When she notices my empty water glass again, she returns with the pitcher.

"You know," she says, filling it to the brim, "at this rate, you'll be the most hydrated drunk in Austin. We should get you a trophy, something classy, like a golden toilet."

I almost choke on my water, caught between a laugh and surprise.

The conversation with Aimi drifts into comfortable silence as she moves down the bar to serve another customer. I reach for my whiskey glass, but something more urgent demands my attention. A pressure builds in my lower abdomen, insistent, impossible to ignore.

I slide off the barstool, and the world tilts slightly. The floor seems less solid than it did moments ago, the straight lines of the bar counter wavering like a mirage. I'm not drunk, I don't get drunk, but I'm definitely feeling the effects more than I anticipated.

"Bathroom?" I ask when Aimi passes by again.

She points toward the back. "Past the pool tables, on your right."

I nod my thanks and navigate around tables and patrons. My usual precise movements have abandoned me; I brush against a chair, murmuring an apology to its empty seat. The room seems to expand and contract with each step, the distance to the restroom stretching like taffy.

The men's room swings open with heavy resistance. Inside, fluorescent lights buzz overhead, casting harsh shadows across grimy tile. Graffiti decorates the walls, crude drawings and declarations of love, hate, and anatomical impossibilities.

I make my way to the urinal, planting my left palm against the wall for stability. The cool tiles ground me as I relieve myself, the pressure in my bladder finally subsiding. I close my eyes for a moment, feeling the room spin gently behind my eyelids.

When I finish, I wash my hands thoroughly, some standards remain uncompromised regardless of my state. I pause for a moment, splashing cold water on my face. The man in the mirror looks unfamiliar: tie askew, hair slightly disheveled, eyes glassy. Is this what losing control looks like? Just a loosened tie and damp collar?

The journey back to my seat requires more concentration than it should. I focus on placing one foot directly in front of the other, as if walking an invisible tightrope. A few heads turn to watch my careful progress, but I maintain what dignity I can muster.

I slide back onto my barstool with a sense of accomplishment disproportionate to the task. The whiskey bottle still waits, but my enthusiasm for it has waned. I reach for the water instead.

Aimi approaches, carrying a plate that sends savory aromas wafting toward me. My stomach responds with an embarrassingly loud growl.

"Perfect timing," she says, placing the burger and fries before me. "Eddie's masterpiece, medium rare as requested."

"Your life raft in a sea of Wild Turkey," she announces. "Try not to weep with joy."

The burger sits in the center of the plate, surrounded by a mountain of golden fries. Steam rises from the food, carrying aromas that make my stomach clench with urgent need. The hunger I've been suppressing all night roars to life, no longer the dark, dangerous thing that lives in my chest but something more primal and immediate.

I grab a fry, surprised by how hot it is against my fingers. The first bite is a revelation, crispy exterior giving way to fluffy potato, seasoned with what tastes like Lawry's salt, basil, and perhaps a hint of dill. I close my eyes briefly, savoring the simple perfection of it.

Then I turn to the burger. The first bite confirms what my eyes promised, perfectly medium rare, pink in the center, juicy but not bloody. The bun is toasted and buttered, adding another layer of richness. I take a second bite, larger this time, and can't suppress the sound that escapes me, half laugh, half something close to a sob of pure enjoyment.

I demolish most of the burger in what feels like seconds, hardly pausing between bites. The flavors explode across my tongue, salt, fat, umami... A symphony that makes even my most meticulous architectural designs seem dull by comparison. I can't remember the last time I ate something this satisfying. Certainly not in any of the Michelin-starred restaurants I frequent to impress clients.

"Holy shit," I mumble around a mouthful of fries. "These are... these are fucking incredible."

I'm not one for profanity, not typically. But the alcohol has loosened something in me, dissolved the careful boundaries I maintain. The fries deserve the emphasis anyway.

Aimi slides back over, watching me with amusement as I stuff another handful into my mouth.

"How's that burger treating you, architect man?" She leans against the counter, her smile warm and genuine.

I try to answer, but my mouth is full. I hold up a finger, chewing frantically before swallowing.

"S'fucking amazing," I slur, trying to focus my mind and vision, both slipping further into a drunken stooper. "Eddie's a... a culinary genius. Should build him a restaurant. Big one. With... with lots of windows."

My tongue feels thick in my mouth, words slipping out before I can arrange them into their proper order. The whiskey that had been warming my blood now seems to have replaced it entirely.

"Whoa there," Aimi laughs, reaching for the bottle I've been nursing. "I think you and Wild Turkey need some time apart."

I make a half-hearted grab for the bottle, but my coordination is shot. My hand swipes through empty air.

"No, no, s'fine. I'm fine." I blink hard, trying to focus on her face, which keeps shifting in and out of clarity. "Just need to... finish my professional... professional breakdown."

Aimi tucks the bottle under the bar, out of my reach. "I'll hold onto this for safekeeping. Consider it a security deposit on your dignity."

"That's..." I point at her, trying to look stern but probably failing miserably. "That's very funny. You're funny. Has anyone ever told you that? Funny. Like a... like a comedian, but prettier."

I hear the words tumbling out and know, distantly, that I should be mortified. But the whiskey has burned away my capacity for embarrassment.

Aimi doesn't roll her eyes or dismiss my drunken compliment. Instead, her smile softens, and she actually looks... pleased.

"Well, thank you. That's sweet of you to say." She adjusts a strand of hair behind her ear. "Even if it's the Wild Turkey talking."

"No, no, it's not the..." I wave my hand, nearly knocking over my water glass. "I mean, yes, I'm drunk. Very drunk. But that doesn't make it untrue."

I lean forward, suddenly eager to make her understand something important, though I'm not entirely sure what that is until the words start pouring out.

"I never say what I actually think, you know? Not to anyone." My voice drops to what I hope is a conspiratorial whisper but is probably still audible across the bar. "I just... I calculate. Every word. What they want to hear. What advances my position. What maintains control of the conversation."

I tap my temple with my finger. "It's all up here. Blueprints for every interaction. But with you?" I gesture broadly, almost losing my balance on the stool. "No blueprint. Just... words. Real ones."

Aimi studies me with her eyes a minute, squinting, her head tilted slightly. She's looking at me differently now, like she's seeing something beyond the disheveled architect drowning his sorrows.

"That sounds exhausting," she says finally. "Living like every conversation is a chess match."

I blink at her, surprised by her insight. "It is. God, it really is. But necessary. Essential."

"Is it though?" She places a fresh glass of water in front of me, her fingers lingering on the glass. "Seems like the unfiltered version of you is doing just fine tonight."

"You know what's strange?" I lean forward, steadying myself with both elbows on the bar. "I can't remember the last time I just... talked to someone. Without an agenda."

She raises an eyebrow. "Everyone has an agenda."

"No, I mean..." I gesture vaguely, searching for words that don't feel pre-planned. "With clients, I'm selling. With women, I'm... pursuing. With colleagues, I'm competing. It's exhausting."

Aimi wipes down the counter near my plate, cleaning up the water I spilled. "And what's your agenda with me, architect man?"

The question catches me off guard. What is my agenda? The hunger stirs, but it's different, less demanding, almost like I can hear it, but from behind a wall.

"I don't have one," I admit as I drop my arms, turning up my hands. "That's what's so nice. Just talking to you. You're... you're really pretty, you know that?"

The words tumble out unfiltered. I haven't called a woman "pretty" since college. It's such a simple, inadequate word, not sophisticated or precise enough for my usual vocabulary. Yet it feels right.

She smiles, neither accepting nor rejecting the compliment. "Pretty enough to earn a decent tip, I hope."

"I'm serious," I insist, leaning closer. "Not just conventionally attractive. You're... authentic. Real." I tap the counter for emphasis. "Do you know how rare that is? To meet someone who isn't performing?"

Something flickers across her face, amusement, maybe, or skepticism.

"Says the man who just admitted he calculates every interaction."

"Exactly!" I point at her, almost knocking over my water. "That's why I notice. That's why it's so... refreshing. Talking to you."

I pause, suddenly aware of how I must sound, drunk, rambling, completely unlike my controlled self.

"The problem with Iris," I blurt out, "is that she's not like you."

The words hang in the air between us. I blink, surprised at myself. Where did that come from?

Aimi's eyebrows rise with interest. "Iris? Who's Iris?"

I wave my hand vaguely, nearly knocking over my water glass again. "She works in my building. Third floor. Not my company. Different company." I'm talking too much, words spilling out without the careful filter I normally employ. "She's... complicated."

"Complicated how?" Aimi leans against the bar, her curiosity evident. She's stopped wiping the counter, giving me her full attention.

"She's..." I struggle to articulate what makes Iris so captivating, so consuming. How do I explain that hunger without revealing too much? "She's like a puzzle I can't solve. Every time I think I understand her, she changes the rules."

"Sounds like you're pretty into this woman." Aimi's tone is casual, but her eyes are sharp, assessing.

"It's not like that," I protest, then immediately contradict myself. "Well, it is. But it's different. With other women, I know exactly what to do, what to say. I'm in control. With Iris..." I trail off, realizing I'm walking dangerously close to revealing too much about myself.

"With Iris?" Aimi prompts.

"With Iris, I feel like I'm the one being hunted." The confession slips out before I can stop it. I freeze, horrified at what I've just said.

Aimi tilts her head. "Hunted? That's an interesting way to put it."

I backpedal frantically. "Not hunted. That's not... I mean, she's just... unpredictable. I can't read her. Most people, I can read them like blueprints. Their desires, their motivations, all laid out in clean lines. But Iris..."

"She doesn't follow your blueprint," Aimi finishes for me.

"Exactly!" I say too loudly, grateful she understands. "And it's maddening because I should be able to figure her out. I'm good at figuring people out. It's what I do."

"Maybe that's why you're so fixated," Aimi suggests. "You can't stand not being in control."

"You're right," I admit, running my finger around the rim of my water glass. "Control is... everything to me. Has been since I was a kid." The memory flickers, my father's unpredictable rages, the constant vigilance required to navigate his moods. "If you can control the variables, you can prevent disaster."

But something tugs at me, a contradiction I can't ignore. "And yet..." I trail off, searching for words that won't come easily. "With Iris, when I finally gave up trying to control everything, just for a moment, it was different."

I remember her toe pressing against my lips. The command in her eyes. The surrender.

"Different how?" Aimi asks, leaning closer.

"Like..." I close my eyes, trying to capture the sensation. "Like falling. Not the terror of it, but the moment you accept gravity. When you stop fighting and just... experience it."

My eyes open, finding Aimi watching me intently. "I've spent my whole life building structures, literal ones, yes, but also... frameworks for every interaction. Calculating angles, anticipating stress points." I tap my temple. "Exhausting, like you said."

I take another sip of water, surprised by my own candor. "But with Iris, when I stopped calculating, when I just let go, it felt like freedom. Terrifying freedom..."

Aimi sets down the glass she's been polishing and looks at me with an unexpected intensity.

"Maybe that's your answer right there," she says quietly. "This control thing, it's not working for you anymore, is it?"

I open my mouth to object, then close it again. The alcohol has dismantled my usual defenses, leaving me vulnerable to uncomfortable truths.

"It's always worked before," I mutter.

"Has it though?" She leans forward, resting her elbows on the bar. "Because from where I'm standing, you look like a man who's drowning in his own rulebook."

The words hit with surprising force. I stare at my half-empty water glass, watching condensation trail down its sides.

"Look," she continues, her voice gentler now. "I don't know this Iris woman, and I definitely don't know what's going on between you two. But I do know something about letting go." She absently touches a small tattoo on her wrist, a bird in flight. "I spent years trying to control everything in my life. My daughter's father, my career path, how people saw me. All it did was make me miserable."

"What changed?" I ask, genuinely curious.

"I stopped fighting the current." She shrugs. "Sounds simple, but it was the hardest thing I've ever done. Had to admit I couldn't control other people, couldn't predict every outcome."

"And that worked for you? Just... surrendering?" The concept feels foreign in my mouth.

"Not surrendering. There's a difference between giving up and letting go." She smiles, a flash of wisdom behind her eyes. "Maybe with this woman, you need to stop trying to write the script. Maybe the most interesting part of the story is the part you can't predict."

I consider her words, turning them over in my whiskey-addled brain. The idea of relinquishing control terrifies me, it always has. But there's something compelling in what she's saying.

"What if it all falls apart?" The question comes out smaller than I intended.

"What if it doesn't?" Aimi counters. "What if letting go is exactly what you need to do?"

"That's what scares the hell out of me," I confess. "Because what happens when you build your entire identity on control, and then discover that what you really want is to let it go?"

Aimi's eyes crinkle with mirth. "You know what they call an architect who can't let go of control? Structurally unsound." She mimics a building collapsing with her hands, complete with explosion sound effects.

I snort loudly, nearly choking on my water. It's not even that funny, but something about the absurdity of it, this bartender psychoanalyzing me with architecture puns, breaks through my whiskey-soaked melancholy.

"That's terrible," I manage between chuckles.

"Hey, I'm a bartender, not a comedian." She grins. "But seriously, even the most perfectly designed buildings need flexibility to withstand pressure. Too rigid, and they crack at the first tremor."

The metaphor lands with unexpected clarity. I've spent my life building rigid structures, in steel and glass, yes, but also in my mind, in my interactions. No room for error, for spontaneity. For joy.

"Aimi," I say, my voice suddenly earnest. "Thank you. For the burger, the drinks, everything. Talking with you tonight has been... illuminating. I can't remember the last time I had a conversation this real."

She waves away my thanks. "Part of the job description. Bartender, amateur therapist, same thing."

I push back my stool and attempt to stand, immediately regretting the decision as the room tilts violently. My legs buckle, and I grab the bar to steady myself.

"Whoa there, architect man." Aimi rushes around the bar, slipping her shoulder under my arm. She's surprisingly strong for her size, taking my weight without strain. "Let's get you a taxi."

She guides me toward the door, her arm around my waist. The physical contact is strangely comforting, not sexual, just human. When was the last time someone touched me without agenda?

At the door, I fumble for my wallet, pulling out several hundred-dollar bills. I press them into her hand.

"For you. For everything."

Aimi stares at the money. "This is way too much. Your tab wasn't even fifty bucks."

"Please," I insist, curling her fingers around the cash. "You've earned it. Trust me."

She hesitates, then nods. "Alright. Thank you."

The taxi arrives, yellow and blurry through my double vision. Aimi helps me inside, gives the driver my address from my ID.

"Get home safe, Sebastian," she says, her voice fading as I slump against the seat.

The taxi pulls away. Street lights streak past the window, blurring into golden ribbons. I close my eyes for just a moment.

And then... nothing.

CHAPTER 19

I barely sleep.

My eyes snap open while it's still dark. I lie in bed, my mind spinning, desire a weight in my chest. I stare at the darkness, thinking of her. Iris.

I rise early, driven by an unfamiliar urgency. My routine is usually meticulous, but today, I'm rushed. I'm not myself. I crave her.

The city is still half-asleep as I step out of my penthouse, the sky a gradient of indigo and orange that promises the dawn. I'm usually the master of my mornings, savoring the calm before the chaos of my workday at Wolfe & Hart. But today, there's a tremor in my hands, a thrum in my veins that won't quiet. It's her. Iris.

I make my way through the awakening streets, my strides purposeful and quick. The crisp air does nothing to clear my mind, which is crowded with thoughts of her. Every morning, without fail, she steps into that elevator at precisely 8:17 AM. It's a ritual, a moment that anchors my day in a sea of predictability. But today, I'm early. I need to see her, to ensure that she's real, that our encounters aren't just figments of my imagination.

I race along the street, pulse hammering in my throat. 8:13 AM. Four minutes until her arrival. Four minutes until Iris.

This never happens. I'm never late. Control slips through my fingers like water, and I hate the feeling. The revolving doors of my building spin as I push through, nodding curtly at the security guard who barely has time to return the greeting. My shoes click rapidly across the marble floor, echoing in the still-quiet lobby.

8:16 AM. I check my watch, breathing hard. One minute. I smooth my tie, adjust my cuffs, small attempts to reclaim control. The elevator stands before me, doors closed, numbers above it indicating it's on its way down. Perfect timing.

I look at my watch again, watching the minute hand as it strikes 8:17. I scan the lobby, my eyes darting from entrance to entrance. No Iris. Perhaps she's running behind as well. Perhaps she's already inside. The elevator arrives with a soft chime, doors opening to reveal an empty car. I step inside, hold the door open button, and wait.

8:19 AM. Still no Iris. This isn't right. She's never late. Not once in all the months I've tracked her movements.

8:23 AM. My foot taps against the elevator floor, an irritating staccato that I can't seem to stop. I release the button, let the doors close, then press the lobby button again to reset the elevator's journey. People approach, but I wave them away with a curt "Out of order, somethings wrong with the button panel" that sends them to the adjacent bank of elevators as I hold the 'Door Open' with my thumb.

The elevator begins to chime its alarm as I continue to hold the button. I start pushing the door open button over and over as I lean my head out the doors.

I see the security guard Ivan slowly walking towards the elevator.

I don't want him coming over to ask why I'm holding this door, I will just sound crazy. I jump out, releasing the button, the doors promptly closing behind me and the elevator begins to ascend.

8:27 AM. Where is she?

I leave the elevator, My hand runs through my hair, disrupting its careful styling. I pace small circles in the lobby, checking every entrance repeatedly.

8:30 AM. My phone vibrates. Ryan.

"Sebastian? You coming in today? The Carmichael presentation is at nine-thirty."

"I'm in the building," I snap, the words short and clipped. "Fucking elevator issues. I'll be up."

I jam the phone back in my pocket, swear under my breath, and stride back to the elevator. Alone, I punch the button for the my floor, my reflection in the polished doors showing a man I barely recognize, scruffy, agitated, unmoored.

Iris hasn't come. And I don't know why.

The elevator doors slide open, and I step out onto my office floor, where the corridors gleam with modern minimalism. My temple throbs with the beginning of a headache. Everything feels slightly off, and why is this sunlight so bright.

Elizabeth stands at my office door, clutching a portfolio to her chest. Her soft blonde hair is pulled back in that severe bun she favors. Her mouth opens before I reach her.

"Sebastian, I've been waiting, the Carmichael presentation needs your final approval on the central atrium design, and they've specifically requested..."

I brush past her, throwing my coat onto the nearest chair. "Not now."

"But they'll be here in less than an hour, and the renderings..."

The tension that's been building since I realized Iris wasn't coming snaps like a steel cable. "I said not now." My voice cuts through the air, sharp enough to draw blood. "Is that unclear? Do you need it written down? Or perhaps you'd prefer I use smaller words?"

Elizabeth's face colors, her eyes widening. The office beyond my door has gone silent. I can feel the attention of every employee shifting toward us, their collective breath held.

"I, I'm sorry," she stammers, clutching the portfolio tighter. "I'll just... leave these here."

She sets the portfolio on my desk, movements quick and nervous like a bird ready for flight. She exits without another word, her heels clicking rapidly down the hallway.

I sink into my chair; my hands pressed against my temples. Where is Iris? Has something happened to her? Or worse, has she deliberately avoided me?

A tiny knock interrupts my spiral. Ryan stands in my doorway, brow furrowed, tie slightly askew as usual.

"Hey," he says carefully. "That was... intense."

"Did you need something?" I don't look up.

He steps inside, closes the door behind him. "What's going on with you today? You're never late, and you just tore Elizabeth apart for doing her job."

"I'm fine."

"Bullshit." Ryan leans against my desk. "I've known you for eight years. You're a lot of things, but 'fine' isn't one of them right now."

I lean back in my chair, pinching the bridge of my nose and closing my eyes. I take in a deliberate deep breath, holding it for a moment, then releasing.

"It's nothing," I say, my voice steadier now. "I'm dealing with some personal matters."

Ryan raises an eyebrow. "Personal matters? You don't have personal matters. You have architectural matters, business matters, and occasionally, restaurant reservation matters." He crosses his arms. "Is this about a woman?"

The question catches me off guard, and I feel a treacherous warmth crawling up my neck. Am I that transparent?

"Don't be ridiculous," I snap, shuffling papers on my desk to avoid his gaze.

"Holy shit," Ryan's voice drops to an incredulous whisper. "It is about a woman. I've never seen you like this over someone. Who is she? Do I know her?"

I shoot him a withering look. "Don't you have work to do? The Carmichael presentation..."

"Is ready and waiting for your final approval, which is why Elizabeth was here." He doesn't budge. "Come on, Sebastian. Consider this an intervention. You just verbally eviscerated your assistant in front of the entire office."

I sigh, running a hand through my hair again. "Fine. Yes. There's a woman."

"And?"

"And nothing. She didn't show up where she was supposed to be this morning. I was... concerned."

Ryan's face softens. "So call her."

"I can't do that." The admission sounds pathetic even to my ears.

"Wait, you can't..." He stops, eyes narrowing. "Sebastian, how well do you actually know this woman?"

I don't answer. How can I explain that I know the exact shade of amber her eyes turn in morning light? That I could identify her by scent alone in a crowd of thousands? That I've memorized her patterns, her movements, her preferences, yet we've only just begun speaking?

"Jesus," Ryan mutters, reading my silence. "You're obsessed with someone you barely know."

"I know her," I insist, the words coming out sharper than intended. "I know Iris."

Ryan's eyes widen with recognition. "Wait, Iris? The woman from your party? Raven hair, killer smile, wore that black skirt that made half the room stop breathing?"

I straighten papers on my desk that don't need straightening. "Yes. That's her."

"Well, no wonder you're a mess." He shakes his head, a hint of admiration in his voice. "She was something else. The way she moved through your place like she owned it. Half my department couldn't form complete sentences when she walked by."

My fingers tighten around a pen, knuckles whitening. The image of other men watching her, wanting her, sends a surge of heat through my veins. I force myself to release my grip before the pen snaps in half.

"She's not just some woman," I say, my tone clipped.

Ryan holds up his hands. "Hey, I can see that. Look, whatever this is, you need to get it together. The Carmichaels will be here soon, and you look like you're ready to put your fist through a wall."

I check my watch. Forty-five minutes until the presentation. I inhale, hold it, exhale. Control. I need control.

"You're right," I admit, the words tasting foreign on my tongue. "I'm not... myself today."

"Take the day," Ryan suggests, leaning forward. "I can handle the Carmichaels. You've already done the heavy lifting on the design. Let me present it."

"That's ridiculous. I don't need..."

"Sebastian." His voice is firm. "Go clear your head. Get some space. Let off some steam. Whatever you need to do to get back to being the terrifying perfectionist we all know and tolerate."

I consider his offer, weighing it for a moment. The thought of sitting through a three-hour meeting while my mind circles endlessly around Iris's absence feels impossible.

"Fine," I concede. "I'll take the rest of the day off." I reply, my voice mumbling, carrying painful resignation.

"What was that?" Ryan asks.

"I'll take the rest of the day off!" I repeat, my tone making sure he hears me this time.

"Great, there's a spa in town I sometimes visit, Alpine Waters. Sensory deprivation, steam room, the works. Helps me realign." Ryan says.

"Perfect," I reply, rolling my eyes.

Ryan nods, already gathering the presentation materials. "Go float in darkness or whatever it is you do to reset. Just come back as yourself tomorrow."

I grab my coat and briefcase, feeling the weight of Ryan's concern like a brand against my skin. What's happening to me? I'm Sebastian Wolfe. I don't lose control. I don't snap at employees. I don't obsess over...

I stop myself. That's exactly what I'm doing. Obsessing.

As I step out of my office, the usual sound of conversation dies. Keyboards fall silent. People suddenly find their computer screens fascinating, their coffee cups captivating. They're all watching without watching, stealing glances when they think I won't notice. But I notice everything.

Kevin from structural engineering suddenly needs to examine a blueprint on his desk. Marina from interior design becomes absorbed in her phone. They're all avoiding my gaze, all pretending they didn't hear me eviscerate Elizabeth moments ago.

My throat tightens. This isn't me. Or perhaps it is, and I've simply kept it better contained until now.

Elizabeth sits at her desk outside my office, her shoulders rigid, her movements mechanical as she types. Her eyes remain fixed on her screen even as I approach. There's a slight redness around them that wasn't there before.

I've made her cry. The realization hits me with unexpected force.

"Elizabeth."

She looks up, her expression carefully neutral. "Yes, Mr. Wolfe? Did you need something else?"

The formality in her voice – we've worked together for three years, and she's never called me Mr. Wolfe – cuts deeper than I anticipate.

"I'm taking the day," I say, keeping my voice low. "I wanted to apologize for my behavior earlier. It was completely unacceptable."

Her fingers hover over her keyboard, surprise flickering across her face.

"I've been dealing with some... personal issues. But that's no excuse for how I spoke to you. You were doing your job – exceptionally well, as always – and I was out of line."

She blinks rapidly, her professional mask slipping for just a moment.

"I'm sorry, Elizabeth. Truly." The words feel strange in my mouth – when was the last time I apologized to anyone? – But it was necessary.

"It's... it's okay," she says softly. "We all have bad days."

"Not like this. Not at your expense." I place the Carmichael file on her desk. "Ryan will handle the presentation. I'll be back tomorrow, and I promise to be better."

She nods, a small, cautious smile forming. "Thank you, Sebastian."

I watch Ryan as I step into the elevator, coffee cup in hand, giving me a reassuring nod as the doors slide closed. He'll handle the Carmichaels. The thought brings less relief than it should. My schedule, my routine, all of it shattered because of her absence.

Ding.

I look up as the doors open, trying to avoid any more run ins with someone I don't want to tear apart. I keep an eye out for Iris as I cross the lobby. *Still no Iris.*

The parking garage is cool and dimly lit, the scent of concrete and exhaust hanging in the air. My Aston Martin waits in its designated space, always the same one, every day. At least something remains constant. The door opens with a soft click, and I slip inside, the leather seat cool against my back. I press the ignition, the engine roaring to life.

I take a moment, leaning back, my eyes closed, taking in deep breaths, holding them and exhaling. The roaring purr of the engine provides white noise, doing well to remove me from the environment I physically exist in.

I take out my phone, tapping the screen to search for "Alpine Waters spa." It appears immediately, a sleek website featuring smooth stones and flowing water. Four-point-eight stars. "Sensory-focused relaxation experiences." Not my typical choice, but today is anything but typical.

I plug the address into my GPS and pull out of the garage, the engine purring beneath me. I put a heavy foot to the throttle and I pull out onto the road and make my way down the streets.

Alpine Waters occupies a minimalist building of glass and stone. I park, straighten my tie out of habit, and stride inside. The reception area smells of eucalyptus and something faintly floral. Calm ambient music plays from hidden speakers. Everything designed to induce a calm state of being.

A menu of services hangs on the wall behind the counter, flotation therapy, infrared sauna, hot stone massage, various "treatments" with names that sound more like cocktails than relaxation techniques.

"First time with us?"

I turn to find a young woman behind the counter, her smile practiced but genuine. Her name tag reads "Mia."

"Is it that obvious?" I ask.

"Just a little." She gestures to the menu I've been staring at. "You look a bit lost."

"My colleague Ryan Adams recommended this place, told me to come in."

Her eyes light with recognition. "Oh, Ryan! He called and said we should expect you. Would you like the same thing he always gets?"

I pause, considering. I have no idea what Ryan does here, what rituals he finds comforting. But I need something, anything, to reset.

"I'm not entirely sure what that entails," I admit, the words feeling foreign on my tongue. "But yes, that would be fine."

Mia hands me a plush white robe and a pair of foam slippers. "Right this way, Mr. Wolfe." She leads me down a dimly lit corridor, the polished concrete floor cool beneath the thin slippers.

"Our sensory deprivation chambers are completely soundproof," she explains, voice hushed as if already honoring the silence we approach. "The water is heated to skin temperature, about ninety-eight degrees, and contains eight hundred pounds of Epsom salts."

We stop before a sleek black door. She pushes it open, revealing a minimalist room bathed in whispers of blue light. At the center sits what looks like a large, white pod, rounded and alien against the dark flooring.

"Inside the tank, you'll float effortlessly. No sound, no light, just you and your thoughts." She points to a small button on the interior of the pod. "If you need anything, press this button. Otherwise, I'll leave you alone for ninety minutes and knock when your time is up."

I nod, taking in the space, shower in the corner, towels neatly stacked on a bench, and dim lighting that can be adjusted with a dial by the door.

"I'll let you change now," she says, placing a small basket on the bench. "You can put your clothes and valuables in here."

I hesitate, suddenly realizing a fundamental oversight. "I don't have any swim clothes with me."

Mia's lips curve into a subtle smile. "That's not a problem. Most of our clients prefer to float without anything at all." She lowers her voice slightly. "I do too when I use the tank. It's the purest experience, nothing between you and the water."

I catch the flirtation in her tone, the way her eyes briefly flutter down then back to mine. Under normal circumstances, I might catalog this interaction, file it away as potentially useful. Today, it barely registers beyond mild amusement.

I return her smile anyway, keeping the social contract intact. "I appreciate your candor. Thank you, Mia."

"Take your time. When you're ready, shower first to remove any oils, then step in and pull the lid closed." She backs toward the door. "Enjoy your float, Mr. Wolfe."

The door clicks shut behind her. Alone now, I remove my watch, 10:17 AM, and place it in the basket. My tie, jacket, and shirt follow in methodical order. Each item folded precisely, placed deliberately.

The silence in the room is absolute. No music plays here, no ambient noise to distract.

I finish undressing, keeping my movements efficient and purposeful. The pod waits, its curved lid partially open, the blue light reflecting off the still water inside.

The water gives gently beneath my weight as I step into the pod. It's surprisingly buoyant, the high salt content immediately trying to push me upward. I lower myself slowly, my body submerged to the chest before I pull the curved lid closed above me.

Darkness. Complete and absolute.

For a moment, I simply sit there, my knees drawn up slightly, hands gripping the smooth edges of the tank. The warm water laps against my skin, neither hot nor cool, but somehow perfectly matched to my body temperature. I can barely distinguish where air ends and water begins.

"Let go," I murmur to myself, the words swallowed instantly by the perfect acoustics of the chamber.

I lean back cautiously, expecting to sink, but my body rises instead, floating effortlessly to the surface. The saltwater cradles me, suspending my limbs without effort. My ears submerge, and the last ambient sounds disappear entirely.

Nothing exists but my own breathing and heartbeat.

I close my eyes, though it makes no difference in this perfect blackness. The absence of all sensory input is both liberating and unsettling. No light. No sound. No texture beneath my fingertips except for water that feels like nothing at all.

I focus on my breath. Inhale for four counts. Hold for seven. Exhale for eight. A technique I learned years ago to maintain composure during high-pressure client meetings.

My mind immediately drifts to Iris.

Her scent. Her smile. The coolness of her toe against my lips.

"No," I whisper into the void. "Not now."

I redirect my thoughts, focusing on the sensation of floating. My muscles begin to release tension I didn't realize they were holding. My jaw unclenches. My shoulders drop away from my ears.

Breath in. Hold. Release.

Iris slips back in, her fingertips trailing across my skin.

I grit my teeth. This isn't working.

Deeper breath. Longer hold. Slower exhale.

I force myself to visualize an empty white room. Clean lines. Perfect symmetry. Nothing but space and light.

A gentle knock disrupts the void. My eyes open to perfect darkness, I must have dozed off.

"Mr. Wolfe? Your session is complete." Mia's voice filters through the pod's shell, distant yet clear.

I blink, disoriented. The weightlessness that had seemed so strange initially now feels natural, too natural. My limbs resist the idea of movement, content to remain suspended in nothingness.

The knock comes again, more insistent. "Mr. Wolfe?"

"Yes," I manage, my voice rough. "I'm awake."

"I'll be just outside when you're done," Mia replies. "Please shower to remove the salt, then change into your robe. I'll be waiting outside to take you to the next part of your treatment."

I push against the lid, cool air rushing in as dim light spills in. I sit up, water cascading off my shoulders, my body unexpectedly heavy now.

The shower's pressure is perfect, strong enough to be efficient without becoming aggressive. Hot water washes away the salt that has already begun to crystallize on my skin in delicate patterns. I scrub methodically, working from top to bottom, watching the soapy water disappear down the drain.

Toweling off, I examine myself in the mirror. Still me.

The robe is unexpectedly substantial, plush against my skin. Reaching around, I grab the attached belt, securing it across my waist.

"How was your float?" Mia asks through the door.

I consider the question. My mind feels clearer. The obsessive thoughts of Iris haven't vanished, but they've receded to a manageable distance.

"Effective," I answer simply.

"Excellent." Mia replies.

Mia waits in the corridor, her posture relaxed but professional. "This way, please." She leads me deeper into the building, past doors marked with symbols rather than words. "How are you feeling?"

"Better," I admit, surprised to find it's true.

She stops before a sliding panel of a white paper Japanese style door, its wooden frame elegant, yet simple. "This is the massage room." She slides the door open, revealing a room with a padded brown floor that gives slightly beneath my feet as I step in. The space is warm, dimly lit, with a undertone of jasmine.

"This is our main massage room," Mia explains, gesturing to the space. "For your deep tissue work."

She hands me a fluffy, oversized white towel from a heated cabinet. The warmth radiates through my palms, unexpectedly comforting.

"Please remove your robe and lie face down on the mat," she instructs, pointing to a large cushioned platform in the center of the floor. It's covered in crisp white linen, thicker than the standard massage table I'd expected. "Use this towel to cover yourself. Nikki will be with you shortly."

I take the towel, noting its weight, substantial enough to provide proper coverage without feeling cumbersome.

"Nikki is one of our senior therapists," Mia continues. "She specializes in deep pressure work and trigger point release, Ryan's usual preference. She'll help with any remaining tension the flotation didn't address."

Mia moves toward the door, her hand resting on the frame. "Would you like some water before I go?"

"No, thank you."

She nods. "Just relax and breathe. Nikki will knock before entering."

The door slides shut with barely a whisper. Alone again, I shed the robe, hanging it on a wooden peg by the door. The air is pleasantly warm against my bare skin, not hot enough to be uncomfortable, but heated precisely to prevent any chill. Another carefully controlled environment. I appreciate the attention to detail.

I position myself on the mat, adjusting the towel across my lower body. The cushioning beneath me yields perfectly, supporting without allowing me to sink too deeply. My face fits comfortably in the padded cradle at the top of the platform, allowing my neck to remain in neutral alignment.

The jasmine scent grows stronger as I settle, likely diffusing from somewhere above.

I focus on my breathing again, matching its rhythm to the faint sounds of water trickling from a small fountain in the corner.

For the first time today, my mind feels clear. Empty. Present.

A gentle knock at the door signals Nikki's arrival.

The door slides open with barely a whisper. I remain still, my face pressed into the cradle, listening as Nikki enters.

"Hello," she says gently. Her voice is a smooth and even elegance of sound.

"Hello," I reply, my own voice barely above a murmur.

"I'm Nikki, your therapist today," she continues. "Ryan Adams recommended you come see us."

I nod slightly against the padding. "Yes, that's right."

"I've been told Ryan enjoys your work," I say, adjusting my position slightly.

"Ryan's a regular," Nikki says, her voice closer now. I hear the subtle sound of oil being warmed between palms. "He specifically thought you might benefit from my meditative hot stone therapy. It's what I specialize in."

"Is that different from a standard massage?" My question comes out more abruptly than intended. Control, always seeking information, parameters, boundaries.

"Very different." Her hands hover above my back, radiating heat before making contact. "Traditional massage focuses on working the muscles directly. What I do combines deep pressure with heated volcanic stones to release tension at a deeper level."

Her palms finally press into my shoulders, fingers finding knots I didn't realize existed.

"The stones retain heat," she continues, working methodically down my spine, "which helps the muscles release more completely. It's not just physical, the weight and warmth of the stones creates a meditative state. The body surrenders when the mind allows it."

I tense at her choice of words. *Surrender.*

"You're fighting it," she observes, hands pausing. "That's normal. Most people who come to me holding as much tension as you do have trouble letting go."

"I'm fine," I insist, the words clipped.

"Of course." Her tone holds no judgment. "But maybe try this, focus on a single point of pressure. Don't try to control it. Just observe it."

She places something warm against the center of my back, the first stone, its weight surprising yet perfectly bearable. Another stone follows, then another, creating a line of heat down my spine.

I inhale sharply, instinctively resisting.

"Breathe into the sensation," Nikki murmurs. "The stones aren't your enemy."

My jaw clenches. This woman doesn't know me, doesn't understand my need for control.

Her hands work alongside the stones, pressing them deeper into specific points. Something shifts, a knot releasing, creating a cascade of sensation that travels from my shoulders down my arms.

Despite myself, I exhale, the breath longer and deeper than before.

"There," she says. "That's the beginning."

Nikki works silently for a while, her hands surprisingly strong for someone of her size. The stones blaze hot trails across my skin, not painfully so, but enough to command my attention. My mind tries to wander, to Iris, to work, to the items appearing in my home, but the heat pulls me back each time.

"You're still resisting," she murmurs, adding another stone to the base of my spine. "What are you holding onto so tightly?"

I don't answer. I don't owe this stranger my thoughts.

"The body speaks when the mouth won't," she continues, untroubled by my silence. Her thumbs press into a point between my shoulder blades that sends a shock of pain-pleasure down my arms. "This knot here? It's where we store unprocessed emotions."

I almost laugh. New age nonsense packaged as wisdom.

"You don't believe me," she says, reading my reaction in my muscles. "That's fine. Your body believes."

She removes the stones one by one, replacing their heat with the firm pressure of her hands. Her movements become deeper, more targeted, finding places of resistance I didn't know existed.

"People think control is about holding on," she says, working her way down to my lower back. "But true control comes from knowing when to release."

Something unclenches deep within me, not physically, but somewhere less tangible. The sensation is disorienting, almost alarming in its intensity.

"There," she says, her voice softer now. "That's what we're looking for."

For a moment, just a moment, my mind goes perfectly blank. No Iris. No mysterious warnings. No calculated plans. Nothing but this present sensation.

The clarity is so startling I almost gasp.

"Turn over please," Nikki instructs, lifting the last stone from my back. "We'll work on your neck and shoulders from the front."

I comply, adjusting the towel as I roll onto my back. For the first time, I get a proper look at her, shorter than I expected, with a compact strength to her movements. Brown hair with blonde highlights frames a face that's neither beautiful nor plain, but somehow compelling in its ordinariness.

Nikki's hands find the junction where my neck meets my skull, her thumbs pressing into points that connect directly to the tension I've been carrying. I close my eyes, surrendering to the pressure, not fighting it now, but allowing it to dissolve something rigid within me.

"Your breathing has changed," she observes quietly. "That's good."

She's right. The tight, controlled rhythm I maintain has loosened, deepened. Each inhale feels like it reaches further into my body. Each exhale carries something away.

"Ryan was right to send you here," she continues, working down toward my collarbones. "You needed this."

I don't respond. Words feel unnecessary, almost intrusive in this state. My thoughts drift, but not to Iris for once. Instead, I find myself thinking about a building I designed three years ago, a museum with a central atrium that captured light in a way that changed hourly. The way the shadows moved across the floor throughout the day, creating patterns only I had anticipated.

Nikki presses her palms against my sternum, a steady pressure that grounds me back in my body.

"Almost done," she says. "We'll finish with some compression work on your shoulders."

Her hands move with confidence and precision, applying careful pressure to points along my shoulders and arms. The sensation borders on discomfort before releasing into relief, much like solving a complex structural problem in a design.

"There," she says finally, stepping away. "Take a moment before sitting up. Let your body adjust."

I breathe deeply, surprised by how different I feel. The obsessive thoughts haven't vanished, but they've receded, creating space for clarity I haven't experienced in weeks.

When I finally open my eyes, Nikki stands at a small sink in the corner, washing her hands.

"How do you feel?" she asks without turning.

"Better," I admit. The word feels insufficient, but anything more would reveal too much.

She nods, drying her hands on a small towel. "Good. I'll step out now so you can dress. Mia will be waiting in the hallway to guide you back to reception."

I dress quickly, each movement deliberate but unhurried. The sensation is strange, my body feels heavier yet somehow unburdened. As I slip my watch back onto my wrist, I notice how the leather band settles differently against my skin, as though the dimensions of my own body have subtly shifted.

The hallway feels longer walking back, the ambient lighting darker than I remembered. Mia waits by the reception desk, her posture relaxed yet attentive.

"How was your session with Nikki?" she asks, moving behind the sleek marble counter.

"Effective," I answer, reaching for my wallet. The word is the same I used earlier, but the meaning has deepened. "More than I expected."

Mia smiles, the expression genuine without being overly familiar. "That's what we aim for. Nikki has that effect on people."

She taps something into the tablet before her. "Your total comes to three hundred and twenty dollars. We accept all major cards or mobile payment."

I hand her my black card, watching as she swipes it with practiced efficiency.

"Ryan mentioned you might make this a regular appointment," she says, returning my card and offering a receipt. "Would you like to schedule your next session now?"

I consider the question. The clarity I feel now is valuable, a resource I didn't realize I needed until experiencing its absence and return.

"Yes," I decide. "Same time next week."

Mia nods, making the notation. "Excellent. We'll see you then, Mr. Wolfe."

"Thank you," I say, the words carrying more weight than such a simple courtesy usually warrants.

Outside, the afternoon sun feels different against my skin, sharper, more defined. I slide into my Aston Martin, the leather seat conforming to my body. The engine leaps to life with a turn of the key, its vibration traveling up through my fingertips.

I sit motionless for a moment, hands resting on the steering wheel. My mind, for the first time in weeks, feels ordered. The obsessive thoughts of Iris remain, but they've taken their proper place in the hierarchy of my consciousness rather than dominating it entirely.

And in this newfound clarity, other patterns begin to emerge... connections I've been too distracted to put together or notice.

Ryan.

The realization hits with such a force that I don't notice the ache of my fingers that are attempting to squeeze the life from my steering wheel.

Ryan Adams, with his perfectly dishevelled hair, earnest blue eyes, and reassuring smile. Always there, always watching. Always positioned to catch me when I fall.

Or push me first.

The Carmichael presentation. The elevator making sure I miss my meeting. The orchestrated destruction of my professional life and sensibilities benefits one person, Ryan...

The pieces lock together with terrible precision. Ryan volunteered to handle today's presentation not out of kindness, but opportunity. Every moment of my distraction is his advantage. Every mistake I make strengthens his position at the firm.

My mind races through the past few weeks, recalibrating events through this new lens. The errors in the Westfield specifications, Ryan had offered to review them before submission. "Fresh eyes," he'd said. The board meeting that was mysteriously moved up, giving me less time to prepare. Ryan had been the one to inform me of the change.

A bitter laugh escapes me. I've been so consumed with Iris that I've been completely blind to the architect of my professional undoing.

And Iris...

My thoughts circle back to her like water finding its inevitable path to the sea.

Not all consuming like the obsessive fool I've been, but as a man reclaiming control. The compulsion remains, transformed but no less powerful, no longer blind devotion but full of purposeful.

What I need to do is suddenly, startlingly clear.

One way or another, I will have a resolution with Iris. Then... Then I'll deal with Ryan.

The clarity stays with me as I drive, my mind crystalline and focused. The streets pass in a blur of intention rather than speed. I know exactly where I'm going, Iris's address plastered at the forefront of my mind.

I park my Aston Martin across the street from her place, its sleek silver form reflecting the streetlights. The engine ticks as it cools while I sit, hands still on the wheel, collecting myself. This isn't impulsive. This is necessary resolution.

The walk to her door feels perfectly measured. Each step lands with purpose on the concrete path leading to her front porch. The night air carries a hint of pollen.

I press the doorbell. Its chime echoes inside, but no footsteps follow. No shadow passes behind the frosted glass panel beside her door.

I wait exactly thirty seconds before knocking firmly. The sound of my knuckles against the wood is sharp, authoritative. Still nothing.

I press the doorbell again, holding it slightly longer this time. The silence that follows feels deliberate, as if the house itself is ignoring me.

My finger jabs the button a third time. A muscle in my jaw tightens.

Three more rings in rapid succession. My foot begins tapping against the porch, a physical manifestation of my fraying patience. The sound seems unnaturally loud in the quiet neighborhood.

The door swings open suddenly. Iris stands there, expression placid, as though my presence is neither surprising nor concerning.

"Sebastian," she says simply.

I don't wait for an invitation. I step forward, forcing her to step back, and close the door behind me with a decisive click.

Her home stops me short. The space is jarringly minimal, not the carefully curated minimalism of design magazines, but something more unsettling. A single recliner faces a wall with no television. The dining area holds only a table with a bonsai orange tree at its center, miniature fruit hanging from its branches like ornaments.

No photographs. No books. No evidence of a life being lived.

"What's going on?" Iris remarks, watching me catalog her barren space.

"Are you going to explain yourself?" she asks, her posture relaxed against the wall. Her voice is calm, but it holds an edge I've never heard before. "Or are you just going to stand there gaping?"

"I've had enough," I declare, stepping toward her.

Her eyes narrow slightly, but she doesn't flinch. "Enough of what?"

I close the distance between us. "This game between us needs to end. It has to stop."

Iris arches an eyebrow, a defiant tilt to her chin. "Does it?"

"Yes." I reach for her, my hands claiming her shoulders. "I can't do this anymore, Iris. I need you. Now."

She lets me pull her closer, her body warm against mine. "You've waited long enough, Sebastian. Perhaps it's time for your reward."

I kiss her, hard, desperate, my hands moving to tangle in her hair. She meets my urgency with her own, her mouth opening under mine. Our teeth clash, the pain a catalyst for even greater hunger.

She pulls back slightly, her breathing uneven. "Take me to my room."

I let her lead me through her barren home. My eyes search for signs of a life beyond these walls, a stray sock, a half-full water glass, anything that proves she exists outside of my fixation, but find none. The air between us crackles with tension, an electric storm trapped within these walls.

In her bedroom, the only hint of color is the crimson of her sheets. The rest is as stark as the rest of the house.

She turns to face me, her eyes searching mine. "Make love to me slowly, Sebastian. Worship every inch of my body before you take me, taste every part of me. Then you can have me however you want."

I hesitate, the challenge of her request clear. But the game has changed, and I'm determined to play it to its conclusion.

She slips her robe from her shoulders, letting it fall to the floor. I trace the gentle curve of her collarbone with my tongue before capturing one taut nipple between my lips. She arches her back, pressing herself against my mouth.

My breath is hot against her bare stomach as I hover just above, before my lips caress her. Her skin tastes of salt and something indefinably sweet. I work the underwear down her hips, letting my mouth follow, leaving a trail of kisses across her soft skin.

She shudders as my tongue brushes the hollow of her hip bone, her breath catching. "Don't stop. Not until you reach the end."

My name for her echoes in my mind, whispered in distorted tones. Angel. Aphrodite. Perfection. But I don't stop. I continue downward, placing open-mouthed kisses along her thigh, the warmth of her breath above me.

A subtle moan escapes her as I kiss the sensitive spot behind her knee, my hands sliding up the back of her thighs. I take my time as I taste her, every movement deliberate and achingly slow, but her request is clear, and I will not deny her. Not this time.

I pull away the final piece of the robe and press my lips to the small scar on her ankle, evidence of a story I don't know. This woman, this enigma, is finally yielding to me, offering herself without restraint.

My mouth finds the sensitive spot behind her knee once more before moving to the hollow of her calf, then her ankle again. My fingers slide beneath her feet, lifting them from the floor. She leans back, leaving her completely bare.

I press gentle kisses along the inside of her thigh, inhaling her scent. Her fingers twist in my hair, urging me higher, but I continue at my own pace. My tongue teases the soft crease where her leg joins her body, her breath catching as she steadies herself with one hand on the wall.

The feeling of her warm, supple skin beneath my lips is maddening. She tastes sweet like, honey and salt, exactly as I'd imagined during those elevator rides. The taste that's haunted me for months.

But as I continue my path across her body, something changes. A subtle bitterness lingers on my tongue, faint but unmistakable. I ignore it, focusing instead on the way she responds to my touch, the meek sounds she makes as my mouth explores her.

My lips trail up her stomach, tasting the hollow beneath her ribs. The bitterness intensifies, metallic, almost medicinal. Like copper pennies soaked in something caustic.

I pause, swallowing hard. My jaw feels suddenly tight, muscles constricting along the hinge. A cramp works its way up the side of my neck, tightening like a vice.

"Don't stop," she whispers, fingers tangling in my hair, pulling me closer.

I continue, pressing my mouth to the underside of her breast. The bitterness floods my senses now, overwhelming the natural taste of her skin. My tongue feels heavy, awkward in my mouth. The muscles in my neck spasm, a sharp pain shooting up into my skull.

Still, I persist. This moment, her surrender, is what I've been waiting for. I won't let some strange sensation derail me.

But as I move higher, trailing kisses along her collarbone, the cramping intensifies. My jaw locks momentarily, teeth clenching against my will. The muscles along my neck cord like steel cables, pulling tight enough to restrict my breathing.

Unease crawls up my spine. Something isn't right.

The bitter taste coats my mouth completely now, impossible to ignore.

I pull back slightly, trying to work the tightness from my jaw. My vision blurs at the edges, the room tilting sideways for a fraction of a second.

My jaw seizes without warning. Teeth clamp together with such force I hear something crack, a filling, perhaps a tooth itself. Pain shoots through my skull like lightning, branching down my spine.

I try to speak, to ask what's happening, but my mouth refuses to open. My tongue presses against clenched teeth, useless and trapped.

The muscles in my neck spasm next, wrenching my head back at an impossible angle. My spine follows, arching violently as though invisible hands are bending me backward. I can't move, can't control anything, as my body betrays me in the most fundamental way.

Iris watches, unmoved by my distress. Her hand presses against my chest, firm and deliberate, rolling me off the bed.

I hit the floor with a sickening thud. The impact should knock the breath from me, but my lungs are already seizing, chest muscles contracting so tightly I can barely draw air. My heels dig into the hardwood as my back bows further, head pulling toward them in a grotesque contortion.

My limbs twist and writhe, muscles clenching with such force I'm certain bones will snap. The pain is beyond anything I've experienced, beyond anything I could have imagined. It's as though every fiber of my being is trying to tear itself apart.

Through tears that stream unbidden down my face, I see Iris squat beside me. That smile, the one I've replayed in my mind countless times, the one I thought held promise and invitation, now reveals itself for what it truly is. Predatory. Calculating.

A sharp prick in my shoulder cuts through the symphony of pain, a needle sliding into muscle. Whatever she's injecting feels cold as it enters my bloodstream.

I want to scream, but my locked jaw permits only a muffled groan. Every second stretches into eternity. My muscles pull against bone with such force I can almost hear the creaking, feel the microfractures forming as my skeleton struggles against the impossible tension.

Tears flow freely now, not from emotion but from the sheer intensity of physical agony. My vision begins to blur, darkness creeping in from the edges.

The last thing I see is Iris's silhouette walking away, her form wavering like a mirage as consciousness slips from my grasp. My eyelids grow impossibly heavy, and as they finally close, I surrender to the darkness.

CHAPTER 20

"Good morning sleepy head," Iris mutters in a sweet yet mocking tone.

I blink, the world coming into focus through the haze of a nightmare I can't quite shake off. Iris is above me, her figure silhouetted against the bright morning light filtering through the sheer curtains of her bedroom. Her voice is a melody, a taunt wrapped in the warmth of dawn.

My head throbs, a dull ache that pulses with the beat of my heart. I try to sit up, but my muscles are uncooperative, heavy with the remnants of sleep, or something else. A bitter taste still lingers on my tongue, a stark contrast to the honeyed sweetness I've come to associate with her.

"What happened?" The words escape my lips, rough and unfamiliar. My memory is a scattered puzzle, pieces missing from the night before. I remember the taste of her skin, the way she commanded me with a touch and a whisper. I remember the overwhelming desire, the hunger that clouded my judgment.

Iris smiles, a small, secretive curl of her lips that does nothing to help the unease twisting in my gut. "You wanted a taste, didn't you?" She moves closer, the scent of her, honey and something darker, enveloping me, suffocating me. "You got what you wanted, Sebastian."

My mind races, struggling to grasp the threads of control that have slipped through my fingers. I am meticulous, calculated in my indulgences. This... loss of control is unacceptable. I take a deep breath to steady my nerves.

"I don't understand," I admit, my voice betraying a vulnerability I loathe. I am not a man who confesses to confusion, to gaps in his memory. But here I am, at the mercy of a woman who has turned my world on its axis.

Iris tilts her head, studying me with an intensity that belies her casual demeanor. "You're not the only one with secrets, Sebastian," she says, her tone light but her eyes sharp. "You're not the only one who knows how to play a game."

A game. The word echoes in my mind, a chilling reminder of the notes, the moved objects, the sense of being watched. The attack outside my office. The clues that someone else is pulling the strings, forcing me to confront a reality I've carefully constructed.

I turn my gaze to Iris, my stare steady despite the turmoil within. "What game are we playing, Iris?" I ask, my voice a low rumble that brooks no argument. "And what are the rules?"

She steps back, her eyes flickering with something that might be fear, or is it excitement? "You'll find out, Sebastian," she replies, her voice dripping with a promise that is both alluring and terrifying. "But first, you should know, my name isn't Iris Klarelle. That's just a clever anagram I created."

"Anagram?" I sputter out in confusion, "for what?"

Iris leans down over my body, her lips close to my ear.

"Serial Killer!" She whispers venomously into my ear.

The implications of her words settle over me like a shroud. Iris is more than just an obsession, more than a fleeting moment in the elevator each morning.

I try to stand, battling the fog in my mind and the ache in my veins, but it is no use. My muscles are clenched in tight spasms, screaming uncontrollably.

I realize that Iris Klarelle is not just a disruption to my order. She is the storm that threatens to tear down the walls I've built around my world. And as much as I fear what that means for me, I can't help but be drawn to the chaos she represents.

My heart hammers against my ribcage as Iris's revelation sinks in. I stare at her, searching for a flicker of truth in her eyes, but all I find is an impenetrable calm that chills me to the bone. The woman who has consumed my thoughts, who has disrupted the precision of my life, is not who she claims to be.

"Serial Killer," I echo, the words tasting like ash in my mouth. The room spins around me, the familiar lines of my architectural sanctuary twisting into a grotesque mockery of safety. I've designed my world to be a fortress against the chaos of human nature, yet here I am, trapped in a web of my own making.

I manage to turn my head, the effort costing me more than it should. "Who are you?" I demand, my voice weak and uneven. I need to understand the game she's playing, need to regain some semblance of control.

Iris, or whoever she is, regards me with a mixture of amusement and pity. "I've worn many names, Sebastian," she says, her voice a silken thread that binds me tighter. "But I suppose you've earned the right to know the truth."

She circles me on the floor like a predator, her movements graceful and deliberate. "I've been watching you, Sebastian Wolfe," she continues, her words slicing through the remnants of my composure. "The way you stalk your prey, the way you believe you're untouchable. It's quite... fascinating."

I feel the color drain from my face as the puzzle pieces of the past weeks click into place. The notes, the moved objects, the too-convenient encounters, they were all orchestrated by her. "You," I breathe out, the realization hitting me like a physical blow. "You've been in my home, my office."

She inclines her head, a queen acknowledging the fealty of her subject. "I had to ensure you were worthy of my attention," she says, her tone almost affectionate. "And you are, Sebastian. Oh, you most certainly are."

My mind races, trying to anticipate her next move, but I'm playing catch-up in a game whose rules I never knew existed. Iris, or the woman who claims to be Iris, has been one step ahead of me from the beginning, manipulating me with a mastery that rivals my own.

"Why?" The question escapes my lips before I can stop it. I've always prided myself on my ability to discern the motivations of others, to predict and manipulate their desires. But with Iris, I am hopelessly out of my depth.

She pauses, her eyes locked onto mine with an intensity that borders on the supernatural. "Because, it's funny, isn't it?" she replies, her voice a mocking tone, "You thought you were hunting me. But I was always tens steps ahead."

The room falls silent, the air heavy with the promise of a revelation that could shatter my world into a thousand pieces. I am a man who has always been in control, who has shaped his environment with an iron will. But as I lie here, helpless and at the mercy of a woman who has outplayed me at every turn, I can't help but wonder if my obsession with Iris has led me to my own destruction.

She reaches out, her fingers brushing against my cheek in a gesture that is both tender and terrifying. "Don't worry, Sebastian," she murmurs, her eyes gleaming with a dangerous kind of pleasure. "It will be over soon."

And with those final words hanging in the air, I am left to confront the terrifying truth: Iris Klarelle, or whatever her name may be, is not just a player in the game of cat and mouse we've been dancing.

She is the game itself.

I stare at the woman who moments ago I thought I knew, my mind reeling. The carefully constructed world I've built around myself, the one that insulated me from the chaos of human nature, is crumbling before my very eyes.

"Who are you?" I manage to ask, my voice barely a whisper. "What do you want from me?"

She smiles, a haunting thing, beautiful and cruel, like the last flicker of a candle before it dies. "Names are such fragile things," she murmurs, her voice smooth as glass but sharp enough to cut. "They shatter so easily, don't you think? And what I want... well, that's the more interesting question, isn't it?"

I swallow hard, my mind scrambling for an escape, but the walls press closer, the air thick with inevitability. There is no way out. She has woven this moment with careful hands, stitched the seams of my fate before I even knew I was wearing it.

"You see," she purrs, gliding around me like a shadow made of flesh, "I've been watching you, Sebastian Wolfe. Watching you stitch lies into gold, sculpt desire into chains, whisper your name into the ears of the willing, over and over again, until they forgot their own."

A shiver claws its way down my spine. How long has she been lurking at the edges of my life? How many times has she passed so near, unseen, unheard, breathing in the scent of my sins? The thought wraps itself around my ribs and squeezes.

"You're an artist," she concedes, tilting her head as if considering a masterpiece. "A master of the human heart, bending it, breaking it, carving it into whatever shape suits you. It's quite something to behold."

I clench my fists, fury and fear warring beneath my skin. This was supposed to be my game. I was the architect, the puppeteer, the unseen hand guiding the dance. And yet, here I stand, outplayed, undone, ensnared in a web I never saw being spun.

She smiles, not soft, not kind. "For so long, you've been the wolf at the door." A pause. A step closer. "Tell me, Sebastian, do you know what it feels like to be the one inside?"

I stare at the woman looming above me, my limbs betraying me like the rest of my carefully constructed world. My body, the vessel that has always obeyed my commands, is now a prison of paralyzed muscle and sluggish blood. The bitter orange taste coats my tongue like a mockery of her honey-sweet scent.

"You've been..." My voice falters, weaker than I've ever allowed it to be. "You orchestrated everything."

A slow smile spreads across her face, the same smile that once seemed coy and inviting now reveals itself as something predatory. "Everything," she confirms, tracing a finger along my jawline. "The elevator meetings, the chance encounters, the way I seemed to always be just beyond your reach."

The thought hits me with nauseating clarity: I never chose her. She chose me.

"The phone call, text messages..." I manage through gritted teeth, "the phone in the book?"

She laughs, a light, musical sound that cuts through me like a blade. "I needed to see how you'd react. Whether you'd run or fight back." Her eyes narrow with appreciation. "You didn't disappoint, Sebastian. You never do."

I attempt to move again, fighting against whatever she's given me, but the effort sends waves of pain shooting through my nervous system. My pride balks at this display of weakness, but there is no hiding it now.

"What was that on your skin?" I demand, desperate to understand at least one piece of this puzzle.

"A concoction of my own," she says, her voice almost tender. "Honey, Bitter Orange, tobacco, cinnamon, amber, hedione, heliotropin and a little something... special. Don't worry, you won't suffer long, it's quite fatal."

My mind races through the possibilities, the implications. If she knows what I've done, why hasn't she gone to the police? Why this elaborate game?

"Why me?" The question escapes before I can temper it with dignity or restraint.

She tilts her head, studying me with the clinical interest of a scientist observing a particularly fascinating specimen. "Because you're just like me, Sebastian. You hide behind your perfectly tailored suits and your architectural brilliance, but underneath..."

She leans closer, her lips nearly brushing my ear.

"You're hollow, always hungry, trying to fill that void. And I wanted to watch you fill that emptiness with me before I devoured you."

The clinical detachment in her voice, as if she's explaining architectural principles rather than my execution, is what terrifies me most. I've always been the one who understood people, who could see through their facades and manipulate the strings of their desires. Now I'm the puppet, twitching helplessly while she holds the scissors to my lifeline.

"You won't get away with this," I manage, the words sounding pathetic even to my own ears. The line of a desperate man, not the calculated predator I've always been.

She laughs, a sound like wind chimes in a hurricane. "I already have, Sebastian. Just as you've gotten away with Jennifer... and all the others."

Jennifer's name from her lips stops my breath. No one knows about Jennifer. No one has ever connected me to her disappearance. The careful disposal, the meticulous cleaning, the perfect alibi, it was flawless.

"How long have you been watching me?" I whisper, trying to contain the panic rising in my throat.

"Long enough to learn your patterns. To understand your hunger." She traces a finger along my collarbone, a mockery of intimacy. "Long enough to appreciate your artistry, even as I planned to dismantle it."

My vision blurs at the edges, whether from the poison or from terror, I can't tell. The paralysis is creeping higher, each breath becoming more labored than the last. I wonder, in a detached corner of my mind, if this is how they felt in their final moments, my indulgences, my collection of perfect moments. Did they too feel this helpless rage as control slipped away?

"You're not like me," I spit out, clinging to this last delusion. "I've never..."

"Never what?" She leans closer, her scent, that damned honey, flooding my senses. "Never played with your food? Never savored the moment when they realized their fate? We're more alike than different, Sebastian. The only real difference is..." She smiles, beautiful and terrible. "I'm better at it."

My consciousness flickers like a dying bulb. The world contracts then expands, Iris's face swimming in and out of focus. Each muscle in my body tightens unbearably, as if invisible hands are wringing me out from the inside.

"P-please," I manage through clenched teeth, hating the weakness in my voice. I've never begged, not once in my life, yet here I am, reduced to pleading with the woman who has dismantled me so completely.

A spasm rips through my core, and I convulse against the floor. The pain is exquisite in its totality, consuming every nerve ending until I can no longer distinguish where my body ends and the agony begins. This must be what my indulgences felt in their final moments, this helpless surrender to forces beyond their control.

"Shhh," Iris whispers, her face hovering above mine. In the blurring of my vision, she appears almost angelic, haloed by the soft light from above. "It won't be long now."

My tongue feels too large for my mouth, my words slurring as I try to form one last defense, one final assertion of control. But there is nothing left to say. She has stripped me of my carefully constructed facade, laid bare the hollow creature beneath.

The room tilts and spins. I feel myself sinking deeper into the floor, gravity becoming a crushing weight. Her scent, honey mixed with something deeper, darker, fills my nostrils, the last sensory input my failing body can process.

Iris leans down, her lips brushing against my cheek in a kiss so gentle it could be mistaken for affection. The sensation burns against my skin, a brand that marks me as hers even in these final moments.

"Goodbye, Sebastian," she murmurs against my ear, her voice fading in and out like a poorly tuned radio. "I'd say it's been a pleasure, but we both know it's been much more than that."

My eyelids grow impossibly heavy. The last thing I see before darkness claims me is her smile, the same smile that captivated me in the elevator all those mornings ago, now revealed for what it truly is: the satisfied curve of a predator's mouth after a successful hunt.

As darkness encroaches on my vision, I find myself contemplating the bitter irony of my situation. I, who has orchestrated every detail of my life with surgical precision, am now undone by someone who saw through my façade from the beginning. How many times had I watched my prey's eyes widen with the realization that they were trapped? Now those same eyes are mine.

The paralysis creeps upward, each heartbeat becoming more labored than the last. I wonder about my legacy, the buildings I've created that will outlast me, standing as monuments to a man no one truly knew. Will they see the hidden corners of my designs, the secret spaces where I poured my darkness? Or will they remain blind to the truth, just as I was blind to Iris?

Iris. Even now, as poison courses through my veins, I can't help but admire her craftsmanship. She studied me, learned my patterns, and used my own hunger against me. Where I saw coincidence, she orchestrated destiny. Where I believed myself the hunter, I was always her prey.

My memories blur together, Jennifer's face morphing into the faces of all who came after, their expressions frozen in that perfect moment of realization. Did they feel as I do now? This strange mixture of rage, fear, and something almost like relief?

The thought surprises me. Relief. Perhaps there is relief in finally being seen, truly seen, for what I am. No more pretense, no more careful construction of the mask I wear for the world. Iris peeled it away, layer by layer, until I lay exposed.

I think of my meticulous routines, the careful ordering of objects on my desk, the precise timing of my morning elevator rides. Such desperate attempts to impose order on a chaotic world. But chaos finds us all in the end, doesn't it?

My consciousness flickers like a dying flame. I feel myself slipping away, falling into an abyss far deeper than any I've created for others. And in these final moments, a strange clarity washes over me: I was never the architect of my own story. I was simply another room in someone else's design.

Acknowledgements

Writing a book is never a solitary endeavor, and I am deeply grateful to the wonderful people who helped bring this story to life.

To my wife, who listened with endless patience to every plot twist, character development, and writing breakthrough, thank you for being my first reader and for believing in this story from the very beginning. Your support and willingness to alpha read through early drafts meant the world to me.

To Tiffany Hepworth of Tiffany Hepworth Books, I am tremendously grateful for your expert feedback and editing services. Your keen eye and professional guidance helped shape this manuscript into something I'm truly proud of.

To Callie Saldana, thank you for being such an incredible author friend and the perfect sounding board for all my story ideas. Your insights, encouragement, and shared passion for storytelling have enriched both this book and my journey as a writer.

This book exists because of each of you, and I am honored to have had your support along the way.

BITTER SWEET - CHAPTER 1

I float in a void between consciousness and oblivion. Am I dead? Is this what waits after life, this nothingness, this sensory deprivation? But then...sound. Voices penetrate the darkness, muffled and distant like I'm submerged underwater. The chatter grows louder, more insistent.

My mind tells my eyes to open, but they remain sealed. I fight against the weight of my eyelids, raising my eyebrows in a desperate attempt to crack them open. The sensation is excruciating, like lifting a barbell for the hundredth repetition, muscles screaming in protest. A straining, helpless feeling.

I strain again. Again. Again.

Finally, a sliver of light breaks through. My vision blurs, then slowly focuses on a form moving nearby. Black hair. Short. Delicate curvy body. Iris!

Panic surges through me. My heart pounds against my ribs like a trapped animal. The sudden acceleration must trigger something because a machine begins to scream, beeping faster and faster, matching the frantic rhythm of my pulse.

The woman whirls around, concern etched across her features as she approaches my bedside.

"Shhhh... it's alright hun," she drawls in a voice that isn't Iris's, it's softer, with a slight accent I can't place.

I look up at her beautiful pale face, studying it with desperate intensity. Not Iris. Beautiful, yes, but not her. Not my hunter. Not my executioner.

She brushes my hair back with cool fingers, and something in her gentle touch calms me. My pounding heart settles, the machine's beeping slows to a steady rhythm.

I blink slowly, willing my mind to clear. The shadow of Iris lingers at the edges of my consciousness, but the gentle Southern drawl of this stranger anchors me to reality.

"Easy there," she says, adjusting something beside my bed. "You've been through hell and back."

My throat feels like sandpaper. When I try to speak, only a rasp emerges.

"Water?" she asks, anticipating my need. She brings a straw to my lips, and I drink greedily, the cool liquid burning as it slides down my parched throat.

"How long?" I manage.

"Five days." She checks the monitors beside me. "Frankly, we weren't sure you'd make it. That poison... it's nasty stuff. Destroys the body from the inside out."

Poison. Iris. The memories flood back, her smile as she watched me collapse, that bitter orange taste spreading across my tongue.

"Who are you?" I ask, studying her face properly for the first time. High cheekbones, expressive eyes, delicate features twisted with a concern that seems too genuine for a stranger.

"Mary Kate Conley." She pulls up a chair beside my bed. "And I've been hunting the woman who poisoned you for nearly two years now."

I try to sit up, wincing as pain shoots through my body.

"Don't strain yourself." She places a firm hand on my shoulder. "Your body's still healing."

"Why did you save me?"

Mary Kate's expression darkens. "Because it's what any person would do. Because, I was too late to save my husband, Joseph." She twists a simple gold band around her finger. "He was one of her first. Found him just like I found you, paralyzed, body shut down from that same poison."

Something in her voice breaks. A single tear falls from her cheek, then takes in a deep breath, wiping away the wetness on her face. "Difference is, by the time I got to him, he was already gone."

She leans forward, intensity radiating from her. "I hired a private investigator, but he disappeared while he was here. I was getting regular reports, then radio silence. When he vanished, I stepped into to investigate myself. I tried to pick up where he left off, following you, watching your movements, trying to make sure you weren't the next victim." She shakes her head. "Almost wasn't fast enough."

Her eyes lock with mine. "Sebastian, I need your help. She's still out there, and she won't stop."

I stare at Mary Kate, trying to make sense of my new reality. Five days gone. Iris vanished. This stranger sitting vigil by my bed.

"I think I know what happened to your investigator." I reply coldly. "Was his name Thomas Grayson?" I ask.

"How'd you know that?" She replies, her face giving a puzzled expression.

"He showed up at one of my work sites a few weeks back, dead, probably the same way I almost died." I reply.

"Poor Mr. Grayson." She says, her lips pouting, her eyes empty as she lowers her head.

"Why did she kill your husband?" The words scrape past my throat, still raw from the poison.

Mary Kate's face crumples. She looks down at her wedding band, twisting it again. "I don't know. That's what's been driving me crazy all this time. Joseph never hurt anyone."

I study her face, searching for any hint that she knows what kind of man I am, what kind of man her husband might have been.

"What was he like?" I ask carefully. "Your husband?"

"The gentlest soul I ever met." Her voice softens with memory. "He was a musician, played guitar at small venues around Nashville. Wrote these beautiful songs." She smiles sadly. "He'd bring me wildflowers after every gig, no matter how late he got home."

"Did he have any... unusual interests?" I press. "Hobbies that seemed out of character?"

She looks puzzled. "Like what?"

"I don't know. Things that might have put him in contact with someone like Iris."

Mary Kate shakes her head. "Joseph was an open book. We shared everything. Some nights he'd stay out late networking after shows, but that's just part of the music business."

"No secrets?" I ask, trying to keep my voice neutral.

"None." Her certainty is absolute. "That woman, she just appeared in our lives one day. Started showing up at his performances. I thought she was just another fan."

"She even opened for him one night, singing and playing her violin."

Her fingers ball into fists on the bed. "Three weeks later, I found him."

I let this sink in. Here she sits, pouring her heart out to me, completely unaware of the monster lying in this hospital bed. She thinks she's found an ally, another victim. She has no idea that I'm the same kind of predator she's hunting, or worse. If her husband was like me, she never saw it either. The thought is almost amusing.

"How did you find me?" I ask, changing direction.

"I noticed that Iris tended to leave the office building about the same time as you every day, arrive just about the same time too. I put two and two together and had a feeling you were her next target."

I take in Mary's words, trying to reconcile everything she's telling me with what I know about Iris, with what I know about myself.

"So your private investigator... he's been watching me?" I ask, my jaw tightening. The thought of being observed, studied like an insect under glass, makes my skin crawl. The irony isn't lost on me.

Mary nods, tucking a strand of hair behind her ear. "The beige Crown Victoria. That was him. We had to know if you were..." She hesitates.

"If I was what?" I press.

"If you were like my Joseph. If you were innocent." She doesn't meet my eyes. "Or if you were working with her somehow."

I almost laugh at the absurdity. Working with Iris? The woman who poisoned me, who bound me to a chair and watched with fascination as toxins coursed through my veins?

"Do you know who she really is?" I ask. "Iris Klarelle. I know that's not her real name."

Mary shakes her head, her expression hardening. "I'm not sure who she is. But I've discovered something..." She pulls out her phone, tapping the screen several times before holding it up for me to see. "She's a musician too. After each kill, she writes and releases a new song."

I stare at the Spotify artist profile displayed on her screen. "Iris Klarelle" in elegant font, with a stylized profile photo that's unmistakably her, though artfully obscured enough that you wouldn't recognize her passing on the street.

Four songs. Only four songs.

"Four victims," Mary whispers, following my gaze. "Including my Joseph. And you would've been the fourth."

My finger hovers over the screen, scrolling through the titles. The last one catches my eye: "Drown for Me."

"Play it," I demand, my voice catching.

The opening notes fill the hospital room, the same haunting melody she hummed as she moved around me that night, the same song that had washed over me like a narcotic as the poison took hold.

"She sang this," I whisper. "The night she..."

Mary's eyes widen. "She performed this one when opening for Joseph's band. Right before she killed him."

I look at the songs, my mind racing. Four songs. Four victims, well, if you could call us victims.

"Have you gone to the police?" I ask, watching Mary's face carefully.

Her expression shifts instantly, a bitter laugh escaping her lips. "The police? I've tried. Multiple times." She waves her hand dismissively. "First time, they were sympathetic. Second time, they started looking at me sideways. Third time?" She shakes her head. "They practically showed me the door before I could finish speaking."

"What did they say, exactly?"

"That there's no evidence linking these deaths together except in my head." Her voice trembles with frustration. "That these poisonings could be from a dozen different sources. That my grief is making me see connections that aren't there."

I watch her twist her wedding band again, a nervous habit that speaks volumes about her loss.

"The detective actually suggested I see someone. A therapist." She practically spits the word. "Like I'm making this up. One even suggested I might have had something to do with my husband's death."

"Why would you kill your own husband?" I ask.

"Insurance. I don't know how much you know about us folks from Kentucky, but we are pretty simple people. Most of us is pretty poor too."

I sit back taking in her words.

Something uncomfortable stirs in my chest as I look at Mary, this woman who's stood vigil by my bedside for days, who risked everything to save a stranger she suspected might be in danger. A stranger who, if she knew the truth, she would run from in horror.

"Please," she says, leaning forward, grasping my hand in both of hers. Her touch is soft, warm, vulnerable. "I can't stop her alone. You're the only one who's survived. The only one who's seen her for what she is."

I feel something crack inside me, a sensation I barely recognize. Regret? Guilt? What is this?

I don't understand why this woman's pleas would affect me in ways my own actions do no. Yet here they are, surfacing like long-submerged bodies finally rising to the water's surface.

This woman has lost everything to a killer. Here I am, saved by her kindness, when I've spent years being the very same kind of monster that she's wants my help to stop. The irony is almost beautiful in its cruelty.

Mary's eyes glisten, and before she can stop them, tears spill over her lashes. One falls on the back of my hand where she holds it, the warm droplet startling against my skin. I stare at the tiny wet circle it forms, watching it seep into my skin like an accusation.

I look up, meeting her gaze. The rawness there, the naked grief and determination, hits me with unexpected force. I've seen tears before. I've caused them. I've watched life drain from eyes more times than I care to count. Yet something about Mary's tears feels different. They aren't the desperate pleas of prey. They're something else entirely.

"Please," she whispers again, her voice breaking. "I can't do this alone. You survived her. You saw things that could help us stop her." She squeezes my hand tighter. "I know you're still weak, but once you're stronger... will you help me find her?"

I study her face, pale and beautiful, framed by that striking black hair. Her vulnerability should disgust me or at least bore me. Instead, I feel an unfamiliar pull, like gravity shifting.

"What would you need me to do?" I ask, my voice steadier than I feel.

"Give me information you remember about her. Like her patterns. What she said to you." Mary wipes her eyes with her free hand. "And maybe... maybe you could be bait to catch her."

I almost laugh at this. The predator becoming prey to catch another predator.

"I don't want anyone else to go through what Joseph did. What you almost did." Her eyes hold mine, refusing to let go. "Will you help me, Sebastian?"

The rational part of my brain screams warnings. This is dangerous. This woman could discover who, or what I really am. Yet some other part, long dormant, stirs to life.

"Yes," I hear myself say. "I'll help you find Iris."

Check out the music referenced in Sweet Hunger by Iris Klarelle and sang in the story on Spotify at the QR code linked below.